THE WORLD WE MAKE

EVERGREEN BOOK 6

MATTHEW S. COX

DIVISION ZERO PRESS

ISBN (ebook): 978-1-950738-50-2

ISBN (paperback): 978-1-950738-51-9

CONTENTS

THE DAY THE EARTH STOPPED

SEPTEMBER 7TH

L oyalty had always come easy to Harper, a side effect of her tendency to attach deeply to people she liked after the ice broke.

Even Tyler, the boy who almost murdered her little sister, still demanded real estate in her mind to hold the strange combination of revulsion, anger, pity, and sympathy she had for him. Simply chasing him off into the wasteland likely killed him as sure as a shotgun blast would have, but it at least gave him a chance of survival, however small. It bothered her that Madison sorta-argued over not shooting him. One didn't share a house with a much younger sister without ever getting into an argument, but their disagreements usually revolved around stupid things like what movie to watch or who took too long in the bathroom.

Madison being pissy over her *not* murdering someone went far past surreal.

Certainly, if not for his being her 'almost boyfriend,' Harper would've shot him for pulling a knife on her little sister.

Fortunately, Madison's 'arguing' over letting him go lasted for only about two hours. Neither of them had thought about Tyler for months. Harper couldn't figure out why he randomly jumped into her mind, or what she happened to be doing standing on an empty shooting course. Thirty feet in front of her stood a large blue plastic barrel in which a shotgun waited for her. She'd competed on ranges like this hundreds of times. Run to the station, pick up the weapon, shoot the targets, replace the weapon in the barrel, then dash to the next station to grab a different weapon. For some reason, the adults didn't want a thirteen-year-old sprinting around the woods carrying a loaded weapon. Go figure.

Harper looked down at herself. Green T-shirt, jeans, and certainly no longer thirteen.

She couldn't explain how she'd gotten to the range or why she appeared to be eighteen but dressed in the same outfit she wore five years ago for competitions. The instant she realized the bizarre situation meant she must be dreaming, the ground began to tremble beneath her.

"Harp!" shouted Dad. "Wake up!"

"Huh?" She blearily opened her eyes, squinting at the glare from the bedroom light overhead.

All the windows remained black. Her father loomed over the bed, having grabbed her pajama shirt at each shoulder to shake her conscious. The fear in his eyes plus the uncharacteristically aggressive nature of being throttled awake stunned her.

"Get moving, now!" yelled Dad.

A whispery voice drifted in from the door to the hall, Madison sleepily asking Mom, "What's going on?"

Harper groaned. "Dad, it's still dark out. It's way too early."

He hauled her off the bed mostly to her feet, then dragged her out of the room. Too shocked to question him and too delirious from her interrupted sleep to think, she stumbled after him, grabbing at the wall to keep from falling over. He'd *never* manhandled her like this before. His death grip on her wrist left no doubt in her mind she had zero choice in the matter of going where he wanted her to.

Voices came from the parents' bedroom, radio news people from the alarm clock. Whatever they said blurred into a haze of words her mind couldn't process. Dad pulled her down the stairs so fast she nearly fell twice. The dark ground floor passed in a blur. Harper caught a glimpse of Mom vanishing through the door leading to the basement.

She barely had time to think *what the heck* before her father practically shoved her down the stairs. Again, she lost her balance, but caught herself on the banister. Dad slammed the door behind them, then ushered her into the basement and over to the corner by his workbench where the air tasted like gun oil and metal. Mom and Madison had already crawled under the giant wooden table. Still somewhat numb and half awake, Harper scooted in after them and sat cross-legged by her mother.

What the hell? Tornados never make it all the way to Lakewood.

Dad plopped down next to her, resting his face in his hands. He seemed as relieved as if they'd narrowly missed being hit by a speeding bus.

"Dad?" whispered Harper, rubbing her sore wrist where he'd grabbed her. "What the heck is wrong?" She almost added 'with you,' but didn't because he looked genuinely scared and gave off a strong sense of protectiveness. "It's not even light out yet. What time is it?"

Mom glanced over at her, but couldn't seem to bring herself to speak.

The black rectangles of basement windows abruptly lit up, the world outside gone from midnight to brighter than an August summer day in an instant. Madison made an 'ooh' noise, as if finding it pretty.

"Holy shit," whispered Dad. "They did it... the morons actually did it."

"Did what?" asked Madison.

Harper's blurry brain finally processed what had been streaming out of her parents' alarm radio. *Multiple reports of detonations along the east coast. We've lost all contact with New York City, DC, Atlanta, Richmond, Miami...* the rest had been a continuing series of city names.

Before Dad could answer Madison, a deafening roar whipped up outside. The house shook like a box of marbles in the hands of a furious giant. Harper might have screamed, but couldn't even hear herself.

The searing glow in the windows faded, but not to perfect black, rather a dim reddish-orange as if the sky had caught fire.

Harper gawked at nothing in particular; the significance of her father acting so out of character, the radio news, the bright flash, the roar all hit her at once. *Nuclear war?* Her brain tried to calculate the distance from the time between the flash and hearing the explosion. How long would it take for the blast wave to reach them?

Wham!

A tremendous impact rocked the house. Random tools, supplies, and junk her father kept on shelves and wall pegs fell to the floor. One five-gallon drum of empty brass for reloading hit the floor next to her, bursting open and scattering its contents all over the floor. Dust blasted off the ceiling. The lights went out. Harper grabbed her family and screamed, expecting a wave of nuclear fire to blow in and roast her at any second.

HARPER SNAPPED AWAKE, BREATHING HARD AND CRYING.

She found herself in bed with Madison curled up beside her and Lorelei sprawled on top of her. It took her a few seconds to process the reality of being safe in Evergreen. Nested nightmares didn't happen often. Dreaming that she awoke from a dream only to find herself still dreaming freaked her out more than she expected possible from an imaginary event.

Those few minutes replayed again in her waking mind. The heavy house-rattling slam hadn't been the nuclear blast wave hitting them, rather a massive chunk of concrete debris punching through the roof—and landing on Harper's bed. Her father woke up a little earlier than he usually did—due to his needing the bathroom—and noticed the emergency warning on his cell phone. If Dad hadn't overdone it on iced tea the previous night, she'd have still been asleep when two tons of former skyscraper landed on top of her.

A long, slow exhale leaked from her nose at the thought she almost never woke up. She'd have either stopped existing entirely or gone into whatever afterlife there might be, never knowing civilization came to a stop. Her ghost would still crave Starbucks and video games or spend all day grumbling about going to school on test days.

The cynical people say those victims were better off.

Harper reached up to brush a hand over Lorelei's head. Her friend Darci's father died in a similar way... the blast wave obliterated their house before the man woke up. Neither she nor her friend knew the exact way in which he died, but Darci had discovered his mangled remains in the pile of scrap wood she used to live in. It baffled her to think about pieces of downtown Denver weighing multiple tons being thrown so far as to land in Lakewood. No one mentioned it yet, but the metal parts of the debris chunk had to have become somewhat radioactive. Harper had never again gone upstairs at all, much less to her bedroom, after the morning of the strike. Along with Darci's father, countless millions died in an instant, most not knowing what even happened.

Instant death is easy, but it also sucked. Sure, a person couldn't suffer after death, but they also couldn't know happiness either. Harper held Lorelei like a living teddy bear, the tiny seven-year-old so far asleep she didn't react.

Madison sniffled, evidently awake and trying to cry without making too much noise.

"You okay?" whispered Harper.

"Did you have a nightmare too?"

"Umm." Harper extracted her left arm from under blankets and bodies, then wrapped it around Madison. "More a disturbing dream than a nightmare. It wasn't scary as much as just ugh."

Madison straightened her legs, stretched, then cuddled against her. "It sucks we have to work today."

Today? Harper blinked in confusion until the fog of near-sleep lifted after a few seconds. *Oh, shit. No wonder I had that dream. It's the seventh.* Exactly one year ago today, idiots reshaped the world in nuclear fire. Perhaps it counted as selfish in a way, but Harper ended up associating more emotional weight to an unknown day roughly two months after the strike: the day the Lawless killed her parents. Hiding in her basement kept the reality of the outside world at arm's length. It felt like a crazy, unexpected break from school and work.

"Don't think of it as work…" Harper kept brushing her fingertips through Lorelei's wild, blonde hair.

"You try farming. It's a crapload of work." Madison sighed.

Harper smiled at the ceiling. "I know. I meant work as in a job. You're not busting your butt for a paycheck. It's not *employment,* it's 'everyone trying not to starve.'"

"Yeah, I guess." Madison yawned. "I hate starving."

"Me, too."

They lay in silence for a while, teasing the edge of sleep but never quite slipping over it.

"What did you dream about?" asked Madison in a semi-whispery voice.

"Umm…"

Madison lifted her head to make eye contact. "If it's bad, you don't have to tell me."

"Not bad. Just… depressing. I had a weird nonsense dream, then in the dream I woke up in bed back home to Dad shaking me awake the morning the bombs fell."

"Oh." Madison rested her head on Harper's shoulder. "Mine was a bunch of radiation zombies chasing us around the mall."

Hearing her sister having an 'ordinary nightmare' composed of nonspecific fears rather than reliving a painful moment came as a relief. Madison had nightmares slightly more often than the average kid before the war, but not to the point the parents took her to a therapist. The girl merely happened to scare more easily than most. Post-war, having serious real things to be scared of, the nightmares got worse… though lately, they'd settled to almost normal frequency. Generic 'radiation zombies' sounded similar to the sorts of nightmares she used to have from movies.

Equal parts worried and hopeful, she gave her little sister a squeeze.

"Ack," whispered Madison. "Not too hard. I gotta pee."

"Well, go do so." Harper lifted her arm out of the way.

"It's still dark and the bed is warm," muttered Madison.

Harper chuckled to herself, remembering *many* early mornings where the same battle raged in her mind. Every so often, her sister truly proved they came from the same parents. They lay under cover of warm blankets, sleepily talking about random things from Darci being pregnant to the new dresses Renee and her 'fabric team' gave Madison. Wearing them made her feel like a peasant kid from a renaissance festival. Neither Madison nor Jonathan had spoken much about dance class for months. Harper figured it reminded her too much of happier times, so she filed it away not to talk about.

Not like she needs to worry about getting enough exercise.

Eventually, traces of daylight appeared in the window to the right of the headboard. Seeing proof they'd soon *have* to get up pushed the discomfort of having to pee past the point of idleness. Madison grumbled as she crawled out from under the blankets, slid to the floor, then trudged into the hall toward the bathroom while whispering about her toes freezing.

Harper playfully rolled her eyes. Early September hadn't gotten cold yet. Chilly, yes. Compared to a modern house with working heat—and not merely a fireplace for warmth, the room *was* cold. However, a few months from now, it would be worse— cold enough she'd resist getting out of bed until on the verge of having an accident.

Slippers. I need to ask Renee to make furry slippers or something.

"C'mon, kiddo," whispered Harper, tickling Lorelei in the sides. "It's morning."

The seven-year-old didn't react.

A faint metallic rattle came from the hallway.

"I'm using it," said Madison from behind a closed door.

"Dammit," mumbled Jonathan, more as a reflex than sounding angry. "Okay."

Harper shifted Lorelei to the side, laying her on her back. She sat up and tickled the child's foot while coaxing her to wake up. Still, Lorelei slept, mouth agape. Taken by sudden worry, Harper checked the girl's pulse and listened to her chest. All sounded normal, so she relaxed.

Poor kid's exhausted.

Lorelei had a reputation for sleeping *hard*. A gunfight could happen in the same room, and she'd barely stir. Harper got out of bed, hurriedly changing from her nightgown into a shirt and jeans, plus socks. One nice thing about being 'an adult,' she didn't outgrow clothing. Mom always grumbled about being 'too fat' to fit into the stuff she wore in high school. Harper disagreed with Mom about her being fat, but the woman *did* have clothing she couldn't fit into anymore. The odds of Harper gaining significant weight post-nuclear-war didn't seem good at all. Most likely, she'd be able to wear these clothes until they disintegrated. Dad had a few shirts he claimed to be thirty years old, ones he'd gotten at rock concerts during his later teen years.

After changing, Harper scooped Lorelei up and carried her out into the hall. A shirtless Jonathan stood with his head pressed against the bathroom door, seemingly asleep on his feet. His pale blue pajama pants tried desperately to cling to his rail thin body, giving him slightly worse than plumber's crack.

"You're about to lose your pants," said Harper.

"Mmmn." Jonathan pulled them up a bit, but they fell right back to the same place as soon as he let go of them.

He's still too skinny. I need to give him more food.

Upon reaching the kitchen, Harper set Lorelei in one of the chairs and gently draped her forward over the table, resting her head on her arms. That done, she tested the light switch to see if power worked. It did, so she proceeded to start on breakfast. Today, she'd make a fair approximation of pancakes, using fruit preserves instead of syrup. Without baking soda or 'proper' pancake mix, they came out denser than normal... but the kids adored them anyway.

Cliff entered the kitchen. "Wow..."

"Hmm?" Harper instinctively checked herself to make sure she hadn't suffered a wardrobe malfunction, then twisted to look at him.

He stood in the spot where the hallway met the kitchen, shaking his head at Lorelei. "That kid sleeps as hard as a hung-over Ranger following a 72-hour mission with minimal rest breaks."

"She feels safe now," whispered Harper in case the girl happened to be awake enough to hear. "I think she's still trying to catch up on all the sleep she missed at home." The heartbreaking idea the girl had to stay constantly vigilant—even against her own mother—knotted a lump in her throat.

"Maybe." Cliff frowned for a second, then shrugged. "Or she's just a heavy sleeper. I knew a guy..."

He related a story of a soldier who slept so deeply the other guys often pranked him, once even successfully dressing him up as a clown without him waking up.

Madison trudged into the kitchen, barefoot in jeans and a grungy pink T-shirt with the word 'dancer' scrawled across her chest in sparkly glitter. The 'ugh' mood her face gave off relaxed to neutral as soon as she smelled the pancakes. Without a word, she took a place at the table, waiting.

The rather obvious sound of Jonathan using the toilet echoed in the hall.

At an uptick in the wind outside, the ceiling light flickered.

Harper peered up at it. "Hmm. Looks like we're on windmill power."

"Is that better?" asked Madison.

"I'm not sure if it's objectively better." Cliff stretched, twisting side to side. "But we can build more windmills and fix the ones we have. Can't make new panels or fix the ones that break."

Madison nodded. "Being able to fix them makes them better."

Maybe we won't have to live without electricity for the rest of our lives. Harper glanced up at another flicker in the bulbs. It didn't seem right for the power to react in real time to fluctuations in the wind. That suggested they had the wires plugged directly into the generator. Maybe the capacitors or whatever they used to even it out failed again. Jeanette's electrical team busted their butts working as hard or harder than the farm crew.

Jonathan walked in, smile-yawning at everyone. He adored the beige 'peasant's tunic' Renee made for him, but still wore jeans under it so it didn't feel as much like a dress. The garment swallowed the boy, making him look even scrawnier. Harper made sure to pour his pancakes slightly bigger than usual. Carrie and Renee arrived from next door, joining them for breakfast as had become normal. Happiness at having a large family who ate together no longer made Harper feel guilty as some kind of slight against her parents. Back when the world had been normal, dinner rarely had more than the four of them at the table. The occasional major holiday added a set or two of grandparents or perhaps a cousin sometimes. More often than not, the last two or three years before the war, her family tended to eat on their own time microwaving leftovers or freezer meals, except for weekends and Tuesdays when Madison didn't have any after-school stuff to attend.

Amazing she never complained about all the shit Mom signed her up for. Dance class... taekwondo, gymnastics... it was all just a human hamster wheel, something to run on in our cages. Harper thought of all the hours the kids—and adults—put in on the farm working. *People long ago didn't need to invent ways to be active.*

Renee and Carrie helped cook, which soon shifted to Carrie cooking and the girls mostly transporting the food to the table. After giving Jonathan his subtly oversized pancakes, Harper paused on the way back to the counter area to mark the day on their wall calendar, a simple spiral notebook.

They'd given up on trying to 'draw a calendar' with boxes for each day. No one used it as a planner, purely a record of time. Harper stared at the list of dates across the page, taken by a sudden sense of awe at having only a handwritten record to know what day of the year it was. She couldn't look online, or check a phone, or Google the current time and date. Harper, and most of the adults in Evergreen, knew how many days each month had, so merely counted them out as a means of telling the date. Hours blurred into more generic descriptions of time such as early morning, morning, late morning, noon, and so on. Almost no one referred to time using numbers anymore. Occasionally, someone would say 'two hours before sunset' or something similar. She hadn't heard the phrases 'o'clock,' 'A.M.' or 'P.M.' in months. Some of the older residents still used wind-up wristwatches, though no one could say for sure if they had them set accurately. Walter Holman joked 'it finally took nuclear war to get the hell rid of Daylight Savings Time.'

Harper grabbed the pen and wrote 9/7/19 in the next space, marking today's date. Her hand shook a little at the significance. She ended up standing there, staring at the numbers, unable to believe it had been an entire year. Half of her brain said it felt like six years had gone by, the other half thought it mere weeks. In either case, one full year didn't seem possibly correct.

Is it weird I don't *want to cry?*

"Yeah," said Cliff in a soft, comforting tone, right behind her. "It's *that* day."

She stuck the pen back in the wire spiral on the notebook. "Is everyone going to pretend it isn't?"

"Sitting around reminiscing where you were when *it* happened is for old folks with nothing better to do." He winked. "Like the Kennedy assassination."

"The what?" Harper kept staring at the date.

"Wow, are you serious?" He whistled. "Schools fail."

"Heh." She sighed.

"Eat." Carrie pointed a spatula at the table. "Don't let 'em get cold. And someone wake the little one."

Madison grabbed a handful of Lorelei's hair, lifted her face off her arms, slid a plate of pancakes under her, and let her face rest on them. The girl didn't react.

Jonathan laughed, as did Madison.

Renee *tsked* and hurried over to pull Lorelei's face out of the pancakes. "They're too hot to use as a pillow."

"Wow. Lore is *out*," said Jonathan.

Cliff squeezed Harper's shoulder and returned to his seat. "Anne-Marie is talking about making it an 'official day of remembrance.'"

"Is that like a holiday?" Jonathan stuffed a forkful of pancake into his mouth.

"No." Madison shook her head. "People don't work on holidays. We gotta work today."

Jonathan held up a finger until he finished chewing. "So

what's a 'day of remembrance' mean?"

Harper flopped into her seat. "It means everyone collects somewhere and stands around feeling sad for a while."

"Why do people have to go to a specific place to feel sad?" deadpanned Madison. "I do it everywhere."

Harper's throat tightened. She couldn't tell if Madison tried to crack wise or meant it seriously. Jonathan offered a tentative smile tinged with concern.

"An official day is like the Perrier of sad," said Cliff, twirling a hand around. "All other sadness is just sparkling melancholy."

Renee and Carrie stifled chuckles.

"So, what do we do on a 'day of remembrance'?" asked Madison.

Cliff overacted a grim face. "Everyone gathers together and thinks really hard about being sad for a few minutes out of respect, then goes back to normal."

"You don't approve?" asked Carrie.

Harper squeezed Madison's hand. Her little sister responded with an 'I'm okay, just being sarcastic' face.

Cliff stabbed a fork into his pancakes. "Seems kinda pointless to me. Everyone knows what happened. Making a big deal out of crap we can't change is the kind of stuff politicians used to do so people voted for them. We don't have elections here yet, so there's no point."

Carrie glanced at him, then Harper. Based on the woman's expression, Harper figured she and her new 'mom' were on the same wavelength regarding him. He didn't like to dwell on negative emotions, preferring to avoid them when possible. Who or whatever he lost to the war, he'd rather not spend an official holiday thinking about it.

Lorelei sneezed herself upright, gazing around at the kitchen with such a bewildered 'where am I' expression everyone laughed. She looked at Harper for a second, then straight down at the plate in front of her, eyes sparkling. "Ooh, pancakes!"

2

CHILD LABOR

SEPTEMBER 7TH

A ttempted murder hadn't even been on the list of things Harper expected to happen on such a poignant day.

In truth, she probably should have braced herself for *some* manner of insanity. Roy Ellis, former cop, had been training the Militia for months in various things from tactics to negotiation and even some psychological stuff: like how people can be unpredictable in moments of high emotion. He frequently told stories about responding to DV calls (domestic violence) where a neighbor called in because a guy got violent with the wife, girlfriend, or kids. Soon after the cops arrived to protect the woman or the kids, the wife-and-or-girlfriend would attack the cops, trying to stop them from carting the abusive guy off to jail.

It made no sense, but happened.

Lots of things made no sense but happened... like nuclear war.

Harper hadn't been expecting a gunfight at Anne-Marie's moment of silence ceremony. An almost elderly resident, Albert Burke, decided to interrupt the silence by telling everyone to be thankful to God for sparing them. This resulted in mostly grumbling until he made the mistake of saying something to the effect of everyone who died to the nukes had been purged by God for sin. At that, Cole Bixby—who'd lost his wife, as well as both of his adult sons and their families—pulled out a handgun and tried to blow Albert's head off.

Fortunately, a fifty-eight-year-old in the midst of blinding rage didn't exactly have the best reflexes in the world. A handful of others went for handguns, some dove at Albert, trying to tackle him to safety. Five adults near Mr. Bixby grabbed him. Three shots went off. By some miracle, no one got hit. Cole screamed at him about what kind of god would allow such vast death and suffering, and even if he *did* exist, he wasn't worth worshiping. This enraged Albert, who then tried to pull his gun from his belt while calling him a heretic. The two guys who knocked him to the ground to shield him grabbed his arm. In the ensuing struggle, Albert appeared to suffer a heart attack. This made Cole laugh and taunt him that his god was punishing him for being an inconsiderate ass.

With Madison, Lorelei, and Jonathan there, Harper hadn't gotten involved, instead shielding her family while other Militia who happened to be closer to the fray intervened. She'd also been a bit too stunned at the old bastard suggesting her parents deserved to die to react. Albert ended up in the hospital while Cole went to the Sheriff's jail in South Evergreen to, as Walter said, 'cool off.' Most people expected he'd be held for a day or two, the incident chalked up to extreme emotion. The way Walter ran the Militia, they really only had two punishments for crimes: exile or firing squad. Putting someone in jail for an extended period of time made little sense to the people running town since they'd be sitting idle, consuming food while offering nothing back in terms of effort at survival.

Sure, Cole tried to shoot Albert, but exile seemed like a harsh consequence given the circumstances. Arturo Rosales, the lawyer, inserted himself into the ensuing debate to defend Cole by claiming it an 'act of passion' and not premeditation or even conscious thought.

Except for the almost-shooting, Anne-Marie's 'moment of remembrance' amounted to most residents of North Evergreen standing around by the Quartermaster's building in silence for about ten minutes at the top of the last hour of daylight. Except for the smallest children who weren't pressed into farm work, all in attendance were exhausted, fidgety, and not terribly interested in milling around in a crowd thinking about tragedy. No one complained about attending, but Anne-Marie kept the ceremony short.

Harper sat on the porch, leaning against the front wall of the house and looking up at the stars. Any sort of holiday or event struck her as inadequate. Even if humanity retained the technological capacity to build a hundred-story monument to the dead, it wouldn't be enough. What could anyone really do in response to billions of lives being lost?

Motion made her look straight up.

The weak light bulb above the front door had attracted a cloud of moths. Darci draped herself across a plastic patio chair facing the porch with five-year-old Elijah asleep in her lap. Renee sat with her back against the wall on the other side of the door from Harper, holding Lorelei in her lap and talking about the girl's various dolls. Jonathan and Madison attempted to play Frisbee in the front yard to varying degrees of success in the dark. Most of their game consisted of searching around for the plastic disc after a missed catch.

Darci hadn't gained much weight either, still so skinny Jonathan said she looked like an elf from D&D. The sight of her pothead friend sober, caring for a little boy, *and* roughly two months pregnant blew her away. Of all her friends, Darci had been the very *last* one expected to 'go domestic' with kids and a husband. They all figured she'd either join a goth band and live the wild life in the music world or end up as a single graphic artist living with two dozen cats and an incontinent parakeet.

Renee won everyone's vote as the one who would be 'first to marry and spawn.' Harper found it ironic, but understandable that Renee showed zero interest in boys now. Considering she'd escaped the Lawless before they touched her, she had a decent chance of mentally recovering.

Can't even imagine... Harper didn't try to think how she'd react to being locked in a room by a violent gang who constantly reminded her as soon as she grew up a little more, she'd become someone's wife whether she wanted to or not. Renee's lie about being only fourteen saved her. Harper also tried not to think about the incredibly remote odds involved in them finding each other. Any thousand different tiny decisions made by multiple people could've meant she never saw her best friend alive again. Of course, they both lived in the same neighborhood and all cars, planes, and other forms of transportation stopped working instantly when the nukes went off. Running into people she knew didn't really seem too farfetched.

Before emotion got the better of her, Harper distracted herself by talking to Renee about clothing. Her friend, and the people on her team, had figured out the process of making cloth from scratch and stitching it into usable clothes. Of course, everything they made tended to look like costumes from a medieval renfest or Shakespearean theater house prop room, but the goofiness of clothing didn't matter as much as having something to wear. Of course, considering the amount of stuff they'd scavenged, it would be years before the people of Evergreen became wholly reliant on new clothing they could manufacture. For now, the recipients of any handmade clothing tended to be those who needed stuff in rare sizes they hadn't been able to scavenge much of.

"This sucks." Madison swiped the frisbee up from the grass and faced Jonathan.

"So, don't toss it around in the dark," replied Renee.

"Not the frisbee." Madison threw it to Jonathan. "I'm talking about the farm. It's September. We should be in school now, but they delayed it. All the kids are stuck on the farm from sunrise to sunset. We don't even have time to play. It's like being in a Russian prison camp."

Darci chuckled.

Jonathan threw the frisbee back to her. "Harvesting food and getting ready for winter. It's important. I'm fine working hard if it means we don't starve. We won't be working on the farm in the winter."

Madison kicked at the dirt. "Becca and Eva are so tired they just went straight home. And seriously. I'm only ten. I'm supposed to be little enough not to be conscripted. Didn't they say it's twelve and older for farm work?"

"Emergency help. It's just a few weeks," said Jonathan. "We need to harvest everything before it rots."

"Then back to school," chirped Lorelei.

"I know." Madison sighed and threw the frisbee over Jonathan's head. "Crap. Sorry."

"I got it." He jogged into the dark.

Madison folded her arms. "I'm just complaining because I miss my friends. I'd rather work on the farm than have people starve. Mr. Rollins said the winter's gonna be colder than it should be."

The frisbee cruised into the light, nailing Madison in the chest.

"Oof." She clamped her hands over it.

"Nice catch." Jonathan snickered.

"Thanks for not hitting me in the face." She winged it back at him.

"If you hate the farm, what do you wanna do when you grow up?" asked Darci.

Madison huffed. "I dunno. The apocalypse happened. I'm not

supposed to be stressing out over my career at ten years old now."

Renee barked a laugh.

"I wanna work with the electric guys and keep the wind turbines running," said Jonathan. "And draw stuff."

"Maddie? You haven't thought at all about what to learn?" asked Renee.

"Not really." Madison tossed the frisbee to the ground near the steps, then sat on the porch in front of Harper. "It's too dark for this. We're gonna lose it."

"Yeah." Jonathan flopped on the steps.

"You just wanna work on power because the electricity is too weak for the PlayStation now." Madison snickered.

Jonathan shrugged. "Yeah. But it's also for the heat and hot water and cooking and light. Having 'lectric is important, not just for video games."

Renee nudged Madison with a foot. "C'mon. There has to be something you want to learn."

"Umm." She squirmed. "I dunno. *Not* shooting. Even if I got good at it, we're gonna run out of bullets. Once we're outta bullets, it won't matter how good someone can shoot. It's kind of a dead skill now, like being a social media expert."

"More a dying skill than a dead one..." Harper exhaled. "It's useful for as long as we have ammo."

Jonathan made finger guns. "They had six-shooters in the old west. Don't need computers to make guns."

"Someone's eventually going to make more ammo." Darci rolled her eyes. "If humans are determined to do anything, it's invent new and better ways to kill stuff. Everyone keeps saying we're stuck in the 1800s again. Well, they had plenty of guns back then. The Wild West wasn't called wild because of the prostitutes."

Madison blushed. Jonathan giggled. Lorelei showed no

reaction to the word. Harper and Renee made 'you did not just say that in front of children' faces at her.

Grace emerged from the house with water for everyone. She sat in the doorway and passed drinks around. "Yes, but they also had lots of mines. Big industry digging up sulfur and stuff to make gunpowder. No one's doing that now. We're decades away from society getting back to that point. We're still not even sure how bad things are. Like, is *every* major city gone? Is the largest collection of people living in one place basically Evergreen?"

"I doubt we're the biggest." Darci puffed at a strand of hair hanging over her face.

"No." Grace gave her some water. "I mean the size of Evergreen… or is there still like a big city left?"

Harper gestured at nothing in particular. "We're just a bunch of little towns in our own private worlds."

"Yeah." Grace handed Lorelei a small cup of water. "Eventually, trading between towns will develop, then more contact, and maybe we'll turn into a nation again."

"You don't know it'll take so long." Darci yawned. "Did anyone nuke like El Salvador or Mexico?"

"No clue." Renee shrugged. "I haven't seen anything about it on the news."

Harper chuckled.

"Maybe I'll be professionally pregnant like Darce," said Madison.

Renee clamped a hand over her mouth to mute a laugh, turning bright red in the face.

For a moment, Harper and Darci stared at Madison. Harper didn't know how to take the remark, though doubted her little sister meant to imply anything about prostitution.

"Umm, what?" Darci blinked.

"You don't do a job. Just sit around being pregnant." Madison patted her belly.

Darci laughed. "It's not a job, it's a condition. Besides, I *do* have a job. Sorta. I help Lucas grow the town's supply of weed. Just can't really be around it right now."

"Really is the end of the world," muttered Harper. "Darce is being responsible."

Darci flipped her off while grinning. "I'm responsible when innocent kids are involved."

The unspoken 'it's just *my* life I gamble with' hung heavy in the air between them for a moment. Darci broke eye contact first, glancing down. Harper took her friend's demeanor as a 'yeah, I was stupid, working on it, but I don't want to talk about it.'

"We're going to have enough food for the winter, right?" asked Renee when the silence grew too awkward.

Harper cringed. "Nee, when trying to shift the topic off something uncomfortable, it's usually better to go happy or funny... not scary."

"Sorry." Renee bit her lip. "But... are we?"

"I hope so," said Harper as more of a sigh.

A woman's voice came out of the darkness from where Hilltop Drive ran past the front yard. "Speaking of food for the winter..."

Everyone on the porch except for Lorelei jumped. Harper mentally chided herself for the tactical stupidity of sitting under a light source, which made the surroundings even darker. *If I can't feel safe at home, where can I let my guard down ever?* Part of her wanted to believe it unlikely anything bad would happen inside Evergreen, but the world no longer had organized law—at least not anywhere in this area. Anyone tempted to do evil things held back only by fear of punishment no longer had such hesitation. On the other hand, innocent settlers could also generally shoot 'bad guys' without any worry a legal system would screw them over. Perhaps it cancelled out.

"What about food?" asked Jonathan.

A creak came from the gate. Footsteps swished in the grass for a few seconds before Leigh Preston stepped into the light, casually carrying her AR-15 on a shoulder strap. A flashlight dangled from her belt, not switched on.

"Since when are you a vampire?" Harper chuckled.

"Saving batteries." Leigh patted the flashlight. "Moon's bright enough to walk around."

Madison scooted closer to Harper and leaned on her, almost defensively.

"You're here to tell me it's my turn to go do something reckless, right?" asked Harper.

"Not really reckless." Leigh hooked her thumbs in her jean pockets. "Walter's looking for a group to take a trip into Denver. Our names are at the top of the list again."

"Why?" asked Madison, pressing herself tighter against Harper.

"Jars," said Leigh. "We have a list of stores likely to stock supplies like mason jars, stuff to preserve food. According to Liz, we don't have enough here. All those vegetables and such they're harvesting now need to be eaten, frozen, or canned... or they'll rot. If we waste too much of it, things are going to get pretty desperate this winter."

"Umm..." Harper fidgeted.

Madison looked down. "It's like working on the farm. Sucks, but we have to do it. Please be safe."

She's not begging me to stay home... "Are you sure? I don't *have* to go."

Jonathan made a 'you kinda do' face at her.

She smirked back at him. She didn't *have* to do anything except protect her family. Protecting them meant staying alive to do so. The Evergreen Militia didn't have contracts or the legal authority to do anything to people for 'disobeying orders.' Hell, Walter didn't really give orders. He asked people to do stuff. If Harper turned down a request to help collect needed supplies, he'd understand. She'd also feel like she let everyone down. If she continued dodging responsibilities to the town, they'd likely ask her to leave the militia. The idea of giving up Dad's Mossberg didn't feel as much of a betrayal of her family anymore, but as the one movie said, she had a 'certain set of skills.' Might as well use them, especially if it gave her the opportunity to target shoot a few Lawless. She would never go out of her way to hunt them down as she still believed the best way to survive a gunfight was to avoid it entirely. However, going into Denver certainly came with a high probability of running into the gang responsible for her parents' deaths. Any chance of her hesitating at pulling the trigger on a person in a blue sash sat in the same grave as her childhood innocence. She also had to think of preserving food in terms of working to protect Madison. Her sister needed to be protected from *all* harm, not merely bad guys with guns.

"Yeah." Madison squirmed around to look at her. "You're gonna be all guilty and stuff if you don't go. Besides… I don't wanna starve."

"Starving is bad." Lorelei shook her head. "We shouldn't do it. Tried it once. Didn't like it. Zero stars."

Renee laughed into an aww, squeezing her.

Lorelei's grin gave away she said it on purpose to get extra hugs.

"All right." Harper nodded to Lorelei. "I'm guessing we're going in the morning?"

"Yep. Bit dark to drive now." The woman chuckled.

"Drive?" Harper blinked.

"Yeah. Rafael's taught a Post Office truck to eat corn scraps. Seems to like it. He hasn't quite managed to get it to fetch yet, though." Leigh laughed.

"Got the biodiesel working?" asked Grace. "Nice."

Leigh shrugged. "So he says. It's the plan, anyway."

"I don't really like you doing dangerous stuff, but this is important." Madison rested her cheek on Harper's shoulder. "Expect me to be extra clingy tonight."

"That's fine." Harper leaned her head against her sister's.

"All right. Meet over by the QMs in the morning." Leigh turned to leave. "No huge rush. Have something to eat first. It ain't all that far a ride. I'm gonna go get some sleep. Too damn dark to do anything else."

Darci grinned. "I can think of a few things one can do in the dark."

"Not Frisbee," said Jonathan.

"Where's Logan been?" asked Grace.

"He moved into the house a little up the street from Carrie's place with his sister." Jonathan pointed. "Kinda diagonal from here."

Harper's cheeks warmed as she associated Logan with the idea of 'things to do in the dark'. "He's spending a lot of time with Luisa. Also, the farm's kicking his ass. He's exhausted."

"Seriously," muttered Madison, sounding tired.

"Okay guys." Harper exhaled. "Bedtime."

"I totally get the cat thing now." Darci gestured at Elijah.

"Which cat thing?" asked Harper.

Darci pretended to be too weak to move the little boy. "The weight of a cat sleeping in your lap makes it impossible to get out of a chair. Kid does the same thing to me."

"You wanna crash on the couch? Kinda dark to walk." Harper pointed her thumb at the door.

"Lucas would lose his mind if I didn't come home." Darci grunted and got to her feet, balancing the boy so his head hung over her left shoulder. "Thanks for the offer, but I can find my way there."

Grace collected empty water cups. "Wow, he really cares for you."

"Yeah. He really does." Darci's smile took on a wistful somberness. "We kinda saved each other. Night."

"Night," muttered Elijah.

Harper made her way into the house, grateful for the electricity still working. Weak lights beat zero lights. Madison and Lorelei followed her to the bedroom where they all changed into their nightgowns. After taking turns going to the bathroom, they crawled into bed.

"Sorry." Madison cuddled up at her side.

"What for?"

"If I wake you up from having a nightmare. I'll try not to. You gotta get sleep so you're alert and stuff."

Harper exhaled, staring at the ceiling, debating changing her mind. Madison didn't seem overly freaked, merely on edge. Last winter had been extremely crappy from a food standpoint. If going into Denver had any chance of making the upcoming winter better, she had to do it.

She also couldn't deny a bit of curiosity.

Maybe the Lawless are all gone. Guns and swords don't make food grow. She closed her eyes, sighing to herself. *Yeah, right. I'm not so lucky.*

3

A QUEST FOR JARS

SEPTEMBER 8TH

T rue to her word, Madison went into super cling mode, hanging on her all morning except for the time it took to visit the bathroom. An almost-eleven-year-old, even a girl her sister's size who hadn't been eating well, made for a less-than-comfortable lap cat. However, Harper tolerated the clinginess during breakfast.

Growing up, no one would ever have accused her of being superstitious. Even when her father encouraged her to take up competition shooting, she hadn't developed any weird habits like the guys who had a 'lucky hat' or 'lucky shooting gloves.' One man legit withdrew from a competition because he'd forgotten said lucky hat at home in another state. He preferred not being on the roster at all than risking a bad showing.

Superstition hadn't truly developed in her, but she also didn't want to take the chance of setting off any argument, no matter how small, before doing something risky. Asking Madison not to sit in her lap or to give her a little space—*any* show of annoyance at all—could set the girl off on an emotional outburst. The idea that her sister storming off to the bedroom in a moody, wounded huff right before a trip to Denver would have any effect on Harper's chances of survival sounded laughable. She didn't believe in woo-woo things or random associations between events. However, *if* something happened to her, she couldn't leave Madison with the memory of their last moments together being combative or full of bad emotions.

Darci had to deal with that in regard to her father. The last words they exchanged flew back and forth on fire in a rather nasty argument.

So, she let her sister do whatever she wanted to feel better about her anxiety.

After breakfast, Cliff headed off to do militia stuff, Renee went to make clothing, and Carrie followed Harper and the kids down Hilltop Drive to the large Quartermaster's building on Route 74 at the heart of North Evergreen. The big Y-shaped building used to be the 'Life Care Center of Evergreen.' It had become the central storage and distribution location for food, clothing, and other supplies. Lately, whenever they had communal meals—most often occurring when deer hunts proved successful—everyone gathered in the parking lot between the Quartermaster's building and the Jewish temple behind it.

Lately, it seemed most everything important started or ended at this building, including today's trip. Rafael the mechanic checked over the guts of a US Postal Service truck roughly the size of a standard passenger van. It looked about as comfortable as riding in a steel wagon pulled by a team of huskies, but it beat walking or riding a bike. Extra metal bits sticking out the sides of the front compartment appeared to be the modifications needed for it to run on biodiesel, possibly even an entirely new engine. The home-brewed fuel also explained why the truck smelled like a fast-food deep fryer.

Leigh Preston, Roy Ellis, and Josh Webb—all fellow Militia—stood by Rafael watching him tweak something under the hood.

Madison sighed at the truck. "You're only gonna be gone for a few hours, right?"

"That's the plan, yeah. Definitely back by dinner time." Harper hugged her.

"Any chance I can come with you? I promise I'll stay in the truck." Madison held on tight, refusing to let go.

"It's Denver." Harper frowned. "Anywhere else, maybe I'd consider it but..."

Madison sighed at her sneakers. "Yeah. I know. You're right. Having to watch out for me is only gonna get us both hurt. Just... be careful, okay?"

"I will."

"Good luck out there, Harp." Carrie hugged them both, squishing Madison into her for a few seconds.

"If you get hurt, I'm going to be so sad." Lorelei overacted a pout. "Please come back."

Harper exhaled hard. "That's the plan."

Lorelei, being too little for farm work, followed Carrie into the Quartermaster's building. Their 'new mom' presently helped with winter preparations and preserving food. She'd been a hobbyist before at making preserves and such, and took on a teaching-slash-supervisory role in terms of the canning process. Madison begrudgingly followed Jonathan down the road toward the farm, peering back over her shoulder at Harper every few steps.

Roy chuckled. "They really are laying quite the guilt trip."

"Aww." Leigh fidgeted at a paper map. "You know Walter would understand."

"Yeah, I know. But I don't want to be that girl who always weasels out of stuff and leaves the crap to everyone else." Harper swung the Mossberg off her shoulder and checked it over.

Roy, Josh, and Leigh all nodded their approval, though Leigh still looked a bit guilty. Harper suspected all three of them would go out of their way to keep her safe, Roy especially. A quick trip into Denver to grab empty glass jars no one else in their right mind would have had any interest in didn't sound like the most dangerous thing in the world. A group like the Lawless would be unlikely to conserve bullets and went out of their way to get into violent situations. It somewhat surprised her they hadn't come to Evergreen, being relatively close. However, 'close' applied to driving cars. On foot, not so much. Also, the Lawless didn't really go for fair fights. If they heard rumors of a well-armed militia in Evergreen, they'd more than likely avoid it, preferring to prey on individuals or small, unarmed groups.

In a better world, we'd roll in there and wipe them out to protect the innocent. She sighed out her nose. *We don't have a better world. We're still trying to keep ourselves alive.*

Harper stared down the road at her sister. *Damn. I promised her I wouldn't leave town again... except for a really good reason. She didn't protest. Suppose 'not starving over the winter' counts as a good reason.*

"Fuel's in the back." Rafael shut the hood before going around to the left side door and pointing inside. "Plastic bottle hangin' here. Second five-gallon bottle there. If you run out on the first bottle, just pull the tube out and swap them. Added a roof hatch, too. Lid's quarter inch plate steel with the guts of a bulletproof vest on top."

Roy leaned in to look around. "Looks good. We'll do our best to get it back to you with as few new holes as possible."

"Appreciate it." Rafael chuckled. "We only have one workin' biodiesel, so best not to lose it."

"You got it." Roy stepped in and moved up front. "Preston, you want the wheel?"

"Sure." Leigh went around to the driver side door. "Crap. Other side, like England."

Rafael laughed. "Yeah. Mail truck. They put the wheel on this side so the driver can stuff mail into mailboxes without having to get out."

Harper climbed in the side door. The cargo area contained empty shelves, empty space, one large plastic bottle mounted to a bracket on the wall behind the driver's compartment, a spare plastic bottle of yellowish fluid, and a dirty canvas USPS sack lying on the floor against the left tire well, seemingly stuffed with undelivered mail. At the front right corner, the seat of an office chair with the back and wheels removed hung from a clamp bolted to the ceiling beside a round opening in the roof. A simple handle held the hatch closed. Someone could pull themselves up onto the chair and sit roughly chest-deep in the roof, taking cover behind the open hatch plate. Unfortunately, it did not appear capable of rotating, so the armor plate only protected from the front.

Yeah, that's a death trap. No thanks.

Noting the conspicuous lack of seats and no shortage of steel surfaces to smack her head on, Harper decided to sit on the mail sack.

The instant she lowered her weight onto it, she realized she'd sat on a small person. *What the heck? No way is this Madison. I watched her walk off down the road.*

Josh ducked inside, his AR-15 clattering. He looked around at the basic open nothingness, then whistled. "Wow. No seats."

"Just a kid in a bag," muttered Harper before standing. "Out."

The bag didn't move.

Harper lightly kicked it twice. "C'mon. I know you're in there. Just sat on you. Not fooling anyone. If you don't get out of the sack, I'm going to shove the whole bag out the door."

Grumbling in a child's voice accompanied squirming. The top end opened, revealing a pair of small hands. Mila Cline pulled herself out of the bag, slithering onto the floor. She'd dressed for ninja work in a black long-sleeved sweatshirt, yoga pants, black sneakers, and—of course—her bandolier of little throwing knives.

Harper folded her arms. "What are you doing?"

"I'm going with you to make sure you stay alive so Madison isn't upset." Mila stood, brushing dust off her sleeves.

Josh and Roy stifled laughter. Leigh peeked in the narrow door between the driver's compartment and the back, mouthing 'wow.'

"If I thought this was even remotely safe enough for kids, I'd have let Maddie come with us. It's *Denver*."

Mila folded her arms as well. "Exactly why you need me."

"I'm not questioning your skill, but"—Harper ushered her to the door—"you're ten. Doesn't matter how good you are, you're a kid and you're staying here where it's safe until you're at least sixteen."

Sighing, Mila jumped down to the pavement outside. "Fine. Had to try. You know we're the same, right?"

"Oh, I gotta hear this," muttered Roy.

"How?" Harper raised an eyebrow.

"Kids who are really good with weapons." Mila let her arms drop at her sides. "They kinda think you're a kid and need to be protected, too."

"Harp's a badass," said Leigh.

"I'd trust her watching my back any day." Roy smiled.

"I'm eighteen." Harper grumbled, more than a little embarrassed at the praise. 'Badass' didn't even make the list of top 100 things she expected people would ever call her, more like 'tree hugger' or 'Greenpeace Girl.' *Get emotional and cry once in sixth grade during a presentation on rainforest destruction and everyone thinks I'm an environmental lunatic.*

Mila kicked at a small stone. "Okay. Fine. I'll go back to the farm. Mom would be seriously upset if I went to Denver anyway."

"Yeah. So would Maddie." Harper ruffled her hair.

The engine sputtered to life, making the whole truck vibrate. It didn't sound as beefy as she thought a diesel engine ought to, but even if this thing only went thirty miles an hour, it definitely beat walking. Also, no way could they carry a crapload of mason jars back on bicycles.

Harper shoved the side door closed, then sat on the uncomfortable metal floor to do the one thing she feared the absolute most: going back to Denver.

4

DANCING ON THE SURFACE OF THE SUN

R iding in the back of a Postal truck while sitting on the floor proved uncomfortable.

Between the vibration of the engine, crummy shocks, bumps, and frequent swerving around debris, holding herself steady ended up being surprisingly exhausting. The vehicle had been designed to carry mail, not passengers, thus the back end didn't have windows. Josh tolerated only about twenty minutes of sitting on the floor before he decided to try out the hatch. Though somewhat precarious, the piece of office chair had *some* cushioning.

Roy and Leigh discussed directions. She pointed out several locations where old phone books suggested they would be able to find jars suitable for canning and preserving. Places like Walmart, Trader Joe's, Ninth Avenue Hardware, Pacific Mercantile Company, Savory Spice Shop, and a few others. According to Leigh, if they stuffed this truck to the ceiling with mason jars, they'd make it through the winter 'comfortably.' She remained hopeful no one would have taken—or smashed—empty glass jars. Even the Militia left them behind on prior scavenging trips, not having anticipated as much need for them. Alas, the stock of such jars already in Evergreen turned out to be insufficient for the farm's yield.

Harper leaned forward to peer through the doorway out the windshield every so often.

The trip up Route 74 to Route 70 and east into downtown Denver came out to around twenty-five miles according to Roy's mumbled calculations.

"How fast are we going?" called Harper.

"About fifty." Leigh paused. "Could probably get this thing up to sixty-five or so but not pushing my luck. It's shaking already."

Harper raised both eyebrows. "Fifty? Nice. We could get there in half an hour if we don't end up stuck in traffic."

Roy, Leigh, and Josh laughed.

Taking Route 70 eastward into Denver cut through Lakewood, her old neighborhood. Harper didn't much mind the lack of windows. Looking at the places she used to see all the time ruined, burned, abandoned, or worse would only throw her into a dark mood. She closed her eyes and clung to her memories of how everything was before the war, a time when she didn't wonder *if* her friends remained alive and she could contact any of them as fast as sending a text message.

I haven't touched a cell phone for over a year. Hmm. Guess Dad was wrong when he said I'd lose my mind if separated from my iPhone for more than three hours.

A sudden, intense pang of sorrow hit her at remembering his joke. With it came a flood of memories, everything from her family to school to the anxiety she felt over going to college. It seemed so damn trivial now. Being afraid of college sounded stupid. In truth, she hadn't been *frightened* as much as merely spoiled and not wanting her life to change so much. College meant growing up, leaving her friends behind, taking on more and more responsibility and not being a kid anymore.

All the emotions faded as rapidly as they'd manifested.

She longed for her old life but accepted her new one. Missing the dead only proved her humanity, not anything wrong with her. Harper couldn't change the world back to what it used to be. The only thing she could do for her parents was to survive—and protect Madison. Harper sat up straight. She had a veritable cannon and three armed friends. In a way, she kind of mourned the Harper Cody who ran screaming from her house a year ago. That girl couldn't kill anyone, even to save her father's life.

Everyone has changed.

The truck slowed to a stop, startling her out of her maudlin daydreams.

"Here's the first place." Leigh cut the engine. "We—ack. What the hell?"

"Whoa," said Roy. "That's messed up."

"What is?" Harper got to her feet, moved to the doorway between cargo area and driver's compartment, and looked out the giant windshield.

In the intersection half a block in front of where they stopped, thirty or so charred human skeletons stood in a circle, arms raised, skulls tilted, legs up, all frozen as if in the middle of a wild dance around a figure seated in a giant throne made from concrete rubble. The man, small compared to his seat, slumped to one side, obviously dead even from this distance.

Harper stared in disgusted, horrified awe at the spectacle. Skeletons did not, as far as she knew, possess the ability to stand on their own, much less dance. She assumed someone had made 'statues' out of them somehow.

"I gotta take a closer look at that." Roy shoved the front door open.

"Okay, but we shouldn't dawdle." Leigh got out.

"We have time." Josh climbed down from the roof hatch. "Not like we went too far from home."

Harper swallowed the saliva building up in the back of her mouth, then crept out the door behind Roy. Mossberg poised, she scanned their surroundings. Leigh had pulled over at the side of a four-lane street somewhere downtown. Despite having visited the city many times, Harper couldn't recognize the exact location thanks to the destruction. Intermittent pigeon noises and the clatter of falling debris echoed across the destroyed remains of buildings. Some former high-rises tilted to the side, away from the direction the nuclear blast came from. Several had collapsed entirely. Others had been reduced to naked steel frames, all the concrete and internal guts blown straight out of them. She searched in vain for even the smallest, recognizable landmark… but the city had changed.

Shocked disbelief rapidly gave way to vigilance. Harper, being on the left side of the group, reflexively 'adopted' the left rear pie quarter of an imaginary circle around them and watched it for hostiles. Every glint of broken glass or flutter of shredded plastic could potentially be a Lawless trying to sneak up on them. She knew a bizarre sight waited for her outside her peripheral vision, but didn't dare look away from their surroundings so fast.

Mom had taught her some things around age twelve: never take a stairwell without security cameras, never cross a parking lot at night alone, avoid dark places, carry keys between her fingers like Wolverine's claws… and so on. Her mother's advice came from an entirely different world exclusive to young women, but still applied. Cliff's training shifted her mindset from prey animal ready to flee when spooked to… she didn't want to say predator. However, any reaction she had to unknown persons or threats would not come from a place of fear anymore.

She looked. She listened. She even smelled.

… and regretted it.

Taking a deep breath in through her nose almost made her gag on the fetid murk of rotting corpse. Given all the debris around, she figured it an almost certainty that many people lay buried under the concrete fragments. Though should they *still* smell after a year? She tried to stifle a cough, keeping her attention on three side streets and two alleys across from the truck. Anyone climbing over or through the numerous mounds of rubble would make a significant amount of noise.

Roy began walking. Leigh, Josh, and Harper formed a lopsided checkmark formation behind him. Roy, Leigh, and Josh formed a three-person V with Harper trailing after Josh on the left side.

Wish we had a working machinegun on the truck. She smirked to herself. *A year ago, I really wanted a new laptop. Now I want a big gun covering me. Guess I'm broken like everyone else.*

The streets of downtown Denver hung in eerie silence.

Harper couldn't believe her eyes. They hadn't gone to Denver. This had to be some alternate reality or an Armageddon-themed attraction at Universal Studios. Somewhat confident no threats lurked in her field of responsibility, she glanced to her right.

Ahead of them lay a large intersection where two four-lane streets crossed. The throne-like chair appeared to be made from various hunks of concrete rubble. By far, the largest one, the seatback, consisted of a single slab ten feet high and roughly four feet wide. Whoever made the 'throne' couldn't possibly have moved such an enormous piece of reinforced concrete, suggesting it had already been there, stuck into the ground like a dropped knife. At this distance, Harper noticed various things holding the skeletons together: wire, duct tape, packing tape, power cables tied around them, even screws and small bits of wood. The vast majority of the bones had serious charring, blackened almost to ash over most of their bodies. Some of the pieces didn't seem to match the rest of the skeletons. One had a too-small arm. Another's skull didn't seem right for the rest of it. A third skeleton's pelvis had two different halves. In some spots, completely wrong bones sat where they didn't belong, such as fingers replacing a rib or two or femurs in place of upper arm bones.

Way beyond any of the destroyed buildings, toppled utility poles, melted cars, or general destruction, the ring of 'dancing' skeletons made the ruined city feel otherworldly. Angry butterflies swirled around in Harper's stomach as she beheld the macabre arrangement. She didn't really believe in ghosts, yet couldn't shake the bizarre sense all the dead of Denver watched her.

If any of these things move, even if it's the wind, I'm going to freak the hell out.

Leigh appeared equally on edge, though she didn't visibly shake like Josh.

Roy raised an eyebrow, glancing around at the spectacle with an expression like he'd caught someone littering. "Wow..."

The man in the concrete throne appeared much more recently dead than the standing skeletons. His clothing didn't stand out as too unusual: a filthy polo shirt, jeans, sneakers, and an old-style Army coat. The general state of grime suggested he'd worn this outfit for months before his death. An upward spreading pattern of blood on the seatback, a hole under his chin, and a revolver dangling from his right hand gave a fairly solid account of how he'd died. Between his feet sat a rectangular metal toolbox, its arrangement deliberate as if for display.

Paintings of mushroom clouds, missiles, bombs, and abstract flames decorated the pavement around the skeletons as well as every flat rubble surface within the circle they formed, including the throne. The dead man slumped perfectly to one side, making a smallish mushroom cloud painted on the concrete appear to follow the trajectory the bullet exited the top of his skull.

Noticing the top of the toolbox slightly open, Harper surrendered to curiosity and crouched to look inside. It contained no tools, rather a woman's wedding band, a youth league baseball trophy bearing the name Brian Watson, a Barbie doll, a tiny white teddy bear, a plastic giraffe head like from a baby's mobile, and a small framed photo of an elderly couple smiling.

Harper stared at the items. *Oh no... this stuff must have belonged to people he loved.* Tears gathered in the corners of her eyes.

"Whoa, check this out," said Josh from behind the throne.

"Sec," rasped Harper, trying to swallow a lump.

The others moved around to the rear of the throne. Harper eased the lid of the toolbox down, took a deep breath, then joined the rest of the Militia people. Crudely carved writing covered most of the ten-by-four-foot slab:

NOT ONE SAT ON A ROCKET SLED
   Seeking travel to the nearby star

NO WARNING SOUND NOR LIGHTS OF RED
   Herald midnight fire sent from afar

FROM YOUNG TO OLD THEIR LIVES UNDONE
   They danced on the surface of the sun

FOR TINY FRAGMENT SECONDS BURN
   In searing light to ashes they turn

BY GLOWING PEACE OR LAWLESS BLADE
   Their lives go dark, loves and fates unmade

HERE UPON A THRONE OF RUIN
   I wait upon the fateful reckoning

. . .

BEFORE THEM ALL MY WORK IS DONE
  Despite my shrine, no silence beckoning

GHOSTS FORLORN IN AGONY SCREAM
  Awaiting me to escape this dream

THE ARTIST HAS NO MORE TO DO
  I dance on the surface of the sun

  Allie - Brian - Erica - Zara - Austin - Mom - Dad
  Jeffrey O. Watson

HARPER'S MIND DREW CONNECTIONS BETWEEN THE NAMES AND THE contents of the box. She assumed the names referred to the dead man's wife, son, daughters, infant son, parents. No telling which ones died to the blast, to the Lawless, or to other misfortunes. Glowing peace had to refer to those vaporized in an instant. It didn't take deep thought to grasp what he meant by 'Lawless blade.'

Stuck between sadness and anger, Harper merely stared at the morbid poem.

"So, umm…" Josh fidgeted. "Is this art? A grave site, or the work of a psycho?"

"I don't think this guy killed anyone but himself," said Roy. "Probably spent months arranging those bones."

Leigh whistled. "Poor bastard."

Harper stared at the names along the bottom of the slab. "This is a grave. We shouldn't disturb it."

"I agree." Leigh pointed at the building next to the van. "Let's check that place for jars and get the heck out of here."

Roy and Josh both nodded.

Harper stood there, too emotional to move, imagining this poor man driven mad with grief, feverishly collecting bones and stitching them together into this... memorial. She thought it tragic he'd survived the Lawless only to take his own life. Before her thoughts could torture her trying to figure out how each person named on the slab died, she shook her head and hurried after the others.

More than anything, she wanted to race home and grab Madison, Jonathan, and Lorelei, just to remind herself why she fought so damn hard to stay alive.

5

THE QUIET ONES

The store appeared to have suffered only casual looting, more rummaging than removing.

Not even the Lawless saw any point to taking objects unlikely to be useful, no matter how valuable or expensive they'd have been before the war. A place full of arts and crafts type supplies didn't hold the same interest as pharmacies or supermarkets. They located a substantial stock of empty mason jars intended for hobbyist canners and began the tedious process of transferring them back to the truck by hand with baskets since it would take too long to clear all the junk out of the aisles so shopping carts could get by.

Harper snagged an entire case of colored pencils—twenty tins —for Jonathan, shocked to see them marked at $90 each. They wouldn't take up much space in the truck, so it didn't bother her to grab one 'nonessential' item.

After nine back-and-forth trips carrying double handbaskets of mason jars, Harper headed back inside to grab another load. They'd cleared off the shelves out in the store and moved on to loot the stock room. Having an unexpected lucky break surprised her. No one else had bothered to take the jars for something like

Molotovs or whatever. Then again, Denver's streets and various trash receptacles had plenty of empty beer and wine bottles for that. Long-necked bottles worked better for flame grenades.

While loading up her baskets for the tenth time, a voice whisper-shouted on the other side of a fire exit at the back of the stock room.

"Shut the fuck up! They got guns. We gotta get em when they ain't looking."

Harper dropped a four-pack of jars into the basket and yanked the Mossberg off her shoulder. None of the other Militia people were in the room with her, either on the way to the truck or back from it. If she yelled 'incoming' or gave any audible warning, the people outside would know they'd given themselves away. Staying quiet, she hurried to the left, taking cover behind a plastic-wrapped pallet of art supplies. Once in cover, she raised her weapon.

The fire door scraped open.

Two men walked in, both in dingy shirts, jeans, and jackets. The lead man looked to be in his late thirties with shaggy black hair; behind him, a younger guy, perhaps not even twenty yet. Both wore the blue sashes of Lawless around their necks. Shaggy carried a crowbar with nails welded onto the curve. The younger guy clutched a silver Beretta 92.

Harper sighted on him first. As if sensing a shotgun lined up with his skull, the younger man turned his head to stare at her. The sight of blue sashes eliminated any hesitation she might've had about shooting, but the instant they made eye contact, she stopped herself.

The kid looked familiar.

He gave a strangled gurgle and froze in his tracks. The older guy glanced back at him, seeming annoyed—until he spotted Harper. For a few excruciatingly long seconds, they stared at each other.

"Harper?" whispered the boy.

"Steve..." She adjusted her grip on the Mossberg, keeping it pointed at his face. It felt beyond wrong to point a loaded weapon at someone she'd gone to school with, but... blue sash. "Pratt?"

"Hey, you remember me." He grinned. "C'mon, Harp. You're not gonna shoot us."

"Lower that thing and come with us," said the older man.

Harper narrowed her eyes. "The only reason I haven't shot both of you yet is I know you. What the hell are you doing with those lunatics?"

"Lunatics?" asked Steve.

"The fucking Lawless," snarled Harper.

Steve raised his left hand in a placating gesture, keeping his Beretta motionless, still pointed mostly up in front of him. "It's different now. Only the strong have any chance. These guys are pretty cool. C'mon, Cody. I'll protect you."

"Cody?" asked the older guy. "Who the hell is Cody?"

"She is." Steve chuckled. "That's Harper Cody. I know her from school."

"Oh, whatever. You wanna keep this one, fine," said the older guy.

Grr. Keep me? Like some kind of pet? "No. Lawless killed my parents. There's no way in hell I'm ever joining them or allowing myself to be kidnapped. Drop the gun. Now."

Rustling in the aisle junk came from the doorway leading back to the store. Backup would arrive in seconds. Steve and his older friend shifted uneasily at the noise.

"Relax, Scorp." Steve smiled at her. "Cody wouldn't hurt a fly. She's a complete tree-hugger. Even wrote a letter to the board of education protesting dissecting animals in bio."

"Heh." Scorp flashed a wicked grin. Perhaps intending to grab her as a human shield against whoever approached the stock room from the store, he rushed toward her.

The instant he started to move, Harper shifted her aim, put a load of buckshot into his face, and had the Mossberg back on Steve before the teen could point his gun at her. Scorp's head whipped back; blood, teeth, and jaw fragments went flying, spattering all over Steve. The rest of Scorp crumpled into a heap on the floor, a dark red puddle spreading out from where his head met concrete.

"You're not the only one who's changed," said Harper.

Steve squeaked, eyes wide.

Josh rushed in, taking cover behind the shelf closest to the door. "Sitrep!"

"Lawless," called Harper, still staring over her gunsight at Steve. "Was two. One now. Watch the front."

A distinct fecal odor rose from Scorp's remains.

"What's it gonna be?" asked Harper, ignoring the ringing in her ears from a gunshot so close to cinder block walls. "Are you really one of *them* or are you still Steve Pratt?"

Images of the same boy—much cleaner with shorter hair—flickered across her mind. He'd been mostly invisible like her socially, except for being the primary harassment target of the school's football star, Kyle Peterson, and his crew. She didn't really know either of them well, behind thinking Kyle a dick and having some pity for Steve. Despite the blue sash, killing a kid she'd gone to school with from first grade would haunt her... even more than the dancing skeletons, which she *knew* had already booked reservations for a future appearance in her nightmares.

Steve stepped back toward the fire door.

"Don't run." She tensed her finger on the trigger. "I will shoot you."

"For running?" He blinked. "That's messed up."

"Yep. If you run, you're going to get more Lawless."

"I won't. Swear."

Josh took a position mostly behind Steve, aiming his AR-15 through a gap in the steel shelves.

She frowned. "Yeah, right. I know you're not going to bring friends, because you are going to just stand there until we're done."

Steve shivered nervously. "Y-you're not really gonna shoot me, Harper. C'mon. we sat like three desks away in Mrs. Carr's class. We've known each other since like forever."

"I've known your name since first grade. Can't really say we *knew* each other." She sighed. "You are wearing a blue sash. The *only* reason I didn't just blow your head off as soon as I had a clean shot is knowing you from school. Toss the Beretta. I won't tell you again."

Most of the color drained from his face. The last time she saw that expression on him, he'd been caught cheating in Algebra. He threw the Beretta into a giant box of silver-spray-painted pinecones six feet to his left. "What the hell happened to you, Cody?"

"Back atcha. Never pegged you for a rapey, murdering gang thug." She lowered the shotgun a little. "Didn't you used to be one of the quiet kids?"

"It's always the quiet ones who cause the most trouble," said Josh.

"Clear out here," called Leigh.

"Let's hustle." Roy whipped around the doorway, making a tactical entry to the stock room. Upon noticing only one hostile, he relaxed a little. "Harp, you wanna keep an eye on this kid or should I?"

"I got him. You can carry more than me." She relaxed and tensed her grip on the gun.

Steve cringed away, seemingly uninterested in looking at the puddle of blood expanding away from Scorp's head.

For a tense twelve minutes, Steve stood in silence making 'you wouldn't really shoot me, would you?' faces at her while Leigh, Roy, and Josh finished grabbing the remainder of the jars.

Roy leaned back into the stock room, making a whirlybird gesture with his finger.

"Steve," said Harper in an almost whisper.

"Harper," replied Steve.

"You can come with us if you want. If you stay with the Lawless, I can't promise I'll hesitate next time."

He looked down. "Yeah, well. It's a different world now."

Harper didn't like the vibe he gave off. It reminded her too much of Tyler. The scrawny kid harassed by the popular boys must have daydreamed about lashing out and never found the nerve or opportunity to do it. Some of the football players sarcastically voted him 'most likely to snap and do a school shooting.' She guessed the Lawless gave him what he'd secretly wanted: a sense of power. Something about his expression, his posture, told her he'd done bad things since the war and didn't have the least bit of remorse. He likely thought his victims deserved it. She'd never have expected him to be capable of violence but... as he said, the world changed.

"I'm sorry they teased you," whispered Harper.

He scoffed to the side. "You didn't tease me. You barely said anything to anyone. I didn't shoot you."

She blinked. "What? Of course you didn't. Your gun's in the pinecones."

"No." He gave a mirthless chuckle. "In my dreams."

Her throat ran dry. The football players had been closer to right than anyone knew. "You always had it in you... didn't you? Just scared of getting in trouble."

"Yeah, basically." Steve shrugged. "Decided it wouldn't be worth it. Would've been epic, though... but only for a few minutes. No matter how much they deserved it, I'd end up dead or in jail for the rest of my life."

"So, you join the Lawless and get off on hurting other people just like the bullies who harassed you. Makes sense... not."

He rolled his eyes. "I don't hurt everyone. Just those who don't properly respect me."

For a fleeting instant, she came close to putting him out of the world's misery, but couldn't do it. Shooting an unarmed boy she used to go to school with for saying dark things crossed a line from defense to murder.

"You're wrong, Steve. It's not worth it to do what you're doing." She nodded at the fire door. "Get lost."

He took a step toward the box of pinecones.

"Don't."

Steve faced her, arms out to either side. "You're robbing me?"

"No. I'm confiscating a weapon from a kid who's too unstable to have one. If I let you go out that door with a firearm, you're going to hurt someone and it will be my fault. You're wearing the blue sash of a Lawless. Be goddamned happy you're still breathing."

Steve backed away from the pinecones, hands up. "Sorry about your parents, Harp. I had nothing to do with that."

She stood there, pointing the Mossberg at him until he bolted out into the alley behind the store. After kicking the fire door shut, Harper grabbed the Beretta and sighed at it. Letting him leave alive bothered her, but not as much as the idea *not* killing someone might have been the wrong choice.

At least he won't use this to hurt anyone else. She flicked the safety on, then ran for the truck.

6

FUTURE THREATS

Riding in the mail truck into Denver had been uncomfortable.

Cramming four people into the driver compartment ended up being paradoxically more comfortable, if a bit awkward. Roy took over driving for the return trip. Leigh got the passenger seat, offering her lap to Harper. Roy jokingly offered to let Josh sit in his lap, too… but the steering wheel got in the way. That, and he hadn't been serious. Josh sat on the floor with his back against the door to the cargo area, which they'd stuffed as full as possible with mason jars. They'd even piled six giant plastic storage boxes on the roof, all containing yet more mason jars. The box of colored pencils remained in the truck, up front between the two seats—with two boxes of jars on top of it. At least being up front let her see the world going by. Harper kept her eyes closed as they crossed Lakewood, relaxing only after they reached the highway leading into the mountains.

With Denver fully in the side mirrors behind them, she finally stopped squeezing her shotgun in a white-knuckled grip. Much as she'd done before, Harper filed away the men she'd shot today with the same emotional insignificance as shooting bad guys in video games. Over nine stores, they'd run into a total of twelve more Lawless, but only two at a time. She hadn't recognized anyone else.

Evidently, the gang had either declined in number or didn't spend much time roaming the area of downtown Harper and her friends visited, considering it scavenged to uselessness. A year after the war, anything they would think worthwhile had long since been taken. Two attacks ended fast, at ranges impossible for Harper's shotgun to matter. She'd kept her head down while Roy, Leigh, and Josh engaged the bad guys. Combat rifles vs. handguns didn't end well for the people using handguns. The other four 'patrols' didn't show up until after Harper and her friends had gone inside the store, forcing close-range fights. None of the Lawless appeared to expect armed victims who wouldn't hesitate to open fire on a known criminal group. She figured they'd heard rummaging plus female voices and assumed solitary survivors who'd be easy prey.

Much better than having a group of ten come at them all at once.

The unusual lack of Lawless made her wonder if she'd been right. A predatory gang might be too stupid or lazy to try establishing a farm or a ready source of food. Existing purely on scavenging ruins and stealing from others would last only so long. By now, the entire city of Denver and the surrounding suburbs had to be completely empty of useful canned food. If the Lawless hadn't been killed off, their numbers quite likely suffered thinning due to starvation, disease, idiocy, or perhaps migration to another major city.

Of the six two-person teams they encountered, only three individuals had guns. Neither Harper nor her friends hesitated shooting at guys armed with axes, knives, and baseball bats. It helped the idiots charged at them. Harper *probably* wouldn't have simply gunned down everyone in a blue sash simply for existing.

Scorp, and the other three she shot, made aggressive moves on her or her friends before she fired.

Going into Denver and leaving without a scratch might have emboldened anyone else, but it made Harper a bit sick to her stomach with nerves. If she'd ever gone to Vegas and gambled, she'd stop as soon as she won even a small prize from a slot machine. No 'I'm on a roll' nonsense leading to her losing everything she won twice over. False confidence bred disaster. Going in and out of Denver without so much as a splinter in her finger encouraged her never to do it again. She'd take her 'winnings' and be satisfied.

Steve, however, haunted her.

The boy had been quiet, simultaneously thoughtful and creepy all throughout high school. For all she knew, he'd only said he daydreamed about shooting up their classmates to sound tough. He hadn't, after all, really made a move to aim the Beretta at her. Of course, he also had zero apparent qualms with the idea of kidnapping her, so perhaps the violence he fantasized about had become more real than anyone from school expected possible.

She examined the silver Beretta. It definitely wasn't fake, loaded with eleven hollow-point bullets in the mag, one in the pipe. Harper cleared the chamber, then added the bullet to the mag before stuffing it back in the handle. Steve had been carrying a real weapon. Whether he'd used the missing five rounds or found it that way, she couldn't tell. Still, she couldn't picture Steve Pratt walking into class holding this Beretta and shooting Kyle, or anyone else. The boy had practically wet himself when she ended Scorp.

He didn't want to spend the rest of his life in jail. Had that been the only thing stopping him?

"Did I screw up?" asked Harper, breaking a long stretch of silence.

"Not as far as I could see." Roy glanced at her. "What makes you ask?"

Josh shook his head. "We got in and out clean. Used a little ammo, but no one's hurt."

She sighed. "I let Steve run away. Does that make me responsible for anyone he hurts? He came into the store hoping to ambush us, wanted to kidnap me… and I let him go."

"He surrendered," said Leigh. "We don't just shoot people for wearing the wrong thing, like a blue sash."

"Exception for anyone in Dallas Cowboys stuff." Roy nodded once. "Feel free to take them out without a word."

Josh and Leigh chuckled.

Harper managed a feeble smile. "What kind of cop lets someone off with a warning after stopping a violent crime?"

"A cop in a world without jails." Roy swerved around a partially molten Ford Explorer.

Leigh exhaled. "Better we don't bring him with us. He'd take one look around and run back to his buddies. If the Lawless knew about Evergreen, they'd try to come take what we have."

"If he hurts someone else… I could've stopped him." Harper stuck the Beretta into a storage cubby below the windshield.

"Nah. You made the right choice," said Leigh. "The only thing separating us from the 'bad guys' is we only kill when absolutely necessary. He wasn't an immediate threat to you. Any crap he does in the future is all on him."

The woman only had her by about ten years, at twenty-eight or so—too young to feel motherly. Harper had no experience being the 'little sister,' but took comfort in the reassurance offered. Lawless or not, she would have been horrified at herself if she thought nothing of executing a kid she'd gone to school with. He'd been reasonably normal until high school. The teasing hadn't kicked into high gear until then. She didn't even know him well enough to understand why anyone picked on him.

Maybe the world's better off without high schools. She rolled her eyes. *Yeah, sure. Less bullying, but we'll have no more doctors and scientists. Not a great tradeoff. Still, Leigh made sense. Maybe watching Harper blow Scorp's head off gave Steve a much-needed reality check. It might not, but whatever he did now wasn't her fault.*

"Thanks," said Harper.

"We'll be back in about twelve minutes." Roy smiled. "Just in time for more manual labor, lugging all this crap inside."

Harper stretched. "Fine with me. No one will be shooting at us."

7

BLOOD AND FAMILY

Harper helped lug the boxes of mason jars into the Quartermaster's building.

Unloading proved far easier than loading, thanks to the help of a giant lumber cart from Home Depot. They didn't need to carry individual boxes into the building, which greatly lessened the time required.

Harper grabbed boxes from the truck's rear door, handing them off to Josh to put on the cart. Leigh, Roy, and a few of the people who worked in the Quartermaster's pulled the giant plastic storage bins down from the roof.

The rapid clap of small sneakers on pavement meant only one thing. Harper handed another box to Josh, then peered around the side of the truck at Madison and Mila running down Route 74. Both girls looked as if they'd tried to go swimming in dirt.

Harper glanced at Josh. "One sec."

"No problem." He laughed and began grabbing boxes out of the truck rather than waiting for her to pass them over.

Madison ran into a hug. Mila stopped a step or two behind her, slightly winded but smiling.

"Sorry," said Harper.

"It's okay," mumbled Madison into Harper's shirt. "I'm not a baby."

Mila folded her arms. "She only threw up from anxiety once. Better than last time."

Harper squished her tighter. "You're not a baby, Maddie. You're traumatized."

"Umm." Madison leaned back to make eye contact. "One: she's teasing. I didn't throw up. Two: we're *all* traumatized. Everyone in this town is messed up in some way or another. If they're not, they're psycho."

Harper resumed grabbing boxes and handing them to Josh. Madison and Mila scrambled into the truck to help unload it.

Madison handed her a box. "Cliff said we can let it own us or we can live for Mom and Dad."

"Yeah." Harper took the box and gave it to Josh before grabbing one Mila held out to her.

"I'm not gonna pretend it never happened or that I'm totally okay..." Madison slouched. "But... it's gonna make Mom and Dad sad if I give up. Cliff's got some PTSD stuff from being in combat, and so do we."

"He hides it well." Mila grabbed another box.

"Not everyone is as tough as Cliff." Harper stepped up into the truck, but didn't really have to with the girls plucking boxes from deeper inside. "It's totally fine if you have trouble coping. You didn't give up."

"You don't wanna lose the last family you have." Mila shoved two stacked boxes toward the back end with her foot while carrying a third.

Madison looked down. "My family is Harper, Cliff, Jon, and Lore... not just Harper."

"But she's your blood."

"Blood's not necessarily important." Josh grabbed four boxes at once. "I can't stand my older brother. He's a racist asshole. Oh, shit. Sorry. Little kids around. I shouldn't swear."

Madison giggled.

Mila flashed the perfect 'give me a break' expression. "We were nuked. I got kidnapped, tied up, put in a jail cell, and held prisoner for months by this psycho who thought he was a spirit ninja. Lorelei almost starved. Maddy watched her parents die. I think we can handle bad words."

At 'watched her parents die,' Madison flinched.

Harper pulled her into a hug.

"I'm okay," whispered Madison. "Umm, Harp?"

"What's up?"

Madison held up a box of jars. "I was thinking. I really miss Mom and grandma showing me how to cook and bake. Carrie's kinda teaching me some stuff now. Can I help out here in the kitchen stuffing these jars instead of breaking my ass on the farm?"

Josh laughed, as did Roy and Leigh.

"Well, she is kinda scrawny for hard labor." Roy peered around the side of the truck and winked.

Madison flexed her noodle of a bicep. "Truth."

"I don't see why not. Go talk to Liz." Harper ruffled her sister's hair.

"Me?" Madison blushed. "Can't you do it?"

Harper passed another box of jars to Josh. "I could, but it would work better coming directly from you. How about I go with you?"

"Okay." Madison's blush lessened. "That's fair."

8

SPOILED

SEPTEMBER 19TH

An unusually warm Thursday made Harper's patrol duty surprisingly pleasant, considering eleven days ago, she almost killed a former classmate.

Any time a week passed without her needing to shoot someone, her overactive hopefulness kicked in and tried to convince her it meant the world started healing. She wanted to believe reality wouldn't end up being *Mad Max*. Not only had all the gasoline already rotted beyond usefulness, Harper couldn't accept the idea a significant number of real people who had known life in the modern world could give in to savagery and tribalism on a large scale. Sure, pockets of idiots existed like the guys Dad used to refer to as 'cosplay soldiers,' who simply couldn't wait for the end of the world so they could swoop in and become the new power instead of the old government.

However, in order for huge roving tribes of marauding bandits to spring up or humanity to experience an overall descent into feralness, everyone would have to thoroughly forget where they came from. Life anything akin to what they depicted in movies about the apocalypse wouldn't come about for several generations if at all. Only when no living people remembered the world that once was, did it seem possible.

As far as Harper and her friends thought, the future would likely end up being a bizarre version of the Old West with scraps of prewar technology. If things went really bad, perhaps a return to medieval style feudalism. In either case, she believed people would cling to some sort of fundamental underpinning of civilization. No one would be racing around the desert in kink leather throwing spears at each other... at least not in her lifetime, or her grandkids lifetimes (if she had them.)

She'd probably spend the rest of her days trying to survive as best she could, seeing constant reminders of the life she almost had. Some random repurposed bit of metal with a Subway logo on the side of a survival shack would fill her head with memories of the time Veronica and Andrea got the giggles in a Subway and the manager asked them to quiet down or leave. A scrap of plastic blowing along the ground would make her think of a world where she could just 'go to a store' whenever she wanted to get food... a concept anyone three or younger now would likely find as alien as her reaction to Dad showing her cassette tapes.

However, as long as Madison, Jonathan, and Lorelei made it at least into their thirties, Harper figured she could accept the fall of civilization without anger... at least not *too* much. Not knowing who to blame complicated being angry. One early morning a year ago, the sky caught fire out of the blue. She had yet to talk to anyone who knew why it happened or who started it. All manner of theories went around, everything from a glitch in the computer systems to hackers to a sudden overthrow-slash-coup somewhere in Russia or China and the new leadership hit the button right away without warning. A few crackpots even blamed aliens, but even they couldn't agree on the same rationale.

Either the aliens made humans nuke each other or humans fired nukes to stop an alien invasion and missed.

She usually laughed at anyone who seemed to genuinely believed little green men ended the world. Thinking about them again took her mind off worrying about Lorelei. The girl hadn't been her usual energetic self, instead complaining of a tummy ache and feeling cruddy. Considering the child's history—having almost starved to death in the aftermath of the war—Harper took her to the clinic to get checked out.

Dr. Tegan Hale (who insisted Harper call her Tegan) looked the girl over. She didn't run a temperature, have a runny nose, or show signs of serious issues, so Tegan thought she likely had a non-contagious stomach bug or perhaps ate something that didn't agree with her. The doctor suggested letting Lorelei take it easy and making sure she drank at least one glass of water each hour. The child didn't appear too out of it, so she went with Carrie to the Quartermaster's, intending to curl up on a chair under a blanket.

The other kids once again headed off to the farm in the morning after breakfast. Madison ended up compromising. Since she adored the animals, she still went to the farm to feed chickens, cows, and so on… then went to the Quartermaster's to learn cooking and canning rather than work in the field carrying crops around. Based on the progress getting food in off the fields and preparing shelters for the livestock, the town managers expected to have kids under fifteen in classrooms within the next few days since it wouldn't be as much of an 'every available pair of hands are needed' situation.

Harper followed her usual route, walking around the residential area surrounding the old Hiwan golf course, now farmland, just south of the school. Enough of her idealistic, hopeful side remained to think she patrolled as a service to the residents in case someone needed help rather than being there primarily to defend the town against hostiles. Of course, she didn't ignore the real possibility 'bad guys' might show up. After all, it took less than thirty minutes to reach Denver from here, along a rather easy and obvious highway. If the Lawless *did* decide to cause trouble, they'd arrive from the north, though they would most likely follow Route 74 into the heart of town rather than jump the chain link fence and cross an overgrown meadow toward a school they would assume empty.

If any Lawless noticed their Postal truck leaving the area, they hadn't cared enough to chase. The gang didn't strike her as the most tactical or thoughtful people. They also had a tendency to laugh and mock their own members for being killed, so not the most loyal group either. If they planned to retaliate, it would've happened by now. It didn't seem at all likely they'd be upset at Harper or her friends for killing a dozen of them. Maybe Steve decided not to tell his buddies about what happened after all. Of course, no one said a word about Evergreen to him. He had no idea where Harper came from. Maybe he still thought she lived in Lakewood.

In addition to the Lawless, she had another worry stalking her on Hiwan Drive: biology.

Based on her instinctual sense of timing, she should have had her period by now. Yesterday, she'd even worn a pad… which she considered more precious than shotgun shells. It remained completely clean at the end of the day, to her surprise. Despite their scarcity and preciousness, she couldn't bring herself to keep it for re-use even though it had no blood on it. Not wanting to waste them—and being more than a little freaked out at the lateness—she opted instead to stuff her pants with scrap fabric.

Naturally, Renee teased her about the old phrase 'being on the rag' as it had become exceptionally literal. Walking around with a wad of fabric down there felt awkward as hell. Going 'full 1800s' happened much earlier than she anticipated. Darci's joke about side-stepping the whole lack of tampons/sanitary pads issue by just staying pregnant all the time didn't sound appealing—or practical. Of course her friend would never do that. She'd sooner parade around pantsless for a few days than ruin her clothes. The mere thought of that—plus knowing Darci really *would* do it— made Harper blush.

She looked left and right at houses as she passed by. No smoke, no screaming, no unusual noises came from anywhere. The area seemed dead and abandoned except for the giant house where Doreen Mack lived with thirteen or so babies and toddlers, various orphans who'd trickled in since the war. She had help now, in the form of Therese and Jen Oliver who lived there as well, along with Jen's almost thirteen-year-old son, Daxton. The boy had walked, alone, to Evergreen all the way from Kriley Pond to beg for help. His mom and a bunch of other people living there faced starvation as well as attack from a weird cult of morons.

Harper stopped by to talk for a bit and ended up helping change a few diapers. Soon after resuming her patrol, she went to check on Mr. Vitelli, the diabetic, but he'd gone somewhere... likely to his job. He'd been a real estate agent before the war, which 'naturally' translated into becoming a maintenance guy who helped fix up and maintain the houses here. She vaguely recalled Tegan saying something about giving him the last of the Metformin pills they had at the clinic.

Her thoughts returned to the uncomfortable mass stuffed into her pants. It bothered her not so much for the physical discomfort but the reminder of being late. Harper found a secluded spot in the trees between houses, opened her jeans, and checked. Still no blood.

Dammit. No. We've been careful...

She zipped up and resumed walking, though caught herself shivering. For some strange reason, the chance of pregnancy becoming a death sentence scared her less than the no-longer-possible scenario of her having to tell her parents she'd gotten pregnant at eighteen before finishing high school. She had no doubt Mom and Dad would have been supportive and not angry. In all likelihood, they'd have taken primary care of the baby so she could continue going to school.

Why am I fixating on telling Dad about it?

The last time she and Logan had sex happened nine days earlier in the same house not too far from Harper's where they had sex the first time. The place had officially become Logan's since he no longer counted as a 'single adult,' having an almost sixteen-year-old sister to look after. Granted, sixteen these days seemed far more of an adult than it did only a year ago. Luisa had been asleep in the other bedroom, forcing them to stay as quiet as possible. Cliff often cracked wise about life in a post-technological society, comparing it to living in the sticks of Pennsylvania.

Harper muttered to herself, trying to do an impression of his voice. "We've only got three things to do for fun here: drink, have sex, or shoot guns..."

He'd follow it by joking about how they only had so much beer and needed to save the bullets for defense, which left one practical option. Somehow, her new dad ended up being able to embarrass her every bit as easily as her biological dad. Still, not being directly related to him made it possible to talk about some stuff she'd never be able to with her real parents. Discussing how to handle sex, for instance, went by with as little awkwardness as setting up a night watch rotation. He wouldn't tell Harper not to do it, just didn't want her to do it around the kids. Not that she would have. He considered her an adult, even at seventeen since 'there are no children in war.' A girl who survived a nuclear strike and could kill people to protect her kid sister had the ability to determine whether or not to have sex as she pleased, according to him.

Nine days... She scratched at her belly, remembering Logan's valiant effort to avoid getting her pregnant. This, of course, led to the super uncomfortable memory of Dad attempting to tell her not to trust any boy who promises to 'pull out' instead of wearing a condom. Even if the boy didn't lie and really tried to, accidents happened. As far as she could tell, Logan had been extremely careful.

Maybe my math is wrong. Could be I'm not late after all, and it's not supposed to start until next week. I do have a lot of shit on my mind. She bit her lip. *Ugh. The last time I wanted to see blood this bad, I aimed a shotgun at the guy who killed Dad.*

Thoughts and images swirled around in her mind as she walked among the empty houses, the images and sounds playing across the theater of her brain simultaneously scary, reassuring, and somber. Children too little to work on the farm went to school. Kids around ten or older pitched in with the harvest—or did lighter work to free adults up for the heavy lifting. Most of the adults occupying the houses here also headed to the farm. A few dozen people came up north from South Evergreen to help, seeing as how the farm fed them, too. Rather than expend the massive amount of time, energy, and materials needed to build a cow shelter, they planned to use the huge Big R store on Stagecoach Boulevard to protect the big livestock from severe temperatures and snow.

She worried about possibly dying in childbirth as well as dreaded how much it would hurt to have a baby in a world without painkillers. People claimed redheads had a higher pain tolerance... but she didn't know for sure. No one could accuse Harper of being fat, especially a year into her apocalypse diet, yet compared to Darci, she felt beefy. The mere thought of her friend going through natural childbirth caused her to cringe.

Having kids didn't exist even remotely in the periphery of Harper's planning before the war, as she'd been focused more on college than anything past the time immediately following her senior year. Nuclear war hadn't changed her 'not now, maybe not in five years' opinion of having kids. If anything, it made her *less* inclined to spawn thanks to the uncertainty of everything. Most of her future had always been as nebulous as her views on what to major in. She hadn't been able to definitely pick a career path and always figured luck or circumstance would make something jump out at her.

Ironically, fate had done exactly that, though not in the way she'd been expecting.

However, if she *did* happen to screw up and let Logan give her a baby, she couldn't surrender to fear or negative emotions. Darci loved all the new-agey stuff. She'd even gone to a weeklong summer 'spiritual retreat' last year. Harper more or less considered it spending a week naked in the woods smoking weed all day long with a bunch of other people who could name 140 different strains of marijuana off the top of their head and tell you exactly how each one differed, a scene straight out of 1969 Woodstock. Any 'spiritual discussions' probably amounted to nothing more profound than 'whoa, man, the trees are breathing.' Darci would certainly tell her spending nine months pregnant while dwelling on how much she *didn't* want a baby would mess the kid up for life due to 'psychic negative energy.' Harper didn't believe it any more than she thought Santa Claus existed. However, a person's mindset would definitely shape their moods and interactions with others. If she did end up with a baby, she'd do what she'd done ever since the bombs fell… roll with it and hope for the best.

Walter would not let her walk patrol while pregnant or really do any militia stuff considered risky. Madison would be thrilled to have her sister 'home all the time.' It irritated Harper in the same way all the sexist crap of the old society did. Of *course* the girl gets stuck home with the kids. However, she couldn't in good conscience risk waddling into a gunfight while carrying an innocent passenger.

I don't want to be a mom yet. Please, not now. I've got Lore and Maddie to watch. They're enough.

Jonathan didn't need 'watching' as much as support. For an eleven-year-old, he had a surprisingly stable head on his shoulders. At times, it unnerved Harper to think about a boy who'd watched his parents die to an angry mob showing little outward signs of trauma. Jonathan only seemed to lose control of his emotions if someone started ranting about blaming Chinese people for the war. Even if China really did launch first, ethnically Chinese people living in the USA had nothing to do with it. The boy's grandparents had been born here.

Japanese internment all over again. Harper sighed. *People are stupid when they're scared.*

If her plumbing betrayed her with a nine-month surprise, she decided to accept it as just one more thing happening she had no control over—like the war. Lying to herself made it a bit easier. She had control. Nothing forced her to have sex with Logan. She'd done that purely out of want... and love. As Cliff said, they didn't have much else to do for fun around here.

The clapping of small sneakers on earth made Harper spin to look behind her.

Jonathan dashed out of the trees at the dead end of Thunderbird Lane and came running up to her, a look of worry in his eyes. "Harp!"

She rushed over to him. "What happened?"

"It's Lore..." He bowed his head, trying to catch his breath.

Harper's brain went crazy with a thousand different explanations from the child attempting to hug a bear to randomly dropping dead for no visible reason. She grabbed his shoulders. "What's wrong?"

"Lore's sick or something." He exhaled hard. "She looks sick."

Critical panic eased back to strong concern. "Where? And what happened to Carrie?"

Jonathan spun around and jogged off. "Home. Carrie's still

working. We got off the farm a little early. Lore didn't feel good, so Carrie sent her home with us."

"Who's watching you?"

"Uhh." He flapped his arms. "I am, I guess."

Before Harper freaked out too much, she recalled Cliff's stories of growing up in the Eighties. No one thought anything of letting ten-to-twelve-year-olds run around outside to play unsupervised back then. The man adored relaying tales of he and his friends riding bicycles around his hometown in the days before cell phones. When the street lights came on, he knew to go home.

Living in a small post-apocalyptic town where everyone more or less knew everyone else and the odds of creepy outsiders randomly driving in from afar were low made the concept of unsupervised kids *slightly* less scary to Harper. The biggest threat any child faced here generally took the form of their own carelessness. Then again, Lawless, a pack of prison escapees, or a similar gang might wander by at any minute. She didn't much care to be alone herself, even with a shotgun, and certainly didn't think a group of kids could watch themselves when the oldest was only eleven.

She ran behind Jonathan, grumbling under her breath at the situation. Dad spent most of his afternoons home alone growing up since both parents worked. According to him, the catchy term 'latch key kids' circulated in the media back then, referring to grade-school-aged kids left home alone while both parents (or a single mom) worked.

Her father hadn't gotten himself killed, so maybe Jonathan could handle being the 'responsible adult' for the few hours between end of school and either herself, Carrie, or Cliff returning from their 'jobs.' Of course, her patrol shift usually ended around the time school did, so the kids had at least her to keep an eye on them. Jaylen, one of the new guys on the Militia, had inherited her patrol route for the later shift. Typically, she went home as soon as he showed up. But he hadn't arrived yet today. Time didn't obey exact clock hours anymore, so variances happened.

With Lorelei needing help, Harper didn't much care if anyone yelled at her for rushing home a bit early. Doing so was no different than if she'd found some resident up here in need of assistance. Once they got back to the house, she'd ask Jonathan to go tell Walter to send someone to cover the area. Things had been quiet as of late, but quiet didn't guarantee anything.

A few minutes later, she jogged down Hilltop Drive toward the house that had become her home. The voices of happy, playing children echoed in the trees. Having woods in and around all the houses no longer felt weird, as if they'd 'gone camping.'

Jonathan raced around the side of the house, heading for the backyard. Harper followed.

Mila, Emmy, Christopher, Becca, Eva, and Elijah raced around with the four kids Cliff discovered a few weeks ago: Allie, Tristan, Rylee, and Elliot. The new arrivals stood out from the others due to wearing 'new' handmade clothing from Renee's team, which made them look like medieval peasants. Elliot, who also happened to be eleven and Chinese, had become close friends with Jonathan. The kids appeared to be playing soccer or something similar to it, making as much noise as a grade school recess yard.

Lorelei sat on the porch steps, arms folded in her lap, bent forward, long blonde hair draped all the way to the ground, covering her feet. Completely unlike her normal self, she appeared totally uninterested in the game or the presence of other kids. Madison sat next to her, rubbing her back and doing her best to be supportive and comforting.

Jonathan scrambled to a stop by the little porch and flopped to sit. Madison looked up at him, then over at her big sister, seeming quite relieved to have her home.

"Lore?" Harper rushed over. "You okay?"

"Not really," mumbled Lorelei. "My tummy hurts. I think there's a food fight."

Madison cringed. "She's been making weird noises."

"Her stomach's growling super loud." Jonathan let himself fall over backward to lie flat on the porch. "She's either real hungry or she's gonna drop an epic fart."

Madison gasped. "Girls don't do that!"

"Yeah you do," said Jonathan. "You just try to be sneaky about it. Be proud of your stench. You almost made me pass out last week."

Red-faced, Madison simply stared at him.

"Hey." Harper crouched in front of Lorelei and coaxed her chin up with a finger.

The seven-year-old's face dripped with sweat. She looked bleary-eyed but not feverish. No mucus dripped from her nose, nor did she sound congested.

"Where does it hurt?" asked Harper.

Lorelei gently patted her stomach.

"She grabbed herself and screamed before." Madison pantomimed clutching her belly and doubling over. "She's really hurting. I told Jon to go get you."

Sweat beads dripped down the sides of Lorelei's face. "Sometimes it hurts badder, like a knife."

Dammit. Okay. This is over my head. "C'mon. I'm gonna bring you to see Tegan again."

"Kay."

Lorelei appeared to concentrate for a second, as if she needed to search for the strength to stand up. She rested a hand on the armrest of Carrie's plastic patio chair, which stood next to the porch, to steady herself as she got up, grimacing in discomfort as she rose. The instant she straightened out, her eyes shot open wide in an 'uh oh' expression. Lorelei yanked her dress up to her armpits an instant before she exploded from the rear end, spraying runny diarrhea all over the ground and lowest porch step. Some of the splatter landed on Madison's leg.

The soccer game came to an abrupt halt.

"Eww!" yelled Rylee.

Elliot, Tristan, and Christopher collapsed to the ground, laughing so hard they cried.

Mila and Allie stared at Lorelei, their expressions full of concern.

Madison clamped both hands over her mouth.

"Told you girls fart," deadpanned Jonathan.

Madison lurched forward and threw up on the dirt.

"Uhh, she didn't fart, dude," called Elliot.

Jonathan sat up and glanced at the 'blast zone.' "Oof. I don't think she's faking being sick."

"Oh, shit," whispered Harper.

"Exactly." Jonathan stood. "I'll get the bucket. Don't rub your eyes, Maddie. You got some on your face."

Madison gurgled and threw up again.

Still holding her dress up high, awfulness running down her legs, Lorelei managed a weak smile. "I kinda feel better now."

ONE EASY THING ABOUT TAKING CARE OF A KID WITH ZERO SHAME, cleanup proved as convenient as a backyard and a garden hose.

While Jonathan dutifully cleaned up the porch, Harper rinsed Lorelei off, then wrapped her in a towel before bringing her to the clinic. They had a short wait due to both doctors already being in rooms with other people. Lorelei slumped in one of the grey waiting room chairs, holding her belly and moaning. At a loud gurgle from the child's gut, Harper scooped her up and carried her down the hall to the bathroom. Lorelei hurriedly ripped the towel off and jumped on the bowl.

After the second explosion, Lorelei burst into tears. "I can't stop!"

Harper held her hand. "It's okay. Let the bad stuff out."

Lorelei groaned and shrieked in pain a few times, but finally, the convulsions stopped, leaving her exhausted. For the second time in twenty minutes, Harper cleaned her up. She decided to remain near the bathroom—and offered up silent thanks to whatever power of the universe allowed Evergreen's water system to still work.

Harper sat on a small chair in the hallway outside the bathroom, holding the shivering towel-wrapped child for about fifteen more minutes until a late-twenties man covered in mud exited one of the treatment rooms with his left hand in bandages. A weary looking Tegan peeked out into the hall, sprays of blood crisscrossing her shirt. She appeared about to scurry off to change but stopped upon seeing Harper.

"Uh oh," said Tegan.

"Is it bad?" Harper tensed, full of dread. Severe, uncontrollable runs stirred fears of dangerous problems like dysentery or Ebola and so on. She'd never seen a little kid break out in cold sweats and constant shivering before... or poop so much they screamed at their butts to stop.

"What's going on with her?" Tegan waved for Harper to follow and crossed the hall to a different treatment room—which used to be someone's office.

The relatively small space had been repurposed with medical stuff brought up from the larger medical clinic downtown, mostly due to it being much easier to supply this old office building with electricity.

Harper set Lorelei down on the cushioned table.

"Bear with me a moment. I need to clean up. Jimmy was

bleeding all over the place, and me." Tegan ducked out of the room.

Lorelei pressed her hands into her stomach. "It's gonna happen again."

"Now?"

"No. Couple minutes."

Harper eyed a wastebasket by the door as an emergency catch device. "Okay. Try to give me enough warning to get you to the toilet."

"Kay."

Tegan returned a moment later, drying her hands on a towel, but still in a bloodied shirt. "Okay then, sweetie… what's happening?"

"Spiky worms in my tummy are biting me."

While the doctor examined Lorelei, took her temperature, and listened around with a stethoscope, Harper described two bouts of explosive diarrhea that appeared to coincide with painful cramping.

"What do you think she has?" asked Harper, again biting her lip.

Tegan wiped sweat from Lorelei's forehead. "Is anyone else in your family feeling off?"

"Not that I know of. I feel fine. None of the other kids complained about being sick."

Lorelei peered up. "Carrie wasn't feeling good last night."

Harper raised both eyebrows. "She's sick?"

"I dunno. She sounded hurt. Kept saying"—Lorelei tried to mimic the sounds she heard—"'oh god oh oh oh oh god' and she was moanin' real loud."

Harper couldn't look at Lorelei without bursting into laughter. She shot Tegan a sideways glance. The doctor appeared to be fighting the urge to crack up as well.

Lorelei cringed, pressing a hand into her stomach. "Daddy was with her, so I wasn't scared."

Snickering, Harper hugged her. "I think Carrie's okay."

"Wow, from the mouth of babes," whispered Tegan, wiping her eyes. "Okay… well… if no one else is feeling sick, this looks like she probably got some iffy food. I'm assuming you're all eating the same stuff. My thoughts are her system might still be on the brittle side since everyone else dealt with it, and she's having a rough time. Looks like she's come down with a mild-to-moderate case of food poisoning."

"Because her system is weakened?" asked Harper.

Tegan shook her head. "Possibly. I wouldn't worry though. She's pretty much fully recovered. There shouldn't be any permanent damage to her system. If anything, she might remain undersized due to being malnourished for most of her life."

Lorelei looked down. "I'm sorry."

"You don't have to apologize for getting sick." Harper lifted the girl's hair off her face. "It's not your fault."

"It is." Lorelei flashed a cheesy smile. "I got special food in a hide place. Can had kind of a dent."

"Special food?" asked Tegan.

Lorelei stared down at the floor, swishing her feet back and forth. She looked as guilty as if what she prepared to say would get her thrown out of the family. "I took some cans and stuff and put them away where no one can take them. Used to do it with bad mommy 'cause she didn't let me have food alla time. I know I don't gotta do it now, but I's scared."

"I understand." Harper brushed a hand over the girl's head. "You're not in trouble."

"I'm not?" Lorelei gasped, gawking at her open-mouthed.

"No." Harper hugged her.

"Don't squeeze me too much or I'm gonna 'splode again," said Lorelei in a serious tone.

Tegan stuck a thermometer in the girl's mouth. "Hoarding food is a fairly typical behavior for children in her situation. If she ate the contents of a compromised can, it certainly explains why she's so sick now."

"Seriously, you're not in trouble." Harper squeezed her hand. "But I don't want you to get sick again, okay? Let me look at anything you're going to eat before you eat it. No one's going to take it from you. I only want to check it to make sure it's safe."

"I don't like cans food anymore," mumbled Lorelei past the thermometer.

"We have some antibiotics left. I'll give her a dose." Tegan appeared satisfied by the readout on the thermometer. "It's important she keep up on fluids until the diarrhea stops. Dehydration can cause more problems than the bug she picked up from the can."

"Understood." Harper nodded.

"How many times has she gone to the bathroom uncontrollably?" asked Tegan.

"Twice," said Harper.

"Ammost three times. Gonna be three times soon." Lorelei fidgeted, seeming frightened. "Tummy's starting to hurt again."

Harper grabbed her under the armpits. "Be right back."

Tegan followed them across the hall to the bathroom.

Lorelei exploded within seconds of being placed on the toilet. She yowled in pain, then screamed, "I don' wanna poop myself to death! Make it stop!" before lapsing into sobs.

Harper ended up crying too, because she couldn't make it stop. Tegan returned with a pill and a large glass of water.

"Can you give her something to stop the runs?" asked Harper.

"It's generally not done with kids her age. Loperamide tends to be a bit rough for children. It can cause serious complications in kids under three, but in my opinion, it's iffy under twelve. And she's small for her age. Also, we don't happen to have any."

Harper sighed.

Tegan patted her shoulder. "Stay with her until the runs subside. Make sure she keeps up on water and give her some bread as soon as she's interested in it. Lorelei isn't feverish or running too high a temp. Her body is coping with the invaders just fine. It's not going to be comfortable, but she'll be okay."

Lorelei struggled to stop crying, trying to put on a brave face.

She's going to be terrified of canned food for a while. Harper thought about Mom staying up with her when she'd been sick around the same age, though she'd been vomiting. *Guess it's my turn to be Mom.*

9

MESSED UP

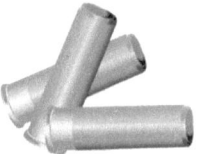

SEPTEMBER 20TH

O f all the unpleasant little details nibbling at Harper's thoughts, the eventual extinction of gunpowder possessed sharper teeth than most.

Competition shooting had been fun, but she'd never gotten wrapped up in it. It wouldn't be true to say she didn't care about it, since she *did* enjoy winning when it happened. However, coming in second or lower didn't throw her into a bad mood. 'Oh well, maybe next time' had been her attitude. Dad got far more upset over losses and far more excited over wins than she ever did. Unlike some of the parents at Madison's dance school, Dad didn't try to live vicariously through his daughter's success. He genuinely seemed thrilled when she did well and offered only support if she failed to place in the top three.

At no point in her life prior to September 7th 2018 had Harper considered the notion guns would stop existing to be even remotely alarming. If she couldn't go to the range anymore, no big deal. She'd find another hobby. *Now*, though, it mattered. Her once 'okay, it is kinda fun' pastime became her only real skill.

In a functional world, being able to shoot six plates out of the air as fast as someone could toss them didn't really serve much purpose beyond a side show attraction. Neither did running from station to station going through various shooting challenges. It gave her some YouTube fame, some prize money for the college fund, and bragging rights she never cared to exercise.

She'd been dragged kicking and screaming over the line between sport shooter and warrior.

Her uncommon skill with a shotgun wouldn't help her once she ran out of ammo, only Cliff's instruction for hand-to-hand combat... which went only so far. Being a master blackbelt only did so much for a girl her size if she needed to protect herself against a 350-pound linebacker. Her personal stash had dwindled down to 208 shells. The Militia probably had some, too. As far as her .45 went, she had forty-two rounds at last count, but didn't feel as comfortable using it as she did the shotgun. Obviously, she'd rather use a gun than her bare hands to defend her life... but the time would eventually come where no one had ammo anymore.

Grace and Renee liked to bring up the copious amount of guns in the Old West, but the 1800s also had functioning industry and global trade. Mines, factories, and manufacturing facilities produced all manner of commodities from gunpowder to consumer goods such as baking soda. The list of things she'd never thought twice about being able to have and now couldn't get left her speechless. Stuff as common as toothpaste or even underwear with elastic couldn't be found anymore. They'd run out of coffee, tea, sugar, spices, and anything even remotely close to candy. Some salt and pepper remained since the Militia had raided the entire inventories of every grocery store within fifty miles, and she'd been trying to make her family's allotment of it last. A chance existed some basic nonperishable supplies might exist in small towns and isolated houses, but no one considered it worth the risk to forage too far from home on the hope something useful *might* be there.

Maybe she'd end up trying to become a teacher when the bullets ran out. She'd done quite well in school without really working hard. It ought to be enough to teach little kids the basics. However, she still wanted to be prepared. The compound bow she'd taken from Walmart could outlast her ammunition supply, though it, too, would eventually break. However, she figured it a much better chance someone in Evergreen would be able to fix a compound bow before anyone resumed manufacturing gunpowder. Making more powder required chemicals and minerals no one here had access to. Until the day came where humanity resumed mining, they'd have to make do.

So, Harper spent time practicing with her bow. The backyard had only so much space—plus an increasing number of children too close for comfort while firing arrows. She'd gotten into the habit of bringing the bow along on her morning patrol time to take advantage of open areas where she could work on long-distance shots. Archery didn't come as easily as shooting, but she'd made noticeable progress. Given the choice, she'd always reach for the Mossberg first. At least she no longer felt 'as good as dead' if she got caught in a shootout with only a bow.

Harper set up for practice in the wooded area between Pinehurst Drive and Medinah Drive, using a roughly 300 foot long 'alley' of open field surrounded by trees between backyards.

She loaded an arrow, aimed, and let fly, staring at the projectile until it struck the old mattress she used for a target. Hitting a specific spot still proved tricky, but she'd gotten to the point where tagging a man-sized area at 200 feet had become relatively simple. Her arrow might land in the knee, thigh, groin, gut or face, but she'd hit someone. Considering the 'bad guys' would soon also not have guns, putting a broadhead arrow into someone's belly drastically changed the odds of a fight.

Four arrows later, she smiled at the reasonable grouping and drew a fifth. Along with not requiring ear protection, archery proved fun as well as practical. She enjoyed shooting, especially since no one stood behind her with a scorecard.

Voices filtered in from the trees on her right as she pulled the fifth arrow back. She started to draw a bead on the mattress, but her brain rapidly switched gears. The voices didn't sound familiar. Strangers likely made their way down Route 74 heading toward Evergreen. As soon as she identified them as unfamiliar, the conversation she'd tuned out came into focus.

"You sure about this?" asked a man.

"Positive. Whole bunch of them hiding out up here in the hills. Plenty of food and girls for the taking."

Shit.

Harper released the arrow since firing was faster than safely unloading a tensioned bow. She chucked it to the ground beside a tree and grabbed the Mossberg.

"None of that nonsense," said a woman.

"You ain't gotta watch." A man laughed.

Dammit. She contemplated using her airhorn can to sound an alarm, but doing so would give away her position. Better to observe what sounded like Lawless—or similar bad guys—and follow them out of sight. As soon as they came within range of the snipers at the bus barrier, she might open fire, sound the alarm blast, or depending on the situation, order the people to drop their weapons.

Harper ran through the nearest backyard, around the house, then across Pinehurst Drive into more trees. Another almost 200 feet separated the street from Route 74. Continued conversation among three men and one woman focused primarily on how many 'pretty young women' they'd find here and whether girls or food would be the bigger prize. The woman muttered occasional one-word responses, suggesting she disapproved of attacking girls and wanted to focus entirely on grabbing food and ammo.

When she got closer to the highway, Harper slowed to a fast

walk, favoring stealth. The instant she spotted motion up ahead through the trees, she froze. Cliff's voice in her mind repeated *the human eye is drawn to motion*. Four people meandered along Route 74 in the direction of Evergreen, slightly shy of being directly in front of her. She held still as a statue until they passed by far enough not to catch her in their peripheral vision, then advanced to the edge of the forest.

Three men in grimy Army jackets, T-shirts, and jeans accompanied a dark-haired woman in an orange Jack-o'-Lantern turtleneck and sweat pants. The sight of her slapped Harper with an almost physical force, leaving her too stunned to do anything but stare.

The woman wore the exact same outfit her mother had been wearing when she died. Harper got light-headed as the moment replayed in her memory. Her mother tried to defend the house, firing a 9mm handgun out the window over the kitchen sink. A Lawless lunged through the window, stabbing Mom in the chest. She'd collapsed instantly, crumpling over the sink before slumping to the floor.

As if somehow sensing Harper's stare, the woman turned to look at her.

Mom.

The orange turtleneck even had a bloodstained hole where the knife had gone in.

She also wore a blue sash loosely draped around her neck, as did all three guys with her.

Harper's stomach churned. Somehow, she stopped herself from projectile vomiting. No way could she shoot her own mother. No way could her mother be alive. No way could her mother be *Lawless*.

What the hell...?

After a long, silent staring contest, Harper somewhat raised her shotgun and approached them, staying on the forest side of the chain link fence separating the woods from the highway.

"Mom? What the hell?" rasped Harper. "You died…"

"Sorry to disappoint you, Harp." Mom picked at the hole in the sweater. "He stabbed me, but it wasn't fatal. I passed out. Why did you and Maddie leave me for dead?"

Harper's head spun. Any second now, she'd go full *Exorcist* and spray vomit everywhere. "No. No way. Not happening. What the hell are you doing with these assholes?"

"Your father couldn't protect us." Mom frowned. "What else was I supposed to do? He was dead, you and Maddie abandoned me."

"I don't believe you." Harper narrowed her eyes. "My mother wouldn't say that. And she wouldn't accuse me of being disappointed to see her alive. Cliff and the others buried you and Dad."

Mom and the three Lawless stood there, staring at her while making 'what are you gonna do about it' faces at her.

"Shit." Harper sighed at the clouds. "I'm having a nightmare."

She jolted awake, seated at the base of the tree against which she'd leaned the Mossberg. Eight arrows stuck out of the mattress target at the far end of the narrow clearing. Memory returned. She'd been too exhausted to want to walk down there to get them back a fifth time. 'Sitting down for a moment' turned into an unintentional nap.

"Ugh." She leaned forward, grabbed her head in both hands, and forced a yawn.

Staying up half the night with Lorelei left her in zombie mode. The poor kid finally stopped crapping her brains out at around two or three in the morning by her best guess of time. Harper didn't think anything would traumatize her as badly as being powerless to help a kid who scream-cried in pain because she'd gone so much it burned coming out. The thought she'd have to sit there and watch a seven-year-old literally shit herself to death while unable to help at all brought a new round of tears. Despite Tegan assuring her the girl suffered a manageable case of food poisoning, the reality of listening to her freak out, screaming and begging for it to stop hurting.

Harper spent most of the night sitting on the bathtub beside the toilet, holding Lorelei's hand, consumed with dread over all the formerly insignificant little sicknesses that could kill them. It all seemed so damned unfair. Lorelei had been born to a drug addict mother, neglected for her entire life, abandoned during the strike, and left to starve on her own. She didn't deserve to die at a mere seven years of age—or to something as undignified and horrible as unstoppable diarrhea.

The worst part had been the poor girl screaming 'make it stop' or whimpering 'I don't wanna die.'

At least Lorelei hadn't put up a fight over drinking water. At some point quite early in the morning, she'd gotten to a point where her guts decided to calm down and promptly passed out in Harper's arms. Since the girls shared a bed, Harper took her to the sofa in the living room and wrapped her in a blanket. Not like they could run out to a store and buy a new mattress if the girl had a disgusting accident. Of course, no one could buy new couches either. They'd slept there, cuddled together, until Cliff checked on them after sunrise.

Harper felt horrible for not telling Walter she needed to skip patrol today to stay home with a sick child—or for being too exhausted to function. *Getting into a gunfight while exhausted is as bad as driving drunk.* Cliff usually went out on a later patrol, so he took over watching Lorelei to give Harper a break and get some air.

After an experience like that, she's never going to want to touch canned food again. Harper rubbed her face with both hands, trying to wake up. She sucked in a huge breath, stood, and collected her stuff before making the trudge across the field to the mattress.

I hope Tegan is right, and her system isn't messed up.

The best response she could come up with to a dream about her—potentially zombie—mother returning was to ignore it happened. She plucked the arrows out of the mattress one by one, replacing them in the quiver hanging from her hip, then walked to the road to resume patrolling.

At the bend in the street, Harper randomly decided to keep on walking into the woods, heading to the clinic. She caught Tegan having lunch, a bowl of stew. The people at the Quartermaster's tended to prepare communal meals for mid-day in order to help stretch resources as much as possible. Noticing the doctor eating, Harper stopped short, raised an apologetic hand, and backed up.

"It's okay." Tegan waved her in. "What can I do for you?"

"Just wanted to ask, since Lore isn't here at the moment..." She leaned against the doorjamb. "How worried should I be about the food hoarding?"

Tegan tilted her hand in a so-so gesture. "It's probably not a serious problem since she confessed so easily. If we were looking at a serious problem, she'd have never admitted it. That behavior is somewhat common in kids who've had situations like her. I had a case about four years ago, a boy with severely abusive parents. They kept him locked in a closet, barely fed him. When he ended up with foster parents, he got into the habit of raiding the fridge at all hours, gorging himself."

"Wow... poor kid." Harper scowled. "Are we more or less savage after a nuclear war?"

Tegan gave a somber chuckle. "Hard to say. How's she doing?"

"Stayed up with her until stupid o'clock." Harper described Lorelei screaming while unable to stop pooping. "I think she went like ten times in six hours. Kept giving her water, like you said. She finally passed out. This morning, she ate a couple pieces of bread with jelly."

"That's good to hear." Tegan smiled. "Let her rest as much as she wants, but keep her hydrated. If she's not interested in food more substantial than bread by tomorrow, bring her in so I can check her."

"Okay. Thanks." Harper exhaled in relief. "She's done with

hiding food, I think... surrendered her stash. Most of the stuff's probably still good from the look of it. Bunch of ravioli and canned pasta. She ate one with a huge dent in it, probably had a break in the seal."

"Sounds about right." Tegan grimaced. "She's lucky it only started to turn. That stuff can be pretty dangerous if it's potent. Though, I don't think she'd have eaten something furry and rancid."

Harper almost chuckled. "Here's hoping. Thanks."

"Anytime." Tegan patted her arm.

Smelling the stew made Harper want some, since she hadn't had lunch—or much breakfast—yet. She headed out of the clinic, pausing to cast a wary glance up Route 74. Upon *not* seeing her mother back from the dead, she hung her head and let out a long sigh.

"Lore's not hiding food anymore and she isn't overeating, just worried about having enough. The kid's being cautious. She's not messed up in the head." Harper again looked at the highway, half expecting to see Mom standing there scowling at her. "Like me."

10

FAR FROM IMPOSSIBLE

SEPTEMBER 29TH

Except for the occasional circuit breaker trip, the electric stove still worked rather well.

Harper hadn't done too much cooking before the war, though she suspected the heating elements should be hotter than they were. Still, they proved more than adequate. Mom rarely cranked them up to max, anyway. Setting the dial on 'high' now probably equated to medium back on 'real' electrical power.

The fragrance of boiling strawberries filled the kitchen. Happy children's voices filled the backyard, Lorelei's among them. She'd bounced back from the bad canned food as if the whole thing never happened. Madison still tried to avoid stepping on the 'blast area' by the back porch, even though Jonathan had done a thorough job of cleaning up. He'd even dug up an inch or so of dirt and carried it off somewhere to bury. They didn't have much bleach left, but he'd used some on the porch step.

Her mood soared into heights of happiness she didn't often experience these days. Not only had Lorelei recovered, Harper's 'monthly visitor' finally showed up two days ago. Never before in her life had she been so happy to be in so much discomfort. Being freed from all the worries that came with having a baby lifted a weight the size of a house off her back.

Carrie tended to the pots with her, making Harper feel a bit like a young frontier wife keeping house while 'the menfolk' went off to do whatever. They'd spent most of the morning into the afternoon talking about everything from Lorelei's health to Carrie finding Jonathan and Mila's budding 'relationship' adorable as well as how—if at all—to officially consider the family whole. Namely, Carrie wondered if it mattered anymore to hold a wedding or if they should all move in together under one roof. Her house had enough space for everyone. The house Harper, Cliff, and the kids presently occupied did not. Evergreen didn't exactly have a population problem, so no pressure existed to be as efficient as possible with space. Still, when the day came Madison or Lorelei wanted (or needed) their own bedrooms, moving them to Carrie's made sense.

Cliff, Logan, Sadie, and a handful of other Militia spent most of their time lately on hunting trips. Jeanette and her electrical people had put together a bunch of wind turbines dedicated exclusively to the Quartermaster's building to ensure the industrial sized cabinet freezers they'd taken from multiple restaurants and the high school down south continued working.

Between canning and freezing, the general mood among the people of Evergreen remained hopeful. The winter would probably be rough, but starvation shouldn't be a worry. Months ago, Jonathan got the idea to take seeds from vegetables and start a garden in the backyard. Quite a few people kept personal gardens to help out. No one cared about pretty lawns or bushes anymore. Every bit of food helped.

Harper presently converted strawberries from their personal garden into preserves, using jars from Carrie's impressive collection. The woman had been into canning as a hobby for years and ended up being instrumental in teaching the process to the survivors. Except for Thanksgiving and Christmas before the world went to hell, Harper didn't often spend most of her day in the kitchen. It only really started seven years ago when Mom asked her to help out, ostensibly to teach her how to cook.

Carrie lugged a pot of hot strawberry goop over and set it on a wooden cutting board beside Harper. "So... I'm probably preggers."

"Cool," said Harper before processing the meaning of the words. She gasped, then gawked. "Wait. What?"

"Heh." Carrie lifted her baggy pale blue sweatshirt to show off a small but noticeable bump. "If I had to guess, I'd say third month. Likely happened near the end of June."

"Holy crap." Harper resisted the urge to touch her 'stepmom's' belly. "You sure it's a baby and not too many potatoes?"

Laughing, Carrie threw a dishtowel at her. "Stop, you. 'Too many potatoes' would go straight to my thighs. For another, a potbelly wouldn't make me feel off in the mornings."

"Oh wow... Umm, did you and Darci plan this?" Harper chuckled.

"Your friend's gotta be a month ahead of me."

Harper shrugged. "I dunno. She's so skinny, she probably started showing at two months."

Carrie gave a nervous laugh. "Being 'too skinny' has never been something I worried about until some idiot decided to light the world on fire."

"You're not too skinny."

"Oh?" Carrie folded her arms, pretending to be offended. "What's that supposed to mean?"

Harper rolled her eyes. "You're a whale, obviously."

Carrie gasped.

Laughing, Harper hugged her. "I'm teasing. You're normal."

Still feigning offense, Carrie swatted at her. "Pour that into the jars before it cools off too much to flow."

"Yes, Mom," said Harper in a younger voice.

Carrie leaned on the counter, watching the pour. "I'm kind of worried."

"Yeah. I was crapping bricks last week myself." Harper tilted the pot back as the first jar filled. "Couple days late."

"Your system got confused because mine missed a broadcast." Carrie moved the full jar out of the way and put an empty in its place. "Renee ended up being late, too, and as far as I know, she hasn't touched a boy."

Harper swallowed a small lump in her throat, thinking of her mother. It didn't take long after her system decided to start punishing her once a month for it to sync up with Mom's. Dad used to joke about needing to build a bunker in the garage so he had a place to take cover once Madison got old enough and they had three ladies in the same house simultaneously going through 'the troubles' as he called it.

Guess my biology thinks we're family now. She managed a weak, but sincere smile.

"At my age, this could be dangerous." Carrie swapped in another empty jar.

"Oh, stop. 'At your age.'" Harper scoffed. "You're what, thirty-five?"

Carrie sighed. "Yeah."

Harper poured the next jar full of preserves. "That's not old. Not even close to being old."

"It's getting a bit too old to have babies, especially in the Old West." Carrie set the next empty jar down. "There's a reason they used to marry at sixteen back then."

"They also had little kids working in mines, too. Doesn't make it right." Harper filled the empty jar.

"Let's go check out the plane crash," said Christopher in the yard.

"Bad idea," replied Mila. "It's too far, and dangerous."

"Umm, yeah." Jonathan made an uneasy noise, part groan, part sigh. "My new mom kinda screamed at us for it last time. We're not supposed to go that far away from home… or play in crashed jets."

"You know what I mean. Past thirty, the chances of complications goes up." Carrie glanced out the window at the kids and raised her voice. "Damn right. I don't want you getting hurt. Stay where I can at least hear you shouting."

Married and pregnant at sixteen. Eek. Harper pictured herself stepping off a steam train to 'start her new life' in a small town somewhere in Bumblefart California in 1849. It would be hot, her dress would be far too heavy and thick for the weather, and she'd be expected to do whatever her husband told her to. "Bleh. Screw that."

"Hmm?" Carrie looked at her. "You think the kids should go play on a crashed aircraft?"

"No." Harper set the pot of preserves down, and set up a row of empty jars. "Just thinking about it being 1849. We still have two real doctors, and society hasn't regressed."

"Regressed?"

Harper flashed a goofy smile. "Women can still vote."

"Hah. Yeah, that's helpful." Carrie started putting lids on full jars. "Thanks for being confident on my behalf."

"I was scared, too." Harper paused with a jar halfway full to look at her. "Honestly, it's silly. Compared to a gunfight, I shouldn't be scared of having a baby."

"Dear, in a gunfight, you can duck." Carrie smirked.

Lorelei let out a tiny seven-year-old's best version of a barbarian war cry. Harper looked up to peer out the window over the sink at the little blonde swinging a pool noodle in a two-handed grip, 'sword fighting' with Becca. For a moment, she couldn't tell if the kids were playing swords or legitimately training to fight.

"Heh. True." She resumed pouring, distracted by random thoughts of the future. "How weird is that?"

"Ducking?"

"No." Harper snickered. "I mean... your baby. *Any* baby... heck, even two-year-olds. They're never going to know the modern world. It won't be long before the kids have no idea what video games were, or airplanes, cars, television shows, movies..."

Carrie shrugged. "No need to be pointlessly depressing. The world changes. Do you miss eight-track tapes?"

"What the heck is an eight-track?" Harper paused pouring again to stare at her, nose scrunched.

"My point exactly." Carrie patted her on the arm. "You can't miss what you never knew."

Harper raised an eyebrow. "Seriously, though. What's an eight-track?"

"It's like a cassette, but bigger."

"Cassette?" Harper blinked.

Carrie laughed.

"Heh. I'm teasing." Harper grinned. "I know what a cassette tape is. Dad had a bunch."

"Not many kids your age do." Carrie let out a long sigh. "I grew up with CDs. Cassettes kinda died out before I was old enough to care about music."

"Crap. Music." Harper stared into space. "I can't remember the last song I heard."

"Wasn't it Madison's rendition of... what was it, Lady Gaga?"

Harper snickered. "I mean an actual song with music and stuff. Professional." She racked her brain, trying to recall the last thing her MP3 player pumped into her ears, but couldn't. She hadn't even thought about music at all much over the past year. *Guess it means I don't really miss it.* A long, slow breath slid out of her mouth. *Wow... so much is different.*

"Hmm. Come to think of it, I don't remember, either." Carrie tapped a finger to her chin. "Wonder if the electricity is strong enough for my CD player to work? Suppose there's one good thing about me keeping my old stuff in the attic."

"Wow. You could put music on and it would be like a concert for the whole town." Harper whistled.

Carrie fake-gasped. "Wouldn't I need a permit for public use?"

"Heh. I don't know whether to laugh, cry, or consider it a win." Harper scooped the last of the preserves into a jar. "One good thing..."

"What?"

"With the new baby, you won't ever have to deal with Barney the dinosaur or the kid wanting to watch the same movie *over* and over and over."

Carrie pantomimed wiping sweat from her forehead.

Memories of five-year-old Madison insisting on watching *Beauty and the Beast* on an endless loop set off an unexpectedly heavy crash of sadness. Harper leaned her weight against the counter, head bowed, trying to play it off as fatigue. The somber spell passed in a moment, chased away by a random kid giggling outside.

"Dodged a bullet with the Barney thing." Carrie chuckled. "You okay?"

"Yeah." She sighed. "I guess it is what it is. People live through the past once. We can do it again. Worst part is medicine being gone."

Carrie stuck the pot in the sink and turned the water on. "Never thought I'd be pleasantly surprised to find the faucet works."

"Right?" Harper huffed.

"Really, it's not much different as far as medicine goes." Carrie began to wash the pot.

Harper turned toward her, arms folded, eyebrow up. "How do you figure? We've lost so much. Like... diabetes is a death sentence now."

"Most people couldn't afford to go to the doctor or hospital before, anyway." Carrie frowned. "Is there really a difference between medicine not existing at all or being financially out of reach?"

"Fair, but what about other countries? Weren't we the only place with a medical industry more concerned with profit than helping people?"

"I suppose." Carrie shrugged. "Why waste time being cynical? We're still here. Life's a lot more work now, but it's far from impossible."

Harper let her arms fall slack. "Yeah. You're right. Gah. I hate hormones sometimes. When I'm as old as you, will the random emotional swings stop?"

Carrie threw the dishtowel at her again, laughing. "You just told me I'm not old."

"So, wow. You and Cliff spawned." Harper whistled. "Congrats."

"Seems that way." Carrie gazed off into space, perhaps thinking about her former husband, David.

At the time of the attack, he'd been across the country in New York City. The strikes started on the East Coast and moved west, allowing the radio news to report most of the entire metropolitan area around NYC had been vaporized in the few minutes they had left before going off the air. Harper lost count of all the people here who had relatives who 'may or may not' be dead. Given the situation in New York, though, the odds of David Rangel being alive were only slightly better than the odds of Harper joining the Lawless or Harper's parents not being dead.

"You and Logan planning on having one?" asked Carrie, ending the awkward quiet.

Harper fanned herself, once again feeling as if she'd narrowly avoided being run over by a speeding bus. "You know that thing in health class they tell you doesn't work?"

"It's been a tick since I was in high school." Carrie chuckled. "Which particular thing are you talking about?"

"Umm." Harper squirmed. Talking sex type stuff with Carrie

didn't bother her as much as bringing it up with her real parents, but she still felt weird having such a conversation with a 'genuine adult.' She whispered, "Pulling out."

"Ahh." Carrie grinned. "Yeah... Cliff and I didn't even slow down enough to think about that."

Harper's cheeks burned. They might not be her actual parents, but the past year had made them close enough she didn't want to picture them doing sexy things. "Yeah, well... I guess Logan and I are playing Russian roulette with the baby cannon."

Carrie snort-laughed, then lapsed into uncontrollable cackling.

"What's funny?" asked Lorelei, sticking her head in from the backyard.

Harper cringed. Carrie continued laughing, unable to speak, forcing her to deal with the question.

"Just a stupid joke." Harper waved dismissively.

Lorelei smiled. "Tell me?"

Harper bit her lip. "Umm, how's a cow hide in a tree?"

The child stared at her.

"She paints her hooves red."

Lorelei blinked. "That's not funny."

"It isn't." Harper couldn't look at the serious glower of disapproval on the little face surrounded by wild blonde hair without cracking up, so she proceeded to put the lids on the last few jars of strawberry preserves. "It's stupid. She's laughing because it was so stupid."

"Oh. Grown-ups are weird." Lorelei rolled her eyes and ducked back outside.

"We sure are," rasped Carrie between chuckles.

DEGREES OF SUCK

SEPTEMBER 30TH

Harper sat on the couch trying to read *Great Gatsby* and ignore the pain in her left shoulder as well as the aroma of Cliff cooking fish.

As if the nuclear apocalypse hadn't been bad enough, most of the books she had access to tended to be the sorts of things English teachers forced kids to read over summer break. *Gatsby* used to be historical, but parts of it now felt almost futuristic. She had trouble concentrating, too distracted by the ache.

Patrolling the town started feeling almost pointless and annoying—until earlier that day. The sight of a five-or-six-year-old boy running naked, wet, and soapy down the street toward her screaming for help didn't prepare her for what came next. The boy's guardian, a late-twenties woman named Cassidy, had apparently suffered a psychotic break during a moment of severe depression and tried to drown him in the bathtub. He got away, but his younger sister remained in the house.

Harper managed to get there in time to save the three-year-old's life... though little Ryan actually pulled the girl out of the water while Harper got into a jiu-jitsu war with Cassidy who kept screaming 'they're gonna die anyway'. The whole scene passed in a blur, ending with the woman unconscious on the floor, bleeding from the mouth and nose. Harper had never pummeled a person's face into the floor until they passed out before, but if anyone deserved it, a crazy bitch who tried to murder two kids certainly did. The little girl, Averie, required CPR—and being dangled upside down to let the water out—but came to. Ryan went running out of the house specifically to find Harper, because he knew she'd be out there in case anyone needed help. He'd seen her go by every day for months. Cliff suggested her growing feeling having to 'go to work' was a burdensome drag meant she'd mentally recovered into being a normal teenager. However, after this morning, she'd never again feel annoyed at having to spend most of a day on foot. The grateful, adoring look Ryan gave her when his little sister sputtered awake broke her heart.

I'm not walking patrol to stop Mad Max raiders... I've gotta protect us from ourselves.

The only good thing about the situation was Cassidy not being the kids' biological mother, thus lessening the emotional damage to the children. Needless to say, Ryan and Averie wouldn't be staying with Cassidy anymore. Last she heard, Summer Vasquez wanted to take them in. Since Cassidy planned to kill herself once she 'spared the children the pain of a torturous death' it remained unclear what Walter and the rest of the town council would do with her. Because a matter of maybe ten to twenty seconds made the difference between murder and attempted murder of a three-year-old, Harper wouldn't be terribly upset if they opted for execution—as long as she didn't have to pull the trigger or watch.

She ended up staring at the page more than reading, debating the idea of responsibility vs. evil vs. mental illness. Tyler almost killed Madison due to being legitimately crazy—on serious meds crazy—and she'd let him go. Part of her credited it to squeamishness at not wanting to 'execute' a guy who wasn't an immediate threat, but if she could excuse a man for attacking Madison due to mental illness, perhaps she shouldn't be so quick to think Cassidy deserved to be shot.

I hope I am never responsible for making a choice like Walter. How the hell did judges deal with it?

Commotion out front distracted her from the book.

The front door swung open, revealing an almost dark sky as well as Jonathan, Madison, Lorelei, and Eva. Madison's pre-war friend looked frightened and worried. Jonathan didn't seem upset. Lorelei appeared normal. Madison zombie-walked over to the sofa and fell onto it face first beside Harper.

"Food," droned Jonathan while reaching for the kitchen.

"About ten minutes," called Cliff. "If Carrie and Renee aren't here in five, someone go get them."

Lorelei flopped on the floor by the fireplace and proceeded to play with her dolls.

Eva walked up to Harper. "Can I sleep here tonight? Mom's sick."

"Of course." Harper set the book down, not-so-accidentally forgetting to mark her place. "What's up with your mother?"

"Coughing a lot. Maybe a cold or flu." Eva ground her toes into the rug. "She's too sick to watch me and gotta stay at the hospital."

Madison mumbled incoherently into the sofa cushion.

"You okay?" Harper prodded her.

Jonathan chuckled. "We spent all day helping overfeed cows so they'll get fat for the winter."

"And cleaning poop," mumbled Madison. "It's not fair. This is child abuse. I'm too little to work this hard. I'm too tired to even eat."

Her sister's tone of voice reminded her of how she used to gripe about being late for dance class or wanting to go to

Starbucks when they didn't really have the time for it. Sad thoughts didn't really set in since Madison appeared to be coping with their new life rather well, all things considered.

"Few weeks of work, then you get to sit around doing nothing for months." Harper patted her sister on the back.

"When did she get a job working IT?" called Cliff from the kitchen.

Madison lay there moaning in exhaustion. Jonathan paced around. Eva joined Lorelei with the dolls. A few minutes of waiting for dinner later, Madison chuckled for no particular reason.

"Gonna let us in on the joke?" Harper nudged her.

"I just had a crazy random thought," mumbled Madison.

"What?"

Madison rolled onto her side, lifting her face out of the cushion. She opened her mouth as if to speak, then looked around at everyone, blushed somewhat, and pushed herself upright. After giving Harper a c'mere nod, she headed down the hall to the bathroom.

Curious, Harper followed.

Once they'd both gone into the bathroom, Madison nudged the door shut and whispered, "Mom said my periods might not start until I'm a little older 'cause of dance, gymnastics, and being skinny."

Harper vaguely remembered something along those lines. Athletics could delay things… nothing she really worried about. Competition shooting didn't come close to the same level of constant physical activity as dance class or gymnastics, never mind both. "Okay…"

"Well…" Madison rubbed her stomach. "I'm even skinnier now, and the farm is kicking my butt way worse than anything Coach Berlin ever did to us. I just had this weird, random thought: I'm not gonna need tampons until I'm thirty."

Harper stifled a laugh.

Madison's eyes went wide in horror. "Oh, crap! There aren't any more tampons. What the heck are we gonna do?"

"Scrap cloth, maybe reusable washable cloth pads or something. We'll figure it out."

"Eww." Madison shivered. "Washable? That's nasty."

"No nastier than cloth diapers on the babies."

Madison made a gagging sound. "Ugh. Maybe I'll just stay ten forever. It's less disgusting."

"Heh. If only." Harper tickled her. "My turn for a weird, random thought."

"About tampons?"

"Actually, yes." Harper grinned.

"You have a stash, don't you?"

"Yeah, but not many. They'll be gone before you're old enough to need them." Harper leaned against the sink. "Honestly, it's probably safer not to use them in a world with no real medical care. It's possible to get some really nasty infections from them. Nature didn't really intend for us to stuff things in there."

Madison blushed as red as she ever had in her life.

"Sorry..." Harper snickered.

"You're not really embarrassing me too much... I haven't run away screaming with my fingers in my ears yet."

"Like you did the first time Mom tried to have the talk..."

"So, umm..." Madison squirmed. "Does it hurt? How bad was your first?"

"Are you talking about tampons or something else?"

"Something else. You know... the first period," whispered Madison so softly she almost made no sound.

Harper found herself blushing at the memory. "Umm, well... no, it didn't hurt at all. I'd been expecting wicked cramps, but the first time, it didn't even feel like gas. I, umm... didn't even notice until Renee poked me in the back during math to tell me I had blood on my chair."

Gasping, Madison clamped both hands over her mouth. "It happened *in school*? Like, in front of *everyone*? I'd die."

"Not really in front of everyone." Harper waved dismissively. "I sat in the middle of the room so only in front of like half the class."

Madison stared at her, her expression saying, 'that's not any better'.

"Seriously, only Renee saw anything. I tied my sweatshirt around my waist, got up, told Mrs. Simmons 'I'm going to the nurse' and walked out, not even waiting for her to say okay. Renee took care of my seat while everyone watched me walk out, so no one else noticed what happened."

"Eww." Madison squirmed. "She touched it?"

"With a tissue... and yeah. It's only blood."

"No wonder she's your best friend."

Harper muttered, "Truth."

"So, umm... no warning at all?" whispered Madison.

"Nope. Just happened. First one's probably going to sneak up on you." Harper rested her hands on her sister's shoulders. "It's natural and normal. Nothing to be embarrassed about. Once it happens, you can start predicting about when it's going to kick in. But... the first red faerie is a ninja."

"Ugh." Madison rolled her eyes. "So unfair."

"What are you worried about?" Harper winked. "It's not gonna happen to you until you're thirty."

Madison stuck her tongue out.

"Seriously, though. You have at least three years, probably."

"How old were you?"

"Eighth grade. Thirteen."

Madison appeared to relax. "Okay... not time to panic yet."

"Dinner!" yelled Cliff from the kitchen.

Madison and Harper exchanged a stare.

"Hungry?" whispered Harper.

"Not really."

"Because you're exhausted or because of what we've been talking about?"

Madison grimaced. "Yes."

"You know you have to eat. Food's not—"

"Guaranteed anymore. Yeah. I know." Madison looked down. "Okay. I'll eat."

Relieved, Harper smiled and pulled the door open.

"Did your day suck as much as mine?" Madison trudged out into the hall.

"No," whispered Harper, thinking of Ryan and Averie. "It sucked more."

12

COCOA BEANS

OCTOBER 3RD

Harper stared at the door to her locker, baffled by the idea 'girl issues' had become so significant a problem. Why did her little stash of hygiene products feel so abnormally valuable all of a sudden?

She looked away from the locker door, worried her friends might discover she kept such a precious commodity there. Veronica, Andrea, Renee, Darci, and Christina stood around her clutching their books the same way they always did for the few minutes they had to hang out between class periods.

Around them, an army of faceless teenagers milled back and forth. Her friends' voices sounded distant, echoing as if far away in the school's shower room despite their standing so close. They complained about Mr. Burroughs making his tests 'so damn difficult'. Christina brought up a party going on at 'this kid Brian's house' later that night, and the whole group began insisting Harper join them there, except for Renee who merely fidgeted awkwardly at the mention of parties.

Going to parties didn't bother Harper, but she also didn't

really adore them. For no specific reason, the idea of going to a party tonight struck her as an awful idea. She'd much rather spend the night at home with her family.

"Sorry, guys," said Harper. "I'm just not feeling real social."

Renee smiled. The rest of her friends stared at her, baffled.

The hallway, the girls, and all the other students blurred away into a peach-hued haze.

The heck?

A momentary spell of dizziness passed. The high school had become Harper's bedroom. She lay sprawled on the bed, her MP3 player pumping Katy Perry's *Dark Horse* into her eardrums. In three days, it would be Madison's ninth birthday. Just so happened the date coincided with Veronica going to an out-of-state karate tournament. Harper traced random patterns in her bedspread, annoyed at being obligated to attend her sister's party. Why on Earth would she have any interest spending the day hanging out with a bunch of eight-and-nine-year-olds? What self-respecting sixteen-year-old went to kiddie birthday parties? Veronica's parents would be in California with them. Not like the girls intended to go on their own.

But, no. She had to miss the trip because of Madison.

Grumbling, Harper plucked her earbuds out. Loud music cut off to heavy silence. She pushed up off the bed and walked over to her desk. Around her computer screen stood an arrangement of small pictures depicting her family as well as friends smiling or being goofy. Discoloration appeared on one photo showing Harper and her friends all lined up at the edge of a swimming pool, arms folded on the concrete deck. Veronica, Christina, and Andrea appeared to be in black and white, unlike the rest of the picture.

The change spread over other photos, Mom and Dad also faded out of color.

One by one, her parents and friends changed from normal pictures to oddly colorless, then withered... rotting away to gore-covered skeletons in mere seconds. Renee and Darci remained normal, though their facial expressions shifted to horror as if realizing they had their arms around rotting zombies.

Harper screamed.

Far-away rumbling outside grew to a deafening roar. The bedroom window flashed brilliant white, then faded to orange, revealing a mushroom cloud rising in the distance. Miles and miles of orange-tinted emptiness surrounded the glowing plume of death as if Lakewood or Denver had never existed, merely endless desert.

Bracing for the concussion wave to slam into the house, Harper crossed her arms in front of her face—and jolted upright in bed. She couldn't see anything but pitch darkness. Despite the nuclear flash existing only in a dream, it had been so bright, reality seemed darker. For a moment, the only sound in her ears came from her own breaths.

Holy shit... Harper grabbed her face in both hands, and sat there shaking.

"Bad one?" whispered Madison.

A crash of guilt fell on her shoulders. True, she had been annoyed at missing Veronica's tournament for Madison's ninth birthday, but hadn't been anywhere near as resentful as she'd felt in the dream.

"Weird, not scary," said Harper. "Why are you awake?"

"Because you threw me off. I *was* kinda half on top of you." Madison yawned. "Bonked heads with Lore, but she's still asleep."

"Sorry." Harper lifted the blankets and swung her legs off the bed. "Be right back. Need bathroom."

"You okay?" Madison stretched.

"Yeah. Whoever said 'you don't know what you got 'til it's gone, I wanna kick them in the balls."

"Me too," said Madison in a sleepy voice. "I could kill someone for a caramel macchiato and a cake pop. What's bothering you?"

Harper stood. "I dunno. Hormones maybe. Just dreaming about how sometimes, I tried to avoid people and now those people are gone so I *can't* spend time with them."

"If your dreams are turning into Hallmark movies, it's time for therapy," deadpanned Madison.

Hallmark would never make that movie. She cringed. *They don't have the special effects budget... and they don't exist anymore.*

"I wish we had some chocolate." Madison sat up. "Now's a perfect time for some. Mom always ate some chocolate when something made her feel sad or stressed."

"If we ate chocolate every time we felt sad or stressed lately, we'd both be the size of cows."

Madison snickered. "No kidding. I think Mom would say it's a waste of energy being upset over stuff we can't change, and if we *can* change something, use the energy we'd waste being upset to do the change instead of whining about it."

Harper chuckled. "She's right, but I'm not about to walk to South America to get cocoa beans."

Madison laughed. "Aww, why not? It's only like a billion miles away."

"I'm only going to walk to the bathroom so I can get back to sleep."

"Dammit." Madison grumbled. "Now I gotta pee, too. Hurry up."

"Sorry."

"Less sorry, more walky." Madison got out of bed and pushed Harper toward the door. "We can dream about having chocolate after we pee."

13

WINTER OF TRUTH

OCTOBER 5TH

The past few days had been quiet.

All kids fifteen or younger finally returned to full time school, relieved of farm obligations until next summer. For the most part, the teachers covered the same sorts of subjects she had in grade school, but eased off on the math to make room for more immediately practical knowledge like animal care, cooking, sewing, basic carpentry, and so on. The teachers working with older kids still offered the complicated math, but only if the student asked for it and after hours. *Someone* probably needed to maintain the knowledge of how to do algebra and trig, but the majority of kids would get more benefit from learning how not to die.

Harper sat in a blue cushioned chair in a conference room at the Militia HQ. Walter intended to keep the meeting brief since having everyone in one room except for Cameron who remained on the bus barricade across Route 74 meant no one happened to be out on patrol.

The bi-weekly status meetings felt simultaneously weird—

like something from a pre-war job—and reassuring. She figured it likely resembled the sorts of briefings police captains used to conduct, since Walter spent the first five to fifteen minutes (depending on how things went) going over recent incidents. He felt it important to keep the entire Militia aware of everything any of them dealt with. Public speaking had always been something she dreaded, but it got easier among a group of people she knew well. One or two newer faces in the Militia didn't bother her so much.

When her turn came up, she gave a brief explanation of the Cassidy situation, trying her best to keep emotion from affecting her perception of what happened. From the sound of it, the town council decided not to exile or kill Cassidy, instead banning her from access to firearms or children. Tegan's assessment stated she felt the woman would not pose a threat to random children, as she felt responsible for Ryan and Averie being 'her kids to protect' and believed she would spare them greater suffering by giving them 'peaceful' deaths instead of whatever 'the wasteland' had in store for them. The woman would spend at least the next few weeks south in the jail at the Sherriff's office. Depending on how she reacted to sessions with Tegan, she'd likely end up being relocated down there to a small house away from kids.

No possible outcome sounded good enough for Harper. Killing the woman felt excessive. Exiling her seemed cruel. Keeping her in jail felt like the most appropriate idea, though it almost felt like a reward: free food and no responsibility to work. No matter what the council decided to do with her, it would feel insufficient or excessive.

Thankfully, the 'crimes briefing' only took five minutes. Other than Harper's awful situation with Cassidy, they had two fights at Earl's between drunks and one minor fire.

"As you all probably know," said Walter, "this is going to be our first winter with zero canned goods left. We are entirely dependent on hunting, fishing, and farming. The estimates I'm seeing from Liz and her people are guardedly optimistic. It's going to be a bit on the lean side, but nowhere near as bad as last year. We might see some grumbling, but I think by now, everyone's more or less gotten used to how things are."

"Damn what I'd do for some freakin' McDonalds," muttered Dennis.

"Right?" Roy chuckled.

"How you getting on in a world without donuts?" Cliff winked.

Roy gave him the finger, grinning. "Says the mall cop."

Walter chuckled. "The good news is, if we can handle this winter well, it means we're over the hump and in decent shape. Every season forward from here will get easier and easier."

The mood in the room held at a level of cautious optimism. People hadn't exactly been feasting lately, but the specter of running out of food entirely had more or less gone away. Of course, the unspoken truth remained: it wouldn't take much to spell disaster. A bad growing season, contamination getting into the farms... Evergreen hadn't made it out of the proverbial woods yet and may never do so.

Discussion continued along the lines of winter stuff, mostly emergency planning for severe weather. The town council considered using either the school or the Quartermaster's building as a temporary communal living space in the event of a bad storm. Both had dedicated electrical generators and heat. The Quartermaster's had the advantage of being where the majority of the food resided. Given distance—and the large number of children living in Harper's patrol area south of the school—it didn't sound like a great idea to make them hike over a mile in deep snow.

"Why don't we use both options?" asked Harper as soon as she had the chance. "The school building has power, heat, and there are working fridges in the cafeteria. We can split the emergency evacuation procedure over both sites. Unless we're going to get everyone over there *before* a severe storm, it's a lot easier to move them up to the school instead of across town."

"Hmm." Walter rubbed his chin.

"We'd be cramped up pretty tight packing everyone in Liz's place," said Anne-Marie. "It could be done, and we've been thinking in terms of a few days to a week. But... we're up in the mountains. We could get some serious snow."

"It's been kinda warm. Still about sixty degrees." Fred gestured at his fairly light shirt. "Doesn't feel like it's gonna be a bad winter."

The Militia all started talking at the same time, debating whether or not an unseasonably warm autumn meant the winter would be mild. Lonnie Blanchard, the 'Safeway sniper' who'd come back to town with them, brought up a historic blizzard in the 1800s that followed an oddly warm fall. The sixty-one-year-old didn't actively serve on the Militia, but as former military, he liked to be involved as an advisor.

Owing to the desire to get everyone back out there on patrol, Walter hurried the discussion along. Ultimately, he and Anne-Marie came to the conclusion they'd split the emergency sheltering arrangements between both the school and the Quartermaster's building. Everyone who lived in the area around the former golf course would be relocated to the school in the event their homes became dangerous due to lack of heat or lack of food.

Also, if a bad storm hit, the Militia would, as needed, be responsible for going around to check on everyone. Walter asked for volunteers to help move some provisions up to the school building so they'd have at least a few days' leeway.

The thoroughness and preparedness of it all surprised Harper. She caught herself thinking in terms more primitive than reality. Even if they did end up in some strange alternate version of the 1800s, society back then had been much closer to the modern world than she'd believed.

She left the meeting feeling both validated and reassured. Her idea went over well. It meant a little more work in the near term (moving food to the school) but could make things a lot easier on everyone if they got a bad storm.

No sooner did her boots hit Route 74 than she stopped short, completely consumed by thoughts of Madison's birthday in four days. Her sister hadn't said or done anything to suggest she even remembered or cared about the day. After taking a deep breath, Harper resumed walking back out to her patrol area. Hopefully, she'd have a boring few hours... but she'd be there if someone needed her. No one had ever accused her of being a particularly violent person, but she'd need to consciously control herself if she ever came face to face with Cassidy again.

Her thoughts drifted from idle daydreams of revenge she'd never act on to her little sister's upcoming birthday—not necessarily a happier subject. Did the girl's complete lack of mentioning it mean she hoped to forget it? Should Harper *not* call attention to the day? Madison's tenth birthday happened a month and two days after the nuclear strike while her family sheltered in their basement not knowing what the hell happened to the world. Everyone had been so shell shocked that no one paid much attention to the birthday other than Mom whipping up a sad cake using the charcoal grill as an oven and topping it with a solitary candle.

Three-weeks and change later, their parents died.

Would Madison forever associate her birthday with the Lawless invading their home? Did her kid sister hope to forget all about it? Or did she simply act normal and not behave in an overly excited manner since birthdays and Christmas no longer came with promises of any cool presents? They couldn't exactly run out to a store or order video games, electronics, or nice clothing off Amazon. Any gifts given or received now came from scavenging or handcrafting.

Might Madison not even want presents at all as much as time

with family? For Christmas, she'd asked only that Harper 'not die.' Trying to decide whether to acknowledge, downplay, or flat out ignore the birthday led her to thinking about the anniversary of the strike. Few people in Evergreen had much of a noticeable reaction.

Everyone's too busy getting ready for winter to have time to be depressed. She sighed out her nose. *Except Cassidy.*

After an hour or so of walking the streets surrounding the golf course, Harper decided to preserve the feeling of normal by having a birthday celebration. It didn't need to be extravagant, but she wanted to acknowledge it. They'd done similar things for all the other kids. She worried Madison would feel left out if she didn't get a birthday, too. If it stirred any bad reactions, she'd tackle them head on. Hiding from painful memories only made them come back worse later, according to Tegan… and Madison seemed to be close enough to her old self to be able to cope. Sure, she'd lost much of her bubbly side, but at least she smiled again.

Maddie would've wanted PlayStation games, nice clothes, or cute plushies for her birthday… probably a Starbucks gift certificate, too. She chuckled. *What do I get her now? A Glock? Ugh.* Harper stared up at the clouds, horrified by her momentary daydream of Madison reacting to being given a gun the way she reacted to getting her iPhone. *Okay, that's psychotic. No, she wouldn't want a gun. She only went to the range with us to make Dad happy. Maybe I can find a plush in the pile of random stuff.*

Harper decided to hit the Quartermaster's as soon as her patrol shift ended. There had to be *something* in the 'miscellaneous room' she could grab as a birthday present. The hard part would be getting it into the house unnoticed and keeping it hidden.

14

ELEVEN

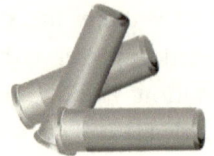

OCTOBER 9TH

Madison didn't act strange in the morning upon waking up, proceeding to go through breakfast and heading out to school like any other day.

Fortunately, she didn't seem *weird* about anything. That told Harper her sister didn't try to 'keep her head down and hope no one remembered.' Perhaps she'd been so exhausted by farm work and happy to have made the transition back to school she'd simply lost track of what day it was. Dad once joked 'without Facebook, I'd never remember any birthdays.'

Harper discovered a small box of sanitary pads tucked inside a pink covered wastebasket in the 'random stuff' room at the Quartermaster's. She contemplated giving them to Madison as a gag gift considering their conversation from a few days ago, but didn't feel totally comfortable her sister would take it as the joke intended. All things considered, such items had become insanely valuable, so she couldn't leave it there unclaimed. She decided to gift it anyway and play it by ear. If Madison laughed, it would be a gag gift. If she didn't seem amused, Harper would stress the rarity of having sanitary products and mean it as a sincere gift—along with a large orange tabby cat plush. Madison always wanted a cat, but the parents wouldn't get one. A stuffed cat didn't quite match a real one, but she had Rosie the Chicken and Mr. Cluck as live pets.

Ugh. We're going to need to bring the chickens inside before they freeze. Harper paced around the kitchen, wondering where the heck they'd put an indoor chicken pen. Obviously, they couldn't let them run around free in the house crapping and peeing everywhere. Maybe they could live in Carrie's house for the season. They'd need to do something like find a plastic kiddie pool to protect the floor or some such thing.

Harper took advantage of getting off patrol an hour early to help Carrie put the finishing touches on a 'birthday cake.' The baked treat looked and smelled closer to bread, but extra eggs and a massive amount of strawberries effectively turned it into a dessert.

A cacophony of children's voices welled up outside, growing louder as the kids came down the street. Cliff hurried in the back door carrying a big aluminum tray of baked potatoes and zucchini with cheese, Renee, Grace, and Darci scooting in behind him.

The front door opened, admitting Jonathan, Madison, Lorelei, Mila, Becca, and Eva.

"Happy birthday, Madison!" said everyone waiting in the house more or less at the same time.

Madison stopped short, gawking. Her expression cycled from shock to disbelief to denial before settling on a look of 'holy shit it is.' "Umm. Wow."

Harper ran over and hugged her.

"Really? It's…" Madison bit her lip.

"Yes." Harper smiled at her. "It's October ninth. You are officially eleven."

Madison exhaled. "Oh. Cool."

"Damn, kid." Cliff chuckled. "You forgot your birthday? That usually doesn't happen until you're in your thirties."

Carrie poked him. "Women never forget our birthdays. We simply ignore they occur after twenty-one of them."

Sensing a large group of people in the house all looking at her, Madison turned in place, still gnawing on her lower lip. "Umm, you guys are gonna make a big deal out of it, aren't you?"

"Yep!" chirped Lorelei.

Madison flapped her arms in an 'okay, fine' manner.

At her sister *not* running off in tears or shutting down on the spot, Harper practically jumped for joy. It appeared her worries about the birthday being permanently chained to horrible memories didn't come to pass.

"What the heck is that?" Madison scrunched her nose at the 'cake' on the table. "Pink bread?"

"Basically," deadpanned Carrie. "It smells like cake."

"It is a cake-like-substance," deadpanned Jonathan. "What planet did it come from?"

Carrie looked around for a dishtowel to toss at him.

"Good enough for me." Cliff rubbed his hands together like a weasel. "I shall go retrieve a cutting implement."

"Oh." Madison raised her eyebrows. "Cool. Thank you for the cake-like substance."

Everyone chuckled.

According to her parents, four-year-old Harper used to scrape the icing off cupcakes and toss it aside. While she didn't remember doing so, nor have any lingering hatred of icing, the lack of it on the CLS (cake-like-substance) didn't bother her. It had been so long since she had real cake, this stuff didn't taste too far off the mark. At a guess, she'd call it denser and drier than cake probably ought to be, but for what they had available, it totally worked.

The kids sat around munching on cake in the living room. Harper and the adults congregated around the dining room table.

Cliff joked about the lack of coffee being one of the greatest tragedies of the century. Once the kids started discussing what to do with the rest of their afternoon, Harper zoomed down the hall to grab the plush cat from her hiding place. She tucked it behind her back and made her way to the living room, sneaking up behind Madison who sat on the sofa with a plate of crumbs in her lap.

"Happy birthday, Termite." Harper draped herself over the sofa back, holding the stuffed cat at eye level.

"Aww!" Madison hugged it. "He's adorable! Thank you."

"Cat's bigger than me," said Lorelei in an awed tone.

Cliff rubbed his chin, raising an eyebrow at her. "Not sure about bigger. Heavier, sure."

Lorelei made a face at him.

Renee gave Madison a faerie music box. Lorelei handed her a 'shiny amulet' she found (a steel knob from an outdoor hose valve). Madison reacted as if she'd been given a solid gold coin, making Lorelei giggle. When Madison looked at Jonathan, he ran to his room. She twisted the other way to make 'what did I do' eyes at Harper.

Jonathan rushed back a moment later carrying a purple document protector. "It's not much, but here…" He offered her the folder. "Happy birthday, Maddie."

Madison took the folder, raising the eyebrow of suspicion.

"Open it," whispered Cliff, fidgeting.

He knows what it is already. Harper shifted her gaze back and forth from Cliff to the folder. *Wow, it must be something huge if he's excited.*

Jonathan appeared nervous, as if dreading she'd hate it.

Madison lifted one side of the folder to reveal a color drawing. At first, Harper thought Jon gave her sister a page out of a comic book—until Madison covered her mouth in both hands and started crying. Caught off guard by the reaction, Harper leaned over the sofa to take a closer look.

Rather than a page out of a comic book, he'd given her a full-page drawing in comic book style, stunningly close to looking done by a professional. The scene appeared to be the girls' bedroom viewed from beside the bed, showing Harper and Madison sitting on the mattress hugging each other. Above and behind them on either side, floated the semitransparent faces of Mom and Dad, both with angelic wings, smiling down on them.

Despite being comic styled, the two angels looked unmistakably like their parents. Jonathan must have rummaged the trunk Cliff brought back from Lakewood with Harper's pictures.

Harper stared at the drawing, stunned speechless.

"Thanks for the pencils," said Jonathan a touch over a whisper. "They're really good."

Madison sobbed.

Harper couldn't stop crying, too.

Lorelei bit her lip, seeming worried. Everyone else stayed tomb silent.

Jonathan winced. "Sorry..."

"No," rasped Madison. She carefully closed the folder and set it on the seat beside her, then leapt to her feet to hug him. "I love it... I'm gonna keep it forever."

Cliff grinned as wide as he'd ever done since Harper met him.

Everyone clapped.

"Little bit of a cheese out, but I've been kinda busy." Cliff winked, reached under the sofa, and pulled out an empty picture frame. "Got ya this. It should fit the drawing."

Madison cry-laughed.

Great. That's going up on our wall, isn't it? I'm going to cry every time I look at it.

Renee and Mila complimented Jonathan on his artistic abilities. Darci slipped in a zinger about how he hadn't drawn Harper like a comic book bimbo with a giant chest, tiny waist, and big curves.

"He won't start drawing girls that way for a few years yet." Cliff winked.

Jonathan blushed.

"Jon's making a comic book and his character's kinda based on me." Mila twirled.

Jonathan blushed more.

"Might as well get this framed right away to keep it safe." Cliff picked up the frame and carried it to the table.

Madison released her hug on Jonathan. "You gotta draw one with our family now."

He smiled. "Okay. I can do that."

Once they had an official picture hanging ceremony—naturally, in the bedroom—the kids migrated to the living room to play board games thanks to it being a bit rainy outside. Cliff, Carrie, and Renee reluctantly went back to their respective jobs for a few more hours, leaving Harper and Darci to watch over the festivities.

Surprisingly, sitting on the couch watching the kids play games and talking to her friend made the afternoon go by fast. Before she knew it, Becca, Eva, and Mila left to go home for dinner. Darci soon collected Elijah and headed out as well. Harper started cooking, essentially warming up the tray Cliff brought over from Carrie's. In celebration of Madison's birthday, they had an all-vegetarian (except for the cheese) meal.

Madison didn't object to cheese since it didn't require killing an animal.

An hour or so after dinnertime, Carrie, Renee, and Darci returned, as did Becca and Eva—who'd both gotten permission to sleep over as part of the birthday event. Grace also popped in, seeming weary. The poor girl had been putting in long hours at the clinic dividing her time between learning and helping take care of everyone getting hurt amid the frenetic rush to winterize.

Jonathan managed to get the PlayStation into a good enough mood for one of Carrie's DVDs to play. It had more to do with the output of the electrical generators being above a certain level and less with the boy being the 'console whisperer.' Watching *Zootopia* felt surreal. It didn't really bother Harper too much until the end when the credits started and she had the awful thought to wonder how many of the people whose names scrolled by died in the attack.

For a while after the movie, she talked with her friends about random stuff. Eventually, she noticed Madison's voice missing from the din of kids. Sure enough, her sister no longer sprawled on the rug with her friends. The other girls' non-reaction to Madison's absence suggested they knew she'd gone somewhere but expected her to be back soon, likely a bathroom break.

Ten minutes or so later without any sign of her, Harper became concerned.

"Sec..." Harper got up from the couch and hurried around it into the dining room.

Worried her sister had been faking composure all day long and finally had a nasty attack of the sads, she practically ran to the bathroom. No Madison. Harper flung herself across the hall, catching the doorjamb of the bedroom and sticking her head in. No Madison. She checked both Cliff and Jonathan's rooms, finding them both empty.

Worry increasing, she fast-walked down the hall to the kitchen, about to raise the alarm with Cliff and Carrie—but stopped short at noticing motion out of the corner of her eye on the left. Madison sat on the back porch, head against her knees, arms wrapped around her legs. She made no noise, nor did she shake as if crying.

Harper crept out onto the porch and sat beside her.

"Hey," muttered Madison, not looking up.

"You okay?"

"Not sure."

Harper rubbed Madison's back. "Wanna talk about it?"

After a moment of silence, her sister sat up. Her eyes didn't appear red. "You know what? I kinda do."

Wow. Wasn't expecting that.

"I'm more angry than I am sad, but I'm confused, too." Madison grumbled.

"About?"

"Who to be angrier at. The idiots who started the war or the Lawless." Madison leaned against her.

Harper put an arm around her. "Hmm. Hard call. It's probably not healthy, but I'm angry with both of them."

"Yeah."

"I've been angry for a while, but it comes and goes. Not like we'll ever find the person who pushed the button that sent the missile to Lakewood."

Madison nodded. "You already shot the man who killed Dad. I know you're gonna say it didn't help and make you feel any better."

"Honestly?" Harper raised an eyebrow.

"What?"

Harper looked Madison in the eye. "You're eleven now so you can handle truth. What they say? It's BS. Killing that bastard *did* make me feel better."

"Wow..." Madison sat up, gawking. "Seriously?"

"Yeah, but not for giving me any sense of power or even revenge." Harper puffed a squiggle of hair out of her eyes. "It made me feel happy—once the crippling sorrow and rage wore off—because I knew that piece of shit would never hurt anyone else."

Madison leaned on her again. "Okay. That sounds like my sister."

Harper chuckled.

"And I understand. It sucks."

"What sucks?"

Madison idly tapped her feet together. "I'm never going to forget September seventh. My birthday is always gonna make me think of being in our basement after everything blew up."

Ugh. Dammit! "I'm sorry... was afraid of that. Full honesty. I was afraid you'd hate your birthday and wasn't sure if I should bring it up or let it go."

Madison fidgeted at the thigh pocket of her cargo pants. "Yeah. Figured. I'm glad you decided to be normal about it and have a party. Thanks."

Tension and dread melted out of Harper. "I'm glad you're glad. You weren't hoping no one remembered?"

"Full honesty?" Madison smiled. "I really did forget. I'm *still* tired from the farm. Not really thinking about much but being happy we're free from the labor camp."

Harper snickered.

"I don't hate my birthday. It's, umm... just not as happy as it used to be."

"Yeah." She squeezed her sister close. "I understand."

"It's still a little happy." Madison held up a pinchy gesture. "Little bit. Thanks for being here."

Harper rested her head against Madison's. "I honestly don't know what I'd have done without you."

"Get real." Madison sighed.

"No, I'm serious. Being very real here. I was so focused on keeping you safe and worrying about where you'd gone mentally, I didn't have time to think about anything else. I'd probably have gotten sad and lonely otherwise, and who knows if I'd have even cared enough to keep on fighting."

"I'm not nuts anymore," deadpanned Madison.

"You weren't nuts. Just traumatized." Harper fussed at her sister's jet-black hair. "You're going to be sitting on it soon. Still like it super long?"

"Yeah." Madison glanced over at her. "Please don't give up, okay? Keep fighting."

"I will. I'm still here to keep you safe."

Madison hugged her, hard.

"Oof. Oh, hey." Harper grinned. "I got you something else, but didn't wanna give it to you in front of everyone. Hang on a sec."

Madison let go, giving her a suspicious 'if you prank me, I will hit you' stare.

Harper ran inside to grab the small box of sanitary pads from the hiding place in the bedroom closet. She tucked it under her sweatshirt and hurried outside again. Not seeing any obvious gift, Madison furrowed her brows even more.

"Happy birthday." Harper pulled the small pink box out and handed it to her.

Madison's cheeks turned bright red. She stared at it for three seconds, then burst into giggles while grabbing the box and hiding it under her shirt as if afraid someone might see it. "You are so bad!"

Once she stopped laughing, Harper grabbed her in a one-armed headlock. "Keep them safe until you need them, okay? They're really hard to find... probably worth more than gold now."

Madison gave her a 'gimme a break' smirk for a few seconds before her expression shifted sincere. "I don't know if I can use them now..."

"What?"

"I mean..." Madison pulled the box out again, holding it in both hands and staring at it. "This is like stupid and emo, but I'm gonna think about this moment every time I see this box. Using them feels wrong."

"Aww." Harper ruffled her hair.

"And... I don't know how to use them."

Harper snickered. "It's not difficult. I can show you when the time comes if you want. They are yours. Do as you will with them."

"Think I'ma keep 'em for the memory."

Easy to say now when you don't actually need them yet. Harper winked. "Okay."

"Hey, let's go inside. I wanna spend the rest of my birthday before bedtime with my whole family." Madison tucked the box under her shirt again. "*After* I hide this."

Seeing her sister smile so genuinely made Harper almost lightheaded from joy. She stood and opened the door. "After you."

Madison darted inside.

Harper paused to gaze up at the stars. *Maybe there is some hope left, after all.*

15

NUCLEAR BLIZZARD

NOVEMBER 20TH

Harper awoke to find Cliff hovering over her, hand still on her shoulder. Her bedroom remained mostly dark, a scant hint of light offering a vague suggestion of the walls and furniture. Fog clung to her brain, leaving her unable to tell if she really woke up too early or if she'd slipped into another bizarre dream.

"Hey," said Cliff. "It's morning. Or, past it."

She shifted her gaze to the right. The framed drawing hung on the wall above the dresser, likely proof she didn't dream. "Ugh." Harper lifted a hand to her face, rubbing it. "Why are we getting up this early?"

"It's not early. You overslept by about an hour or so." Cliff stepped from the bedside to the window. "It's bad out there."

"Wait, what?" Harper's eyes widened on a sudden wave of consciousness. "It's not like five in the morning?"

Madison's shriek echoed from the bathroom.

"Crap." Harper scrambled to get up.

Cliff caught her before she French-kissed the rug. "Toilet's a bit chilly."

Harper stared at him, then shifted her gaze to the door. "Maddie? You okay?"

"It's f-freezing in here," yelled Madison.

It occurred to Harper her toes had gone numb. "Ack."

"Ack indeed." Cliff chuckled.

Motivated by shocking cold air, Harper hurriedly changed from her relatively thin nightgown into long underwear, jeans, two shirts, thick socks, and a sweater, not caring that Cliff happened to be in the room. Apparently caught off guard by her deciding to get changed before he could leave, he stayed by the window, not looking back at her.

"What the heck happened?" rasped Harper, slightly out of breath from moving so fast.

"It got cold. And it's snowing." Cliff gestured at a buildup of white stuff on the outside of the window.

Harper stepped up beside him to look out. He hadn't shaken her out of bed at a ridiculously early hour: the world forgot to get bright today. Between snow buildup on the window and a dreadfully gloomy sky, it looked as dark as twilight. A storm of massive snowflakes blocked out the scenery, making it difficult to even see the fence along the back of the yard.

"Shit. Rosie and Mr. Cluck..." whispered Harper.

"Got them." Cliff smiled. "They're next door in the pen."

Harper exhaled in relief. Madison didn't much care for frozen chicken anyway, and she'd absolutely hate it if the chicken in question happened to be her pet. Hopefully, Rosie the Chicken and Mr. Cluck the Rooster preferred a six-by-six-foot enclosure in Carrie's living room to being outside in this mess. Thoughts of freezing chickens leapt to freezing cows. She started to dread having to go outside in such a storm until it hit her the Militia didn't have the responsibility to move livestock to the shelters. In fact, the overnight farm watchers probably got the process started as soon as they noticed the first flakes.

"Holy crap," whispered Harper.

"Yeah. It went from like fifty something degrees to eighteen in less than an hour."

She raised both eyebrows. "Whoa."

"Feels like. Not real numbers." He chuckled. "We kinda missed the weather report. TV stations are slacking off."

"Right..." She watched the giant snowflakes gliding downward.

Cliff hooked his thumbs in his pants pockets. "This looks like it's gonna be a big ass storm. Came out of nowhere."

"Wouldn't *any* weather kinda 'come out of nowhere' since there's no such thing as meteorologists anymore?" She sighed. "The only weather report we have now is 'looking outside.'"

"Pretty much." He nodded. "Some things you can see coming... like tornadoes. Good thing we don't get them here."

She raised an eyebrow at him. "Think the nukes messed up the planet enough to change the weather?"

"I dunno. It probably had an effect. I mean, you don't kick that much dust and crud up into the air and *not* expect something." He gestured at the window. "We got lucky and managed to avoid a nuclear winter scenario."

"Umm. Did we?" She chuckled. "This looks like a mutant blizzard."

"This might be a nuclear snowstorm, but it's not nuclear winter." He glanced back over his shoulder as Madison walked in, teeth chattering.

Harper gawked at her. "What are you still doing in your nightie? Put something warm on."

Madison stared at Cliff.

"Message received." He overacted being in a hurry and 'ran' out of the bedroom.

Harper looked around. "Where's Lore?"

"Here," said a lump of blanket in the middle of the bed. "It's too cold. I'm gonna stay here all day."

"It's going to be warmer in the living room with a fire going," said Harper. "C'mon. Don't you need to use the bathroom?"

"Yeah, but it's cold."

While Madison got dressed, Harper tried to coax Lorelei out from under the blankets. Ultimately, she passed warmer clothing under the bedding so the child could get changed while completely covered, shielded from the freezing air. Eventually, they made their way to the kitchen. Jonathan stood beside the dining room table wearing an oversized beige angora sweater, jeans, and giant pink 'moon boots' with rainbow-maned unicorns on each side.

"You look adorable," said Harper.

Jonathan shrugged. "I don't care what they look like. They're super warm and they fit."

Madison, who wore similar boots but more of a purple color, offered to swap.

"Umm." He stepped next to her, comparing boots. "Yours are a little smaller. Probably wouldn't fit me. It's fine. I don't mind pink. No one's gonna make fun of me any worse for wearing pink boots than I got it for being a boy going to dance class."

"Used to mean something when a boy wore pink boots," said Cliff in a tone as if mocking a stodgy old guy.

"Yeah." Jonathan nodded. "It means his feet are cold."

Carrie and Renee ducked in the front door amid a swirling blast of snow. For a fleeting instant, Harper caught sight of an already foot-deep trench in the white stuff.

Holy shit. This is gonna be bad.

Jonathan tended to the living room fireplace while Cliff finished cooking breakfast: oatmeal with strawberries. Despite having watched the farm develop from empty land to the crazy complicated project it became, Harper still found it kinda weird to eat oatmeal that not only grew where she lived, but had been milled and prepared by hand. The farmers continuously surprised her with their ingenuity in repurposing various things into useful equipment: such as a giant steel drum full of concrete to crush oats.

"I can't believe this storm," said Carrie. "Like four days ago, it seemed over sixty degrees. We had Eva's party outside and no one needed a jacket."

Harper stirred her bowl of oatmeal, making the sliced strawberries float and sink. Eva and Madison had been friends since kindergarten. As far as Harper remembered, the girl's birthday parties after age six *always* involved some manner of day trip to a fun place. Obviously, no Chuck E Cheese restaurants, malls, hands-on science museums or amusement parks remained in operation. Eva's father died and her mother still hadn't quite recovered from the ordeal of the strike and the months she spent in the Army survivor's camp. Harper had zero doubts Mrs. Parsons would've committed suicide or simply stopped eating until she died, if not for having Eva to look after. Heck, the woman had almost even given up on her daughter at the camp.

Mrs. Parsons sat quietly in a chair as the birthday party happened days ago on the sixteenth. After dealing with Cassidy, Harper had become worried she might snap at some point and think Eva better off 'spared' from the post-nuclear world. However, Mrs. Parsons didn't seem the type to be able to harm her own daughter. If anything, the woman might slip off alone and check out. Perhaps she waited for Eva to be old enough to survive without her. Or... maybe Harper read too much into Mrs. Parsons' blank stare and uninspired smiles. People dealt with grief and trauma in different ways.

It amazed her how most of the kids under twelve just kept on going, like losing the world as it was didn't bother them much at all. The really small ones didn't know enough about anything to miss it, but the children Madison's age, plus or minus a few years, certainly could miss video games, Instagram, and so forth. Yet, for some reason, they didn't make a big deal out of it.

Cliff brought her up to speed on the situation out in town as they ate. He'd been out on night patrol when 'the white shit' as he called it started coming down. The majority of the cows and other large animals migrated to the shelter in the Big R store before sunrise. Smaller livestock like chickens already had covered shelters at the farm. He'd been intermittently shoveling snow to clear a path between their house and Carrie's. No one in town that Cliff spoke with since the storm began had any idea how long it would last or how much snow to expect.

"Jon, you mind going up to clear the roof after you eat?" Cliff pointed upward. "It's flat and you're about the ideal combination of light and strong. Can't let too much snow build up."

"Sure." The boy nodded.

"Are we gonna have 'nuff food?" asked Lorelei.

"Between these cabinets and the ones in my place, we should be able to last six days," said Carrie. "Nine if we ration to minimum."

Madison cringed. Lorelei looked up from her oatmeal, her permanent smile taking a rare moment of absence.

"Not you, kiddo." Cliff winked at Lorelei.

"Yeah." Renee nodded. "You can give me less so she has enough."

"Same," muttered Jonathan.

"Me too." Madison put an arm around Lorelei.

"I think that's pretty much all of us." Carrie smiled.

"Not all of us." Cliff leaned over to kiss her. "You're eating for two now."

Madison and Jonathan stared.

"She's not fat." Lorelei frowned. "Don't be mean. She's not two people."

"No." Madison went wide-eyed in glee. "She's gonna have a baby!"

Lorelei appeared confused.

Cliff looked at Carrie, then Renee, then Harper. "All you. I catch shoplifters at the mall. I don't do the 'explaining to seven-year-olds where babies come from' thing."

"I meant everyone." Lorelei raised her arms out to either side. "Are we gonna run outta food?"

Harper scraped the last of the oatmeal out of her bowl. "From what I hear, we should be okay if we're careful. Glad we went to get all those jars."

"Definitely helped." Carrie whistled. "I see mason jars in my dreams now."

"Why do they call it canning when you're using jars?" asked Madison.

Renee laughed.

"No clue." Carrie shrugged. "Language doesn't always make sense."

Jonathan got up, carried his empty bowl to the sink, and ran down the hall toward his bedroom. "Grabbing a coat."

"You're sending the boy onto the roof?" Carrie stared at Cliff.

"Yep. My fat ass will fall right through it." He patted his non-belly.

Harper chuckled. When she'd first run into him, he had a bit of mall security guard paunch. Despite their 'natural' and often limited diet plus constant work giving him back the physique of a Special Forces soldier, he still routinely joked about being overweight.

"What if he falls? He's only ten." Carrie nibbled on her lip.

"I'm eleven!" yelled Jonathan from the hall. "And it's only a one-story house. Plus, there's snow. If I fall, it won't hurt."

Carrie sighed. "He's just like you. Brave to the point of foolish."

"There is a fine line between bravery and stupidity." Cliff scratched at his beard. "I'm still trying to figure out where it is."

"I wish I could be as confident as you are," muttered Renee.

Cliff winked at her. "Honestly? Those damn donuts at the mall were deadlier than most things we're facing now."

"What's a donut?" asked Lorelei.

"A tiny cake with a hole in the middle," said Harper.

"Oh." Lorelei sighed at her empty bowl. "I like cake."

Jonathan emerged from the hall in a winter coat that covered him to the knees, plus a scarf wrapped around his face. "Ready. Do we have a ladder or are you gonna throw me onto the roof?"

Cliff got up. "No ladder. Not gonna toss ya, but you'll need a boost."

Undeterred, Jonathan walked over to the front door and opened it. "Whoa. It's really falling hard."

Harper stretched up in her seat to see out the door. The snow *did* seem deeper already, two inches or so had coated the previously shoveled path. "Time to go."

"Huh?" Madison stared at her. "You're going out in this?"

"Gotta." Harper stood. "We've got severe weather plans. Militia's responsible for checking on people, making sure they've got enough food and probably relocating the older people to either the Quartermaster's building or the school."

"I'm not going anywhere," said Carrie. "Might as well stay over here since the fire's going."

Harper headed down the hall to the bedroom to grab her coat and boots. The Mossberg felt like more of a burden at the moment, so she decided to leave it here and trust carrying the .45 on her hip would be enough.

Can't shoot a blizzard. Pretty sure not even the Lawless want to go out in this mess.

AFTER SEVERAL EXHAUSTING HOURS TRUDGING AROUND increasingly deep snow to check on people living around her patrol area, Harper returned home before her feet froze off.

She'd left the house in not-quite knee-deep snow. By the time she returned, the shallow spots came up to her hips. Giant flakes gave her hope the stuff might collapse under its own weight and not remain so high. It drifted over ten feet in places with the shallows being not quite half that much.

Harper spent the rest of the day inside at home with her family. With no real planning or discussion, Jonathan and Renee joined Harper, Madison, and Lorelei in their bed for the night. That no one, especially Madison, complained about sharing a bed with a boy spoke volumes about how cold it had become. They couldn't in good conscience demand Jonathan sleep all by himself in an unheated room. Sure, it was a little awkward, but less so than him sharing a bed with Cliff and Carrie. Renee likely felt uncomfortable at the idea of sleeping next to Cliff as well.

Still, no one complained. It didn't get too uncomfortable considering no one bothered changing into pajamas or nightgowns. The only clothing anyone shed before crawling in under the blankets had been shoes. Like a group of hikers stranded after an avalanche, they all huddled close for warmth.

16

DAY TWO

NOVEMBER 21ST

Harper woke to a dark room. Not being overly tired caused a bizarre disconnect between her brain and time. It *looked* like midnight but felt like morning. Lorelei and Madison whispered about snow elves. Renee lay beside her in a tangle of mouse brown hair, mouth wide open, one arm above her head.

The sight of her best friend sleeping there set off a momentary storm of emotions. They hadn't shared a bed since a sleepover roughly eight years ago. Her friend originally expected to use an air mattress on the floor next to Harper's bed, but the electric pump wouldn't work. It struck Harper as weird, funny, and sad how little Renee changed since age ten. She'd obviously gotten taller and filled out a bit more, but loose clothing—or a pile of blankets—easily created the illusion she hadn't aged much.

It's beyond cruel to make Nee go through the apocalypse.

Rather than sad, Harper nursed a spike of anger toward who or whatever was responsible for her best friend having to suffer the death of her parents, being kidnapped by the Lawless, and forced into an uncertain future. They'd never again stay up too late together watching anime or science fiction movies, and her friend didn't giggle much anymore. Renee used to complain about having such a baby face, but it saved her backside—rather literally. Harper didn't even want to think about what the gang might've done to Christina or Andrea. Unlike Renee, they both looked a touch older than their age. Christina got mistaken for twenty-one at seventeen, a 'talent' she used more than once to obtain beer without being carded.

Paradoxically, Renee happened to be the most mature of her friends despite looking like the youngest.

Before her mind ran away with scary daydreams about how each of her missing friends coped with 'the day the world caught fire', Harper forced herself to sit up.

"What time is it?" asked Madison.

"How should I know?" Harper glanced at the window. "I don't think it's still night."

"It's so dark," said Lorelei. "It's gotta be night."

A brief high-pitched fart broke the silence.

"Jonathan!" rasped Madison. "Really?"

"Wasn't him," whispered Lorelei. "Sorry."

For some reason, the notion of the little one ripping an unrepentant fart struck Harper as hilarious. She flopped over sideways and laughed tears out of her eyes. Madison caught the contagious giggles, as did Lorelei. Over the next few minutes, Jonathan and Renee both woke up, proving everyone had been asleep for a reasonable amount of time.

Despite being fully dressed except for shoes, climbing out from under the blankets felt chilly. Harper hurried into her boots, then made her way down the hall. Light coming in the front windows illuminated the living room like an overcast day. Cliff rattled around in the kitchen, which remained dark while Carrie attempted to light the fireplace. The strong scent of wood smoke and a detectable note of dampness saturated the entire house.

"Ugh." Harper wiped her eyes. "What time is it?"

"Morning." Cliff chuckled.

Harper looked back and forth. "Why is it dark in there but not out here?"

"The house is half buried in snow. It's as tall as the roof on the back side," said Carrie. "A lucky wind kept the front windows clear."

Holy shit. Harper crept over to the kitchen and stared at the window over the sink. She fumbled at the wall for the light switch, but hesitated, afraid it wouldn't work. A few seconds later, she got up the nerve to try it… and the light came on.

Whew.

Snow completely filled in the kitchen windows.

"Oh wow…" She looked up. "Is the roof okay?"

"It's still snowing." Carrie tossed a log into the fireplace. "I just dug another two feet out of the path to next door."

Cliff leaned into the living room. "I got that. You shouldn't be—"

"I'm not *that* pregnant yet." Carrie blew on the smoldering tinder.

"Okay…" Cliff raised both hands in surrender.

Lorelei shuffled in with her jeans down around her ankles. "We have a problem."

Cliff, Carrie, and Harper looked at her.

"Toilet's frozen," said Cliff.

Lorelei nodded. "There's a big ice cube. Should I pee on it an' try to melt it?"

"Use a bucket." Cliff grabbed one from the kitchen closet, walked over, and set it down by Lorelei.

The girl glanced at the bucket as if contemplating using it right there in the dining room, but picked it up and shuffled off down the hall to the bathroom before Harper could open her mouth to tell her to do so.

Cliff grumbled. "Pretty lucky the bowl didn't shatter. Think we're going to need to take extreme measures for the next few days."

"Extreme measures? Like pooping in a bucket?" asked Harper.

He chuckled. "That, too. I meant keeping a fire going 24/7 so the house doesn't get cold enough to where the pipes freeze and shatter."

"Aww damn. I need go check my toilets," said Carrie.

"You gotta be kidding," said Madison from down the hall. "What the heck are you doing? That's… eww."

"We have'ta use a bucket, now." Lorelei sighed. "Toilet's ice."

Harper paced around, trying not to think about how badly she needed to use the bathroom. Both the cold air and idea of having no usable toilet made it worse. "What are we going to do?"

"Fair bet no one is going to be going anywhere for a while." Cliff set his hands on his hips, firing an annoyed look at the kitchen window. "Can't say anyone expected it to snow *this* hard for so long."

"Lonnie did." Harper sighed. "He kept talking about some massive blizzard."

Jonathan walked into the kitchen, going straight to the back door. He opened it to reveal a wall of snow from floor to ceiling bearing an imprint of the door pattern. "Wow. Are we trapped?"

"Front door's okay." Carrie pointed.

"Roof?" asked Jonathan.

Cliff patted him on the arm. "Yep. After breakfast."

"Oatmeal?" asked Jonathan.

"How did you guess?" Cliff feigned surprise.

HARPER PACED AROUND THE LIVING ROOM. CARRIE AND JONATHAN kept the fireplace going strong, perhaps using wood a touch fast, but they *did* try to save the pipes. Neither of Carrie's toilets froze to the point of shattering—because Renee already shut the water valves off without mentioning it to anyone. Her parents used to own a vacation cabin near the ski area of Aspen. Though, being they fell far short of rich, the place was quite... 'rustic' so to speak. At least, Dad described it that way trying to be nice. She knew the drill regarding cold weather and water pipes.

Snow kept falling, though had fortunately tapered off from torrential blizzard to a gentler flurry. Cliff went outside at least once per hour to shovel the buildup out of the passage connecting the two houses. It gob-smacked Harper to be standing in a literal trench taller than her head, like something World War I soldiers would've been running around in only made out of snow rather than dirt. The last time she'd seen snow deeper than her height, she'd been six years old. It existed only because Cliff, Carrie, and Jonathan had been going outside every twenty minutes to keep up with shoveling. The mere thought of attempting to excavate a path in the snow at full depth made her exhausted.

At least there's zero possible chance any bad guys will attack us in this crap.

She stood in the 'snow hallway' connecting the two houses, staring up at the falling flakes. Other than the soft murmur of the kids talking inside the house behind her, Evergreen had fallen under a spell of wintry silence. If not for facing a wall of snow so high as to be frightening, she'd have found it peaceful. Technology could no longer intrude on the quiet. No jet engines going overhead, no helicopters, cars, sirens, or train horns.

It really sucks it took nuclear war to remind humans that nature exists. This would be kinda nice if I wasn't constantly worrying we're going to run out of food or get sick and die.

A distant, sharp crack echoed over the hills.

Harper twitched. It sounded like a single gunshot in the distance. She couldn't tell if a handgun went off on the other side of town or a rifle fired miles away. Then again, with all the snow coming down, the noise might well have been a tree breaking in half. Not like Lawless, other gangs, or even wild animals would be a problem at the moment. A year ago, she might not have even considered the sound had been a gunshot. Whether her assumption it had been someone firing a gun and not a tree surrendering under the weight of snow came from recent experience or pessimism, she couldn't say.

Being unable to patrol bothered her. As 'normal' as things had become, some people—like Cassidy—hadn't coped with the apocalypse well at all. Everyone being stuck in their houses might make things worse. A single (possible) gunshot had a grim connotation. Harper hugged herself, taken by a strong sense of dread at what might be going on when she couldn't be there to offer anyone help.

"Harp?" asked Madison from the doorway behind her.

"Yeah?" rasped Harper, then coughed, not quite ready to speak.

"Do you think Becca and Eva are okay? This is a lot of snow." Madison kicked her sock-covered foot at the porch. "I miss them already."

The question worsened Harper's anxiety. *Mrs. Parsons is not okay. She's hanging on, but it's not going to take much for her to have a bad case of the screw-its.* Her gut said Mrs. Parsons would never hurt Eva, but she couldn't shake worry. *I really need to check on them.*

"They're probably okay... but I'm gonna go make sure."

"Okay." Madison scrunched her nose up at the falling white flakes, beautiful and seemingly harmless. "Be careful."

Harper grabbed at the wall of the snow trench, intending to climb up to the surface. Unfortunately, her valiant attempt to venture across town to do a wellness check on Madison's friends failed catastrophically as she plunged into the freezing fluff. Ten minutes of exhaustive flailing later, Harper found herself trapped armpit deep in snow barely ten paces from the house. Worse than quicksand, she could neither drag herself forward, push herself backward, or even haul herself straight up out of the hole. She did manage to get her head above the level of the snow… barely. The entire area around Hilltop Drive had become an expanse of undisturbed white fluff dotted with roofs. Almost no recognizable houses remained in snow that varied from six to ten feet deep in drifts.

Cold seeped in, numbing her skin through her jeans.

"Uh oh," said Madison, somewhere out of sight behind her. "Dad! Mom!"

Hearing her little sister refer to Cliff and Carrie as 'Dad and Mom' stirred mixed emotions. Even though Madison had no intention to forget about or dismiss their real parents, it still seemed strange. Of course, at ten, her kid sister still felt awkward calling adults by their first names. Heck, Harper did too. She only recently managed to make herself refer to Walter as 'Walter' and not Mr. Holman. The use of 'Mom' and 'Dad' not only avoided said discomfort, it revealed the depth of Madison's attachment to them already. For her sister, it had become a sign of healing—so Harper didn't question it.

"You rang?" asked Cliff in an overly deep voice.

"Harp tried to check on Becca and Eva. I think she's stuck." Madison emitted a soft grunt as if trying to jump up to see.

"Hmm. So, you're saying that's not a big fluffy red rabbit sleeping in the snow?" asked Cliff.

"Funny," shouted Harper. "Yeah. I'm stuck."

Cliff and Carrie dug into the trench wall until the snow trapping Harper collapsed out from under her, allowing her to slide backward. Like a bowling ball, she swept her new parents off their feet, all three of them landing in a heap by the front porch.

"Yay!" Madison thrust her arms over her head.

"Go inside, hon." Carrie extricated herself from the pile. "You don't have shoes on."

Harper sat up. Cliff got to his feet, then pulled her up to stand.

In addition to a safe passageway between the houses, they now had a short spur into the front yard. Luckily, her winter coat kept her shirts and sweater dry. Alas, her jeans had become soaked. The breeze presently blowing by made her thighs sting from the cold. Harper rushed inside and hurriedly changed into a dry set of pants, then wrapped herself in a blanket on the couch by the fireplace. Madison and Lorelei obligingly crawled under the blanket with her to help her warm up.

"We can't just sit here. What if someone out there needs help?" asked Harper.

"Hmm." Cliff stroked his beard. "This is not the usual sort of snow we deal with in the US too often. Thinking we take a page from the Swiss Army."

"Knives?" asked Jonathan.

Chuckling, Cliff shook his head. "No. Snow shoes... there's gotta be something around here we can rig."

"I'll go... once I dry off." Harper smiled. "I'm not as heavy as a mall guard."

"Go where?" asked Madison. "You got stuck right in front of the house."

Harper, Jonathan, and Lorelei laughed.

"I mean..." Harper tried to massage warmth back into her legs. "If we can come up with something like snow shoes, I'll try them out."

Cliff mimicked Lorelei and stuck his tongue out at her.

Everyone laughed, including Cliff.

17

DAY THREE

NOVEMBER 22ND

If any sporting goods stores in the area stocked legit snowshoes, no one had bothered to take any. Harper had no idea if they existed around here. Colorado didn't exactly have a reputation for frequent snowfall deeper than the rooves of houses… at least not in Lakewood.

Carrie's former husband David had been a big tennis enthusiast. She still had a bunch of rackets in a closet, which Cliff decided to try using as improvised snowshoes. According to him, 'real' snowshoes looked fairly similar to tennis rackets. The open mesh didn't matter as much as greatly increasing the surface area on which a person walked. Someone his size probably couldn't manage too effectively on tennis rackets without breaking them, but Harper felt up to giving it a shot.

Late on the morning of the *third* day of continuous snow, Harper shuffled out the door with a pair of tennis rackets tied to her boots. Cliff and Jonathan expanded the spur where they dug her out the previous day, turning it into a ramp leading from ground level to the top of the snow dunes.

Armed with an empty backpack and her .45 pistol, Harper walked up the snow hill to the top and proceeded gingerly along. The rackets proved surprisingly effective, keeping her from sinking into the frozen mess. Her stomach knotted up in anxiety, worsening with each step farther from home she went. If she lost her balance and fell, she'd end up plunging into ten feet of snow and may or may not be able to get out. Also, while walking with tennis rackets on her boots made it *possible* to traverse the snow, it remained far from easy. Jogging with ten-pound lead weights strapped to her ankles would've been less work.

Harper tried not to think about freezing to death if she tipped over and got stuck. She didn't attempt to rush and exhaust herself, instead following a deliberate step-breathe twice-step pace.

Evergreen looked nothing like itself. She gazed around at rooftops in some places, mounds in others where houses had been completely buried. Falling snow stuck to the wool scarves she'd mummified her head in, forcing her to continually reach up to pluck gobs of ice off her face so she could see.

This is crazy. I'm more afraid right now than I was having Lawless shooting at me. One bad step and I'm an icicle. No one will find me until spring. At least getting shot is over quick. She considered aborting her mission and going home, but couldn't stop thinking about resuscitating little Averie after her brother pulled her out of the bathtub. Most of the families living in her patrol area relocated to the school building late on the 20th, a few holdouts not moving until it became clear how epic the blizzard really was on the 21st. She didn't know for sure how many moved since she'd been forced to go back inside and rest to avoid frostbite.

Here and there, the scraping of shovels from of people excavating pathways broke the oppressive silence. She couldn't see anyone, as they labored to dig out trenches in snow taller than people. Without snowshoes, they couldn't travel effectively on the surface, limited to digging their way anywhere. Most would probably give up, exhausted, after only clearing a few feet.

We should have moved to the Quartermaster's building when we had the chance. She sighed. *We're not that far away, though.*

She decided to trudge over there and see about getting food to bring home. The massive snowfall would take much longer than six days to disappear. Digging a trench down Hilltop Drive would also take longer than their food stores would last.

The Quartermaster's building looked like a giant model built in a hole. All three of its dedicated power windmills still spun. The largest one's housing looked about the same size as a small fridge. Rattling and squeaking from the mechanisms didn't fill her with a ton of confidence they'd last long, but they'd survived four months already. Someone had kept up with the snowfall, digging out a small space around the entire structure to keep all the windows and doors clear as well as continually sweeping or shoveling it off the roof. Drifts covered the lower half of the pine tree she remembered growing next to the 'Life Care Center' sign. Alarmingly, the electrical lines on poles hung so close to the surface of the snow they looked more like a strange sort of fence in her way.

Harper stopped short, staring at the wires. She had about three or four feet of clearance between the lowest one and the snow surface, but didn't know how dangerous it would be to go near them. Not every wire carried power anymore, only the ones Jeanette and her team spliced into the new system. She only possessed a basic understanding of electricity, but doubted the lines in front of her carried the same voltages they used to.

If I fall here, someone will hear me screaming.

Gingerly, she lowered herself into a squat and duck-walked under the power lines. Thankfully, she did not receive a shock. Relieved, she rose back to her normal posture and walked the rest of the way to the edge of the snow cliff surrounding the building.

Three men out shoveling the area by the main entrance spotted her and made their way over. She didn't recognize them thanks to heavy coats, hats, and scarves, even when they gathered directly below her.

"Harper?" asked Roy.

"Yeah. How'd you know?"

Walter laughed. "The hair is kind of a giveaway. How the heck did you get up there?"

For a second, Harper felt foolish for being surprised. Less than ten people in town had red hair, and not one of them other than her happened to be a teenager. Wrapping two scarves around her face for warmth didn't hide the rest of her long hair, which presently whipped around in the wind. She balanced on one foot and raised the other one to show off the tennis racket.

"Damn fine thinking," said Walter.

"Not my idea. Cliff." Harper flapped her arms. "They're kinda small, so I volunteered since I'm light."

"We might be able to rig something similar," said the third man, who sounded like Dennis. "Shouldn't be too difficult."

"What'cha need?" Roy shielded his eyes, peering up at Harper.

"Hoping to get some provisions. Can you guys dig me out a ramp? Or just load the pack for me?"

Walter reached up.

Harper shrugged the empty backpack off her shoulder and handed it down to them. While Walter headed inside to collect food, she chatted with Roy and Dennis. They grumbled about being 'stuck' there, though also told her the majority of residents decided to take advantage of the communal sheltering idea.

"After I drop the food back home, I can go around and check on anyone who stayed home."

"Appreciate it," called Roy.

Dennis and Roy tossed around ideas for making snowshoes big enough for people larger than teenagers, as well as the odds of potentially finding some in a store around here. Harper decided not to point out they'd need to have working snowshoes to go anywhere. Being from Lakewood, she didn't really have any idea if stores here would even have them. Lots of people in the area used to love doing outdoorsy stuff, but she'd never even heard of snowshoes as a thing until Cliff mentioned them yesterday.

Walter returned carrying a stuffed backpack. "Here, this should keep you and your family going for another two days or so."

He and Roy gently tossed the backpack up to the top of the snow.

"Thank you!" Harper crouched to pick it up. "Gonna run this home, then take a look around."

"Be careful." Walter waved. "Until we have more people equipped for such deep snow, don't take risks. If you lose a tennis racket or fall over, help is going to have a damn hard time getting to you."

Harper shuddered. She already knew falling over would be bad, but hadn't even considered the idea one of the improvised snowshoes might fail. Tying a tennis racket to her boots with clothesline cord seemed invincible—until she thought about it for more than four seconds. "Yeah... umm... right. Will do."

"We're planning to dig a passage out to 74," said Roy. "Gonna take a few days, probably. If we can make it to the highway, we should be able to get a small network of tunnels going."

"That's a lot of ass-busting work." Dennis chuckled. "Why don't we try going *over* the snow instead of through it."

Harper waved and left the guys to discuss their plans. Carrying a backpack stuffed with jars and frozen meat made walking three times more arduous. Not only did she teeter at the verge of falling over, it took significant effort to lift her feet out of the snow. Her life flashed before her eyes each time she felt her balance giving way. Something like a mere 2,200 feet separated home from the Quartermaster's building, but it may as well have been twenty miles.

Her fingers and nose lost feeling. Snowy ice caked her scarf and eyebrows. Her hair hung heavily, burdened by collected snow. She glared at the grey sky overhead, as if her scowl had the power to make Mother Nature ease off with the stupid white crap. Never before in her life had she seen it snow for three days straight. It rained like that once or twice, but not snow. At least it no longer came down in whiteout conditions. Still, a trickle of flurries worsened the already-too-deep mess.

After a few minutes of attempting to follow the path of Route 74, she started to feel like a lost Antarctic explorer. Fatigue from walking plus the mental exhaustion of being so on edge the whole time made the world seem strange and wrong. Roofs sticking out of the snow all started to look the same. Behind her, the 'fence' of power lines offered something of a reference point to where she'd come from.

For a moment or two, Harper stood still, breathing, resting, trying to get her bearings. While she didn't have to rush—the outside temperature more than preserved the food she carried— she couldn't take too long, or she'd end up as frozen as the venison in her pack.

Determined, Harper opened her eyes. The Quartermaster's building sat across the highway from Earl's Brewery. The auto garage came next, then the 'Evergreen Fine Art' building that kinda looked like a modern art version of a giant Adobe hut. It had a second story, so recognizable beige cubes offered a useful landmark above the endless white surface. Hilltop Drive, the street she now lived on, was the next one leading away from 74... by the place with the State Farm sign. The relatively short building vanished completely under the snow, but the line of utility poles pointed the way.

It felt surreal to walk past telephone poles only half as tall as they ought to be. Fortunately, these stood a bit taller than the ones by the Quartermaster's. She didn't need to duck to get past the wires.

By the time she spotted Jonathan up ahead standing on the roof of their house, clearing snow, she wanted to fall over and sleep for the rest of the day. Out of breath, parched, and shaking from exhaustion, Harper plodded down the snow ramp to the ground in front of the porch.

Carrie and Renee pulled her inside and fussed over her while Cliff took the pack to the kitchen to pack stuff away.

"Water," rasped Harper. "So... thirsty."

They peeled her scarves and coat off. Harper sat on the sofa by the fireplace, chugging water.

Renee reached to start untying the tennis racket on her left boot.

"Not yet." Harper grabbed her arm. "I gotta go back out."

"What?" Carrie blinked at her. "You look ready to collapse. You're not going anywhere."

The offer of staying safe and warm almost tempted her. In fact, it tempted her enough to feel guilty. A back-and-forth trek to the Quartermaster's kicked her ass. The idea of walking her patrol route in snowshoes while constantly in fear of freezing to death if she tripped did *not* appeal to her. However, she wouldn't be carrying forty-some-odd pounds of food.

"I have to... but after lunch." Harper chugged more water. "Just a quick check on people. I'm not going to stay out there for hours on patrol. I'm the only one who can go anywhere right now."

Carrie clucked her tongue. "You care so much about other people. It's okay to care about your own safety, too."

"I know." Harper smiled. "I do... but this is important."

A HUNDRED AND THREE STEPS INTO HER SECOND TRIP—AN HOUR later—Harper almost changed her mind.

She'd managed to ease her worries about a fall turning into guaranteed death by rationalizing danger came from going under the surface. If she fell, she'd just stay as flat as possible and drag herself to the nearest roof, pole, tree, or whatever. As a precaution, she'd brought along a bundle of extra clothesline cord, a knife, and a spare 'tire,' meaning a third tennis racket slung across her back. Carrie had almost a dozen of them. Harper didn't know much about tennis, but suspected they'd been expensive. David Rangel worked as a lawyer who used to commute several times a month to New York City. A lawyer who commuted across most of the continent several times a week couldn't be poor. The thought of his horrified reaction to some random girl using his precious tennis rackets as snowshoes made her laugh.

Of course, she didn't know anything about him. Even a reasonable person would be angry with her for treating expensive sports equipment like this—if nuclear war hadn't happened. For all she knew, David's ghost watched her and felt pleased some part of his life managed to help people now.

Still, traveling across the snow had to be the most physically grueling thing she'd ever done.

"At least I had a year of warmup." She chuckled to herself, imagining going straight from her comfortable bedroom back in Lakewood to attempting cross-country snow hiking. Months spending six-ish hours every day walking around had gotten her used to a level of exercise she'd never have been able to tolerate a year ago. Not that she'd been lazy or sedentary, but snow hiking *sucked*.

Harper bee-lined to her usual patrol route, astonished at her ability to recognize where she was based on the trees alone. The thicker forest cover among the houses surrounding the old golf course protected it somewhat from the wind. Few houses here had been swallowed entirely by the blizzard. Most had at least a foot or two of wall visible before the roof.

She went from house to house, knocking on windows and peering inside, finding almost every one of them abandoned for the time being. It reassured her to see so many people decided to seek shelter at the school. Not only did it help with food distribution, it reduced the reliance on firewood. As long as the electrical system on the school's roof held out, they'd have heat without needing fire.

Her hopeful mood took a nosedive when she spotted a trail of white smoke leaking from the window of Doreen Mack's house. She stopped short, staring at it, trying to process the sight. It didn't appear like the house full of babies and toddlers had caught fire. Burning houses tended to produce thick black smoke, not thin wisps of white.

"Help!" shouted a child from the direction of the house.

Harper's attention shot to the rapid motion of a waving hand in a blue glove. A smallish child no older than ten floundered, stuck in the snow a short distance from the house the same way Harper got stuck the first time she tried leaving the house. Throwing caution to the wind, Harper attempted to run toward the kid in such an ungainly stance she felt like a duck tiptoeing around land mines.

She found nine-year-old Emmy chest-deep in snow at the end of the trail she'd made from the front door. The poor kid had witnessed people vaporized by the nuclear flash and still feared the 'sky fire' would come back and get her at any moment. Being trapped outside would be unusually terrifying for her. As soon as Harper got close enough, Emmy grabbed her, trying to drag herself up from the snow.

"Mommy won't wake up!" wailed Emmy. "Miss Oliver, too. Dax… they're not moving. I tried to get help, but I got stuck."

"What happened?" Harper pulled the shaking girl into a snow-covered hug, rocking her.

"I dunno!" wailed Emmy. "They just didn't wake up." The girl lapsed into hard sobs.

"Em," said Harper. "I need you to be strong, okay? They need help. I can't sit here holding you right now."

The child sniffled, but nodded. "Yeah. Okay."

Emmy let go, trudge-tumbling back down the channel she'd cut through the snow trying to climb up. Harper held her arms out for balance and followed to the edge, where a six-foot drop led to an area of relatively shallow snow on the front porch. She sat on the edge, then let gravity pull her down. She could worry about getting out later.

The problem became obvious as soon as Harper reached the porch. A four-foot-thick haze of smoke clung to the ceiling in the living room. Tiny voices murmured inside the house. Harper crouched and made her way through the doorway. Three five-year-olds: a dreadlocked black boy, a frizzy-tow-headed boy, and a little redhead girl, stood watch over a literal pile of smaller children and infants in the middle of the living room. A few of the babies didn't seem to be moving. The toddlers all appeared to be awake, tightly bundled up in blankets and shivering. Both boys had winter coats, jeans, and sneakers on. The little red-haired girl wore a nightie and moon boots, seemingly unfazed by the cold.

Doreen Mack lay unconscious on the floor between the giant blanket mound and the fireplace. The prematurely grey fortysomething woman *did* appear to be breathing in shallow, labored gasps.

It took Harper all of two seconds to process what happened—blocked flue. Anyone little enough to be low to the ground remained conscious, others had succumbed to toxic fumes. Emmy had a habit of hiding under her bed at night instead of sleeping on it.

"Stay there by the door." Harper pointed Emmy at the porch. "Don't come inside. The air's bad."

She grabbed a random towel off the floor, wet it in the snow, then wrapped it around her face instead of her scarves. As best she could with tennis rackets tied to her feet, she rushed around the house opening every window not blocked off by snow. In successive back rooms, she found Therese, Jen Oliver, and Daxton unconscious in their beds beneath a haze of smoke. All had reasonably strong pulses and appeared okay, merely hadn't been able to wake up. She hurriedly dragged them off their beds to the floor, then rushed back to the living room.

Doreen didn't appear to be breathing anymore.

The black boy and the redheaded girl worked on changing the diaper of an infant while the frizzy-haired blond boy went around poking the babies one after the next as if checking to see if they remained alive.

Harper stared at the scene, horrified and overwhelmed.

"Hurry up and clean him, Colton," yelled the tiny girl holding the loaded diaper. "Before his weewee freezes off."

The dreadlocked boy scrunched up his face in disgust, then proceeded to do his best to clean the infant boy without looking at him.

"Wimp," muttered the girl.

Doreen gave a strangled, gurgle and stopped breathing.

Harper pounced on Doreen. She still had a pulse. After rolling the woman onto her back, she got started on rescue breathing.

The frizzy-haired boy tapped her on the shoulder. "Fire's out. Kimmy opened the back door. We're gonna get cold."

"There's smoke," shouted the redheaded five-year-old. "Hadda open doors."

"What should I do?" yelled Emmy from the front porch.

"Keep opening windows. Dig snow out so air can get in," said Harper.

Emmy darted off into the hallway.

Harper resumed breathing into Doreen's mouth.

"Ugh…" Daxton staggered into the room, one hand pressed to the side of his head. "I'm gonna throw up."

"Me too," said Colton, still cleaning poop off the back end of an infant.

"Wimp," muttered Kimmy before carrying the full diaper down the hall.

Colton made a face at her back. "I ain't no wimp. 'Least I'm doin it. Braeden's just watching."

The frizzy-haired boy held out a hand as if to ask 'fine, give me the rag.' "Hurry up. He's gonna freeze."

"Harper?" asked Daxton in a sleepy voice.

She took a deep breath and blew it into Doreen's mouth.

"Aww, crap." Daxton stumbled over to her. "What happened?"

"All the moms got sick, so we hadda help." Braeden pointed at the infants and toddlers in the blanket mound. "They're crying 'cause we didn't eat yet."

"Get down," rasped Harper. "Smoke. Fumes."

Daxton collapsed to sit on the floor. "I feel sick. Where's my mom?"

"She's sick, too. I moved her into better air. She should be okay." Harper breathed for Doreen again. "Come on. Come on. Wake up!"

The little girl returned with a clean cloth diaper. Between the two of them, they got the baby cleaned, dried, and wrapped in a blanket again.

"Dax, can you check the other babies? I think some of them were sick," said Harper.

"Okay." Daxton crawled over to the blanket pile.

Emmy ran back into the living room carrying a saucepan, which she used as a shovel to scoop snow out of side windows, making passages for smoke to escape.

Doreen gurgled, coughed, and—astonishingly—resumed breathing.

Harper practically melted into a puddle of relief.

Prior to the war, Doreen had been a large woman. She'd lost quite a bit of weight, but remained tall and wide-shouldered.

Harper doubted she had the strength to lug her anywhere, especially across ten-foot-deep snow. The tennis rackets couldn't possibly support their combined weight. Anything Harper did to help would have to happen here. Worse, no other assistance could feasibly reach them.

She knelt beside Doreen watching her breathe and Daxton examining infant after infant, feeling wholly inadequate for the task in front of her. More than anything, she wanted her parents to show up and take over... or at least Cliff and Carrie. Alas, given the conditions outside, Cliff and Carrie had as little chance of showing up here as her real parents.

This is on me. I can do it. Umm. Shit. What do I do first? Everyone's breathing. Windows are open. The place is airing out... Can't start a fire. It's going to get cold in here. We need a fire, but the flue is blocked... probably snow. The kids haven't eaten anything. Important shit: make sure everyone is breathing. Air the place out. Clear the flue. Food. Keep them warm. Fire.

"Emmy?" called Harper.

"Yeah?" replied a small voice from another room.

"Is the power working?"

A light flicked on and off in the hallway.

"Uh huh!" yelled Emmy.

Okay. I can make oatmeal. That'll warm the kids up and most of the little ones can eat it.

"Sec. I'm gonna feed you guys." Harper pushed herself up to stand.

"Your boobs aren't big enough," said Braeden.

Harper stared at him, unable to decide between gasping or laughing. The idea of breastfeeding at all, much less feeding nine babies in one sitting sent a twinge of pain across her chest. "Not gonna do that. There's milk here, right?"

All three five-year-olds nodded.

Daxton adjusted the blankets around another infant. "Mom's

kinda been helping out with the two tiny ones. Mrs. Mack's boobs don't work. But, yeah, they have milk in the fridge."

Harper looked the boy over. He seemed woozy but not too sick. Already, the haze of smoke had thinned to less than a foot. Of course, she'd let all the warmer air out as well as the smoke, so the living room had become almost as cold as the outside. "Do you have a snow shovel here?"

"I don't think so." Daxton scratched his head. His longish hair covered half his face, hiding one of his blue eyes.

She figured a kid his age who had the nerve to hike all the way to Evergreen from Kriley's Pond on his own could handle dealing with some snow. "Grab a pot like Emmy. Can you go onto the roof and dig out the chimney? This happened because snow plugged the top."

Daxton peered up at the ceiling. "Yeah, sure. Lemme go grab a coat and shoes."

As the boy hurried off, Harper checked over the little kids one by one. The infants who hadn't been moving turned out to be sleeping peacefully. It appeared Doreen got them all bundled up warm before losing consciousness. She must not have been aware of the buildup of toxic fumes prior to passing out.

"When the smoke started, I opened the door," said Kimmy.

"Emmy pulled us outta bed." Colton pointed at her. "Or we'd be sick, too."

Harper headed to the kitchen and got started making a giant pot of oatmeal. Fortunately, the electric stove both worked and wouldn't generate smoke. Daxton made his way up to the roof. Harper didn't worry about him. As deep as the snow had gotten, even if he went headfirst off the side, he'd be fine.

Jen Oliver staggered into the kitchen, scrunched her nose at Harper and babbled non-words.

"That's not good." Harper stared at her. "Fireplace got blocked up. Fumes filled the house. You're probably disoriented. Go outside and take some deep breaths."

After a moment of staring, Jen crossed the kitchen to the already open back door and went out onto the rear porch.

Emmy ran up to Harper. "Mommy's not breathing!"

"F—art!" yelled Harper, barely catching the F-bomb before it slipped out.

She ran to the small bedroom where Therese lay on the floor. A small pile of snow sat on the rug beneath the window by a saucepan. Emmy had dug out enough of it to let air in, but the room still had a scary amount of smoke. The pale nine-year-old flopped on the ground beside Therese, holding her hand and sobbing.

Emmy's mother of circumstance looked even thinner than Darci.

Once again, Harper pounced, intent on starting rescue breathing. As soon as their lips made contact, Therese opened her eyes and coughed.

"What the 'ell ya doin', girl?" rasped Therese in her thick, possibly Nigerian, accent.

Harper blushed seven shades of scarlet. "Uhh, you weren't breathing. Was going to, uhh, you know. CPR."

"Ah. Is dat why I be so damn dizzy?" Therese rubbed her head. "What's goin' on?"

Emmy burst into tears and hugged her. "Mommy…"

"Snow built up on the roof. Blocked the chimney." Harper wobbled to her feet, nearly tripping over the tennis rackets. "The house is full of smoke and toxic crap. Uhh, need to get back to the kitchen. Oatmeal's going to boil over."

"A'rite then." Therese nodded. "I am okay now."

The sound of Daxton coughing outside came in the window.

Harper tromped to the kitchen to find Jen tending the oatmeal pot. "Oh, whew. You okay?"

"Headache from hell, but I've had worse." Jen leaned against the counter. "Ugh…"

"Why do you have those things on your feet?" asked Kimmy—right behind her.

Harper nearly screamed at being snuck up on, but contained herself. On the way to the living room to check on the babies, she explained the concept of snowshoes. Four diaper changes later, she felt satisfied the small kids were in decent shape. Jen and Therese took over feeding the babies and toddlers.

Daxton, covered in snow, tromped in the front door. He stood there for a second catching his breath, then swatted at his coat, knocking flurries to the floor. "Got the chimney open. Had a bunch of ice on top."

"Harp?" shouted Madison from outside. "Harper?"

Harper stared at the window. *What the hell is she doing here?* She got up and went over to the front door. Madison crouched at the edge of the snow wall, peering down through the gap between the porch roof and the white stuff.

"What the heck are you doing here?" Harper's already overstressed system couldn't handle much more worry. "It's too dangerous."

Daxton removed his coat, shook more snow off it, then hung it on a peg by the door.

Madison lifted a foot to show off a tennis racket affixed to her puffy boot via small bungee cords. "You were gone a super long time. Everyone got worried, so I went out to find you. Chill. I didn't sneak out. Got permission. Cliff practically ordered me to go find you. At least you left pretty obvious tracks."

"Ugh." Harper pulled the no-longer-wet cloth off her face. "Sorry I was gone for so long. Had a serious situation here. Hey, I need you to help."

"What's up?" Madison went wide-eyed.

"Can you make it to the Quartermaster's?"

"Easy." Madison nodded.

"Awesome. Go tell them that Doreen Mack's chimney got blocked by snow and the house flooded with smoke. I *think* the kids are all okay, but they're kinda woozy. Doreen still hasn't regained consciousness. Jen and Therese are awake but a little out of it. Dunno if anyone can get here to help, but at least ask Tegan or Dr. Khan what we should do."

"Got it. And holy crap!" Madison stood out of her crouch. "I'm on it!"

Harper lingered in the doorway watching her little sister fast-walk off. On her, the tennis rackets looked goofily big, but came much closer to the right size ratio for snowshoes. Madison moved across the snow seemingly with ease despite her ungainly stride.

"Be careful and don't fall!" yelled Harper.

"I won't!" shouted Madison.

"Should we start a fire?" asked Daxton. "Chimney's clear now."

Harper bit her lip, thought it over for a second, then turned to look at him. "Yeah. We gotta warm this place up."

18

LITTLE HELP

While Therese took care of the fireplace, Harper bundled Doreen up in blankets saturated in the aroma of wood smoke. Scraps of heat radiating from the developing flames chipped away at the pervasive, chilly dampness hanging over the room.

Braden, Colton, and Kimmy burrowed into the blankets to keep warm. All three five-year-olds appeared much happier no longer having to take care of their fellow orphans. Therese and Jen both praised them repeatedly for how they handled being the 'adults in the room' for half a day.

Jen appeared dizzy while Therese came off as more hung over, her reactions a few seconds slow. Both women, as well as Daxton and some of the toddlers coughed frequently. Doreen finally regained consciousness about twenty minutes after Madison left, erupting in a serious fit of coughing that verged on choking. Harper handed her a cloth, then patted her back and tried to be reassuring while the woman spat up dark mucous.

Eek. That's not good.

Once the hacking subsided, Doreen lay back and wheezed, incoherently rambling about 'keeping the babies warm.' Harper encouraged her to take deep, slow breaths. Emmy and Daxton hurried around closing the windows and doors. Therese added another piece of wood to the fireplace, trying to prod the flames higher. No smoke billowed out into the room, proving Daxton had indeed cleared the chimney of snow and ice. Over the next half hour or so, the house warmed up from deathly freezing to 'holy crap it's cold'.

"Harp?" called Madison from outside.

Doreen looked up, seemingly surprised to find Harper sitting on the floor next to her. "What are you doing here?"

"You had a little situation with the fireplace." Harper squeezed her hand. "How are you feeling?"

"Dizzy as hell. Headache. Chest hurts," said Doreen in a hoarse voice. "Room's sorta spinning, but not really."

"You sound much closer to normal than you did a few minutes ago." Harper smiled. "Keep taking deep, slow breaths. I'll be right back."

Doreen nodded.

Harper got up and went out to the porch.

Madison, Jonathan, and Mila all crouched at the top of the snow wall, peering down at the porch.

"What the heck are you guys *all* doing here?" Harper gawked up at them.

"Technical difficulties." Jonathan laughed.

Mila snickered. "They're having trouble making snowshoes for big people."

"Weren't you stuck at home?" Harper peered at the gaunt black-haired girl—who no longer radiated quite so much creepy as she once did.

"I was." Mila put an arm around Jonathan. "He brought me, uhh… 'tennis shoes.'"

Madison groaned.

"No idea you were gonna need help." Jonathan blushed slightly. "I wanted to see her. Madison went by and yelled for us to go with her, said something serious happened and you might need help."

"We went to the clinic. Neither the doctors nor anyone else can get out here yet." Madison held up a small bundle. "So, they sent us. And... here." She tossed the bundle down.

Harper caught it. "What's this?"

"Cough drops... and a note," said Mila.

"Freakin' cough drops?" Harper had to laugh. "People almost died to breathing fumes and they sent cough drops?"

The three kids looking at her all shrugged.

Harper opened the wadded-up towel. Inside, she discovered a blister pack of pharmaceutical cough drops and a handwritten note. The handwriting had a feminine quality to it, overly neat and precise. "Hmm. Maybe Tegan isn't really a doctor."

"Huh?" asked Madison.

"I can read her handwriting."

Jonathan and Mila scrunched up their faces in confusion.

"She didn't write it. Dr. Khan spoke and Miss Ruby wrote it." Madison shrugged.

"Oh." Harper read the note.

The residents of the house are likely suffering a combination of smoke inhalation and carbon monoxide poisoning. Unfortunately, given our limited supplies, there is not much at our disposal to do for them. The good news is, if they are regaining consciousness, they should recover naturally. Remove them from the contaminated area, give them fresh air, rest, and water. The cough drops will help throat irritation. Symptoms may include disorientation, agitation, or sleepiness.

She frowned, then sighed at the cough drops. "Great... basically said they can't do anything."

"What did they tell you to do?" Mila tilted her head.

"The same thing I already was doing, except the cough drops." Harper leaned back in the door. "Jen?"

"Hmm?" The woman looked up from the baby in her lap.

"Here... for you, Therese, and Doreen. Maybe Dax, if his throat's bothering him from the smoke." Harper frisbeed the cough drops across the living room to Jen, then peered up at her sister. "Okay, so what are you three doing here? It doesn't take three kids to carry a dozen cough drops."

Jonathan laughed. "We're small enough to walk on tennis rackets and big enough to carry babies."

"Carry babies?" Harper raised both eyebrows.

"Yeah." Mila twisted to show off a small, empty backpack. "Mr. Holman and the doctors said we're supposed to carry all the little rugrats to the school where they'll be safe and have electric heat. We would have been back faster, but it took Anne-Marie and Miss Vasquez a while to make these baby carriers."

Madison nodded. "Yeah. Since no one can get here in the deep snow yet, they asked us to help."

"Hmm." Harper couldn't deny the wisdom in moving the little ones to the school building. It honestly annoyed her Doreen, Jen, and Therese hadn't done so already. Of course, if their fireplace hadn't blocked up, there likely wouldn't have been an issue. Still, it would take hours to warm the house, plus it continued snowing. If the flue got plugged again, the consequences could be tragic. "Okay. Drop down here. We're going to dig out a ramp first."

Since it came from the doctors and Walter, Harper treated it like an order from her 'commander' at the Militia that the children were to be moved to the school. Even though she totally agreed with it, she could claim not to have made the decision herself if challenged.

Madison, Jonathan, and Mila made their way down the narrow passage Emmy originally made in the snow. For the next hour-ish, the kids and Harper used pots and pans to enlarge the 'slide' into a ramp suitable for snowshoes. Excavated snow went into the house pot by pot, dumped in one of the two bathtubs to melt. By the time they had a passable route back to the snow surface, Doreen appeared to have returned completely to her senses.

She explained the situation to Doreen, Jen, and Therese, who seemed either too out of it to object or agreed with the idea. The kids' backpacks appeared to have been converted into blanket-lined papooses. The three five-year-olds and two next largest toddlers wouldn't comfortably fit in backpacks, so Harper decided to carry them the normal way.

Thankfully, the large house off Augusta Drive turned orphanage sat only about 850 feet from the school, so they didn't have too far to go. After packing the three tiniest babies in the papoose-i-fied backpacks, Harper wrapped Colton in a blanket and picked him up. She led the way up the ramp, with Madison, Jonathan, and Mila following her in single file.

The people at the school appeared shocked to have someone show up at the door given the massive amount of snow. Harper explained to the teachers what happened and to expect them to make several trips bringing babies to warmth and safety. Al Gonzalez, who had temporarily relocated to the school to serve as the medic, promptly began checking the little ones out. Also, Mr. Simon, a former high school teacher who'd taken over working with the older kids, helped out as well since he had EMT training.

It took three trips to transport all nine babies as well as Colton, Braeden, and Kimmy. Two four-year-olds and a three-year-old remained, all too big to fit in the backpacks. Jen Oliver attempted to rig snowshoes via creative use of duct tape and baking pans, but couldn't get up the ramp without wiping out since the flat steel surfaces offered zero traction on snow.

Madison, Jonathan, and Mila headed off, carrying toddlers wrapped in blankets.

"Guess we're stuck here, huh mom?" asked Daxton.

Jen kicked one of the pans across the living room. "Dammit."

"You should be okay as long as you keep an eye on the chimney." Harper pointed at the ceiling. "The snow covered the opening and trapped all the smoke and fumes in the house."

Daxton blinked. "How does snow cover a chimney? Isn't it like hot?"

"You'd think it would melt." Harper exhaled, trying to come up with an explanation. "It's been extremely cold and windy, plus it snowed a crapton real fast. Probably overpowered it. Maybe the fire went out for a while. You said it had ice on it, right?"

He nodded.

"Sounds like it was partially melting, but it just got cold enough to freeze it into a plug. The more ice blocked it, the colder it got, and eventually the snow collected on top." Harper flapped her arms. "I don't really know how it happened. Just that it did."

Doreen grumbled. "Well, I guess it's better the babies stay at the school until this white shit melts. You mind givin' me a hand goin' there? Gotta stay with my little ones."

"Umm." Harper cringed. "Maybe if we could rig a sled, I could pull you there. It's difficult to walk on snow as deep as it is out there. Even with these tennis rackets, it's really tiring."

Annoyed, Doreen paced, muttering about the 'damned snow.'

"Maybe it would be better if you moved everyone to the school building?" Harper tilted her head. "That way you wouldn't have to worry about bad weather like this. Kids wouldn't have to get wet going to school either."

"Augh, no." Daxton fake shivered. "Living *at* school? Being always at school? That's horrible."

Jen, Therese, and Harper chuckled.

"Maybe, but they have electric heat." Harper swatted snow off her sleeve. "You wouldn't be as cold there."

"How long we got 'til de 'lectric conk out?" asked Therese.

"No idea." Harper sighed. "They say they can keep fixing the wind turbines. Maybe they can. It's really not that high tech compared to solar panels. They could've had wind-powered electricity in the 1800s if they managed to think of it."

"What are the odds we'll get snow like this again?" asked Doreen. "And, that school's at basically the edge of town. Seems kinda risky to put children there. If we get attacked, the school's the first place gonna get hit."

Jen raised her eyebrows. "Didn't think about that."

"This house isn't too far away from the school." Harper folded her arms. "And it's been a year so far. Figure if any big army of bad guys was out there to attack us, it would've happened by now. We went to Denver two months ago and only saw like twelve Lawless. Only three had guns. They're probably dying off for being stupid and not trying to establish farms and stuff."

"Hrm." Doreen set her hands on her hips. "So, you're saying I'm stuck here? How bad is it out there?"

"Most one-story houses are roof deep." Harper traced a wavy line in the air. "Some drifts are close to fifteen feet tall."

"Damn," muttered Jen. "Is this a nuclear snowstorm or just freakishly bad luck?"

"Dunno."

"I gotta get to my little ones." Doreen paced.

Jen rested a hand on her shoulder. "They'll be fine, Dor. We have plenty of food here to weather a few days. You heard Harper. You need to rest. We all do."

"And watch the chimney." Daxton coughed into his hand.

"Maybe you're right." Doreen rubbed her forehead. "I do feel kind of woozy still."

"Haaaarp?" called Madison from outside. "Are you coming home?"

"Go on, hon." Doreen hugged her. "I'll be fine now. Thank you for helping my babies."

"You're welcome." Harper returned the hug. "Do you want Emmy to stay here or go to the school? She's small enough I could probably carry her."

Emmy clamped onto Therese, giving both of them a 'no, please' stare.

Harper grinned. "Okay then. And it's not really me you should be thanking. Emmy woke up first, got the others out of bed, opened the doors. She even tried to go for help but got stuck. She let enough air into the house to, um… yeah, you know."

Sniffling, Emmy buried her face in Therese's chest.

"Aye." Therese brushed a hand over Emmy's hair. "Tank ya, girl. Ya kept me on this Eart' a bit longer."

"You saved me, too," whispered Emmy.

Doreen wiped a tear, as did Jen.

Daxton cringed. "Too mushy."

"Haaaaaarp," yelled Madison. "Come on. I gotta pee."

Chuckling, Harper waved and headed outside. Madison, Mila, and Jonathan waited for her at the top of the snow ramp. Going home—and spending the rest of the day huddled under a blanket—certainly sounded like an awesome idea.

19

DAY FOUR

NOVEMBER 23RD

Careful not to spill, Harper crept down the hall carrying the plastic bucket serving temporary toilet duty.

They'd come up with a relatively fair system. Anyone who used the bucket had to dump it right away... except for Lorelei. Certain exceptions happened, such as a whole bunch of people needing to go in rapid succession, in which case someone got stuck carrying everyone's donations. Rather than cause fighting and a rush by requiring the last one to go to carry the mess outside, they ended up choosing somewhat randomly. Harper had the present misfortune to be the loser of rock paper scissors, thus carried the morning bucket.

She went out the front door to avoid bringing it through the kitchen while Cliff made breakfast. As soon as she stepped into the snow trench that towered over her head, Harper stopped to gaze up at clear blue sky.

It had finally stopped snowing.

For a fleeting moment, she felt like cheering... until the smell ruined the moment.

"Ugh." Grumbling, she lugged the bucket along the trench toward Carrie's house. Not quite halfway there, a T-intersection led into the empty lot between the two houses. Cliff had managed to dig out an impressive six-foot-deep hole in the frozen earth using a pick-ax, a shovel, and a whole lot of foul language. They'd been using it as a place to dump the bucket ever since the toilet froze. She cringed away and gingerly poured the contents of the bucket into the hole. Ideally, they'd dump such things much farther away from the house, but the epic amount of snow presented certain difficulties in regard to doing so. Namely, the amount of work it would take to excavate a tunnel.

Ugh. Septic tanks need to be pumped out, right? Who the heck is going to do that now? No one. Is this house on sewer or septic? What are we going to do if the tank fills? What the heck did people do for toilets in the Old West? She sighed at the mess in front of her. *Holes in the ground. By the time I'm thirty, we'll be using outhouses again.*

Given the tremendous snowfall, she figured the pipes would remain frozen for a while. Keeping the fire going in the living room hadn't quite freed up the toilet, though thus far, the bowl remained unexploded. She shook the bucket to chase away the last few drops of awfulness, then scooped a bit of snow into it to provide 'base water' to help reduce the stink of the next donation.

On the way back to the house, she randomly worried about the town's water system. How long would the faucets and bathtub continue working? Cliff said something about it all being way lower tech than most people thought. Sure, the town's water supply used modern pumps, but similar pumps had been used since the 1930s. If Jeanette's team could build wind turbines for electricity, they could keep some manner of pump going.

Or we wind up having to go to the damn lake whenever we want water and boiling it. Maybe wells.

Harper returned to the house. No sooner did she walk in than Renee grabbed the bucket from her, an urgent look on her face

"Sorry." Renee grimaced. "I know you just went out. I'll dump it when I'm done."

"No worries." Harper let go of the bucket and unzipped her coat.

"Ugh. This sucks so much." Renee started for the bathroom.

"Totally." Harper tossed her coat on the sofa. "I'm sorry for every time I complained about my alarm going off on a school morning."

"Seriously." Renee darted out of sight and shut the bathroom door.

Harper headed to the table where everyone else had already started on breakfast. "It stopped snowing!"

"Really?" Jonathan went wide-eyed.

Madison and Lorelei ran to the front door to see for themselves, then cheered.

Wow. She chuckled to herself. *First time I've seen kids cheer snow stopping.*

"About damn time," muttered Cliff, setting a bowl of oatmeal in front of her.

The portion appeared large, but one thing they had in abundance turned out to be oats. Whoever did the planning overestimated how much the horses would eat. Harper didn't mind. It might be plain as hell, but it warmed her up and she'd never again complain about food being bland. Having enough food—no matter what it happened to be—made her happy.

"We're going to have a whole lot of mud come spring." Carrie chuckled. "Good thing is, we won't flood here, being so high up."

"So, what's the plan for today?" Harper stuffed a full spoon of oatmeal into her mouth.

"Damage control mostly." Cliff stirred some strawberry preserves into his oatmeal, then offered the jar to Harper. "Check on everyone who didn't move to the Q. Probably ask you and the kids to head up to the school and see if they're doing okay on provisions or need a supply run."

"Any word on better snowshoes?" Harper took the preserves. "Thanks."

"Nope. Forgot to charge my cell phone." Cliff ate a spoonful of oatmeal. "Haven't gotten a call from Walt."

Harper rolled her eyes, feeling dumb for asking. Of course, he had no way to get to the Quartermaster's and ask. As soon as they rigged snowshoes, they'd drop by.

"What about Warbonnet?" asked Carrie.

"I don't think scary hats are gonna help." Madison laughed.

"No, it's an outdoor sports place." Carrie shifted her jaw side to side. "I want to say it's off Bryant Drive near the storage place. They might have actual snowshoes there. Definitely skis. Cross-country skis might work as well to get people moving around."

Harper shrugged one shoulder. "I could check it out. Pretty sure I can find it. Hell of a walk in this crap, though. Remind me which one Bryant is?"

"If you're heading south down 74," said Carrie, "Hang a left at the intersection just past the Walgreens."

"Right. Okay." Harper nodded.

"I wanna go, too." Madison set her empty bowl down.

"Sure." Harper added more preserves to her bowl.

Madison blinked. "Really? You're not gonna tell me it's too dangerous?"

"Nah." Harper chuckled. "We're not leaving town."

"Cool." Madison grinned. "I need some outside time. Getting sick of being in the house all day."

Renee appeared from the hallway and hurried out the front door carrying the bucket, not bothering to slow down long enough to put on a winter coat.

"Yeah, seriously." Harper watched her friend zoom by. "We're all getting a little cabin fever."

Cliff leaned back in his chair. "Not me. I'm happy we have this cabin to get sick of."

"Good point." Jonathan scraped the last of his oatmeal out of the bowl. "I'm gonna check the roof again."

Harper ate a little too fast, mostly because she wanted to finish it while it remained hot enough to create a core of warmth in her stomach. "'Kay, Termite. Get your coat and crap on. Let's go."

Swapping the clothesline rope out for the bungee cargo cords made the tennis racket snowshoes more manageable. It offered a bit of flexibility, lessening the odds a mis-step would destroy the racket. Also, if needed, she could remove them much faster than attempting to untie hard knots with frozen fingers.

Upon reaching the path of Route 74—she had a good idea of its location thanks to the power lines and lack of buildings—she paused long enough to turn in a full circle, surveying the area. The blizzard had entirely buried the buses set up across the highway as a barricade. Not having any snipers or lookouts stationed at the unofficial entrance to downtown from the north made her a little nervous, but then again, it's not like anyone dangerous—or harmless—would be traveling in snow this deep.

While it had stopped coming down, little melted. The whole of Evergreen lay blanketed under rippling white dunes ranging from six feet deep to easily double that where the wind piled it. Places on the opposite side of buildings from the wind created shallower voids, some low enough to still see the roofs of dead cars. Most of the snow fell within the first day and a half when the wind blew at its fiercest.

Harper had never seen so much snow, a blizzard powerful enough to conceal entire houses. Storms like it had, according to some of the older people, happened before. She hoped the rarity continued and the next 'hundred year storm' happened well after she'd grown old and died.

Please don't be nuclear craziness.

"What's up?" asked Madison.

"Just looking around." Harper smiled at the small figure next to her, mummified in scarves, jacket, and gloves.

The sudden worry her sister appeared *too* small came out of nowhere. Even at eleven, she still looked like a child. None of them had been eating 'well' compared to their pre-war diet, though the past four months probably counted as 'decent.' Harper couldn't remember when she stopped getting taller. It had to be around fifteen, so her sister still had a few years. Maybe she'd hit a growth surge as soon as puberty started—assuming her hormones hadn't gotten all out of sorts due to crazy amounts of stress, strange diet, and whatever radiation they'd been exposed to.

"See anything good?" asked Madison in a teasing tone.

"Snow. Lots of it." Harper sighed, then proceeded to walk onward along the path of Route 74.

Madison followed.

The soft, repetitive crunch of tennis rackets sinking an inch or two into snow with each step floated off on a constant west-to-east breeze. Harper divided her attention between her feet and the surrounding rooftops, looking for any sign of the Walgreens on the left. She knew the Militia—or at least the original survivors who collected here—had already gone around to every business and collected all items of potential use. Even if Warbonnet Outdoors *had* snowshoes, it seemed unlikely anyone would have bothered to take them. People in the US didn't need those things, only crazy adventurers in remote parts of Siberia, or whatever, did.

Maybe Canada, too.

She glanced at Madison, trying to figure out if her brain played tricks on her or not. Her sister didn't look any bigger than she did a year ago. It's possible she *had* grown some, but so gradually as to escape notice. With everything else going on to worry about, she figured her memory fogged up. Kids didn't simply cease growing, after all. Though, given their food situation, she worried Madison hadn't grown as much as she should have. Her neurotic fears kept circling back to the first few days they spent outside after fleeing their house, covered in likely irradiated ash.

When Harper experienced genuine nightmares, it almost always involved radiation. Running into a man so sick from exposure to gamma rays his skin had swollen up like an inflatable doll and turned purple left a deeper mark on her psyche than she admitted. Of course, such *obvious* problems didn't scare her. Someone in such condition received a megadose. Within days of exposure, they'd be dead—an agonizing, horrible death, but still dead quite fast. That man didn't spend months or years wondering if he'd been irradiated and what effect it would have.

Harper's true fear came in the dread she and Madison might have picked up enough radiation to cause other problems she considered worse than dying rapidly: like cancer or genetic damage leading to severely malformed babies. Maybe they'd make it to their fifties before their kidneys shut down or some other part of their body called it quits thanks to gamma rays.

Having sex with Logan on and off always thrilled her in the moment but came with an inevitable period of being scared once it finished. She'd compared sex to Russian roulette, as both had a chance to kill her. Maybe her fears of dying in childbirth were excessive, but she also didn't want a baby yet. She might never feel like having one deliberately. Guaranteed if she and Logan kept tempting fate, it would happen sooner or later.

The random worry she hadn't gotten 'lucky' thus far as much as radiation microwaved her ovaries into useless raisins made her gasp, then start laughing uncontrollably at the silliness of the mental image.

"What?" asked Madison.

"Stupid thoughts. I think I'm going snow crazy."

"Okay. Whatever. You don't have to tell me if it's about sex."

Harper stared at her sister's wool-wrapped head.

"Hah. Knew it."

"Since when can you read minds?"

Madison flailed her arms for balance while walking up the incline of a snowdrift. "I can't. But you suck at lying. The only thing I can think you'd wanna lie to me about is sex type stuff since I'm 'too little.'"

"Ahh." Harper gave a sad chuckle. "Eleven years old now is a bit different than eleven years old before."

"I have seen some shit," said Madison in a voice only part teasing.

Harper stopped walking. "Okay, Termite. You're right... guess you don't have that much innocence left to shatter."

"Ha. Ha. I don't wanna hear about what you and Logan do when no one's watching. Eww."

Laughing, Harper put an arm around her. "Nah. Wasn't planning on sharing those details..."

As she resumed walking, Harper explained her worries about unexpected pregnancy, radiation possibly causing damage they didn't know about, and randomly wound up going into the whole 'self-defense' spiel her mother gave her when she'd turned twelve. Perhaps a little early to burden Madison with the need to stay alert for creeps, however... the world no longer had cops or organized law. Men who'd prey on young girls would have *much* less fear of being held accountable.

By the time they reached the spot where the big Walgreens building stuck out of the snow, Madison had gotten quiet. Harper avoided going into any great detail beyond saying some sick people out there might try to force Madison to do the same sorts of things Harper did with Logan.

"Eww," said Madison after a long silence. "Okay, that's freaky. Makes the way that guy watched me all different."

"Which guy?" Harper's breath caught in her throat.

"Some dude at the dance studio. Not here." Madison exhaled.

"Mom told me to stay away from him. Didn't say why."

Harper scowled. "Well, now you know."

"Wish I didn't." Madison made a disgusted gurgle. "Harp?"

"Yeah?"

"There's no cops anymore."

"I know that."

Madison looked up at her. "If someone tried to do that to me or Lore, would you shoot them?"

The question forced thoughts into Harper's mind she didn't want to deal with. "Probably. Depends."

"On what?"

"If I caught them grabbing you, or if I found out about it later." Harper gingerly navigated the downhill slope of a snowdrift. "But, yeah... if someone hurt you like that, I'd probably use up a few shotgun shells."

Madison clapped her gloved hands together with a soft *thump*. "Topic change. Do you like unicorns more than faeries?"

Harper laughed.

"Fuzzy!" said Madison in a mimic of Lorelei's higher pitched voice.

"Right."

"No, seriously." Madison grabbed her arm while pointing her other hand to the left.

Harper looked up from the snow, following her sister's mittened finger to a rectangular metal building not quite 200 feet away. A group of five fluffy snow-caked wolves congregated on the corner of the roof above a yellow sign with green lettering 'Evergreen Vacuum.' The plain steel-walled building sat higher on a hill, so the snow only came about halfway up its walls. Harper thought they looked like a pack of animals stranded on a raft adrift upon an enormous snowy ocean.

The wolves all stared fixedly at Harper and Madison, their paws teasing at the edge of the roof as if they contemplated diving into the snow at any second.

Shit. Shit. Shit. Harper glanced down at the tennis rackets strapped to her boots. No way could she run from wolves. Even walking felt laboriously slow. The white aluminum 'Goodyear' garage to their right didn't offer much in the way of shelter as the snow came right up to its roof. She'd have to dig five feet down to reach the door.

Her air horn alarm wouldn't do any good whatsoever. Only a handful of adults had managed to piece together workable snowshoes, and they wouldn't be able to get to her fast enough to matter. She pulled her long winter coat up off her hip to reach the .45.

"I'm an idiot," whispered Harper.

"Sorry. I shouldn't have asked to go with you."

Harper shook her head. "No, not that. I left Dad's shotgun at home. Didn't think I'd need it."

"No…" Madison grabbed Harper's arm in both hands. "Please don't kill the wolves. They're beautiful."

"Termite… they're pretty, yes, but they're hungry. Would it bother you more being mauled to death or me shooting them?" *Yeah, right. If all five of them come after us, we're screwed. I'm not going to be able to take them all out with a handgun. Only chance we have is if the noise spooks them into running.*

"Umm…" Madison fidgeted. "Okay. Just… don't shoot them unless they try to eat us."

"Nice wolvies," whispered Harper. "Go find a fat rabbit or something. We're not food."

Madison tugged on her arm. "Wolves aren't really dangerous to us."

"Right…"

"No, seriously." Madison took a step, trying to pull Harper forward. "Almost all wolf attacks are from animals who lost their fear of humans due to idiots trying to domesticate them who didn't know what they're doing. Or when someone tries to stop a wolf from attacking their small dog. They will almost always avoid humans."

Harper kept staring at the wolves, squeezing and relaxing her grip on the gun. "What do wolves do when their food supply runs low? Will they attack people if they're starving?"

"Uhh. Crap." Madison bit her lip. "Maybe."

The wolves continued to gather at the edge of the roof, staring at them. Despite their size, their tentative demeanor made Harper think the animals didn't trust the super deep snow. They didn't snarl, growl, or appear angry. Curious, if anything.

"They look kinda calm. Almost worried," whispered Harper.

"Yeah... I don't think they wanna attack us. If a wolf's gonna attack, it'll act like an angry dog... snarling and stuff." Madison sidestepped along. "Keep looking at them. Don't turn your back and don't run."

"Okay... how do you know so much about them?" Harper walked sideways behind Madison, putting herself between the wolves and her kid sister.

"Internet research." Madison sighed. "Lots of morons think wolves are evil and dangerous. I got into *so* many flame wars online."

Harper smiled nervously, not that anyone could see it under her scarves. She'd have made a joke about Madison being a 'mini PETA' member, but didn't want to start an argument. Her sister didn't like PETA either.

The largest of the wolves, a big white one with amber-colored eyes, licked the sides of its mouth.

"What do we do if they come after us?" whispered Harper.

"I don't think they will. They look calm."

"But if they do?" Harper accidentally stepped on her sister's left tennis racket due to staring at the wolves instead of the ground.

When Madison tried to move again, the tennis racket remained embedded in the snow as she picked her boot up a few inches. The bungee cords yanked her foot back down, causing her to spill forward onto her hands and knees. "Ack! Watch where you put your giant feet."

"Sorry..." Harper helped her up. "Was kinda paying attention to the wolves."

"Ugh." Madison dusted snow off her jeans. "If they come after us, make noise, throw rocks, basically fight. They'll probably give up if we're too much trouble."

"We're six-to-ten feet above any rocks." Harper squeezed her handgun. "Except for a few really little rocks made out of lead I can throw extremely fast."

"I don't think they're gonna chase us in snow this deep." Madison hustled a little faster. "Come on. Just keep going, don't look away."

Harper let Madison get a little distance before she continued moving, to avoid tripping her again. The five wolves continued watching until they moved far enough up Bryant Drive to break line of sight behind the Evergreen Rentals building.

Still shaking from adrenaline, Harper faced forward and walked as fast as her improvised snowshoes let her. A few inches of sign reading 'Lakota Park' stuck up from the snow to her left. The hike along Bryant Drive—or on the snow where she assumed the road to be—proved a moderately grueling uphill trudge. Harper felt as if she'd walked back and forth to Denver twice by the time she reached where the incline levelled off. Not far ahead on the left, their destination came into view.

The long, two-story tall wood-brown building resembled three plain, rectangular 'Monopoly hotels' stuck end to end. It looked nothing like stores or retail space, having multiple large garage style doors along the lower story and a row of tiny square windows up top. Brown wood siding and green-painted frames around the windows and doors made it look weird to her. She'd never seen garage doors like that on any place other than mechanic garages or shops that worked on cars. Only a few small signs peeking out from the snow suggested it housed businesses. She had no idea what 'Stud108' meant, and didn't really have much interest in learning. Hopefully, they intended it as an edgy way to write Studio 8 and not Stud 108.

"Wow, where's the sports store?" asked Madison.

"Maybe on the other side. Bryant loops around. Let's keep going." Harper gestured at the building. "It's like a whole bunch of small businesses in a shopping center."

"Looks like a giant garage."

"Yeah. It does. Weird."

Madison looked back and forth between the building and Harper. "Why does it have so many garage doors?"

"How should I know?" Harper shrugged. "Maybe they built it as a garage but someone else bought it for store space. Doesn't really matter now. Gonna be decades before anyone has working cars again on a large scale."

Madison sighed. "Yeah. Dammit. Not fair."

"A lot of things aren't fair about nuclear war." Harper patted her on the head. "What particular thing bothers you now?"

"Just making a lame joke." Madison flapped her arms. "I'm never gonna learn how to drive."

"You might... I mean... Rafael got the Post Office truck working." Harper wagged her eyebrows. "Think of it this way... no written test. No traffic lights. No bizarre rules to have to remember."

Madison chuckled. "True. So, umm... You ever break into a place before?"

"Nope. First time for everything." Harper whistled innocently. "But the doors should be open. Walter and his people checked every structure in town before we even got here."

"Okay." Madison peered back. "Hope the wolves go somewhere else before we go home."

"Yeah... me too." Harper put her .45 back in its holster and let out a long, slow breath. "Me too."

20

WELLNESS PATROL

NOVEMBER 26TH

The happy voices of children echoed across the snowscape engulfing Evergreen.

Harper snowshoed down Hilltop Drive as she'd done each morning for the past three days. Again, Madison wanted to go with her. Jonathan stayed home to look after Lorelei while Cliff attended to whatever task Walter gave him. Carrie and Renee would spend most of the day making clothing at her house, thanks to a delivery of fabric and thread. If the team couldn't get to the Quartermaster's building to work on garments, people capable of traversing the snow could bring materials to them. It beat sitting around bored all day.

Madison didn't complain at all about the walking. The tennis racket snow shoes didn't bog down so much for her, thanks to her smaller size and weight. Harper figured if her little sister wanted to spend time with her hiking around town rather than staying warm at home or playing in the snow with the other kids, fine. She'd likely change her mind if Becca and/or Eva showed up. However, Eva's mom and Becca's parents followed the advice of the town council and relocated to the school to ride out the blizzard. No matter how much they wanted to, the girls couldn't hike roughly a mile in snow this deep to hang out with Madison. All the kids playing around here belonged to either Militia parents, those who lived in Evergreen before the war, or anyone who needed to stay close to the town center.

Warbonnet Outdoors surprisingly *did* have a couple sets of snowshoes hidden away behind mostly camping gear and small kayaks. Stuff like sleeping bags, hiking boots, knives, or anything potentially useful to survivors had already been taken. Skis, and other items not obviously useful as anything more than fun stayed behind. Three days ago, Harper and Madison lugged eight pairs of snowshoes and a bundle of skis back to town using a kiddie pool as a sliding cargo platform.

Thanks to their efforts, plus Liz Trujillo and her team getting creative with PVC and duct tape, the Militia gained the ability to travel across snow and resumed making the rounds. Since the blizzard made the area around Evergreen largely impassable, they primarily checked up on residents rather than kept alert for outside hostilities. Harper and Madison set about doing the same thing they'd done the past two days: going door to door to conduct wellness checks on anyone who hadn't relocated to the Quartermaster's place. They'd make their way around the homes on Hilltop Drive and north of it before proceeding farther north into Harper's usual patrol area.

Her plan involved a significant amount of arduous walking, but it would go faster as the day progressed. Most of the homes around the former golf course stood empty thanks to the people who normally lived in them now relocating temporarily to the school. She also figured Madison wanted to come along to see her friends when they got to the school.

The kids who lived around the area of Hilltop Drive (including Lorelei and Jonathan) played in the snow, sliding off the roofs of houses into the white stuff, building snow forts, and otherwise having fun. Snow this deep had to be amazing to small children. Two boys even attempted digging out tunnels to make a 'military base,' until their dad freaked out, worried it might collapse and bury them.

Harper paid enough attention to the squeals and cheers of the kids to react in the event glee became something else. Except for thirteen-year-old Noah Bowden thinking it a great idea to dive headfirst off his house and get stuck in the snow like a lawn dart, the past two days had been accident free. Noah hadn't hurt himself, but he did have quite a scare when he couldn't get out on his own.

After two-and-a-half hours of going door to door, Madison began dragging her feet.

"You okay, Termite?"

"Yeah." Madison stretched, yawning out a huge puff of fog. "Just tired. I like this more than working on the farm."

Harper laughed. "That's not saying much. You hated working on the farm."

"I disliked busting my ass from sunrise to sunset for three weeks." Madison held a mittened finger up. "I don't mind being on the farm in general."

"Makes sense, but those weeks of butt busting is why we have food to eat now."

Madison rolled her eyes. "I did it, didn't I? Grumbling about it while doing it is way different from trying to get out of doing it."

"True." Harper gave her side-eye. "So, you like patrolling?"

"Chill. I don't wanna be a cop, or Militia, or whatever you guys call yourselves."

Harper chuckled. "Whew."

"I still can't believe *you* do this." Madison flapped her arms.

"Yeah… neither can I sometimes."

"What would you have done if the world didn't stop?" asked Madison.

"I have no idea. Why do you think I was so anxious about

going into my senior year?" Harper chuckled. "My friends all knew what they wanted to major in. Not me."

Madison stepped on an ice patch. Her right foot shot out from under her while her left tennis racket embedded itself in the snow, anchoring in place. She fell into a full-on front-to-back split, bracing her hands on the snow to avoid falling over sideways.

"Oof," whispered Madison. "Haven't stretched like this in a while."

Ken Zhang, who happened to be close enough to see her go down, groaned as if he'd been kicked in the groin. "You all right, Maddie? That looked painful."

"I'm fine!" yelled Madison. "Three years of dance class prepared me for this moment."

Harper grabbed her by the armpits and hauled her upright, laughing. Madison wobbled to one side, mostly giggling but also cringing.

"Did you pull something?" whispered Harper.

"I haven't stretched in months." Madison lifted one knee to her chest, held it there for a few seconds, then repeated with her other leg. "But I'm still young and flexible, not an old lady of eighteen."

"Hah! I'm not old."

"Prove me wrong." Madison clapped, throwing snow off her mittens. "Splits time."

Harper waved dismissively. "I'm wearing jeans, not yoga pants."

"These aren't yoga pants. They're leggings."

"Whatever."

"Excuses, excuses," said Madison in a humorous tone as she resumed walking.

Over the next few hours, they brought food to three older residents who'd been too stubborn to relocate to the Quartermaster's for the duration of the snow. Madison seemed happy to be helping out, even if her assistance took the form of carrying jars of green beans and potatoes.

About thirty feet past the fork in Oxbow Road, Harper spotted an unusual divot in the snow.

"That's not good." She stared at the spot.

"What?" Madison shielded her eyes from the sun under two purple mittens. "I don't see anything."

"There." Harper pointed. "Yesterday, a big block of snow was there. It's gone."

"That's Mrs. Michaelson's house. She used to make cookies for us until she ran outta stuff."

A heavy dread settled in the pit of Harper's stomach at the sight. She could come up with only one explanation for how a house-sized block of snow vanished overnight: the roof collapsed. Cliff had been fairly insistent on sending Jonathan onto the roof of their house to keep the snow from piling too high. Their little blue house had an angled roof, but it wasn't steep enough to make the snow slide off by itself. As fast and heavy as the white crap came down, he feared it might crush.

The relatively small pit where a house ought to be lent grim validation to Cliff's concerns. Mrs. Michaelson's place was about the same size as the house Harper lived in. She couldn't quite remember it in great detail, but it probably had a similar style roof.

Her mouth dried out at the thought it must've collapsed sometime between late evening yesterday and this morning, probably in the middle of the night since she didn't hear anything unusual. A house caving in had to make more than a little noise.

She crept up to the opening. Snow ringed the edges of a hole looking down into what had likely been the living room. Only a bit of sofa arm sticking out from the cave-in gave any clue as to which part of the house lay exposed to the elements.

Without even really thinking about what she did, Harper slung the Mossberg off her shoulder and handed it to Madison before turning her back to the hole and easing herself downward on all fours. Madison stood at the top, clutching the shotgun sideways across her chest in both arms like a piece of firewood.

Harper only got about a third of the way down before the tennis rackets on her boots became more of a hindrance than a benefit; they kept snagging on broken wood pieces sticking out of the avalanche. Even from where she perched, it appeared obvious the majority of the snow on the roof had fallen straight down into the house. The structure likely would have completely pancaked if not for the snow surrounding it holding up the walls.

While looking around for places to either grab or place her foot, Harper spotted a greyish-blue hand sticking out from under a pile of crushed lumber and ice. It appeared Mrs. Michaelson had been on the sofa at the time the roof gave out. The faint fragrance of damp ash saturated the cavity.

She must've had a fire going. It happened before dark. She's been there all damn night.

The color of the woman's frozen hand left no doubt Harper got there too late to matter. Even if the collapse occurred while she watched, Mrs. Michaelson could easily have been killed instantly from the weight of the roof and snow landing on top of her. The more she stared at the woman's hand—and undamaged fingernails—the more certain she felt the woman died right away. Nothing gave any indication Mrs. Michaelson had struggled to dig herself out.

Knowing the forty-nine-year-old lived by herself, Harper decided it not worth the risk to continue trying to get down into the house. It could collapse even more at any second. Also, she could destroy the tennis rackets strapped to her boots and end up stranded here. She looked up at Madison. For no particular reason, she got stuck trying to decide if Madison made the shotgun look massive or if the shotgun made her sister seem tiny. Perhaps her brain attempted to distance itself from the reality of a dead woman being less than seven feet away. It made no sense.

She'd killed Lawless and other dangerous people... but none of them ever made cookies for her little sister and her friends. Mrs. Michaelson never hurt anyone. The poor woman lived alone with nothing but pictures of her little grandchildren and daughter to keep her company. She didn't even know if any of them survived the war, as they'd moved across the country to Virginia, North Carolina, or one of those states in that general area where the husband worked.

Harper sighed, bowed her head, and whispered, "I'm sorry."

Madison stood there in silence for a few minutes before sniffling.

The intrusion of human-made sound on the peacefulness of nature snapped Harper out of her melancholia. She hauled herself up out of the hole and dusted snow off her coat.

"Mrs. Michaelson's dead, isn't she?" asked Madison. "I see her hand."

"Yeah, Termite. She didn't make it." Harper took the Mossberg back and slung it over her shoulder. *Mom would have yelled at me for giving her a loaded weapon when we weren't on the range.*

"What should we do?" Madison let her arms drop to her sides.

Harper backed up, turning to peer down at the ruins. "I don't think we *can* do anything yet. It's too dangerous. It sucks, but we're not going to be able to get her body out of there until most of the snow melts."

"Ack." Madison cringed. "At least it's cold."

"C'mon... we've got more people to check on."

Madison apologized to Mrs. Michaelson for having to leave her there for now, then ambled around in a somewhat ungainly 'tennis rackets tied to her shoes' turn before fast-walking to catch up to Harper. After a few minutes without saying anything, she blurted, "I don't want anyone else to die."

"That's why we're out here, Termite."

"Now I understand." Madison hugged her. "Why you stayed a cop."

"I'm not a cop. Just a kid with a gun."

Madison gave a weak chuckle. "You're not doing it because you get to have a gun. You wanna stop people from getting hurt."

"Totally." Harper smiled. "Idiots like Zach want to join the Militia because they feel important."

"Huh?" Madison squinted at her. "I thought he just wanted to get in your pants."

Hearing her kid sister say that shocked Harper as much as it made her want to laugh. It also gave her a sense of hope at the normalcy of her sibling starting to talk about such things. The war had certainly made everyone grow up a bit faster than expected. "Yeah, pretty much."

"I still don't wanna join the Militia, but I'm okay helping you make sure people are okay."

Harper squeezed her sister's shoulder. "Slow down a bit. You're going to tire yourself out. We still have a lot of walking to do."

"I know. Most of the houses left are empty. Everyone's at the school."

So stupid. She peered back at the collapse. *Why the hell did you stay there alone?* The somber thought Mrs. Michaelson might have wanted to be around the photographs of her daughter and grandchildren more than the people of Evergreen—and didn't much care if she died for it—lodged a lump in Harper's throat for the rest of the afternoon.

BORROWED TIME

NOVEMBER 27TH

News of Mrs. Michaelson's death caused a mild stir.

No one in the Militia had the callousness to say out loud they thought the woman brought it on herself, though Harper suspected a handful of the guys felt that way due to their lack of reaction. As a result of the collapse, Anne-Marie decided to order everyone to shelter at the Quartermaster's or the school—until Walter pointed out they really didn't have the ability to *order* anyone to do anything. The Militia simply happened when people with military or law enforcement training came together to protect everyone else from—at the time—the biggest threat: looters and criminals.

Anne-Marie, who by most people's estimation served as the leader of Evergreen in much the same way as a mayor or governor might, hadn't been elected or given her position by anyone else. She'd stepped up to lead when no one else appeared to want the responsibility. In the end, she decided to 'strongly suggest' people gather in one place, or at least clear their roofs of snow.

For the most part, anyone still living in their homes had already taken care of their roofs. Mrs. Michaelson lived alone and kept to herself, with the exception of making cookies and such for kids who stopped by to visit her—at least until she ran out of mix. Both days Harper and Madison checked in on her before the collapse, she'd insisted she was fine. Short of dragging the woman physically across town to safety—something not possible in such deep snow—she couldn't have done much else to help. Clearing off the roof probably would've been a good idea, but she hadn't thought of it. The roof appeared to be holding up, and she didn't lug a shovel around with her.

Today offered a much-needed break. Yesterday, she'd made sure all the holdouts on her temporary route had at least a week's worth of food. She and Madison basically did the same thing her friend Andrea did last summer for a job: delivering groceries.

Going for such a long time without a usable bathtub bothered her more in thought than practice. As everyone in the house gradually became filthier, no one really noticed it standing out. She felt like a scrub, but couldn't do anything about it. Lorelei had certainly lived in worse conditions during her short life and didn't show any signs of caring it had been ten days since they had a bath. Every so often, Harper caught a whiff of herself, or Renee, or Jonathan. Cliff had become the most noticeably ripe owing to his being a grown man who spent most of every day doing physical work.

That no one really seemed to care felt as strange as her dreaming about a frozen zombie Mrs. Michaelson dragging herself out of the collapse to thank Harper for checking on her.

Harper, Madison, and Lorelei huddled together under a blanket on the couch watching 'fireplace TV' as Lorelei called it. Jonathan lay on the floor, working on a drawing of their family in comic book style. Naturally, he somewhat exaggerated everyone into heroicness—but not *too* much so. Harper's 'character' standing there with a confident swagger, shotgun, and tactical gear struck her in a farcical vein like the movie poster for *National Lampoons*, which showed the family in the same painting style as *Conan the Barbarian*. Jonathan had sort of Rambo-ized Cliff. Carrie's cartoon doppelganger reminded her of Linda Hamilton from the *Terminator* movies, even though Carrie had yet to shoot anyone. The kids appeared relatively normal, though he depicted Lorelei as overly adorable with somewhat-too-large eyes. Jonathan even added Mila to the group 'photo' in an almost superhero costume with cat ears and two fistfuls of throwing knives.

All in all, the illustration made Harper want to laugh, get misty-eyed, and hug him all at once.

Wow. He's really good. Who'd have thought grabbing a whole case of expensive colored pencils on a whim would be such a good idea?

Renee sat sideways across Cliff's favorite recliner, reading *The Secret Garden*, now that Harper had finally finished it. Except for a handful of Militia people wandering outside, all of Evergreen had essentially shut down to ride out the snow.

Crunching footsteps outside overpowered the repetitive light scratching of Jonathan's pencils.

Everyone looked at the door.

A moment later, it opened, revealing Cliff in a heavy blue coat and winter hat.

He looks so different with a big beard. Harper smiled. "Hey."

Cliff waved in a 'come with me' gesture. "Okay, everyone. Throw on shoes and a coat. Follow me."

"Everyone?" asked Harper. "Not just me?"

"Everyone." Cliff grinned.

"Ugh." Madison rubbed her legs. "More walking? Where are we going?"

"Quartermaster's."

Jonathan groaned. "I thought we could stay home?"

"We can. This isn't relocation." Cliff stepped inside and shut the door to keep what little heat they had inside. "A surprise."

Madison shook her head. "We can't. We haven't had a bath in a month! I stink."

"More like two weeks." Jonathan continued shading 'Rambo-Cliff's arm. "And we *all* stink. I don't even notice it anymore."

Renee closed the book. "What's the emergency?"

"No emergency." Cliff grinned as if proud. "We bagged a couple deer. They're almost done cooking."

Jonathan practically left a smoke cloud hanging in midair from how fast he darted off to his room.

Madison looked down. "I hate this world."

"Aww." Harper rubbed her back. "I know it's hard, and sad, and painful, but—"

"Not that." Madison let her head loll back against the sofa, staring at the ceiling. "I'm not whining about having to eat meat. I'm upset because I really want to have some... so damn hungry."

Harper bit her lip, unsure what to say. 'Having enough food to get through the winter' didn't necessarily mean everyone got to eat until satisfied and full. While much better than last winter, she couldn't say she wasn't hungry more often than not. Eating pretty much the same thing over and over again: oatmeal in the morning and preserved vegetables every other meal with the occasional gift of bread should have bothered her... but it didn't. That she hadn't gotten sick to death of eating mushy potatoes, carrots, or beans from mason jars yet proved they still rode a fine line between 'enough food' and strict rationing.

It's gotta be worse than I thought if Maddie wants *venison.*

Mrs. Michaelson made the sixth person to die that winter. A guy named Rory she didn't really know had an accident on the farm, gashing his leg open while harvesting corn. The injury hadn't been too bad, but he decided not to go to the clinic. The recently snow-shoe-equipped Militia found him barely conscious at home and dragged him to the clinic where he succumbed to the effects of an infection they no longer had the medications to treat. Dr. Khan attempted to amputate the leg but it didn't help.

Two other residents collapsed and died trying to shovel snow. Cliff and Roy found their frozen bodies in the west yesterday by the houses given to single men, mostly farm workers. Annapurna discovered Mr. Luna, a seventy-two-year-old, dead in bed during a wellness check two days ago. Being on the skinny side, she'd been the first to attempt walking on the PVC-and-duct-tape snowshoes. No one knew for sure if his death had been unnatural. It might've been, but his house was also freezing cold. The fifth death happened on the twenty-first. Paul Moore, one of the players from the Colorado Springs High hockey team who arrived on the same bus as Logan, shot himself. He hadn't left any sort of note or said anything about having troubles, not even to Zach, his best friend.

She vaguely recalled thinking she'd heard a gunshot that afternoon and mistaken it for a tree cracking under the weight of snow. Even though Harper did *not* like Zach and didn't really know (or have a high opinion of Paul thanks to his association to Zach) his death bothered her the most due to his being half a year younger than her. It also made her want to squeeze her family closer. Having people to fight for made it much easier to cope with a broken world.

"Vennnnison!" cheered Jonathan while running back into the room. He tossed Madison and Lorelei's coats at them. "Real food!"

Drifting back and forth from somber thoughts to being happy to have a family, Harper kept quiet as she put her boots and coat on, then followed everyone out the door. The Militia had excavated enough of a passage down Hilltop Drive to allow travel between the houses in the area and the Quartermaster's building. Even though it had only been a week since the storm hit, going outside and not having tennis rackets on her boots felt as weird as leaving the house without pants. Enough snow remained on the ground in the trench to make the passage slippery. Unlike everyone else, Lorelei made no effort to avoid falling over, finding it hilarious. Before she hurt herself, Harper picked her up and carried her, much to the girl's delight. She'd never known a kid so addicted to hugging people and/or being held.

She's an affectionate cat in human form.

A few minutes of relatively easy hiking later, they crossed Route 74, made their way up a 'snow staircase' of small logs, and entered the parking lot in front of the Quartermaster's building. Massive snow walls on three sides enclosed the paved area, lending it the feel of being a 'room' rather than outside. Roughly a hundred people gathered around while four skinned, beheaded deer roasted on spits over cinder block fire pits, their spindly legs jutting out like the tines of forks. The tantalizing aroma of meat and wood smoke made her stomach growl.

People waited patiently for food, gathered in clusters and discussing various things from placing bets on how long it would take for the snow to melt to who slept with who, which women expected babies, surprise at the wind turbines still working, and so forth. Jeanette Vasquez and a few of her electrical people stood in a circle with Anne-Marie and Walter. Harper caught enough of their conversation to understand the solar panels were having some issues. Jeanette didn't sound ready to abandon them, but she did try to convince Anne-Marie to send scavengers out in search for copper wire, magnets, and anything useful to build more wind turbines as soon as it became possible.

Fortunately, no one danced around the firepits singing praises to ancient forest spirits. In the somewhat enclosed area of a snow-walled parking lot, the four massive fires made it almost uncomfortable to keep her coat zipped up. The sight of whole animals being roasted would have made Madison shriek not too long ago, yet she didn't. In fact, the girl stared at the deer with almost the same facial expression Dad used to have whenever he grilled steak in the backyard.

The look in her little sister's eye unsettled her.

People appeared in generally good spirits, enjoying the chance to get some air and socialize. The promise of a decent meal played no small part in the upbeat mood. A group of those who staffed the Quartermaster's eventually began carving off hunks of venison into serving trays. The citizens of Evergreen gathered in a more or less orderly line for a feast of deer meat, roasted corn cobs (from the freezers) and canned potatoes. The process of preserving spuds in mason jars made them taste a bit strange and have an odd mushy consistency, but Harper had long since gotten used to it.

About two-thirds went inside to find somewhere to sit and eat, others remained outside, too hungry to care about standing while chowing down. Harper followed her family inside to the large room where they usually handled food distribution. It already had cafeteria-style tables, though not many chairs.

Madison wasted no time digging into her meal, grabbing hunks of venison in both hands without the slightest hesitation.

Watching this stabbed Harper in the feels. Ever since she'd been five years old, Madison threw tantrums over people eating animals. She'd done presentations at her school about vegetarianism, even wrote a letter to the state government asking them to make killing animals for food illegal. Given all the cattle ranchers in the state, Harper assumed the governor had a good chuckle over the letter.

Love for animals—perhaps taken too far—had been such a part of Madison's personality for so long, the sight of her tearing into deer flesh like a partially feral wolf-child felt as though the war really had killed her little sister beyond repair.

Overcome with grief, Harper rushed away from the table. In the quiet solitude of a small corridor inside the building, she surrendered to tears. The world had broken her little sister. She couldn't save her after all. Madison Cody devouring meat like that felt as wrong as the idea of mice hunting cats.

"Hey," said Logan. "You okay?"

Harper jumped, spinning to face him while raising her left

hand in a defensive posture and grabbing the handle of her .45 in the other. It took her a second to process the person who snuck up on her had no bad intentions. That her reaction to being startled had changed from shrieking like an ordinary high school student to going for a gun piled on top of her feelings regarding Madison and made the tears come harder.

Logan raised both eyebrows. "You're obviously not okay." He gently grasped her forearm as if to hold the gun in the holster. "I'm here if you want to talk about it."

She stared at him for a moment until fully realizing *who* snuck up on her, then fell against him, clinging. "Just having a moment."

"Heck of a moment." He patted her back.

"It's not you. I grab for a gun whenever anyone startles me now." She exhaled hard. "Sorry. I'm just being weird again. Overly emotional. Damn hormones."

He stared. "Uhh… are you saying?"

"No." She buried her face against his shoulder and cry-laughed. "I'm not pregnant. Dunno why it got me so bad."

"What got you?"

"Madison," whispered Harper. "No complaints at all about meat. And she's tearing into it like a wolf. It's so surreal to watch the kid who lectured her entire school on the evils of meat-eating to do that."

Logan grinned. "Hope Cliff isn't teasing her about it."

"No, he's cool. I'm sure Maddie's fully aware vegetarians are a rare breed during times of starvation."

His expression fell to one of concern. "We're not really in times of starvation, are we?"

"Not exactly"—she leaned back from the hug to make eye contact—"but we're also far from rolling in tons of food. We have stuff to eat, but it's all kind of the same. No complaints. Just saying I can understand why everyone's so happy about the hunters bringing back meat." Harper ran a hand up through her hair. "I'd go nuts for some lake fish right about now, too."

"C'mon." Logan tugged her along. "Your food's getting cold. Someone else is gonna swipe it if you leave it sitting there."

Harper followed, sighing at the floor. "It doesn't make any sense why it upset me so much. Everything that's happened to us and Maddie giving up on being vegetarian is such a small thing."

"It's upsetting you like this *because* it's so small." Logan squeezed her hand. "It's right there in front of you, easy to process. You understand everything about this one little situation, so it represents the significance of everything that's happened in the world in a way that resonates."

"I guess that makes sense." She let him take her by the hand and walked with him back outside.

Fortunately, no one had run off with her meal. Jonathan and Lorelei appeared to be guarding it for her. Then again, they had plenty of meat to go around. No one would be leaving this communal meal the least bit hungry.

Cliff rumbled various interesting words like 'meatgasm' in between bites.

Harper sat by her plate.

"Be right back." Logan jogged a few rows over to grab his plate as well as his sister Luisa, relocating to sit beside her.

"Hi." Luisa waved at everyone, then sat to the left of her brother.

"Hey." Madison took another bite while giving Harper a sideways 'what the heck's wrong with you' glance.

Cliff, Carrie, Renee, Jonathan, and Lorelei all waved, mumbled 'hello' or nodded at Luisa.

"You should've seen her the first time Dad tried to give her a burger after she decided to go veg," said Harper, a hint of a smile forming at the memory.

"Ugh." Madison blushed. "Don't embarrass me."

Logan chuckled. "I bet. No one commits fully to anything like a five-year-old."

"She's getting all emo over me eating meat, isn't she?" asked Madison.

Harper sighed. "Yeah."

"I still think humans should be herbivores, but… I'm also thinking this tastes freakin' awesome right now." Madison gnawed another hunk off her portion of venison. "Maybe I overdid it a bit on the vegetarian thing before."

"Naw." Cliff bumped his elbow to her shoulder since he had greasy hands. "Before crap fell apart, we had the luxury to eat whatever we wanted. Doing what we need to do to survive is the most natural thing out there."

"Yeah, yeah." Madison rolled her eyes. "He's going to hit me with the 'wolves eat rabbits, not salad' speech now."

Harper ate a few bites, savoring the grill-essence melting out of the perfectly cooked meat. Perfect, at least to her. Snooty chefs might call it dry or undercooked for all she cared. After days of mushy vegetables and oatmeal, it didn't matter. Any status not considered 'raw' seemed perfect. "So, Madison decides meat is bad. Dad drops a plate of burgers on the table. Maddie scream-sobbed like he killed and cooked our dog."

Luisa glanced over at her. "Aww."

"Must you?" Madison overacted a sigh, her cheeks reddening. "I was five."

"You had a dog?" Logan tilted his head.

"No. Just being metaphorical. Mom wasn't into the idea of pets. Too much work." Harper stuffed an entire potato quarter in her mouth.

While she chewed, Logan leaned over as if to kiss her, but ended up whispering in her ear, "We've survived nuclear war. By any reasonable prediction, most of us shouldn't be here right now. And yet, here we are. All of us, we've defied the odds. Every moment from here forward gets easier."

Harper swallowed potato. "I hope you're right."

"Don't hope." He put an arm around her. "Make it real."

She stared at him, too choked up to speak.

"He really loves you." Madison wagged a deer rib at them. "He's not just trying to get in your pants."

Luisa blushed and stared intently at her plate. Cliff launched a glob of green bean across the table on a cough. Jonathan got a bad case of the giggles. Lorelei, likely not understanding the comment, ignored it. Carrie snickered. Renee gawked at Madison, who simply wagged her eyebrows at Harper the way she usually did whenever she exacted revenge.

Harper's face burned. She wanted to crawl into a tiny hole so none of the twenty or thirty people staring at her, making suggestive winks or laughing could see her anymore. She couldn't crawl into a black hole, so she did the next best thing and buried her face against Logan's shoulder.

Madison examined her fingernails. "I asked you not to embarrass me."

You little... her sister's old self coming to the surface for a moment of petty—and honestly hilarious—revenge chased away Harper's bizarre obsession with the 'death of vegetarianism.' Madison hadn't changed so much after all. Despite being mortified, Harper lifted her face away from Logan's shoulder and smiled.

Yeah... he really does love me. And wow... maybe we're gonna be okay after all. She bit her lip. *As long as we don't step on any rusty sharp things.*

22

SLIGHTLY LESS THAN FERAL

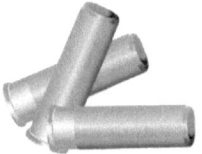

FEBRUARY 4TH

H arper leaned against the kitchen counter, clutching a mug of hot apple cider in both hands while observing the kids play in the backyard. The downfall of civilization might've resulted in the extinction of coffee and tea, but the cider offered a passable substitute. Mostly, she missed the sensation of slowly sipping a hot drink.

The day ended up being warmer than seemed right for February. Weather over the past three months zigzagged as unpredictably as a drunk guy with a cloud of hornets chasing him. Thanks to several oddly warm days in late January, the snow had lessened to more manageable levels, enough for people to return to their homes and kids to be able to play. The warm day truly brought out the aroma of... not bathing for months. Except for the steam rising from her cider mug, every breath made her feel disgusting.

In a twist she'd never expected, Christmas had lost much of its significance among the kids. Almost none of them got wound up for the entire month of December begging for time to hurry up and get to the twenty-fifth. According to Cliff, since kids didn't spend the entire year bombarded by 'thirty-minute commercials' for toys masquerading as cartoon shows and had no expectation their parents or caretakers could buy electronics, video games, or phones anymore, the focus shifted. People, even the young ones, exchanged gifts valuable for their significance rather than their 'coolness' or expense. For example, the beat-up old doll Lorelei had done her best to turn into Harper by tying red yarn to the head and giving it a 'sorta-shotgun-shaped' stick would live in a place of honor on her dresser forever, more precious than any PlayStation or Xbox.

Still, the kids tended to regard Christmas with only slightly more excitement than an average birthday. If not for the big communal dinner, it would've felt like any other day with a 'yay, presents' break two hours before bedtime.

Perhaps due to the massive snowfall or maybe simple luck, the past few months had been quiet and largely uneventful. Aside from now eight deaths, the worst part of the snowstorm ended up being Cliff's suggestion they all take 'field showers' until the pipes became usable again. None of them had been able to have a proper bath since the cold snap. However, in the interest of staying healthy, he'd brought up the concept of 'face, pits, crotch, and crack,' in that specific order. As if he needed to tell anyone to wash their face first before using the same cloth elsewhere.

Standing in a frigid bathroom hitting the critical spots with a rag soaked in almost boiling water straight off the stovetop might have protected against various health annoyances—which could become serious problems since they lacked real medicine—but it also made for an incredibly effective way to wake up in the morning.

As made painfully obvious by the unusually warm February day, Harper suspected the house and everyone in it reeked to hell and back. The aroma of unwashed bodies had likely seeped into all the furniture the way the walls smelled of fireplace smoke. No one had taken a real bath in months. Weeks ago, Lorelei suggested getting a metal tub and putting it in the living room by the fireplace and melting snow for a bath. Unsurprisingly, only she had any interest in taking a bath in the middle of the house in front of everyone. Madison's "I'll just keep stinking, thanks" had become something of a recurring joke catch phrase.

Today happened to be Becca's eleventh birthday. Madison's friend lagged a few months behind her, age wise. Harper smiled to herself at memories of being little again, how a three-month difference in age used to make her feel 'all grown up' compared to some of her friends. Alas, a legal number no longer carried any weight. No one really cared about 'being eighteen' anymore or having to wait for twenty-one to drink. Earl tended to let anyone he thought looked 'old enough' have a beer or two. His opinion of 'old enough' tended to be about fifteen and up. What did it really hurt? Not like any teenagers could drink and drive anymore.

They again treated themselves to the strange 'cake-like substance' Carrie came up with for the party. None of the kids complained about it or vocalized missing real cake. After two hours of loud, happy children in the house, Harper finally had some peace. The kids went outside to adventure in the snow.

She sipped cider, thinking about Cliff's commentary regarding how children now played outside when the weather permitted, which reminded him of his childhood in the Eighties, before video games really caught on. She still had no idea what a 'BMX bike' exactly was—other than some form of bicycle—but Cliff evidently had one as a boy. He loved talking about it.

Estimates for food storage missed the mark by a moderate margin, thankfully not enough to be terrifying... merely uncomfortable. They'd gone back to rationing. To help ease everyone's constant hunger and grumpiness, Jonathan spent several hours after school each day making his way down to the lake to fish. He didn't always catch anything at all. Some days he'd bring back only one or two small fish, but it helped. When he didn't get much, everyone insisted Carrie eat the fish due to being pregnant. Lorelei got second priority. Cliff and some of the militia going out to hunt also offered sporadic relief from worry about starving.

Jonathan's black eye had mostly faded. A few days ago, he'd made the mistake of jokingly saying 'Chicken ala Rosie' in response to Lorelei asking what they'd be having for dinner. Madison, thinking him serious, freaked out. After Harper pulled her off Jonathan, Madison spent the rest of the day over at Carrie's house holding her pet chickens. In a strange way, the kids having a serious fight—well, more Madison pummeling Jonathan who didn't raise a hand back at her—felt normal and reassuring. All three kids being so super nice to each other all the time had been eerie, like they all knew they could die at any minute. A spark of disagreement, and violence, showed proof they (or at least Madison) felt reasonably secure and safe.

Harper took a large swig of cider, trying to down it before it faded from hot to tepid. Having a noticeable warm spot in her belly helped her not think about being hungry. The food situation this winter didn't seem as dire as last winter.

Maybe it's the same and I'm just used to it. She frowned. *The first winter was more of a shock. Modern life had too much. Junk food everywhere. Huge portions at restaurants. Maybe they're right about the whole karma thing and this is what we get for being excessive while people in other parts of the world starved.* She rolled her eyes. *Yeah, okay, Mom. Ugh. I sound like my mother now.*

After finishing the cider, Harper set the mug in the sink and decided she'd had enough of feeling filthy. The day *had* to be warm enough for pipes to work. Due to the snow, she couldn't get under the house too easily to turn the bathroom water back on, but *draining* the tub shouldn't be a big deal. Also, since Carrie slowed down due to becoming more and more obviously pregnant, she couldn't in good conscience ask for help doing laundry. All the clothes had been going without, much like the people due to the limited use of water. A quick rummage confirmed the various collected mounds of clothing needed serious attention. Jonathan had drawn signs labeling three piles in his room: 'eww,' 'omfg,' and 'achieved sentience.' In the midst of gathering stuff to wash, she discovered a fourth collection in his closet under a sign: 'danger, will bite.'

Considering the closet smelled like he'd been storing half a year's worth of farts in it, she handled the clothing by pinching it out at arm's length. To notice *any* smell at the moment meant bad things.

Screw it. I can't take this anymore.

Harper loaded two large stock pots of water from the kitchen sink (the only active faucet in the house) and turned the heat on. Using another, not quite as big pot, she ferried water down the hall to the bathtub over a series of trips. Jumping in the cold water proved almost tempting... but she forced herself to wait until the massive pots came close to boiling.

By the time she dumped the second stock pot of hot water in the tub, her anticipation at being clean took over. She stripped and jumped in so fast she forgot to shut the door. While paralyzed by the sudden shock of slightly-too-hot water covering her from the stomach down, she stared at the doorway—and decided not to bother.

Cliff wouldn't be home until close to sunset. Carrie and Renee were next door, and probably wouldn't come over. Even if they did, a year living 'post-apocalyptic' made the thought of them seeing her naked trivial. Her best friend and basically stepmom walking in on her in a bathtub felt like just 'one of those things' peasants living rough had to deal with. Madison and Lorelei had been bathing in the same tub with her ever since they moved into this house. It had gone from a little weird to completely normal, like something from an early 1800s frontier family putting all the kids in the basin at the same time to save water. At the thought it wouldn't horrify her even if Jonathan stumbled into the bathroom and caught her, she laughed into her hands. Though, honestly, such an event would likely embarrass him more than her.

"Holy crap, I've gone full feral."

Harper didn't hop in the tub to enjoy the water. She wanted to enjoy not smelling like a dying cow on the side of the road. She scooted forward and submerged herself completely, letting her hair soak for as long as she could hold her breath before grabbing the lump of soap and cleaning herself. The true extent of her lack of forethought didn't hit her until she got out of the tub and stood there dripping, staring at the reeking pile of clothing she'd been wearing not twenty minutes earlier. The mere thought of even touching it now made her skin crawl.

"Oops."

Fortunately, no one bathing over the past few months resulted in at least one blue towel being reasonably clean to the point she didn't want to throw up upon sniffing it. Harper wrapped herself up, then glanced at the tub. The murky water mocked her as if the universe called her filthy. She felt five pounds lighter. Alas, she couldn't in good conscience use the same water for laundry, so she opened the drain.

Hopefully, it'll get completely out of the house pipes before it freezes. She chuckled, amused at herself for feeling like taking a bath amounted to doing something naughty. Today had to be in the fifties at least. Cliff wouldn't be upset she sent some water into the pipes. *It's above freezing. Stop panicking.*

Clutching her towel, Harper went on a hunt for something to wear. The house contained only a few items of clean clothing: eight pairs of underpants too small for Madison and too big for Lorelei, still in their packaging in the closet... and bathing suits.

"Ugh." Harper cringed away from the horribly dirty laundry. "Towel it is."

Since nothing came close to being wearable at the moment so soon after taking a bath, she proceeded to get started on the task at hand. Realizing she'd rather run around wearing only a towel than put any of this stuff on further underscored how nasty it had become. Of course, such an attitude came from remembering the modern world. The next generations wouldn't be used to showering every night or using scented shampoo, fancy soap, or body wash with 'skin-scrubbing microbeads.' However, the third time the towel fell off while she carried bundles of laundry around, she decided to put her bathing suit on under it... just in case the towel decided to surprise her again while she wasn't the only person in the house.

Once again, she boiled water in the big stock pots and filled the bathtub by running back and forth with a smaller pot. A few people in town made a generic sort of plain soap—which worked surprisingly well—but she didn't yet use it for clothes. Her stash of 'real' laundry detergent would probably last at least another two years if she continued being stingy with it. Might as well take advantage of the stuff while she could. Of course, grabbing the bottle of detergent reminded her of doing laundry back home before the world went crazy.

A metaphorical little black cloud started to form above her head as the completely silent house allowed her mind to dwell on all they'd lost. However, being *clean* for the first time in three months made her happy enough to shrug off the doldrums after only a few minutes. Having her arms elbow-deep in laundry detergent for hours didn't sound like a healthy idea, so she'd grabbed a pair of dishwashing gloves from the cabinet under the sink—a gift from the house's former owner.

Resigned to spending the entire rest of the day doing laundry, Harper ignored how silly it felt to tromp around wearing giant rubber dishwashing gloves, a bikini, and combat boots. It didn't bother her *too* much except for having to run outside whenever she needed to hang stuff up on the clothesline to dry. A winter coat only helped so much when worn over a bathing suit.

Looking ridiculous is a small price to pay for clean clothing.

AROUND FOUR HOURS AFTER HER BATH, HARPER KNELT ON THE bathroom floor, manually sloshing yet another load of clothes around the tub. She didn't care to sort stuff by fabric type, color, or anything a modern person would care about. She went by importance, washing everyone's underwear and socks first, then making sure everyone had two complete outfits before moving on to other garments. Later that night, she'd try to convince the kids to take a bath before putting on anything she'd cleaned.

After loading up the basket with a bunch of wet clothes from the tub, she hauled it up off the floor and lugged the burdensome, dripping load down the hall to the kitchen where she set it on the table. She peeled off the dishwashing gloves, then the towel—so she didn't lose it outside in the snow—and reached for her winter coat.

The door to the backyard opened, admitting a pack of wet, muddy children: the usual suspects, her three siblings and their friends. Harper looked over at them, unsure if she should gasp, yell at them for being so dirty, or simply laugh. Jonathan and Mila had overly serious, urgent expressions. Becca and Eva blinked at Harper standing there in a green bikini and combat boots, then cracked up laughing.

"We goin' swimming?" asked Lorelei, eyebrows up.

Mila whispered something to her.

"Oh." Lorelei sighed. "Darn."

"What happened to you guys?" Harper shook her head. "You look like a pack of feral children."

"Found a mud spot." Lorelei grinned. "Alla snow went away there."

"Obviously." Harper chuckled. She debated announcing bath time, but didn't for two reasons. One: the tub water had laundry detergent in it. Two: all of the children's clothing was either wet from being washed or too filthy to put on. She couldn't have all the kids sitting around in towels for hours. "Don't track it all over the house."

Jonathan scrunched his nose in confusion. "Why are you wearing a bathing suit? It's *way* too cold to go swimming."

"Gah." Madison shivered. "I'm freezing just from looking at you. Seriously. What's wrong with you?"

Harper shrugged. "All our clothes are months overdue for being cleaned. I snapped. Couldn't take it anymore. Been doing laundry all afternoon. This swimsuit is all I had to wear that didn't feel crusty."

"Eww." Becca gagged.

"You didn't open my closet, did you?" asked Jonathan.

"Yep. The beast is dead." Harper struck a triumphant pose.

Jonathan mouthed 'wow.'

"Go back outside and try to brush the mud off." Harper shooed them at the door.

"Wait. Harp." Jonathan stepped closer. "We kinda found a dead guy."

For a few seconds, the *pat, pat, pat* of laundry water dripping off the table to the floor became the loudest sound in the world.

Harper stared at him. "What?"

"We found a dead guy and ran home to tell you." Jonathan sounded sincere and a little worried. "You gotta come look."

"Ugh." Harper looked down at her bikini. *Figures. All my shit is wet. Screw it.* "Hang on."

She bit her lip, torn between grabbing something better than a swimsuit to wear, but everything not soaking wet smelled horrible. Going outside in wet clothes would not only be uncomfortable, it would be stupid. Without going across the way to Carrie's, her options consisted of borrowing a shirt from Cliff or putting on her still-filthy stuff. Not that his giant flannel shirts would be any less dirty. Running outside wearing a swimsuit in February sounded almost as dumb as wet clothes, even if the temperature had crept up into the fifties. Urgency coming from the kids made her momentary indecision even worse. *I just took a damn bath. I... ugh. Hell with it.* She tied the bath towel around her waist as a skirt, threw her winter coat on over the swimsuit, then ran down the hall to grab her Mossberg. At least she had a reasonably long coat.

Jonathan darted out the door. Madison, Lorelei, Becca, Eva, Christopher, and Mila followed in a disorganized cluster. A dead body didn't make for an incredibly urgent situation. However, she couldn't ignore it for hours while continuing to do laundry. Despite feeling like some crazy, idiotic cartoon character for running around in such a ridiculous outfit with a shotgun, she had to at least check out a report of a dead body. Worse come to worst, she could send the kids to the Quartermaster's building to report the find to the rest of the Militia. Technically, she was 'off shift' at the moment and an already-dead person didn't really count as an emergency... not like the person would get any deader if it took an extra hour for someone to respond.

WADING INTO A THIGH-DEEP SNOW DRIFT WITHOUT PANTS NEARLY made Harper turn around. Alas, she'd already followed the kids almost a quarter mile away from the house. Jonathan's assurances that 'he's just up here' kept her moving. It would take less time to find the body at this point than going back home.

Teeth chattering, she pressed on.

I am so done with snow.

On an isolated section of Spruce Road not far past the branch to Aspen Lane, Jonathan stopped walking and grabbed Lorelei to keep her from going any closer. "He's right up there by the side of the road."

Harper looked around at white tree-covered hills. Spruce Road continued uphill into more trees, bending to the right not far from there, out of sight. The steep terrain around her didn't allow for much of a view distance in any direction, raising the hairs on the back of her neck. It looked like a good spot for an ambush. Her first thought was someone must have been sniped or attacked by parties unknown, considering how close to the outer limit of Evergreen they'd gone. Only two or three houses existed any further east from here, the rest of the land being all forest for about two miles until the town of Kittredge.

"Why were you guys out this far?" Harper sighed. "You know you aren't supposed to."

"It's not past the edge." Jonathan flapped his arms. "It *is* the edge. We didn't go past it."

"Eww!" whispered Eva.

Lorelei pointed. "He's there."

"Stay back." Jonathan tugged her closer. "It's not safe."

"What do you mean, not safe?" Harper crept forward toward the indicated spot. "Think he's booby trapped or something?"

"No." Mila shook her head. "Look at his arm. We should all take ten steps back, now."

When the kids actually listened to Mila, Harper's nervousness mounted. She forced herself to move faster until the sight of a rotting corpse came into view in the dirt a few feet past the edge of the paving.

A man dressed in green camouflage lay slumped on his side, posed almost as if he'd been attempting to sleep. He'd evidently been there and dead for some time, as his skin rotted to the point she couldn't guess his age more precisely than 'somewhere between mid-twenties and fifty.' His left hand rested on a rifle, possibly an M-16. Canteens, backpack, and other stuff hanging off the remains made him look like a soldier. Caked residue down his chest and on the ground by his mouth suggested he'd vomited profusely at some point before death. Her gaze settled on a shiny gold watch dangling from the near-liquefied remains of his right wrist. From midway down his palm to six-inches deep in his forearm, most of the skin and muscle looked burned and decomposed, much more than any other part of his body.

He's too far gone to be recent. This body was here before it snowed. She stared at the shiny, gold watch. The flesh around it appeared to have melted in an effort to get away from it. "Everyone back up."

"Told you," whispered Mila.

Sensing fear in Harper's voice, Lorelei shivered. "Is he a zombie?"

Harper turned away from the body and rushed over to the kids, ushering them away from the corpse. "No. Not a zombie. He's radioactive."

"Really?" Eva gasped, grabbing Becca as if to hide behind her.

"How do you know that?" Becca scrunched her nose. "He's just nasty."

"Did any of you touch the body or get close to it?" asked Harper.

The kids all shook their heads.

"No." Christopher frowned. "Mila freaked out and yelled at me. Said she was gonna stab me if I didn't listen to her."

Harper raised her eyebrows at the girl.

"I wasn't really gonna hit him with a knife." Mila gestured toward the corpse. "I just wanted him to listen. He was gonna take the watch."

"Crap." Harper exhaled. "Good. You're not in trouble."

"Really?" Christopher blinked. "She said she was gonna stab me."

"She saved your life." Harper whistled. "And she wasn't really going to stab you."

"Saved his life?" chorused Becca, Eva, and Madison at the same time.

"The watch is radioactive." Harper encouraged the kids to resume walking back toward home.

"Is he a real soldier? Did he get nuked?" asked Madison.

Harper looked back at the curve in the road, relieved at not being able to see the body down the slope. "I don't think he got nuked. He wouldn't have lived long enough to make it here. That watch was exposed to a serious radiation blast. I don't really know the chemistry involved, but remember gamma bombardment can irradiate gold permanently. This guy probably found the watch on a skeleton and didn't notice it was radioactive."

"Eek," chirped Madison.

"We're leaving?" Jonathan scratched his head. "We can't just leave a dead guy lying there. It's not right. *And* he's dangerous."

Harper nodded. "I don't intend to leave him there. But I'm also not equipped to deal with a radioactive watch—or anything else on him that might be glowing. I'm also not going to talk to Walter in a damn bathing suit. Jon, would you and Mila go to the Q and tell them about it?"

"Yep." Jonathan nodded.

"Sure," said Mila matter-of factly.

"You guys are totally sure none of you touched the dead guy?" Harper looked the kids over. "Where'd all the mud come from?"

Madison laughed. "The mud has nothing to do with the dead man. Lore slipped down a hill way before we walked up here."

Relieved, Harper allowed herself to breathe again. "Okay. Guys. Promise me… don't touch anything that's shiny, gold, literally glowing, or leaking unrecognizable liquids, okay?"

The kids all swore to follow the rule.

"Okay. Good." She puffed at a squiggle of hair hanging over her face. "Let's get you home and cleaned up."

23

SMUGGLING THE WATERMELON

MAY 3RD

I t seemed all of Evergreen cheered the arrival of May.

Even though it had only been a few months, it felt as if Harper lived on the snow planet Hoth for most of her life. *Finally*, the ground outside had more 'not snow' than snow. The inevitable result of warmer temperatures combined with epic amounts of the white stuff—mud—existed in copious amounts, much to the delight of the children.

The overall mood among the residents of Evergreen improved along with the weather. As the icy grip of winter relaxed its claws, people brightened. In Madison's case, she adored going to school more than at any other point in her life— because it kept her off the farm for the time being. Preparations for the upcoming planting season already started.

With the exception of a small memorial ceremony for the eight people who died over the winter—plus the irradiated soldier—everyone's spirits remained high. Deacon, Walter, and Roy volunteered for the grim task of relocating and burying the poor man a 'safe distance' away from town. They used a 'lead apron' from the dentist's office to cover the gold watch and buried everything he had on him, including the rifle and ammunition since no one trusted any of the metal parts. Cliff said he thought the man had been an actual soldier, but no one could come up with any explanation for where he'd been to become irradiated. Harper shared her assumption he'd survived the strike in good health, but later found the contaminated watch and put it on, leading to his death.

Mrs. Michaelson's house finished collapsing as the snow melted. Harper still felt weird about leaving the poor woman's body there for weeks, but between the incredibly deep snow and freezing temperatures, they didn't have much choice. Some people thought the worst part about the winter had been the farm people burning cow manure to heat the Big R store where the animals took refuge from the elements.

A thousand years from now, that place is still going to smell like poop.

Winter had passed, and at least for the time being, took with it gloomy skies as well as gloomy thoughts. The food situation remained borderline, though with the thaw came easier access to the lake for fishing and the land for hunting. Word going around among the Militia offered the hopeful notion the farm planners had already made adjustments in hopes of next winter being even less lean.

The morning of May third started off with an awesome surprise: fresh cornbread.

Carrie, too pregnant to stand, instructed Renee from the comfort of the sofa. She'd successfully made it the 'old way' using actual corn liberated out of the freezer cabinet at the Quartermaster's as opposed to buying a box of mix. The awesome treat offered a much welcome break from oatmeal for breakfast.

Harper forced herself to eat at a human pace. A stinky oil lantern sat at the center of the table, unlit. Electrical power had been on and off the past few days owing to repair work and broken power lines. The lamp used fuel made somehow from animal fat and gave off a smell somewhere between dead thing and cooking meat. Thankfully, they didn't need to light it in the morning in order to see.

Sitting there with her family and having a legit oil lamp on the table made Harper feel like she'd walked into a role in an Old West movie. Those stories of 'mountain people' being stuck in their cabins for months had taken on an entirely new—and too real—meaning. It had been rough, but nothing quite strengthened the intimate bonds of family like everyone trapped in close quarters, changing, bathing, using the bathroom bucket, and huddling together under blankets. As much as she disliked not seeing Logan for days at a time, she considered it a hidden blessing. If he'd been in the house with them, the two of them would definitely have gotten caught doing stuff.

Life certainly made her think of being on the Frontier. Unlike movie settlers, they didn't have to worry about angry Native Americans upset at Europeans stealing their land. However, they *did* have the Lawless. Along with all the relief and joy of springtime, the thaw brought the possibility outsiders could travel here again. Worse, the films she remembered set in cowboy times often portrayed frontier life as romantic and adventurous. They tended to gloss over or ignore the harsh reality where people died from seemingly minor injuries or children lost their lives to preventable diseases like measles, polio, or other ones she'd never even heard mentioned outside history class.

Harper peered over her hunk of cornbread at Lorelei, Madison, and Jonathan, all smiles and laughing. *They're all vaccinated and stuff. Well, maybe not Lore. Her mother didn't give a shit.* She shifted her gaze to a very pregnant Carrie. *Her baby isn't going to be. Neither is Darci's or any other kid.* Worry got her fidgeting. They lived in a mountain town relatively isolated from the outside world. A once-eradicated disease like measles probably wouldn't swoop in out of thin air and kill half the town's children in ten years. It might, however, arrive with a traveler. As she and the rest of the population grew older, replaced by successive generations of new babies who never knew the inside of a genuine doctor's office, humanity would again become vulnerable to a host of problems it had once conquered.

Stop. It's not going to be as bad as you're thinking. People back then didn't have old books to read with all the answers. We can get back to where humanity used to be much faster than it took us to get there in the first place... I just hope they aren't stupid enough to make nukes again.

She stopped chewing a wad of cornbread mush at the sudden realization Darci ought to 'pop' any day now. Her friend lived with Lucas in a fairly nice house up by the old golf course, conveniently in her patrol area. The guy legit owned the house before the war, mostly as a vacation spot away from the craziness of LA. By sheer luck, he happened to be there on the day of the nuclear strike. Harper often joked the reason the guy managed to play such a convincing 'perpetually drunk on rum' pirate was his weed habit. He hadn't been acting drunk as much as seriously high.

I gotta check on her today.

After breakfast, Harper escorted the kids to the school, preoccupied with how weird it felt to be able to walk on the road again—and not be six feet up in the air atop snow. Lorelei simply adored being social with other kids. Madison and Jonathan appreciated school mostly due to it not kicking their butts like farm work.

The community sheltering idea worked reasonably well. Harper only learned last week the school experienced a power loss due to water getting into a place it didn't belong. Heat went out, but only for about thirteen hours. Violet Olsen, the first person in Evergreen to assume the role of teacher, trekked across the 'glacial wasteland' to Jeanette's place to ask for help. After that, they decided one of the electrical techs would live at the school for the duration of the sheltering.

By now, everyone had returned to their homes. Even Mrs. Parson's mood showed improvement. Eva, likely aware her mother's emotional state had become incredibly brittle, often overacted being happy around her. Cassidy, the twenty-six-year-old woman who almost drowned two small children, ended up moving in with an older guy named Bryce Ward. She largely kept to herself as word of what she almost did spread across town. Around half the people of Evergreen wanted to exile her. A few threatened to 'beat sense into her.' Harper suspected their relationship had more of a father-daughter quality than a creepy 'older man dating a young woman' vibe. She hadn't spoken to Mr. Ward at great length, only chatted with him a few times at Earl's where everyone went to have a beer or two. The man had to be a few years shy of sixty and seemed like the type of man who'd want to try and 'fix' a young woman like Cassidy or at least take care of her.

Harper spent the first few minutes of her patrol grumbling about the whole situation. Every possible outcome from a stern 'don't do that again' to executing the woman seemed inappropriate. Reducing her to a status similar to a child in need of a caretaker—someone constantly watching her—kinda worked. As long as she stayed away from small children, Harper would try to stop dwelling on it. Tegan didn't think the woman would randomly attack other kids, merely ones she considered herself responsible for, believing she 'saved' them from the cruel death she'd convinced herself awaited everyone. It sounded way too much like Tyler's rationale for attacking Madison. Though, he hadn't wanted to murder her, merely 'remove the alien control chip from her brain.' Brain surgery was risky in the best circumstances, but an out-of-his-gourd schizophrenic doing *unnecessary* brain surgery in the woods at night with a combat knife on an unwilling child could only end one possible way.

Maybe I should have shot him. If I didn't know him, I definitely would have blown him away.

To stop herself from going down the mental rollercoaster of beating herself up for possibly poor decisions clouded by emotion, Harper began humming *Despacito*. Nothing could so thoroughly consume her brain and shut out everything else the way that song could. Sure, she'd be humming it for the next six weeks, but it beat driving herself nuts over events she couldn't change.

She followed her usual route, checking in on the handful of residents with kids too small to be in school yet. Much like the beautiful weather, everyone looked to be happy and healthy. Not quite a full hour after she left her siblings at the school, she arrived at the huge house where Lucas Garza lived. From the road, she had a good view down into the giant backyard, which would soon be filled with marijuana plants again. Darci stretched out atop a lounge chair on the back deck, a burgundy-colored blanket covering her. The girl looked wrong being pregnant, as if someone strapped a fake silicone belly onto a waifish runway model.

At the corner of the deck, a wooden pole held a flag depicting a big pot leaf over a plain white background.

Those two were made for each other. Harper chuckled. It still shocked her Darci willingly gave up weed for the baby. Such an apocalyptic event paralleled Madison ignoring vegetarianism in the interest of not starving to death.

Harper left the road, walking down the muddy hill into the backyard and up the steps to the deck. "Hey, Darce. How goes?"

"Getting knocked up was worth it just for the food." Darci grinned. "They're feeding me like they're fattening up a turkey for Thanksgiving."

Lucas laughed from inside the house. Harper chuckled.

Her friend sighed. "Honestly? I'm really starting to get anxious. It's scary like I'm on death row or something."

"You know what's depressing?" asked Harper.

"A lot of things, but what, specifically, are you thinking of?"

"Tegan told me the maternal mortality rate in the US prior to the war was actually worse than in some Third World countries. We might actually be better off now."

"Wow…" Darci whistled.

"Hey, I mean… we exist, right? People in the original Frontier had babies all the time."

"True." Darci grabbed Harper's arm, her expression revealing a rare moment where her unserious, sarcastic side completely vanished to sincerity. "Please be there holding my hand when I explode."

"Definitely. They'd have to shoot me to keep me away."

Darci rolled her eyes. "Careful. These days, that might actually come true."

"Heh. Ugh." Harper huffed. "So, any idea when?"

"I'm waiting for the little bastard to rip their way out like the Alien any day now." Darci patted her belly. "Dr. Hale estimated around May fourteenth, but the little one is squirming around a lot. Probably wants a bigger apartment."

"Think it's gonna happen sooner than the fourteenth?" asked Harper.

Darci groaned. "I freakin' hope so. I feel like a goddamned whale."

"I'm not sure how you did it, but you're not even close to fat. Just…"

"Yeah. I'm aware I look ridiculous. Don't care." Darci rolled her eyes. "Feels like I'm trying to smuggle a watermelon through customs after stuffing it up my hoo-hah."

Harper cringed. "Ouch."

"Yeah ouch." Darci exhaled hard. "It's gonna hurt coming out. Swear, if they try to give me a C-section, I'm going to pop like a balloon the instant the blade touches me. Blood all over the walls, one surprised baby stuck to the ceiling. At least almost starving did one good thing. Probably won't have bad stretch marks. My skin was kinda loose already."

"Ack." Harper cringed.

"Hey. Help me get to the bathroom? Gotta pee." Darci flung the sheet off, revealing she lay there naked.

"Oh, ack." Harper glanced away, unsure why she felt surprised. After all, Darci *did* go to a hippie resort at least twice where most people 'embraced nature.'

"What? I'm a whale. I can't even stand up without someone helping pull me to my feet. No clothing fits anymore. This is comfortable."

"Umm. You really don't understand shame, do you?" Harper tried her best to ignore her friend's casual nudity and helped her up.

"Nope. Shame is overrated. It's an artifact from a religiously obsessed patriarchal society." Darci wobbled along beside her, holding on for support. "The expensiveness or lack of a person's clothing has no bearing on how smart or savage they are. Guys in $10,000 suits are more vicious than natives in loincloths. It's all bullshit. Besides, haven't you seen those little figurines they found? I look like some primal nature goddess. People should be worshipping me."

Harper chuckled. "You seriously happened way too late. You should've been here for the Sixties, living in a hippie commune permanently, not just for a week at a time in the summer."

"Totes." Darci chuckled. "That would've been awesome."

Harper couldn't help but glance sideways at Lucas in the kitchen with only a towel around his waist like a skirt. His black hair had gotten kinda long and wild. *He totally looks like a pirate now.*

"Besides." Darci fluffed at her hair. "I love making the squares squirm."

"You sure do." Harper chuckled.

Darci shuffled into the bathroom. She had to grab onto the sink as well as Harper's arm to lower herself into position. "Don't expect you to watch, but I'm going to need a hand getting up again."

"Right." Harper backed out of the room. "Just say when."

A MOMENT AFTER HARPER HELPED DARCI BACK TO HER LOUNGE chair on the patio, Lucas emerged from the sliding glass door carrying two mugs. He looked hot in a 'Hispanic Thor stranded on a desert island' sort of way. Somehow, living rough after the end of civilization only made him *more* appealing. She wondered if he wore the towel skirt normally or if he'd thrown it on once he realized she'd come to visit. Not that Harper had serious thoughts regarding doing anything with a man in his thirties, celebrity or not. About the most she'd do would be put a poster of him on her bedroom wall and have daydreams. She could separate fantasizing about an unattainable hot guy who she saw in movies and TV from the reality of anything happening. Darci, apparently, could not. She'd originally sought him out because he had the only source of weed in the area and freely admitted to making the first romantic move a few weeks after basically moving in.

"Hey, Harper." Lucas offered her the mug in his left hand. "Here, enjoy."

She peered down at a mug of orange herbal tea. It smelled like the stuff her parents got all the time, Tazo or something. "Whoa. Wait. You have *tea*? Like *real* tea?"

"Yep." He wagged his eyebrows over a roguish grin. "Still have a whole cabinet full of it."

The idea a mug of ordinary herbal tea could make her feel as if she'd gone to a celebrity's house and been offered a $600 glass of wine as casually as anything struck her as beyond surreal. She could probably resist the urge to tell everyone he had tea. However, if he admitted to concealing a coffee stash, she'd have to activate her Militia authority and commandeer it in the interest of the people.

"Wow… umm… thanks." She accepted the mug.

"Back in a moment." Lucas paused to check on Darci, then went back inside to grab his cup.

Harper sat on a nearby chair. "Wow. I haven't even thought about this stuff in so long…"

"Perk of being rich." Darci idly bobbed the teabag in her cup. "He'd buy a shitload of things at once, stuff them in a closet somewhere, and forget about them a week later."

Ugh.

"Don't make that face." Darci snickered. "Most of the stuff, like clothes and whatnot, he's already given away to the town. He's not really like his character trying to hoard treasure. Lucas is a sweet guy."

Having observed the two of them on and off for the past almost year, Harper did believe he cared about her. It still struck her as a little weird for her eighteen-year-old friend to basically be 'married' to a man almost double her age. Lucas had to be around thirty-three. She'd been tempted repeatedly to ask Darci if he initially tried to talk her out of initiating a romantic relationship or leapt at the chance to have such a young woman as a lover. It really wouldn't change much other than her opinion of him. Darci was happy, and the guy *did* seem happy with her. When Harper first met Lucas, he used to spend all day in a bathrobe, standing on his patio and drinking whiskey, scotch, or whatever else he had, largely ignoring everything going on around him. She still didn't know if he'd been depressed over going from a multimillionaire to having zero money overnight or his emotional state came from something far less shallow, such as the inability to process all the death and suffering. Since Darci showed up, he'd gone back to being a normal guy, even seeming upbeat.

Lucas returned to the deck and sat in another chair beside Darci.

They chatted for a while in between sips of tea. Her friend's pale skin, black hair, and slightly large eyes made Harper think of an old timey starlet lounging in the company of the Hollywood 'aristocracy' back in the Twenties or Thirties. The two of them definitely existed on the same vibing wavelength—or however Darci would describe it, totally at peace with each other's company. Harper assumed the reason her friend didn't mind—or even actively sought out—such an age gap in a relationship had to do with losing her father. Darci hadn't fully admitted it, but Harper suspected she felt alone and vulnerable in the world, not at all ready to be out on her own. Her father died during the strike when either the initial shockwave or flying debris smashed their entire house, crushing him in his sleep. Harper hadn't seen the place herself. Darci said she woke up staring at open sky— from her basement bedroom.

Harper couldn't even begin to imagine how high or drunk Darci had been to sleep through the nuclear explosions. To call her friend's family 'dysfunctional' wouldn't be quite right. For the most part, Darci got along with her father, but they both spent more time high or drunk than sober.

At some point, one of Harper's parents commented about how women who dated much older men had 'unresolved daddy issues' when large sums of money weren't involved. She couldn't remember if Mom or Dad said it, or what made the topic come up, though it sounded more like a Dad-ism.

Everything seemed okay here. Darci looked healthy but damn close to going into labor. Tea done, Harper begrudgingly got up to leave.

"Thanks for the tea. That was amazing." Harper sighed. "I'd

love to stay all day, but I need to be making the rounds in case someone needs help."

"Go." Darci made a shooing gesture with the hand Lucas didn't hold. "I understand."

"Yeah, totally." Lucas started to smile at her, but ended up with a worried expression. "Is it true about that girl who drowned her kid?"

Harper shivered. "Kinda. She *tried* to. The boy got away from her. He couldn't get his baby sister, so he ran out the door looking for me because he knew I always walked around in the morning."

"Aww." Darci grimaced. "Is the girl okay?"

"Barely. She had a lungful of water. I'm no doctor, but she did wake up. No idea if there's brain damage or how long she was out." Harper absentmindedly picked up her empty mug and tried to drink from it, felt like an idiot, then put it back on the table. "The woman is staying with Mr. Ward now."

Darci snapped her fingers. "Damn. I'm not the most shockingly age-inappropriate girlfriend anymore."

Lucas sputtered into laughter.

"I don't think they're doing *that*," whispered Harper. "Pretty sure he's basically treating her like a daughter with some serious mental issues. Needs to be watched."

"Ahh." Darci nodded, then glanced at Lucas. "Help me waddle to the bathroom, 'kay?"

Lucas stood. "You got it."

"Oh, the glamour of a Hollywood romance." Darci pulled the blanket aside and stood with Lucas's help.

He appeared more uncomfortable at her nudity with company around than she did.

"Chill." Darci put an arm around him. "Nothing Harp hasn't seen before."

Harper held a finger up. "Not by choice. She adores shocking people."

"I adore being comfortable." Darci laughed, then proceeded to stand there leaning on Lucas, not a scrap of clothing on, rambling. "… this Saturday, right? I wanna say sophomore year. Harper and the guys show up at my house to collect me for a trip to the mall. You know me, I was up kinda late. So, I'm still dead asleep. Next thing I know, Harper's standing next to my bed screaming."

"Ugh…" Harper blushed, but couldn't help laughing. "The day I learned you sleep naked."

"Yep." Darci snickered. "The funniest part… the others were still upstairs in the living room with my dad. They heard Harp scream. And my dad goes, 'Harper just discovered my daughter sleeps naked' without even looking away from the TV."

"Oh, wow. Just a little… awkward." Lucas chuckled.

"Your fault for not knocking." Darci winked.

"You didn't have a bedroom door."

Darci's eyes widened. "I absolutely did have a bedroom door. It just so happened to be at the top of the basement stairs."

"That's not the same." Harper whistled. "I reach the bottom of the stairs, turn left, and there's your ass in my face." She glanced at Lucas. "Her bed was right out in the open."

"How is that my fault?" Darci examined her fingernails. "Anyway… bathroom please."

Harper shook her head, chuckling. Another one of Darci's apparent superpowers: she could talk about memories of the world before and not want to cry. Sober Darci definitely counted as weird for being so loud and strong-willed. Harper still thought of her as the perpetually high 'whatever you guys wanna do' girl who tended to have no firm opinions and acted more like a piece of furniture decorating the room, occasionally gaining enough coherence to say random things.

Lucas escorted Darci into the house via the sliding glass doors. Harper went down the deck stairs and resumed walking her patrol route.

Any day now. I think she's scared shitless. Damn. That's my fault. I shouldn't have been talking so much about childbirth being deadly.

She took a breath, resumed hum-singing *Despacito*, and walked down the road.

A FEW HOURS LATER, HARPER CAME AROUND THE BEND IN THE road leading to Lucas's house again.

Without any emergencies or other distractions pulling her away from walking around in circles, she passed the place about once every hour and a half. The last two times she went by, all sounded quiet.

"Fuck the blanket," yelled Darci from inside the house. "It's soaked. Leave it. Get Elijah."

Lucas said something Harper couldn't make out because he didn't yell. She sped up to a jog, hurrying down the street toward the house. The front door opened. Darci, naked except for her spike-studded goth 'Frankenstein' boots, staggered outside, flailing her arms for balance. Yellowish liquid ran down her legs.

Oh crap! Her water broke!

Darci stumbled across the porch to the top of the steps, where she fell against the railing and grabbed on. Lucas rushed up behind her and wrapped a bed sheet around her like a toga.

"Stop wasting time with bullshit. The baby's not gonna wai—" Darci turned the word 'wait' into a scream. Her legs buckled, dumping her to her knees. "Where's 'Lijah?"

"It's too cold to be outside with nothing on," said Lucas. "He's right behind me."

Harper pointed at the open doorway. "No boy."

"Do I look like I give a shit about cold right now?" rasped Darci.

Harper skidded to a stop at the base of the porch. "Darce?"

"Fuck, this hurts." Darci grabbed her stomach and groaned, her normally lily-white face red.

"Pain means you're alive," said Harper.

"Ugh. Stuff the Rambo shit up your butt, Harp." Darci attempted to laugh but grimaced instead. "Please do something useful and grab our other kid. Luke has a fixation with fabric. He should be paying attention to the boy."

"She's not bleeding, is she?" Harper moved up the stairs.

Lucas shook his head, seeming a bit lost for words. "No, just… uhm… uterus juice."

Darci laughed until she screamed again.

Harper stared at him. "Seriously?"

He shrugged at her. "I don't know what the heck they call it. I'm a dumb actor. Barely got my high school diploma."

"I didn't even finish high school and I know it's amniotic fluid," muttered Harper.

"You're also kinda closer to the issue than me." He chuckled.

"Less argue more hospital," yelled Darci. She made a gurgling nose, then growled, dragging herself down the steps to the street, walking right out of the sheet toga.

Most of the color drained out of Lucas's face. "What's happening to her? Is she okay?"

Harper shooed him down the stairs after her. "I think she's going into labor. It's normal. Let's get her to the doctors. Be right back." She cleared the porch in two steps and went inside.

Five-year-old Elijah lay on the floor in the living room, surrounded by an assortment of dolls, action figures, and toy spaceships. As if nothing at all unusual went on, he waved hello and continued playing.

"Hey, bud." Harper hurried over and crouched near him. "Your new mom and dad need to go see the doctor, okay? Can't leave you here alone."

"Aww. Okay. Is mommy hurt?"

"Not exactly. She's going to have a baby."

As if understanding the concept entirely, the boy offered a sagely nod, selected a spaceship toy to bring with him, and stood. Harper took his hand and led him outside.

Lucas, having re-wrapped Darci in the sheet, carried her away down the street. Harper picked Elijah up and rushed to catch up. In between moments of delirious pain, Darci kept peering up at him adoringly.

"Dad?" asked Elijah.

"Hey, champ." Lucas smiled at him.

"Why'd you stick a baby inside her if the doctor has to take it out?"

Harper and Darci burst into laughter.

"It's just how it's done." Lucas gazed adoringly at Darci. "You'll understand when you're older."

The boy didn't appear satisfied with the answer, but also didn't bother pestering him for a better one, instead making *pshh* sound effects while 'flying' his toy spaceship around. Harper decided to save time by cutting straight west into the trees, heading for the highway. Darci occasionally gasped or moaned in pain, but for the most part, appeared quite content to be carried by Lucas.

With the exception of Logan, no boy Harper ever dated would have physically carried her to a hospital in similar circumstances. At least two she could think of wouldn't even have stopped playing video games. If she stood right next to Joey Elkins with amniotic fluid gushing down her legs, he'd have simply tossed her a roll of paper towels and a phone, then gone right back to playing Fortnite. Dale wouldn't have even noticed her—probably why she only dated him for three days. Maybe Darci adored being the damsel carried off by the handsome movie star, maybe she adored having an older guy to protect her, or perhaps she truly loved him. At the moment, the look on her face could've meant any of those things.

Harper also didn't have time to ponder it.

Lucas didn't appear to be doing the 'clueless guy' thing and trying to avoid being aware of or involved in childbirth. He seemed freaked out at the idea something might be wrong with Darci, and his hesitance came from not knowing how to fix it. Having Harper there to keep him focused on the initial need to get Darci to the clinic put him in focus mode. He totally looked like a character in a movie about to carry his injured love across a literal minefield.

Soon, they emerged from the forest onto the grassy area separating the trees from the highway. Harper set Elijah down so she could hold Darci while Lucas hopped the chain link fence. For the moment it took him to do so, the girls exchanged a mutual stare of surprise. Harper couldn't believe how little her friend weighed. Darci seemed impressed Harper had the strength to hold her up without faltering.

Lucas reached across the fence. Harper handed Darci over, then boosted Elijah to the other side before jumping it. She took the boy by the hand and walked beside Lucas across the grass to the highway. Taking 74—a straight line—would be much faster and easier despite having to go over a fence than navigating the twisty streets in the residential areas. As soon as Lucas took her back, Darci grabbed onto him and cried out in pain, her lithe body shuddering in a series of convulsions.

Harper had no idea if she witnessed normal pregnancy stuff or if some crazy complications happened. Seeing her friend shake like that scared her up to a fast walk. It appeared to have a similar effect on Lucas. They hurried down the highway.

As soon as the bus barrier came into view, one of the two figures on top of it pointed a sniper rifle in their direction. Harper didn't panic. The guys did that as a matter of routine, using the scopes to take a closer look at anyone who approached. Anyone 'veteran' enough to be given the fairly cushy job of bus sentry would immediately recognize Harper and—barring serious brain damage—*not* shoot. Assuming the guy with the rifle looked at them, she traced her finger over her belly in a 'super pregnant' gesture, pointed at Darci, then gestured by grabbing her right fist in her left hand and pushing it out through her fingers, simulating a baby's head breaching.

The sniper—probably Cameron—appeared to get the message. He lowered the rifle, turned, and shouted. A minute or two later when Harper, Lucas, and Darci reached the bus barrier, Dr. Khan met them there with a wheeled gurney. Lucas set Darci down on it, then helped push her across the highway over to the clinic while answering the doctor's questions about her condition. Harper followed instinctually, all the way to the treatment room. Ruby Dorsey, the woman who basically ran the clinic as receptionist/administrator, leapt from the front desk to join them. Lucas helped Dr. Khan transfer Darci from the gurney to the exam table. Tegan and Grace appeared a moment later, the entire clinic staff involved in checking Darci out and preparing for the delivery.

Dr. Khan asked various questions about when the water broke, what she'd been feeling, the timing of contractions, and so forth. Darci answered in between groans of pain or mild convulsions. Both Tegan and Ruby kinda gave Lucas shifty looks, but he ignored them, continuing to stand at Darci's side, holding her hand.

Elijah contented himself to sit out of everyone's way in the corner, playing with his toy spaceship.

Harper hovered by the door, somewhere between concerned friend and security detail. The doctors washed their hands at a small sink in the counter. Grace pulled the sheet aside and wiped Darci down with a warm, soapy cloth.

"Sorry, I know it's a bit embarrassing," whispered Grace.

"Don't care," rasped Darci. "Do whatever. Bring in a live studio audience. Take pictures. Reach on up there and yank the little bugger out if you can."

Tegan rinsed soap from her hands, then stepped up beside the examination table. "I think your baby is quite ready to see the world. We're not going to need to go in after them."

A blood-curdling scream came from down the hallway.

Harper blinked. *That sounded like Carrie.*

Darci lifted her head, peering between her knees at the door. "What the heck was that?"

"Carrie Rangel," said Ruby. "She's been here a few hours. Water broke a little before noon, but labor hasn't started yet. Been resting comfortably."

"Doesn't sound too comfortable anymore," wheezed Darci.

Harper leaned back out the doorway into the hallway, looking to her right toward where the scream came from. *Shit. That did not sound good at all.*

Cliff raced out of a room four doors away and ran over to Harper. He appeared bewildered to see her there for barely a second before leaning past her into the room. "Dr. Hale, I think she's finally ready for you."

Another horrible scream filled the hallway.

"That came from Carrie?" asked Darci, seemingly unconcerned whatsoever she lay there stark naked in full view of Cliff. "Harp… if I start screaming like that, just shoot me like a horse with a busted leg."

"No," said Harper. "You're being sarcastic. I am not going to kill you."

"This is gonna suuuuck." Darci let her head flop back on the small pillow. She grabbed two fistfuls of sheet, closed her eyes, and screamed past clenched teeth. "Ugh. Am I having a baby or a pissed off porcupine?"

Carrie screamed again.

Dr. Khan and Tegan seemed to do rock paper scissors with a stare. Dr. Khan remained in the room with Darci while Tegan hurried out, patting Ruby on the shoulder as she went by and giving Grace a 'you should come see this and learn' look. Ruby followed her and Cliff back to the other treatment room.

Harper watched Darci gasp and writhe for a few minutes before another scream pulled her down the hall. She hesitated for a moment outside, afraid of what she might see, then peeked in on her stepmom. They had Carrie on an exam table. Unlike Darci, her head was closest to the door, long, wild light brown hair draped over the end. This room hadn't been a medical suite prior to the war, rather a conference room. The building now serving as Evergreen's hospital formerly contained multiple small offices of different kinds. One or two happened to be dentists, but most didn't involve health. This room lacked a sink or anything more professionally medical than the cabinets and stuff the doctors moved in here after the war.

A blue flannel shirt covered Carrie's upper half, a clean sheet formed a tent across her raised legs. Her jeans and boots lay in a pile on the floor. The palpable sense of urgency coming from Tegan and Ruby at the sight of Carrie scared the hell out of Harper. Grace also appeared quite worried but more in an 'overwhelmed student trying not to screw up' way. Harper didn't want to know what went on under the sheet spanning her stepmom's knees. If the expression on Tegan's face meant anything, an alien tentacle popped out.

Time blurred into a panicky haze. Harper ran back and forth between the two rooms, attempting to 'be there' for both her stepmother and her friend. Both Carrie and Darci screamed on and off, though Carrie's sounded heavier and more painful. Tegan also appeared to be dealing with blood where Dr. Khan's shirt remained clean. She picked up on some conversations between Dr. Khan, Grace, Tegan, and Ruby. Apparently, Darci's water broke and she'd immediately gone into labor. Carrie didn't. Labor started a few hours after. Not optimal, but she'd gotten close enough to term for it not to be a serious problem. Tegan worried more about Carrie's age and the unusually large size of her belly. More than once, she grumbled about not having any ultrasound equipment to know what went on in there.

Cliff stayed with Carrie, holding her hand the same way Lucas did, though he didn't seem worried or scared. He fired the same sort of glare he usually put on right before he killed someone at the wall. More than Carrie's screaming, seeing him apparently angry freaked her out. The man appeared to be furious at the world because the woman he took a chance on loving wouldn't make it.

For no reason worse than out of control anxiety, Harper started crying. No one told her bad news, nor had Tegan said anything seriously alarming, yet she'd somehow ended up convinced her stepmom would die any minute. Somehow, the worry cascaded to include her friend as well. The war had already taken Veronica, Andrea, and Christina away from her. She didn't know if she could handle losing another friend. Trying to tell herself they would've graduated high school by now and gone off to different colleges, still not seeing each other much, didn't help.

Carrie drifted between silence, pained screams, and growling, at one point yelling, "Get out ya damn freeloader. Breathe for yourself." Darci alternated between screaming in pain and crying like a kid who stubbed her toe. After maybe twenty minutes of zooming back and forth between the rooms, Harper flopped on a seat in the hallway and grabbed her head in both hands.

Holy shit. Was it like this for Mom when she had me and Maddie? It couldn't have been this *bad with me since she willingly went through it a second time.* Harper bit her lip. The idea of lying on a table naked from the waist down while a crowd of people tended to her scared her more than the pained screaming. Getting 'female checkups' from Tegan still felt awkward. *Probably because she's more like a friend than my doctor I only see once a year. It's like me going over to Renee's to hang out and casually breaking out a speculum and a flashlight while we talk about random crap.* She stared at the ceiling and burst into laughter. *Ugh. I am losing my mind.*

Hopefully, Walter realized she'd gone to the clinic and sent someone out to cover her patrol route. Neither staying here without knowing for sure or going to check (and leaving Darci and Carrie) seemed like the proper thing to do.

A break came in the form of Jonathan, Madison, Mila, and Lorelei arriving together in a bit of a rush. Upon seeing Harper sitting in the hallway, they froze. Jonathan seemed relieved. Madison lapsed into tears. Mila smiled in an 'oh, whew' sort of way. Lorelei beamed and ran into a hug.

"What happened?" Jonathan dashed over and grabbed her hand. "They said you were here. We thought you got hurt."

Madison sat in Harper's lap and sniffled.

"Darci's having her baby. I helped bring her here. That's all." Harper sighed. "Who told you I was here? I need to have a chat with them about being clear."

"Ken." Madison wiped her eyes. "He said you couldn't meet us at school because you were at the clinic."

"Ugh." Harper stared at the ceiling. "Yeah, I'm physically at the clinic but not because *I'm* the one who needed help."

Madison giggled past relieved tears.

Both treatment rooms quieted down in terms of screaming. No one emerged looking grim, so Harper decided to continue breathing. Being in the building close by had to count for something. She couldn't really do anything to help other than going to fetch a bowl of warm water like someone always seemed to do in movies.

The kids sat with her for a while. Initial shock of assuming Harper had been shot, stabbed, or hurt wore off surprisingly fast. They chattered about school, what they'd have for dinner later, and random baby-related questions.

Cliff appeared, taking one step out of the door to Carrie's room and stood there, facing the opposite wall like a bearded Frankenstein's monster with an expression as if he'd just been drafted to go to Vietnam.

Harper and the kids all turned their heads to look at him. A lump of unease tightened her throat… until a faint twitch in his lips gave away he overacted grimness.

"What happened?" whispered Harper.

Cliff turned ninety degrees to face them. "Carrie had twin boys."

Harper gasped.

"Wow," said Madison.

"Ooo." Lorelei clapped.

"Ouch." Mila grabbed her stomach.

"Nice!" Jonathan jumped to his feet. "Is she okay?"

Cliff tilted his hand in a so-so gesture. "Thirty-five, multiple birth. Bleeding. Risk factors. Doc wants to keep her here for a few days. She's not too happy about it but isn't protesting."

She's still alive… Harper exhaled. "Did you guys come up with names yet?"

"Yeah." Cliff hooked his thumbs in his pants pockets, trying not to smile too much. "Owen and Emmett. I wanted to call them Igg and Ook, but Carr had some light objections."

Harper snickered.

"Weird names." Mila scrunched her nose. "Igg and Ook?"

"Yeah." Cliff chuckled. "A pair of cavemen from an old newspaper cartoon."

"Oh." Mila tilted her head. "What's a newspaper?"

Cliff slouched in a 'damn, I'm old now' manner.

"Harp!" shouted Darci. "Where'd you go?"

"Ack. Gotta go. Promised." Harper stood, lifting Madison, and set her sister on her feet, then ran to the second treatment room.

Darci had turned red over most of her face and chest. Dr. Khan stood at the end of the exam table like a major league catcher waiting for the pitch. Lucas held Darci's right hand in both of his. Her friend flapped her left hand frantically. Taking the hint, Harper rushed over and grabbed it. Madison poked her head in, raised both eyebrows at the sight of Darci, but remained in the doorway watching.

"Here the baby comes," whispered Dr. Khan. "Push like I told you, and keep pushing."

Darci screamed an F-bomb so loud the Lawless in Denver probably heard it. Her grip on Harper's fingers nearly cracked them. Soon after her voice shifted from screaming to a heavy grunt, an infant's cry broke the silence. Elijah promptly echoed the F-bomb in the form of a gleeful cheer.

"Dar said a bad word," said Lorelei out in the hall.

"I know how she feels." Cliff laughed. "I've had a few like that. Military rations will tear you up."

Harper gawked, unsure if she should be disgusted or laugh.

Dr. Khan held a scrawny little baby up to the light. "Congratulations, Ms. Sutherland. You have a healthy daughter!"

CARRIE AND DARCI OCCUPIED ADJACENT BEDS IN THE BACK ROOM of the clinic.

Darci cradled her infant daughter to her bare chest, sharing body heat under a blanket. Lucas could hardly sit still for more than a few minutes, overjoyed. Despite all the screaming, Darci didn't say much about the pain or discomfort, brushing it all aside as if it hadn't really happened.

Since Carrie *had* a functioning sense of embarrassment— unlike Darci—she'd changed into a clean white T-shirt Jonathan ran back home to get for her. Emmett and Owen resembled little blue footballs, wrapped entirely in towels. Cliff paced around pretend-griping about how the next two or three years would be a 'hell without sleep.' If his poorly concealed smile and tone of voice didn't give away the joke, Harper knowing the man had been trained to function on four hours of sleep for extended periods proved he wasn't serious.

"Harp," said Darci.

She looked away from the dozing boys to her friend. "Hey. You're awake."

"I've been awake for a few minutes." Darci smiled hazily, then sighed. "Still can't touch the leaf for a bit or the baby will get high on my milk."

Elijah crawled out from under the bed. He tugged on Harper's arm, then pointed at Darci's chest. "Baby's magic. She gave mommy boobies. Mommy didn't even have boobies before."

Lucas hid his face in his hand. Darci cackled. Carrie got the giggles. Cliff shook his head.

Harper started to laugh… until Elijah poked her in the boob.

"Where's your baby?" asked the boy.

Eep! She leaned back so his finger ceased jabbing into her chest. "I don't have one."

"But you have boobies." He scratched his head.

Laughing, Lucas plucked the boy up off his feet. "I got it."

"Oh, wow," whispered Darci while peering under the blanket at herself. "The titty faerie paid me a visit. So, this is what it's like."

Harper had already been in a weird, excited mood at both Carrie and Darci surviving childbirth. Her friend's fake surprise at 'suddenly having breasts' pushed her off the edge. She cracked up laughing so hard she cried, even though the comment hadn't been *that* funny.

"Hey…" Darci nudged her. "Question."

"Sec." Harper took a moment to wipe her eyes and collect herself. "Okay. Shoot. Not literally."

"Hah." Darci snickered. "Would you mind if I named her Piper?"

Say what? Harper raised an eyebrow. "Why would I mind?"

"Because I'm naming her that kinda after you. Not exactly the same name, but you know. Piper, Harper… both kinda musical."

Harper squirmed, slightly awkward the same way public speaking made her feel. "I guess. It's fine."

"You got me out of that hellhole, and you've like, been there for me this whole time." Darci took her hand. "I don't know if I'd have held it together without you."

"Umm. Wow. That's..." Harper puffed hair off her face. "Really didn't think I did much out of the ordinary, but okay. Thanks."

"It's not only what you did..." Darci grinned impishly. "I figured if the timid little redhead who couldn't even kill bugs could turn into a shotgun-toting ass-kicker, I could not be a complete wimp."

"Hah!" Harper succumbed to laughter again. "Fair enough."

24

FRONTIER MEDICINE

While Harper would have been happy to spend all day with Darci and Carrie, she couldn't let the kids go fend for themselves at home, nor did they seem terribly thrilled at spending hours at the clinic.

Once the worst of the nerve-wracking parts had passed and Harper felt reasonably secure everyone would be okay, she gathered the kids—plus Elijah who she'd offered to watch until the doctors let Darci go home—and headed out after the obligatory round of hugs, congratulations, and admonitions to rest.

Feeling a bit like a red-haired pied piper, she led the small army of kids down the hall to the clinic's front door. A few people sat in the waiting room up front, biding their time until one of the doctors could see them. Harper waved at the ones who looked up at her.

The kids followed her home. Becca and Eva sprang up from the front porch and rushed over, confused as to where everyone had been for so long. While the girls squealed in delight upon hearing the news of three new babies, Harper headed inside to get started on dinner.

A KNOCK CAME FROM THE FRONT DOOR A FEW MINUTES AFTER she'd dumped all the cut vegetables into a pot to make her bastard hybrid of stew and soup. She tended to follow a 'meh, that'll work' recipe when deciding what to toss in the pot. Every time she cooked or watched someone else cook, Harper pondered suggesting another scavenging trip into Denver to grab as many spices and seasonings as they could find. Since people generally didn't eat such things straight, she figured a good chance existed they might find some still sitting on store shelves and in stockrooms. Whether or not the Lawless cared enough about flavor to raid the seasonings aisle remained unknown.

She daydreamed about kicking in the door of a supermarket, racking her shotgun, and muttering, 'Welcome to Flavortown.' The idiocy of it made her laugh.

"Hello?" called Walter from the front door.

The muscles in Harper's back tensed. Walter coming to the house meant one of two things: either he wanted to ask her to go on a mission or something... or something bad happened to someone in her family. However, he probably wouldn't call 'hello' in an optimistic tone of voice if he came bearing bad news.

She hung her head and sighed out her nose, realizing he probably wanted to send her somewhere. The bubbling surface of the sorta-stew held no answers, merely an insufficient amount of black pepper. They didn't have much left, so she tried to be sparing with it.

"Yeah, one sec," called Harper. She set the wooden spoon down too fast, missing the little plate she used to keep food off the counter and sending it flying into the sink. "Grr."

At the clattering, Walter stuck his head in the front door. "Everything okay in there?"

"Yeah. Just dropped the spoon." Harper paused to take a breath. *I am already anxious. Not a good sign. Calm down.* She crossed the house to the living room, then pulled the door open the rest of the way. "What's up?"

Walter Holman, the 'commander' of the Militia, looked more like a retired cop on his way to play golf in a white polo shirt with a Sheriff's Department logo and khakis. The past year aged him noticeably, stress making his fifty-one appear closer to sixty-five. He'd once joked that he'd gone fully grey-haired in his late thirties, but preferred it to his brother ending up bald around the same age. Something about his friendly, quiet demeanor always put her at ease. Looking at him, she had trouble believing he'd ever shot anyone dead... but then again, not one of her former classmates would *ever* in a billion years believe she'd killed people.

Harper couldn't either, really. Mostly because she didn't consider the Lawless to be 'people.'

"Little thing kinda came up." Walter's slate blue eyes softened, giving off a 'feel free to say no, but I'm going to ask anyway' vibe. "We got word there's a young woman in need of a doctor's attention. Dr. Hale is going to make a long-distance house call. We're looking for some volunteers to escort her and make sure she gets back here in one piece."

"Umm," mumbled Harper to buy a few seconds to process. He said Tegan *is going*, which meant the decision to send help had already been made. It sounded like something out of a Western movie. A person running in from the countryside to town asking for a doctor's help. "Where? How far?"

Walter pointed two fingers off to his left and behind. "Ranch house near Hartsel. Southwest of here, farther away from Denver. Figure it's about sixty-five miles of road. I know you went out to get jars and aren't at the top of the list at the moment..."

"Yeah." Harper glanced back over her shoulder at loud bubbling. "Hang on. Soup's gonna boil over. C'mon in." She fast-walked to the kitchen, turned down the stove, and resumed stirring. At least the spoon landed in the sink and not on the floor.

"You're probably wondering why I'm asking you about going." Walter strolled into the kitchen, giving a dry chuckle. "Fair question. I don't want you to feel obligated or anything. My thinking is you're small and light enough to share a horse with Dr. Hale."

"A horse?" Harper blinked. "The Express people are letting us use one?"

"We have a few officially part of the Militia now." He smiled. "Not many, though. Exactly why you'd be doubling up with her."

"Can she ride? I have no idea how to. Last time I touched a horse I was ten years old and it didn't go well."

"What happened?" Walter raised both eyebrows.

Harper kept stirring the soup-stew, chuckling. "I was terrified of the horse. Horse knew it. Don't remember too much other than it stopping short and me going sailing right over its head to the ground."

"Why did you want to go riding if you found horses so scary?" Walter smiled.

"Not my idea. Mom. She did the whole horse thing as a kid and figured I'd like it." Harper whistled. "Once it became abundantly clear it wouldn't work, she backed off. Sometimes, I think she got pregnant with Madison specifically so she'd have a daughter she could take to dance class, gymnastics, and so on."

"You were a tomboy?"

Harper laughed. "No. Just a lazy, timid geek."

He stared at her for a long moment. "I'd never imagine anyone calling you any of those things." He shifted his gaze to the Transformers Autobot logo on her shirt. "Except maybe the geek part."

"I'm not really the same person I used to be." She set the spoon down, leaning on the counter. "It's a lot easier to be lazy and timid when there's no real consequences for it. After the war... I basically stopped giving a crap what happened to me as long as Maddie was okay."

Walter crossed the kitchen to the back door, peering out at the kids in the yard. "They say you never really know what a person's made of until the shit hits the fan."

A rumble of nuclear warheads going off echoed in the back of Harper's mind. "What if the wad of shit is so huge it *breaks* the fan?"

"Then we really see what a person's got inside them." He turned away from the door. "It's all right, hon. I understand."

Harper cocked an eyebrow at him. "I'm not saying no. I'll do it. As long as Tegan's able to control the horse. So silly."

"What is?"

"I'm more nervous about the idea of riding a horse than people might shoot at me."

Walter chuckled. "The unknown is scary."

"Yeah. Just gotta do it, right?" She exhaled hard. "So, when are we going? Someone's sick, so I'm guessing it's soonish? Tonight?"

"Morning."

She nodded once. "Hartsel... don't think I've ever been there."

"It's not too far away. Not technically part of Evergreen, but we're the closest civilization." He stepped closer and sniffed at the pot. "Smells pretty good."

"Food at all smells pretty good." Harper resumed stirring. "I've entirely forgotten what the stuff I used to eat tasted like. Pizza... chicken nuggets, Chinese food. Burritos."

"Ahh, healthy living." He winked.

"Teenage living." She shrugged one shoulder. "Didn't really pay too much attention to food other than what was quick and tasted good. So, umm... is it just me and Tegan going?"

"Well, we don't have too many people we can spare, but... Ken's already agreed to go." Walter looked over as the back door opened. "And the guy who came looking for help."

Walter sniffed at the pot. "Oh, wow. You still have black pepper. Nice."

"Been trying to make it last." She sighed at the huge 'restaurant sized' container of ordinary black pepper. Roughly a quarter of it remained.

Madison crept into the kitchen, making *that* face at her.

Ugh. I promised her not to keep leaving town so damn much. Going to protect Tegan while she visited a sick person seemed much more urgent than a scavenging trip. Not only had the woman saved Renee's life when the idiot accidentally shot her, she'd talked Harper through some of her worst anxieties. Dr. Tegan Hale had somehow become this combination of therapist, big sister, confidant, and friend... not to mention gynecologist. She also held the almost mystical status of being a real doctor. Harper totally got how people in Old West movies tended to revere them almost the same way kids looked up to their parents. If Tegan needed protection, she couldn't say no.

Here I go again, doing the thing I told Maddie I'd try not to do. Harper raised her arm, inviting her sister to scurry over and grab onto her. *Well... I clung to Dad's gun, joined the militia without really thinking about what it would really mean. Can't just hide in here worried only about my family. I don't really have any other skills. Either I do the Militia thing or it's go full frontier woman, play uterus bingo, and hope I don't die.*

The idea she had just as much chances of ending up dead to childbirth as she did pretending to be a Wild West lawwoman stranded her on an island between wanting to laugh, cry, or scream. She'd probably have laughed if not for Madison clinging to her.

Harper thought of Logan taking his shirt off, and smiled. Not a great sign; all her fears of pain and death melted away in the heat of the moment as soon as she got in the mood with him. Or perhaps it *was* a good sign. Having kids had never been something she thought about before, but neither had running around the wasteland with a shotgun. *Maybe when she's a little older, I'll roll those dice with Logan. Assuming it doesn't happen by accident sooner.*

Realistically, she'd probably never make it to old age. Late fifties, maybe late sixties amounted to 'doing great.' Future generations might consider a person in their forties 'elderly,' depending on how much medical knowledge and technology returned.

"The world coming is the world we make of it," whispered Harper.

"Are you trying to talk yourself into doing something dumb?" asked Madison.

Walter grinned.

Harper patted her sister on the back. "Not dumb. Helping other people is never dumb."

"Dangerous."

"So is breathing." Harper bit her lip. "So is having babies. It's probably safer for me to go with Tegan to Hartsel than it was for Carrie to have twins."

"Ugh." Madison shivered. "It's so unfair. How come it's only the girl who might die? Why can't the boy's nuts fatally explode?"

Walter grunted.

Harper cackled.

"Nature is strange." Walter leaned on the counter. "Take praying mantises, for example. The males *do* die in the process."

"I'm not biting anyone's head off." Harper ruffled Madison's hair. "There's someone not too far away who is sick and needs a doctor. Tegan's going there whether I'm with her or not. I'd like to help keep her safe. They can't really ask Deacon to share a horse with her."

"Poor horse," whispered Madison.

"Right?" Harper smiled. "The horse would probably complain about having to carry him alone."

"Umm, Harp?" Madison peered up at her. "Is this the kind of

trip I can go with you, or do you want me to stay here where it's still dangerous but for different reasons?"

"I honestly don't know." Harper raked a hand up through her hair. "You'd really rather stay with me even though we could be attacked by wild animals, shot at, kidnapped, or anything?"

Madison clasped her hands in front of herself. "Yeah. I realize it's an abnormal attachment and I'm being super clingy and needy."

"She's been talking to Dr. Hale, hasn't she?" Walter patted her shoulder.

"Little bit," muttered Madison. "It's dangerous to go, but it's also dangerous to be here. Everything's dangerous. I'd rather get hurt *with* Harper than have her disappear and never know what happened. Just…"

Harper choked up too much to speak.

"Just?" asked Walter.

Madison kicked the tip of her sneaker at the floor, looking down. "If me going with her is gonna be like distracting and stuff and make it harder for her to be okay, then I'll stay here."

"What do you think, Walter?" asked Harper with only a little bit of squeak in her voice.

"Wow. You called me Walter." He clapped.

Harper shrank in on herself a little.

"It's fine. Been telling you to drop the Mr. Holman thing for a while." He waved dismissively. "Well, the fella who came looking for a doctor isn't too conversational in English. He didn't say much about having trouble getting here, and he's about your age."

Madison stared. "Really?"

"Not your age. Her age." Walter nodded toward Harper.

"Oh."

"Look…" Harper grasped her sister by the shoulders. "I'm not only worried about your physical health. If you go out there with me, it might happen that you end up being forced into a situation where you have to kill someone to protect yourself, or me, or someone else. I really don't want you to have to be put in that position."

Madison cringed. "I already shot someone."

"Yeah, but you didn't kill anyone."

"Like you…" Madison hugged her. "I don't wanna kill people."

"Good." Harper held on tight for a moment. "It's one thing if you're here at home and bad stuff goes down. Running off into the world looking for trouble is totally different."

"You're not looking for trouble. You're going to help someone who's sick." Madison flapped her arms. "Trouble would be looking for you. Might look for me, here, too."

Harper narrowed her eyes. "We're not in Kansas anymore… maybe I should stop trying to wrap you in packing foam and let you learn how to handle this new world."

"She's a little young yet," said Walter. "Teaching her how to survive is a good idea. Sending a child on a trip she doesn't *need* to take is another."

"None of us *need* to do this." Harper glanced at him. "This is an act of mercy, not personal survival. We're trying to keep civilization alive."

"It's like the bugs." Madison laughed. "You don't *have* to carry them outta the house, but you do. That's who you are. You just like helping people. I wanna go with you if I can help, but not if I'm gonna get in the way."

"Hey," said Logan as he breezed in the front door holding up a cloth-wrapped bundle. "Got some venison from the freezer. Not much since it's 'my portion,' but I figured you could add it to the pot."

Luisa trailed in after him, waving hello.

"Nice." Harper eyed the simmering soup/stew. "I can toss it in right now. Hey… Walter?"

"Hmm?" He gave her an anticipatory smile.

She couldn't help but smile back at him. "You're welcome to eat with us tonight, but I was gonna ask… you said the guy who came looking for help didn't speak much English? I'm assuming he speaks Spanish?"

Walter nodded. "Yes. And I'd love to join you for dinner."

Logan entered the kitchen, set the venison on the counter, and kissed Harper.

"Can Logan go with us?" Harper looked up at him. "If he wants to come, that is. He can speak Spanish."

Luisa's eyes widened much the same way Madison's did whenever she learned Harper had to leave town.

"I don't see why not." Walter rubbed his chin. "Mr. Ruiz isn't part of the Militia, so his absence won't compromise security here."

"What's up?" Logan looked back and forth between them.

Harper explained needing to escort Tegan to check on a sick woman. "If the guy they sent here for help is iffy with English, he might be the only one there who knows *any* English. Doesn't make sense they'd send a guy who can't communicate well to get help."

"Yeah, no problem. Just gotta let Mr. Rollins know I won't be on the farm for a day or two." Logan put an arm around Harper, his body language exuding protectiveness.

Staring down, Luisa ground her toes into the rug like a girl half her age. She appeared worried to death but too shy to openly protest her brother going. They'd likely have more of a discussion about it once Walter left.

Madison squeezed in between them. "I'm not crazy anymore. This is totally superstition now."

"What?" asked Harper, half chuckling.

"I'm not being clingy because I'm having emotional issues." Madison smiled. "I'm trying not to jinx you. Every time you go somewhere, I get clingy. Don't wanna risk the first time I'm coping okay enough not to be clinging to be the time you get hurt."

Harper opened the venison pack and grabbed a carving knife. "Cling away, Termite."

"Are you still gonna call her that when she's as tall as you are?" asked Logan.

"Probably." Harper started cutting the deer meat into stew-sized chunks. "It's not really a size thing."

"Where'd the name come from?" Logan leaned on the counter.

Madison's face reddened. "It's kinda embarrassing."

"Up to her if she wants to share." Harper tossed a handful of meat into the pot.

"Wow. Really?" Madison blinked. "You're not going to seize the opportunity to embarrass me?"

"Nope."

"Wow." Walter whistled. "Must be bad."

Madison frowned. "Not really. When I was like two years old, I had this thing with chewing on the furniture. Don't even remember it, just heard stories about it."

"Mom almost bought a bottle of the stuff they use to discourage dogs from chewing on table legs." Harper chuckled.

"Bark, bark," deadpanned Madison. "And no, I do not have pica. I grew out of it. Probably a teething thing."

Logan grabbed the spoon and stirred the stew. "When are we going?"

"Morning," said Walter and Harper at the same time.

"Ahh." Logan feigned disappointment. "Guess that changes our plans for tonight."

"Good idea." Madison wagged her eyebrows. "She's gotta ride a horse tomorrow."

Harper blushed, as did Logan.

Walter found the ceiling rather interesting all of a sudden.

25

ANOTHER ROLL OF THE DICE

MAY 4TH

During dinner last night, Walter went over all the information he had about the situation.

A man named Jorge Ochoa arrived in Evergreen late in the afternoon yesterday, claiming to have come from Hartsel, or in the general vicinity of it. He and several others lived in a big ranch house with the Overton family. The name didn't strike Harper as a family who wouldn't know how to speak English. However, the young man didn't have much trouble convincing Tegan, Walter, and some of the Militia of his sincerity.

He'd spoken of a sick teenage girl, Rebecca Vargas, daughter of his uncle, Manuel. That eased Harper's worries about a trap. A guy weak with English being the one sent to ask for help made more sense when the sick person happened to be his relative. She still wanted Logan to go with them, both for his ability to translate as well as having another person. The idea of bringing her boyfriend on a potentially dangerous trip worried her, but unlike Madison, he had a chance to defend himself without being forced to use a gun. The *only* chance her sister had winning a fight against an adult started with nine and ended with millimeter.

Thankfully, Madison's request to go with them stemmed mostly from wanting to spend time with Harper and not out of an irrational, neurotic fear of separation. While the girl certainly didn't love the idea of watching her older sister—and only surviving blood relative—take another trip away from the comparative safety of Evergreen, she tolerated it reasonably well.

The morning started like most others. Harper got out of bed, everyone took turns using the bathroom, then gathered in the kitchen for breakfast. They finished off the last of the 'W stew' as Lorelei named it because it contained 'vegetables and venison' or two v's, hence a W. Along with some 'not quite stale' bread, the leftovers provided a filling, if unconventional, start to the day.

After walking the kids to school, Harper headed to the town center instead of proceeding to her usual patrol. Mild worry nibbled at her brain over the kids. Luisa would essentially babysit them until Cliff returned to the house, though Logan's fifteen-year-old sister still had a heap of emotional issues from her experience after the strike. At times, she acted much more like a nine year old than a teenager, being shy, fearful, and prone to crying at seemingly random moments. Still, she'd made visible progress back to something closer to normal compared to how she'd been after they first found her.

A small group waited on Route 74 near the Quartermaster's building, consisting of Walter, Anne-Marie, Ken Zhang, Logan, Tegan, and another young man who looked a little older than Logan. The stranger had sienna skin, black hair, and a face too boyish for the rest of his body. She figured him for around twenty or twenty-one. A plain, though dirty, tank top revealed sinewy muscles and a lean build. His cowboy hat definitely went along with the 'ranch house' story, as did his boots and dirt-caked jeans. She studied him for a few seconds, until satisfied the nervousness in his eyes didn't hold the same predatory quality she'd sensed in Steve Pratt.

The boy from her class seemed nervous like someone who feared not being able to get away with bad deeds. This guy gave off unease and worry more as though frightened they might not get to the sick girl in time to help, a 'c'mon, let's get going' vibe more than 'don't look at what my hands are doing'.

Had she let Steve go right away, she felt certain he'd have come back with reinforcements. It saddened and disgusted her how a kid who'd sat a few desks away from her for years could join the Lawless. Hopefully, her humanity—in not shooting him on the spot—wouldn't result in anyone innocent being killed.

In addition to the people, four horses stood patiently nearby, saddled and packed for a multi-day trip. Three had dark chestnut coats and black manes, one pale with a champagne-colored mane. That one had to belong to Jorge, since Harper didn't remember seeing an animal of its coloration here before. The saddles on two of the darker horses looked like the 'Militia style' ones, which differed from the Express saddles by trading cargo-carrying satchels for rifle slings.

At the sight of Harper making her way down the road from the north, the stranger appeared to relax. He looked at Logan, said something in Spanish, and the boys spoke for a minute or so before Jorge bowed graciously to everyone around him.

Tegan also appeared on edge, probably the same expression Madison would've been wearing if Harper had decided to let her come with them. Ken appeared the calmest of everyone, ever so slightly wary. He'd dressed in a blue police jumpsuit, complete with bulletproof vest and utility belt. His demeanor reminded her of something Cliff said about bravery being bullshit. According to him, everyone whose brain hadn't broken knew fear. Some people could do what had to be done despite their fear. Others acted tough, made fun of anyone who showed the slightest bit of fear, and generally fell to pieces first when 'shit got real.'

Of course, they hardly prepared to 'ride into enemy territory' or even confront a single crazy person with a gun. In an ideal world, they'd simply enjoy a nice ride across the country, spend a few hours—likely overnight—at a place, then come home. Harper had no illusions she lived in the ideal world, though.

She checked over her stuff: shotgun, nine rounds loaded, fifty more in her hip satchel. Handgun, three extra magazines in her hip satchel. Two canteens, knife, and a light backpack containing a blanket and a couple small bread loaves. Maybe she'd regret not bringing additional clothing, but they didn't plan on going far. After going through yet another winter wearing clothing so dirty it came close to breathing on its own, spending a few days in the same outfit wouldn't bother her at all.

Walter looked around at everyone. "All right then. You'll want to be underway. Horses are packed with enough provisions for six days if you're sparing. Expect to cover about thirty to thirty-five miles before the horses will need to stop and rest."

"So, we'll be camping out in the middle of nowhere tonight?" asked Harper.

"Pretty much." Walter set his hands on his hips. "Everyone still good to go?"

"Yes." Tegan nodded. "Can't say for sure what, if anything, I'll be able to do for the girl, but I have to at least try."

Jorge bowed to her. "Thank you, doctor."

"Try to return that horse unhurt." Walter gestured at the dark brown horse not wearing a Militia saddle. "Adriana was kind enough to let us borrow it for Logan. Extra points if you bring the boy back in one piece, too."

Logan grinned, patting his AK-47. "I'm interested in bringing myself back in one piece."

The horses seemed much bigger than she remembered up close. Harper tried to act casual around them, worried the animals might sense her apprehension and react poorly. Tegan mounted with relative ease, tricking Harper into thinking getting up behind her would be simple.

She managed it—with a fair amount of help from Logan and a lot of flailing. Wrapping her arms around Tegan felt a bit awkward. Trying to brace herself on the saddle behind her butt felt both precarious as well as uncomfortable, so she opted to cling to the doctor.

"First time on a horse?" asked Tegan.

"No. It will hopefully be the first time I *stay* on a horse longer than five minutes." She laughed nervously.

"Hah. Everyone starts off like that." Tegan made a clicking noise, which got the horse moving forward at a walking pace. "Don't try to fight the sway, you'll only end up sore. Settle in, relax, and let your body move with him."

"You giving her riding advice or tips for Logan?" called Ken after hopping up on the second chestnut horse.

Harper gasped. Tegan shook as if laughing in silence.

Logan wisely kept his mouth shut. He climbed into the saddle somewhat more smoothly than Ken. Harper figured he'd ridden more often than her—no surprise—but not as frequently as Tegan, who appeared completely at ease in a saddle.

She must be one of those 'horse girls'. Bet she's been riding since childhood. "I'm kinda exaggerating. Had a bad experience when I was little, but I have been going to see Adriana a few times a month, trying to get familiar with riding horses. Not exactly comfortable with it yet, though. So far, I've basically just sat on one while she led it around in circles, like giving some little kid a horsie ride."

Tegan chuckled.

Jorge leapt into the much smaller saddle on the pale horse so easily he looked like a movie stuntman. He led them down the highway and across Evergreen onto Route 285. Initially, Harper didn't pay much attention to anything beyond the reality of sitting on top of an enormous animal. Paradoxically, it made her *more* nervous having no control and nothing to do but hold on. At any second, she expected to go flying.

Spanish conversation drifted back and forth between Jorge and Logan for the entire ride out of town. Soon after they reached open highway, Logan looked over at Ken, Tegan, and Harper.

"He says he didn't see much of anything on the way up here. However, they've been having some problems with people he calls 'bandits.'"

"What kind of problems?" asked Ken.

Harper leaned to one side to peer past Tegan. "Are we riding into an ambush? Should we bring more people?"

"He says the bandits try to raid the ranch sometimes at night. They also sent threatening messages demanding food and supplies or they'll do worse. Mr. Overton hasn't given them anything, so there's been some vandalism." Logan asked Jorge something in Spanish, nodded, then continued in English. "He doesn't think we'll have any problems riding during the day. We won't reach their territory by tonight. Tomorrow, at the house, we should be safe inside after dark."

"Great," muttered Harper. "So glad I talked Maddie out of going with us."

"That kid's not gonna learn." Ken shook his head.

"Sure, she did. She's not here, right?" Harper sighed. "Didn't even really argue too hard."

"Check saddlebags." Logan laughed. "Make sure she didn't sneak on."

Harper glanced back in the direction of town. "I just walked her to school. No possible way she could've gotten into any of the saddlebags without being seen. Also, she's not *that* small. It would be pretty obvious if she tried to stuff herself in one."

"Any idea why he didn't mention these bandits before?" asked Ken.

Logan chuckled. "Yeah. No one asked."

Tegan and Ken groaned.

"Seriously, though…" Logan faced forward again, smiling. "He didn't know how to explain it clearly enough in English. Figured Mr. Overton could tell us when we got there."

"Bit late once we're already there." Ken shook his head, sighing.

Logan shrugged. "He doesn't sound too worried about them."

"What sort of things do these bandits do?" asked Harper.

"He said they demand food and supplies. If people don't give them what they want, they cause trouble." Logan glanced over at Jorge, then asked something in Spanish.

Jorge gestured as if holding a rifle. "They shoot at house. Start fires. Open gate so the cows run out. Make trouble. Not real fight. Mr. Overton call them idiots."

"These bandits… are they responsible for Rebecca being ill?" asked Tegan.

"Sorry. I…" Jorge glanced at Logan, who repeated the question in Spanish. "No. Not unless they have magic."

Ken, Logan, and Tegan almost laughed.

"Sounds like they're not really equipped for or looking for an actual fight." Harper gazed down at the Mossberg riding in the saddle sheath. "Just trying to scare people into giving them what they want."

"Yeah." Logan smiled up at the clouds. "Not saying we should be careless, but… yeah. Maybe I shouldn't say it won't be a big deal. Don't want to jinx us."

"Good plan," said Ken. "I'm sure they'll change their mind once our shotgun prodigy explodes a few heads."

Harper blushed. "The best way to win a gunfight is not to get into one."

"I hear that." Ken nodded.

Logan raised an eyebrow at her. "Do you mean shoot the

other guy before he can point the gun at you, or completely avoid a dangerous encounter?"

"Yes," deadpanned Harper.

"Uhh." Logan gave a halfhearted chuckle. "I can't tell if you're serious or not."

"The seriousness of my statement depends on if they're wearing a blue sash or not." *And I don't know them from before.* She sighed. *That's how I'm going to die, isn't it? See someone I think I know and they show me how much they've changed.*

Harper spent the next hour or so mourning any sense of being able to trust people. Honestly, she couldn't claim to really *know* Steve Pratt. Sitting near him in class but never really talking to him did not make them friends. Most students in their group thought of him as the 'weird kid' who'd probably snap and start shooting people.

Seems they were right. If he hadn't been afraid of going to jail...

Two simultaneous daydreams—day nightmares—played out on the movie screen of her imagination. In one, pre-war Harper panicked and freaked out as Steve barged into the classroom and opened fire. In the other, she mysteriously had her shotgun with her and took him out before he could kill anyone. Rather than some manner of hero fantasy, the idea of it made her sad at how unlike her former self she'd become. She rolled her eyes at the ridiculousness of the scenario, then got pissed off all over again at whatever moron hit 'the button.'

A TOUCH OVER EIGHT HOURS AFTER LEAVING EVERGREEN, JORGE suggested they stop for the night by Snyder Creek.

Harper remembered taking Route 285 when they'd gone to Fairplay. Fortunately, they wouldn't need to return to the crazy town of Wild West re-enactors any time soon. They'd gone about a mile south from signs for Kenosha East Campground, veering off the highway at a bend where the road went from southerly to going west, close to the end of the hills. Past the curve up ahead, the terrain flattened out in a vast expanse of open ground.

Closer on the left, a D-shaped loop stuck out to the east side of the road. They rode past the end of the guardrail, heading down the tree-studded hill to the edge of a small creek. Harper didn't care how ungraceful it looked getting down from the horse; she adored the break from riding. The horses weren't the only ones in need of rest. She volunteered herself to build a fire and take care of warming up some of the canned beans, mostly to avoid having to deal with horses. Tegan and Jorge tended to the animals, removing the saddles and other gear, watering, feeding, and even brushing them.

The weather ended up being somewhat chilly but mild enough not to make anyone regret the lack of tents. They ate a basic dinner of beans and bread, then settled in for the night, running a standard hour-and-a-half-long watch rotation. Harper got the second shift, which completely sucked. Waking up after a mere ninety minutes of sleep and needing to stay alert while surrounded by near-total silence proved one of the most daunting tasks she'd attempted since the bombs. Cliff's old wind-up wristwatch she borrowed made the rounds again, inaccurate in regard to actual time, but good enough to measure shifts.

Mostly, she spent the time awake listening for signs of danger and worrying about her family. Every so often, she caught herself being more protective of Madison than the other kids… but her sister needed the extra attention. She'd kill or take a bullet for all three of them. Did it count as favoritism to indulge Madison's insecurities? Not like Lorelei had insecurities at all. Jonathan managed his fears quite well for a boy his age. Of course, Lorelei had no blood relatives left alive and hadn't really cared much about the one she used to have. Jonathan never had siblings before, and idiots who blamed Chinese people for the bombs murdered his parents. He, too, had no family left other than the one they'd made.

A handful of gunshots went off in the distance, way too far off to be of significant concern. Harper looked eastward in the direction the noise came from. *Bandits? Jorge said they shot randomly at places where people didn't give them food and stuff.* She frowned. The world had three kinds of people. Those who tried to survive by doing, those who tried to survive by taking, and batshit crazy people. The second and third types sometimes experienced overlap. Cliff's 'profound' statement on humanity also applied to before the war. The only real change amounted to the lack of organized law enforcement leading to a significant increase in the 'takers' compared to the doers.

She counted four rapid shots, then two more spaced thirty seconds apart, then a flurry of ten or so more. It sounded like a fireworks display going off in the next town. The pacing of the shots suggested an opening volley, then retaliation or engagement. If anyone screamed, she didn't notice due to how far off the shooting happened. Might not even be violence... could be morons shooting into the sky for kicks. She didn't really think anyone would be stupid enough to waste ammo like that. Even those who had no interest in killing people would keep bullets for defense.

Following the brief skirmish miles to the east, the night returned to almost oppressive silence.

An hour and thirty-three minutes after she groggily opened her eyes, Harper nudged Logan awake for his watch shift, then tried to go back to sleep.

A WEIRD DREAM OF MOM TAKING HARPER AND MADISON TO THE mall turned into a freakish episode part Tarantino movie, part LSD trip. She, her mother, and Madison tore the place up, shooting Lawless, zombies, and even mutant scorpions while Christmas music blared from the sound system overhead. For some unknown reason, Harper's brain gave Madison a pair of Uzi submachine guns that never seemed to run out of ammo and a pink wool hat with floppy rabbit ears. After the shooting spree, Mom took the girls to Starbucks.

She awoke to Logan tickling her side at the narrowest part of her waist. He'd discovered her 'weak spot' months ago... far more effective at waking her up than shaking her by the shoulder or patting her cheek. Too tired to squeal at him to stop, she merely squirmed and gave a halfhearted moan of annoyance. A few seconds later, the reality of lumpy ground seeped into her brain, reminding her of their present mission and lack of safety.

Yawning, Harper sat up.

"Morning." Logan stood, stretched, and yawned. "Ken wants to get moving quick. Figure we'll just eat bread on the way."

"Works for me." Harper got to her feet and stumbled off to a relatively private distance where she could empty her bladder. It shocked her how casual she'd become about going to the bathroom outside, especially while three guys happened to be fairly close. Completing the mission and getting home as fast as possible outweighed any bashfulness.

Before long, Tegan and Jorge had the horses loaded up and everyone resumed riding. Getting back in the saddle on day two hurt a bit thanks to soreness. However, she'd been up and down off the horse six or seven times yesterday for small breaks. *Practice makes perfect, as they say... or at least less clumsy.*

Jorge again took the lead, continuing to follow the highway. They rode for several hours over mostly empty road, every so often passing an abandoned car. Skeletons lay draped over the steering wheels of few of the more molten ones, which tended to be off the road. Harper leaned away from them, fearing the metal might be radioactive. The scorched cars had obviously been close enough to a blast to suffer heat damage, which meant they—and their drivers—likely absorbed a huge dose of radiation. She didn't think anything around here had been significant enough to attract a nuclear warhead... but obviously, one had to come down nearby. As high-tech as multi-warhead nuclear weapons were, it remained quite possible strays went places they hadn't been intended to hit. The cars couldn't have gotten too far after the EMP blast.

A little shy of an hour after they got underway, they passed a dirt road on the left leading to a gate made from a polished rough-cut tree log set atop two faux stonework columns. It had no fencing on either side, so appeared to be mostly decorative.

"We turn after water," said Jorge.

Not long after the gate, they reached a spot where a decent-sized creek passed under the highway. There, they stopped to let the horses drink, stretch their legs, and go to the bathroom.

Once past the creek, Jorge left the highway behind, heading generally south over the plains. It finally made sense to Harper why they'd taken horses and not the Postal truck.

"We are almost there," said Jorge with a thick accent. "Eighteen mile."

A few more destroyed cars as well as what appeared to be a former cellular phone tower stuck into the ground like a javelin confused Harper. "What the heck did they nuke around here? It's all open land."

"I don't know what you ask," said Jorge.

Logan gestured at the mangled cellphone tower. "¿Qué fue bombardeado por aquí?"

Jorge pointed to the left. "La ciudad que solía estar allí."

"He said 'the city that used to be there.'"

Harper, Ken, and Tegan stared in silence at seeming miles of open nothingness... scrub bushes and grass dotted with a handful of wild cows.

"Holy shit," whispered Harper. "There used to be a city there?"

Jorge laughed, waving in a 'not that bad' gesture. "Four, five miles away. Not close. No está completamente aplanado. Hay muchos escombros, probablemente también radiación."

"He says it's not flattened totally. Mostly rubble and radiation." Logan pointed to the left. "We should probably avoid going that way."

"Agreed." Ken chuckled. "I'm not looking to work on extreme suntanning."

"Did the sick girl go there?" asked Harper. "What's wrong with her?"

Jorge scrunched his eyebrows together.

Logan repeated her question in Spanish, then listened to a relatively long response. "He says she didn't go to the city. Just got sick. Sounds like a rash all over her body and her throat is swollen."

"What do you think she's got?" whispered Harper.

"That could be a few things…" Tegan exhaled. "Need to see her before jumping to any conclusions."

Logan and Jorge chatted in Spanish, seemingly having a routine conversation about nothing of particular importance. Harper fought the temptation to ask for translations. She had taken Spanish in high school, but only because she *had* to take a language and most kids chose Spanish. A few oddballs took French or German. If she ever had to ask how to get to the library or tell someone her age, she'd be set. The boys spoke way too fast for her to follow along. She picked up on the occasional word like 'years' or 'family' or 'house,' enough to assume Logan asked about the place they went to.

Around an hour after they left paved roads behind, they approached what appeared to be a trailer park, though not one from before the fall of civilization. Someone had gathered a bunch of house trailers, camping trailers, buses, and even a few semi-trailers into an arrangement like a model town. It didn't give off a 'lived in' feel, more like a paintball course. Perhaps in a manner similar to the guy who made the macabre scene of dancing skeletons, this place served as some manner of shrine to lost technology. More likely, some survivors tried to make a little town and either died off or abandoned it.

Each time the wind stirred up, metal doors flapped, shutters clattered, and bits of torn sheet metal rustled. The place seemed eerie enough to make her want to go around it instead of through it. For no particular reason, she reached down and pulled the Mossberg out of the saddle sheath.

Noticing this, Logan grabbed his AK-47. "What? You see something?"

"Bad feeling," whispered Harper. "This isn't a settlement. Almost looks like someone set this up as a paintball course. I don't think anyone's playing paintball these days."

"No." Ken readied his M4. "Best if we go cautiously."

"Not around it?" asked Harper.

"If there's a problem in there, better we have some cover than nothing." Ken gestured randomly at the open meadow. "I'd rather check it out and know for sure than get shot in the back."

"I should hop down and walk then." Harper shifted her weight to one side. "It would be way too awkward trying to shoot past her."

"Much appreciate not being a body shield," said Tegan.

"Let me sit in front then." Harper eyed the collection of trailers and buses, thinking about the gunfire they heard last night. This place could be far enough away from where they'd camped to be the site of whatever violence went on. Anxiety— and the hairs on the back of her neck—rose.

"If I'm going to hide behind someone..." Tegan chuckled. "They're going to be my age, preferably tall, dark, and handsome."

Harper flashed a nervous smile. "Not short, pale, and average?"

"You are way prettier than average," said Logan.

"Easy there, Romeo," whispered Ken. "Think I saw a shadow move."

Dammit. Harper swallowed saliva. Sitting on the horse any longer started to feel like asking for death. She wanted to be mobile, able to duck, run, or dive flat if need be.

"Flapping door?" asked Logan.

"Possible." Ken bent forward, rifle up. "Hope it is, but be ready in case it isn't."

As they approached the nearest trailers, Harper pulled her left leg up, then jumped off the side of the horse. She landed with a reasonable amount of grace insofar as she avoided eating dirt. Once she got her balance, she jogged to the front of their formation.

Partially from playing *Call of Duty*, partially from what Cliff taught her, Harper dashed forward and right, taking cover behind the corner of the closest house trailer. Her heart raced; sweaty hands made her grip on the shotgun slippery. She took two breaths, then came around the corner, aiming down the 'street' between trailers and two buses. Seeing nothing alarming, she broke cover and sprinted to the end of a tour bus ten feet further ahead on the left side, again flattening herself against the metal.

Am I being ridiculous or properly tactical? She swung around the corner, aiming down the street. Having cover on her left side made shooting much easier, being right-handed. A metal-on-metal scrape came from the trailer across the 'street' on her right. Harper shifted her gaze to a door easing itself open.

A man in a light brown jacket and bright orange baseball cap leaned out, pointing a bolt-action rifle in the direction of the rest of her group. Another guy peeked around the front of the same bus she'd sheltered behind, raising a pump style shotgun. At least two more people tried to run silently a few 'streets' away to either side, no doubt circling to get behind everyone.

Harper locked stares with the dude at the front end of the bus. His expression, body language, and stance made him seem quite intent on shooting. His weapon also happened to be one second further away from aimed than the guy in the doorway across the 'street.'

The man in the orange hat moved his finger onto the trigger. Harper pivoted to the right, firing a fraction of a second after the guy snapped off a shot toward her friends. A pattern of buckshot holes tore up the flimsy steel door. As the man collapsed into the trailer, she swung the Mossberg back and fired at the front end of the bus, hoping to throw buckshot at the other guy before he lit her up. Her shot shattered the lower part of the side mirror and flung a blast of feathers from a rip in a puffy green jacket. Only a pellet or two grazed the man; he must've started to duck the instant he'd spotted her, without making any attempt to shoot back.

She kept her weapon aimed at the spot, listening for footsteps in case he tried to run around the other side. A brief exchange of gunshots rang out from multiple directions, then fell silent. Moaning came from the trailer to her right. The man had fallen mostly out of sight except for one foot in the doorway.

"Two left," yelled Logan.

"One right," shouted Ken. "Got one."

"Stop!" yelled the man at the front of the bus. "Abort ambush."

"The fuck?" shouted another guy two trailer rows to the left. "You serious?"

"How stupid do you think we are?" yelled Ken.

"What he said," shouted Harper.

"Wait just one damn minute," called the guy behind the front end of the bus. "This don't gotta get worse."

Orange Hat Guy moaned. "I'm hit, Theo. Vest got some of it, but"—he gasped—"bleedin."

The horses nickered nervously. Tegan muttered soothing things to her steed. Harper didn't dare take her eyes off the gouge she'd blown into the front corner of the bus. Lack of scuffing in the distance indicated the two men trying to flank them had stopped moving, hopefully pinned down behind cover by Logan and Ken.

"Cody, right?" called Theo—bus front man—"Harper Cody?"

"What's it to you?" shouted Logan.

She chuckled to herself at the defensiveness in his voice.

"I kinda know her," yelled Theo. "Don't wanna shoot someone I know."

"Umm. Who the heck are you?" yelled Harper.

"Theo Fulton."

Harper sincerely tried to remember the name, but couldn't. "Uhh, sorry. Don't remember you."

"Heh. Course not. You probably didn't even notice me, kid." Theo laughed. "I remember you, though."

"Just a little bit creepy," called Ken.

Harper gripped the Mossberg tighter. *Yeah, a little.*

"Not like it sounds. We shot together in a competition, think it was 2015. You were like fourteen or something. Smoked us all. Craziest shit I'd ever seen. I came in third," yelled Theo.

"Hah!" yelled a man on the right. "You're scared of that kid."

Theo sighed. "Look... She's got a semiauto. I got a pump. I'm not really liking our odds here. This kid's no joke. And her friends have AKs. We're outgunned. And, really, I kinda know her."

A faint memory gave Harper an image of a slightly overweight guy in a green 'Fulton Contracting' shirt and white ball cap gawking at her. She'd found his reaction to her win amusing at the time. Watching guys in their thirties and up stare open-mouthed at the young teenage girl they all thought to be a mascot, or simply the daughter of some adult shooter end up storming the competition course never got old.

"Fulton Contracting," said Harper.

"Hey... you *do* remember me."

Harper started to feel a little sick in the stomach. How had the guy known to exploit her weakness? She no longer hesitated when needed, but killing someone she recognized remained difficult. Even watching someone else kill the Starbucks barista had been rough, especially since she probably could have talked him into surrendering.

"Kinda," she rasped. "How the heck did you turn into a road bandit?"

"Ehh, you know," said Theo in a remarkably casual tone. "Been having trouble getting renovation jobs lately. No one's putting any money into their property."

"Is this guy serious?" whispered Ken.

He just tried to ambush and kill us, and he's cracking jokes?

"Let's call this a misunderstanding and go our separate ways," called Theo.

"You ambushed us," yelled Logan. "You were going to kill us for our stuff. Now you wanna walk away like nothing happened?"

"That would be my preference, yeah," said Theo. "Shit happens. It's a rough world. Sorry. Irwin's hit. None of you are hurt."

Irwin—Orange Hat Guy—moaned.

"Ike's dead," yelled a man a distance to the right. "Shot him right through the damn wall. Vest didn't stop it."

"That's an AK," yelled Theo.

"M4," said Ken. "Still got some green tips. Humor me. How do we know you won't shoot us in the back if we agree to walk away like nothing happened?"

"I can't kill anyone I know, and I kinda know Miss Cody there."

"Mr. Fulton…" Harper lowered her weapon a little, but not so much she couldn't blow his head off if he stuck it out into view. "Have you killed anyone doing this shit?"

"Only if they shot at me."

She frowned. "Your guys opened fire on us first. People tend to shoot back when they're attacked. It's not self-defense if you kill someone you tried to rob for firing back at you."

A long, uncomfortable silence hung over the weird little 'city' of trailers and buses.

Irwin groaned. "Can y'all make up yer damn minds already? Think my rib's broke."

"Guys," yelled Theo. "I'm sure no one here wants to get shot. World's gone to crap. Just doing what we gotta do to survive."

"Doing what you gotta do to survive is stuff like farming… not mugging people." Harper grumbled.

"You gonna hunt us down then, kiddo?"

She exhaled out her nose. "Only if you shoot at us."

Theo stuck his shotgun out into view, pointed up. "Gonna step out. Appreciate ya not blowing my face off." A second later, he sidestepped out into view, hands up. Other than no longer being even close to chubby, he looked more or less the same. "How's your dad doing?"

Harper narrowed her eyes. "He died when a gang broke into our house."

"Ack." Theo cringed. "Sorry. Didn't know. Geez, that sucks. Guys. Serious. Come on out. Not gonna do anything here."

"Theo?" moaned Irwin.

"Yeah?"

"Eat a dick."

Theo glanced to his left. "What?"

"I can't fuckin' move right now, dammit!" yelled Irwin, before moaning again.

Harper flicked the tip of her Mossberg up, indicating the bus window. "Toss the Remington inside."

"Yeah. Sure. No problem. Only thing I want now is everyone walks away alive. Gonna flick the safety on." Keeping the shotgun pointed straight up, Theo pushed the safety, then tossed the weapon into the blown-out bus window.

"You guys should go do something productive and stop

robbing people." Harper backed away from the bus, not quite aiming at Theo.

Logan and Ken still had their weapons pointed to either side, covering the positions where Theo's people likely hid. After a few tense silent minutes, three other men walked into view, not carrying weapons.

Theo removed his ball cap and re-seated it on his head. "We don't actually run around doing this sort of thing all the time. Just happened to be here. Hard to tell who's a threat and who isn't."

"Yeah, no shit," muttered Ken.

"Do you or don't you rob people?" asked Logan.

"Generally not…" Theo shrugged. "We only take stuff from people who attack us. But, you know… sometimes waiting long enough to tell what someone's intentions are is a good way to end up dead."

"Riiight." Ken grumbled.

"Are these the guys harassing the people who live around here?" asked Harper.

"Huh what?" Theo blinked. "We haven't been in the area but a day or so. Kinda keep moving, you know."

Logan whispered in Spanish.

"No lo creo," replied Jorge. "No, he visto a estos tipos antes."

"Probably not the same people." Logan briefly looked at Ken. "You okay?"

"Yeah, just a graze."

Harper didn't really like the idea of trying to walk away from these guys, but it appealed more than executing them. If Jorge seemed sure these men didn't belong to the group of bandits attacking the ranch where he lived, perhaps the situation really had been no more complex than two groups of survivors being overly cautious and assuming the worst of the other. Theo and his friend didn't feel totally innocent, though. After all, he told his friends to 'abort ambush,' which suggested they had intended to attack. It seemed as soon as Theo recognized Ken and Logan had weapons powerful enough to render body armor useless—and Harper could easily hit people in the face to bypass the armor—they lost all interest in trying to take their stuff. Irwin, the guy in the orange hat, definitely fired first, proving the men had bad intentions. It might've only been a fraction of a second first, but still. Harper didn't have to feel responsible for starting an unnecessary gunfight. She'd only tried to stop an unknown person from killing a friend.

Despite the iffy circumstances, Harper didn't see anything about Theo that led her to expect a trick. The man really did seem mildly afraid of her, or perhaps still thought of her as a child he didn't want to hurt. Normally, someone treating her like a kid would be annoying... but if it kept people from dying, she wouldn't complain.

She backpedaled to the group of horses, still outside the area of the 'trailer park.' Trusting Logan and Ken to cover the guys, she looked away from Theo long enough to climb up behind Tegan.

"Okay. Guess we're going to do this and try to be peaceful." Ken guided his horse to the left, following Tegan. "Don't do anything stupid. I'm better at hitting medium-to-long range targets than close."

Theo waved at Harper.

She, Ken, and Logan kept watching the men while riding away. Jorge didn't appear too frazzled by the gunfire. The man carried a pistol, though she didn't think he'd fired it. Over the next few minutes, they rode steadily south over the uneven ground, no one speaking or making much sound until they'd gone far enough away from the cluster of trailers for a surprise attack to seem unlikely.

"Think they're going to follow us?" asked Logan.

"It's possible." Ken glanced back at them. "I liked thinking of them as bandits more than what probably happened."

"Huh?" Logan raised an eyebrow at him.

"The guy in the hat tried to shoot me." Ken frowned. "Why do you think he'd decide to open fire on *me* before anyone tried to talk?"

Logan shrugged. "Because you look like a badass cop? Probably thought I'm a kid, and they didn't want to kill the women."

"Thanks." Ken chuckled. "But I don't buy it. That idiot blamed me for the 'Chinese nukes'."

"Oh. Think so?" Logan whistled. "I think they just wanted to kill us and take our stuff… and women."

Harper shifted her jaw side to side. "Didn't really get that vibe from them. Don't think they'd have kidnapped us. More like they'd try not to shoot us if they could, then take all our weapons, food, and ammo."

"Whatever they wanted to do, it doesn't matter now." Logan stuffed the AK back in the saddle sheath. "On the way home, let's avoid that place."

"Yeah." Harper slid the Mossberg into the holder as well. It wouldn't work at this range, anyway.

Ken glanced over at her. "I'm surprised you didn't suggest he go to Evergreen. A contractor could come in handy."

"Don't really trust him." Harper smirked. "Besides, he's not that good of a shot. Came in fifth."

26

THE OVERTON RANCH

K en and Logan appeared to relax once distance reduced the collection of old trailers and buses to a whitish discoloration on the land.

They paused for a break to allow Tegan to check on Ken. The bullet grazed along the left side of his head above the ear, leaving a shallow but bloody cut. Had Irwin aimed a few millimeters to the left, Ken would've been dead. His shot missing to the right could've been due to him flinching away from Harper the instant before he pulled the trigger. It just as likely could have been due to a misaligned scope, nerves, or simply Irwin being a lousy shot at ranges much closer than normal for a bolt-action hunting rifle.

She chalked it up to luck and mentally took no credit for saving Ken's life beyond preventing a second shot once Irwin realized he'd missed.

"So, you knew the guy?" asked Ken, while Tegan dabbed at his head.

"You ever play a sport in like high school or something where you traveled to other cities to compete against their schools?" Harper randomly walked around to give her legs and backside a break from sitting on a horse.

Ken nodded.

"Same thing. Would you remember one of the players from another team you went up against four years ago?"

"Not really." Ken laughed. "But if a little kid managed to steamroll me on the lacrosse field, I'd definitely remember her."

Harper rolled her eyes. "I wasn't *that* little. Fourteen isn't a 'little kid.'"

"Compared to a bunch of thirty-year-old dudes?" Ken grimaced in pain at Tegan pressing an alcohol-soaked pad to his head.

"Not only a young teenager, a girl, too." Logan walked over to stand next to her. "Bet half those guys couldn't believe you knew which end of a gun to point at the target, much less out-shoot them."

"Most of them assumed my dad was the competitor and I just tagged along." She laughed, rolling her eyes. "Once they realized *I'm* the one competing, they were shocked... but cool about it. Guys at the range never gave me a hard time, but you wouldn't believe some of the nasty crap people wrote in emails to my YouTube account. The way some of them ranted at us, my Dad teaching me to shoot was worse than if he'd pimped me out."

Ken grumbled. "What's wrong with people?"

"If we could answer that," said Tegan, "we'd all probably still be comfortable at home going on about our normal lives."

"Right?" Logan gazed up at the sky. "At least it's a nice day. Less hazy than it's been... or am I imagining that?"

Harper shielded her eyes and peered at the clouds. "Can't tell. I like your optimism though, so I'll say it looks clearer."

"We have blue sky again before the Starbucks." Jorge grinned.

"That guy had to have watched your videos." Logan nudged her. "You still have a fan left."

"Ugh." She chuckled. "My luck. Out of a couple hundred people, one of them *has* to end up about to shoot me."

"That's it? Only a couple hundred?" Ken whistled.

Harper blushed. "Okay, it was a bit more than that. First vid where I was only like two weeks into being thirteen got a couple million views. Wasn't even a competition. Just me running the stations."

"Wow… a couple million?" Logan whistled. "Damn."

She sighed. "Oddity factor. People couldn't get enough of seeing a 'little girl' act like a commando. Gun nuts thought I was adorable and awesome. Normal people were just sorta shock-curious, and the wingnuts who believe guns are the greatest evil in the world freaked the hell out."

"Right." Ken took a deep breath as Tegan finished up. "Thanks, doc."

"You're welcome." She winked. "Really dodged a bullet there."

Logan and Harper chuckled.

Ken groaned. "Not really. It missed. I didn't move."

"Think he's like a stalker or something?" whispered Logan.

"Nah. Didn't get that feel from him." She blush-frowned. "I think I remember him telling my Dad how I made him feel like a complete failure or something."

"Failure?" Logan tilted his head.

"Yeah, like the old guy who's decent at playing piano, then he sees some six-year-old shredding Beethoven like it's no big deal?"

Ken stood. "That's called jealousy."

She headed back to the horse. "Whatever it was, he didn't creep me out. Kinda embarrassed me more than anything, like he made a super big deal out of something I didn't think was special. Not like I popped out of the womb with a shotgun. I might've only been fourteen, but I had five years of basically training and practice."

"Okay." Ken held a hand out at her. "A guy who starts teaching his nine-year-old daughter how to shoot probably counts as a gun nut."

Harper laughed. "Some people sure thought so. He wasn't. Dad's whole world didn't revolve around guns. He loved sport shooting the way some guys love football or hockey. It wasn't about being macho or a survivalist or collecting as many giant toys that go boom as he could fit in his garage. We used to think of guns as sporting equipment. And yeah, he liked hunting, too."

"Wow." Logan coughed. "I'm sure Maddie *loved* that."

"Yep." Harper climbed up on the horse behind Tegan. "She's the reason he gave up hunting. Kinda ironic our new dad is one of the primary hunters for Evergreen."

"How does she handle it?" asked Tegan.

"I think she really understands the difference between people in the world before hunting just for fun... and people now *needing* to hunt so we can eat. It doesn't thrill her, but she's coping."

Harper sighed past a sad smile. "You just described us all. Not thrilled, but coping."

A LITTLE OVER AN HOUR LATER, THEY REACHED THE EDGE OF A VAST fenced-in field.

At the center sat a huge one-story house, barn, and two smaller buildings of plain white wood. Behind the house, roughly a third of the property consisted of farm in the process of being planted. Opposite the crops, another fence surrounded a herd of cows as well as some pigs. This early in the season, she couldn't tell what they'd planted yet. Open ground continued for miles in all directions around the ranch. From her position atop the horse, she spotted at least three other ranches in the distance, the nearest one likely five or six miles off.

"Home," said Jorge, a note of hopeful excitement in his voice.

The group sped up to a fast canter, racing over a long stretch of downhill to a dirt road leading into the ranch. Several horse trailers stood in a row by the front of the house, along with a few pickup trucks. None of them appeared to have moved in quite some time, even the white truck which looked like someone bought it mere months before the nuclear war.

At least they don't have to make payments anymore.

Two men appeared in the house windows holding rifles, though didn't yet point them at anyone.

Jorge waved and called out in greeting. At that, the men darted away from the windows. Seconds later, the front door opened. Two fortyish guys, a man in his early thirties, and a woman around Carrie's age hurried outside. All wore handguns on their hips. The older white guy also carried a rifle, likely a .30-06. They more or less looked much the same as Harper imagined ranchers might look before the war... except for no one having a cell phone clipped to their belt.

"Well, how about that," said the guy with the rifle. "You found people."

"A doctor." Jorge gestured at Tegan.

The other fortysomething guy exclaimed something in Spanish before blurting, "Thank God" in English. "Rebecca, my daughter, is not well."

Harper got down from the horse. Without thinking too much about it, she grabbed the Mossberg from the saddle sheath and slung it over her shoulder on its strap. The ranchers didn't react much other than wary observation. Ken and Logan both shouldered their rifles after dismounting as well.

Jorge introduced everyone. Carl Overton, the guy with the rifle, looked like a stereotypical 'older cowboy,' at least to her. Everyone past twenty-five seemed old. The woman, Lena Bennet, reminded Harper of her sophomore year chemistry teacher, at least in terms of looks. Ms. Bailey had a Jamaican father and British mother. The woman could switch back and forth from both extreme accents or speak without any, a trick she used often to keep class interesting.

I hope she's okay... wherever she is.

Manuel Vargas approached Tegan with an almost reverential

demeanor, as if the Pope himself had come to visit. It made Harper feel as if they really had gone back to the Old West, a time when legitimate doctors commanded awe as if literal wizards.

Loose chickens roaming around the front yard wandered over to investigate newcomers.

The younger man, Drew Bullock, regarded Tegan in a decidedly different manner. Harper almost laughed at his cartoony starstruck expression, as if he witnessed a literal angel manifest in the real world. It seemed unlikely they'd manage to return to Evergreen before the guy asked Dr. Hale on a date.

"Welcome, all." Carl stepped over to shake hands with Ken, then Logan before tipping his hat to Tegan and Harper. "Wasn't real sure what we heard would be true. Been quite a while since anyone came by talking about a survivor town up in the hills. Appreciate you coming out here to help."

Tegan nodded. "Happy to offer whatever assistance I can. Where is Rebecca?"

"Inside." Lena waved for her to follow, then headed to the door.

Jorge and Drew escorted the horses around to the barn. Harper followed the group into a huge living room with natural wood finish walls liberally decorated with animal heads. A giant stonework fireplace took up about a third of the interior wall. From the look of it, the people who lived here used it frequently for cooking as well as heating. It occurred to her she hadn't seen any electrical lines outside nor solar panels on the roof. No sooner did she realize they had no power, she began noticing oil lamps, candles, and other signs of 'frontier life.' Having ridden here on horses added to the sense of going back in time.

Three children raced into the room from a hallway on the left. A girl a touch older than Madison with light brown hair clung to the back of a recliner chair, half hiding behind it while staring hopefully at everyone. Her plain white dress and lack of shoes totally fit the 1800s vibe saturating everything. A slightly younger boy who resembled the girl enough to be an obvious sibling rushed right up to everyone without fear, fascinated by the weapons. His football jersey, jeans, and beat-to-hell sneakers firmly placed him in the modern era. The smallest kid, a blond boy about eight or nine ran around in circles. He, too, appeared to be out of the past, shirtless, barefoot, in denim overalls a little too big for him.

Tegan followed Lena and Manuel down a different corridor leading to the right from the massive living room. Carl invited the two older kids over, introducing them as his daughter and son, Lilly and Billy. Harper snickered at the rhyming names before she could catch herself. Both kids rolled their eyes at her.

"They did that on purpose," muttered Billy.

"Dad's not the most creative." Lilly laughed. "Our older brother is Carl Jr."

"Like the fast food burger chain?" asked Logan.

Carl Overton Sr. threw his head back and cackled at the dumbfounded looks on the kids. "Wow. You're the first one to catch that."

Lilly stared at her father. "You named CJ as a joke on purpose?"

"I sure did." Carl chuckled, then his expression turned sad. "Your mom would'a kicked my ass if she figured it out."

The kids looked down.

"Don't worry." Billy shrugged. "CJ might still boot your butt when he finds out you named him after a burger place."

Carl ruffled the boy's hair. "I didn't name him after the restaurant. I named him after me… just ended up being a bit of a pun."

A pretty Hispanic woman breezed in from a third hallway near the fireplace, carrying a water jug and glasses. She looked mid-twenties, with long straight hair and a permanently worried expression. Harper got the weird idea the woman used to be contagiously happy all the time, but the past year since the war had done a little damage to her optimism. She greeted everyone, introducing herself as Jen while handing out water.

"Please… make yourselves comfortable." Carl gestured at the sofa and various chairs. "You'll of course be joining us for dinner and spending the night. Don't expect you to head right back out. Can arrange ya among the empty beds we've got if you want… or shuffle around a bit so you're all in the same room. Whatever ya prefer."

"Thanks." Ken scratched the unbandaged side of his head. "Don't want to be too much of a hassle."

"We'll figure it out." Carl smiled, then went with Lena and Jen to the kitchen.

Harper took a seat on the sofa. Lilly flopped beside her, seemingly the most comfortable around another girl somewhat close in age. She didn't come off as being afraid of Logan or Ken, merely uneasy around new people. Perhaps due to nervousness, the girl began asking Harper all sorts of questions about where they came from, what she'd seen, and life in general.

Harper learned the Overtons lived on this ranch for years, Carl Sr. having grown up here. Her mother had been in Denver at the time of the nuclear strike, in the hospital battling lung cancer. Doctors gave her about a sixty percent chance of recovery. Lilly's father, along with Drew and Manuel, tried to go get her the day of the strike. Being all the way out here in the middle of nowhere, their truck avoided the EMP wave. Unfortunately, Denver had been in such chaos, they got bogged down in crowds of people trying to climb onto the truck in hopes of a ride to safety.

Alas, when they finally made it close enough to see Denver reduced to a smashed mountain of concrete, steel, and glass, Manuel and Drew had to practically force Carl away. They'd likely gotten close enough to ground zero to have absorbed radiation, but thus far hadn't shown any signs of illness from it. By their reckoning, they'd spent less than twenty minutes near the Denver Ground Zero. Tegan's subtle cringe said they'd likely experience problems someday. Lilly confessed her worry about her father getting sick from the radiation and spoke of having nightmares he'd die of cancer.

Stunned at the girl opening up with such personal, painful memories, Harper reflexively shared what happened to her parents. Fortunately, their conversation took a less somber note when Lilly distracted herself by talking about the ranch. Drew and Manuel used to work as hired hands. Lena Bennet, Jen Carrillo, and Chase Holland—the boy in overalls—all found their way to the ranch in the months after the war. A few other former employees had been here on the day of the strike as well. Everyone had become more or less part of a new giant family.

Lilly continually circled back to talking about how scared she was for Manuel's daughter, Rebecca. Despite the girl being three years older than her, they'd become best friends. Lilly hadn't seen or heard from any school friends since the bombs. She occasionally went to visit kids from nearby ranches, but none of them really liked hiking several miles each way, so it didn't happen too often. The last time she'd gone to visit her friend Sage about four months ago, the girl's parents sent her away, saying her friend had become too sick to get out of bed. Lilly suspected Sage might've died since her Mother couldn't talk about her without crying.

Chase appeared to be a boy version of Lorelei, being that he had seemingly limitless energy, zero fear of strangers, and a perpetually happy mood. He hovered around Ken and Logan, asking them about guns and shooting stuff. Ken's blue police-style jumpsuit and vest made the boy mistake him for a soldier.

Billy drifted back and forth from helping in the kitchen to sitting around in the living room observing the conversation without adding much to it.

A little over a half-hour after Tegan disappeared, she re-emerged from the hallway. Manuel appeared to be crying, but also smiling.

Everyone stopped talking at once to stare at the doctor.

"Is she gonna die?" asked Billy.

Lilly squeaked.

"No. At least, she shouldn't." Tegan went to wipe her forehead, but stopped herself. "Rebecca is sick with mononucleosis, likely infectious. She should be okay in a week or two. However, it is important to avoid contact with bodily fluids, especially saliva. Any forks, spoons, or glasses she uses need to be boiled. Same goes for her clothing and bedding. Bleach is good if you have any left. Handle any bedpans or waste with extreme care."

Manuel nodded.

"Umm..." Lilly shivered. "Am I gonna get sick too?"

"How much contact have you had with her?" asked Tegan.

"Just holding her hand or wiping sweat off her face." Lilly bit her lip.

"One moment." Tegan went to wash her hands. When she returned, she approached and looked Lilly over for a few minutes, mostly peering into her open mouth and checking around her neck. "Seems like you're in the clear. Manuel said his daughter has been symptomatic for over a week. If you aren't feeling sick by now, you're good. Just... wash your hands."

Lilly nodded.

Mono... Harper knew a kid or two from her school who got it. They missed like two weeks of class but came back just fine. On one hand, it felt like a giant waste of time to come all the way out here only for Tegan to say the girl would recover without needing anything done. However, better that than bad news or not visiting if the girl had something the doctor needed to act on. Also, they had given her father—and everyone else here—relief from worrying. Seeing the girl with a swollen throat and rashes all over her body had to be terrifying for anyone who didn't know much about diseases, especially for her father.

Perhaps overly cautious, Harper decided not to go anywhere near the hallway leading to Rebecca's bedroom. Dad used to say 'no good deed went unpunished,' so she didn't want to accidentally bring mono back to Evergreen and make the kids there sick.

They spent the rest of the afternoon socializing and talking about random things from farming to Tegan checking on a few minor health issues. Chase decided Ken and Logan absolutely *needed* to see every one of his toys, mostly robots or action figures he'd basically inherited from sixteen-year-old Carl Jr. and Billy.

Harper found the gathering about as awkward as going to a wedding or funeral for a tangential relative she didn't really know. Despite being eighteen and serving on the Militia, having killed people, the everyday tone of conversation made her feel like a kid. She also felt too old to interact primarily with the kids here, ending up in an uncomfortable non-space between child and adult. Too mature to play with Chase and his toys, too young and geeky to give a crap about the theoretical sports talk circulating among the men.

She ended up sitting beside Logan, unable to really talk to him about the things she wanted to talk to him about thanks to Lilly being right there. The girl jumped at the chance to have another female somewhat close in age around, and chattered away. She alternated between seeming happy and worried, as if she pestered Harper too much and would make her angry. Something appeared to be lurking behind the rapid topic shifts and trivial stuff she continued babbling about. Since it appeared highly unlikely she and Logan could distance themselves from the room of unfamiliar people, Harper asked Lilly to show her the bathroom as a cover for going off somewhere quiet.

The girl led her down the hall, and around a corner into another hall that led to a small rear foyer full of coats, boots, and boxes of stuff on shelves. They went out the back door and crossed sixty some odd feet of ground to a small wooden shack.

"Wow, an outhouse?" asked Harper.

"Yeah. The septic tank's been full a while. Can't use the house toilets no more," said Lilly. "If you have to do the, umm, other thing, there's a box of corn cobs."

Harper squirmed. "Corn cobs…"

"Yep. We ran outta toilet paper, too. It was weird at first with the cobs, but you get used to it. Use the cob to get most of it, then there's rags in the bucket for the last part. Don't use the rags first on account of we wash and reuse 'em."

Ugh. Holy cow. I really hope we never have to deal with that. "Wow, umm. So… Lilly?"

"Hmm?" The girl looked up from the ground, making eye contact.

"I kinda got the feeling you've been wanting to say something but haven't been able to say it in front of everyone." Harper raised her arms a little to each side and let them flap down. "What's up?"

Lilly ground her big toe into the dirt. "Oh, it's nothing important. Sorry for talking your ears off. Just… Rebecca's been so sick. Haven't had anyone to really talk to for a while. You, umm… mentioned you lost your parents?"

"Yeah." Harper leaned against the outhouse, folding her arms. "Two months after the bombs."

"I never got to say goodbye to my mom." Lilly looked down. "She was in the hospital since May. Visited her a couple times a week. Dad got busy with stuff, so we missed two visits. We were supposed to go into Denver that Saturday to spend the whole day there… but, Friday…"

Harper closed her eyes. "I'm sorry."

"Not your fault. Thanks, though." Lilly bit her lip. "How did you deal with losing your mom? I mean… mine was dying for months, and I guess I kinda expected to lose her. Just wasn't ready for it when it happened."

"I..." Harper sank to sit on the ground by the outhouse. "Nothing seemed real. We hid out in our basement after the bombs fell. I don't know that I really processed what happened or understood exactly how much danger we were in. Not until the Lawless kicked in our door and started ransacking the house. They didn't know we were in the basement. Or maybe they saw Dad going out to grab canned food and stuff and followed him. I'll never know. It's all kind of a blur now. Really didn't have any chance to say goodbye to my parents either. Couldn't even tell them I loved them. I had to run so fast to keep my sister safe."

"Oh, wow. I'm sorry." Lilly sat next to her. "This is kinda weird to talk about this stuff with someone I just met. Sorry."

"It's all right." Harper stared off at a line of billowy white clouds on the eastern horizon. *I've had a bunch of practice at this with Maddie.*

"I guess... I dunno. You're just easier to talk to than Lena or Jen." Lilly chuckled. "Maybe 'cause I don't know you and you'll go home and never be back. Maybe 'cause you're kind of a kid, too."

"It's weird. I don't feel like an adult *or* a kid." Harper plucked a strand of grass, twirling it between her fingers.

Lilly twirled a sprig of green between her fingers, silent in thought for a moment. "My friend, Sage... her parents keep saying she's sick and won't let me see her. If she died, why wouldn't they just tell me?"

"Maybe she really is sick?"

"For this long?" Lilly scrunched up her nose. "It doesn't feel right. They're sad like she's dead but won't say it."

Harper let a long sigh slide out of her throat. "Could be, they can't say the words. Too painful."

"I dunno." Lilly tossed the bit of grass aside. "It's not fair. They should tell me. I been walking over there couple times now and they keep sending me home. It's like two hours one way on foot."

A brown chicken wandered over to say hi, nosing around her boots.

"You ever have to shoot someone?" asked Lilly.

"Yeah. Not so much these past few months." She tossed the bit of grass aside. "Before that, had to shoot some people."

"What is it like?"

Worried, Harper looked over to stare into the twelve-year-old's eyes. The kid gave off mostly fear, not bloodlust. *Whew...* "Umm... it really wasn't easy the first time. My dad died because I couldn't kill a guy. Another one tried to grab my sister and... stuff happened."

"Stuff?"

"Buckshot. To the face." Harper cringed. "It's not really something I think about much more than trying to avoid as much as I can. When it happens, it's like being in a video game. The bad guys stop being people and turn into random enemies. If they force me into a situation where it's a choice between shooting a guy and something horrible happening to me or someone I care about, sucks to be them."

"Oh." Lilly nodded. "I wish you could shoot the sads."

"The sads?" Harper blinked.

"I have them all the time. I miss my mom, and my friend." Lilly bowed her head. "Sometimes, I have nightmares about her in the hospital, stuck in her bed watching a nuclear bomb go off out her window and she can't get away from it. I feel like I did something wrong 'cause I didn't see her for a week."

Harper let out a silent sigh. "You could have stolen a truck and driven yourself to Denver."

"Don't be silly. I was only eleven then. Can't drive."

"Walk it?"

Lilly huffed. "You know it's too far to walk. I'd have gotten hit by a car."

"Is there anything reasonable you could have done to get to

Denver that week that you didn't do because you wanted to do something else?" asked Harper.

"No." Lilly plucked another bit of grass and fidgeted with it. "You're right. I shouldn't be upset. It just sucks. No one's fault."

"Oh, it's definitely *someone's* fault. Just not yours." Harper scowled at the distant field. "Whatever idiot hit the button."

"Yeah…"

Harper sat there talking with Lilly, oddly grateful to be away from the room full of people. Despite the grim, sad nature of their conversation, she preferred it to feeling like an outsider in a crowd of strangers. Somehow, Ken fit into their conversation easily, as if he'd known the ranch people for years. Logan, too, could keep up with the sports talk even if they debated and guessed which teams would have made it to playoffs that never happened rather than discussed actual events.

Talking to this girl gave Harper the sense she'd helped out in some small way. Lilly had been holding in her feelings of pointless guilt over not being able to see her mom for a week prior to the day she almost certainly died. She couldn't talk to her father about it because he, too, blamed himself for the death. As if he should somehow have known the missiles were on the way and raced to Denver to get her out of the hospital before everything exploded.

Lilly might not have been on the verge of doing anything drastic, but helping someone cope with undeserved guilt made Harper feel a deep, ephemeral sense of satisfaction. Probably the same way Tegan did when she did 'psychology' on people and helped them.

Their conversation drifted to less serious subjects like music and boyfriends and movies… a fairly typical sort of rambling ten-topics-a-minute discussion for teenage (or almost teenage) girls meeting for the first time. Harper let go a little, falling into a headspace like she'd gone back to being fifteen. A six-year age difference might not seem like much to Cliff or Ken, but to

Harper, it still made the difference between 'child' and not. At twelve, Lilly felt like a child to her and tugged at the same sort of need she had to protect Madison, even if the protection in this case purely took the form of being there to listen and talk.

When the back door opened, Harper gasped, momentarily worried they'd been giggling too loud.

Jen Carrillo leaned out the door. "C'mon, you two. Dinner's ready."

"Be right there..." Harper pointed a thumb back over her shoulder at the outhouse. "Need to use the facilities." *Thankfully, not with a corn cob.*

DINNER AT A TABLE WITH SEVENTEEN PEOPLE RANKED IN HARPER'S top ten unusual experiences.

Along with the Evergreen Four, Carl Overton, his three kids, Lena, Jorge, Drew, Manuel, Chase, Jen, three additional former hired hands, Clayton, Will, and Julio, joined them. The food shocked Harper in its normality: baked ham, mashed potatoes, green beans, and bread. This place might have lacked electricity and toilet paper, but they appeared to have the food situation quite well managed.

Lilly took a plate to the bedroom for Rebecca, who lacked the urge to get out of bed. Over the meal, Tegan repeated her opinion that the teen would almost certainly recover with rest and adequate fluid intake.

After dinner, Carl Jr. Lilly, Billy, and Chase scrambled to get started on the dishes. The nine-year-old hadn't been asked to, but appeared insistent on helping out. Lena showed Ken and Logan to the boy's bedroom, which contained a pair of bunk beds. Billy cleared a bunch of toys off the unused lower mattress on the right. Chase would share a bed with Billy for the night, giving Ken and Logan a spot to themselves. Next, Lena took Tegan and

Harper deeper into the same hallway, pointing them at a small room with two normal beds. Relieved to learn she wouldn't get sick from simple proximity, Lilly wanted to sleep in her usual bedroom again, the one she shared with Rebecca.

As awesome as it was to be *full* for once, Harper couldn't wait to go home.

It didn't take long for the house to go from dim to dark after dinner. Like people from the old days, bedtime coincided with the lack of daylight. The ranchers tried to avoid using up lamp oil unless necessary.

Harper looked around the tiny bedroom, then at Tegan. *I'd say this is awkward, but she's seen me in way less than underwear already. Kinda hard to have a gyno exam with pants on.* Acting casual, she undressed to her tank top and panties. It struck her as weird to go to bed with underpants on. Cliff said something to Jonathan months and months ago about not sleeping in the same pants he wore all day, bacteria or some such thing. Harper figured it wouldn't be exclusively a male issue, so from that point onward, she decided to let her body 'get some air' at night. Not like she owned enough underwear to wear a clean pair every day. Undies had been the first garments to reach the 'oh hell no' pile during the winter. Still, being in a stranger's house, she didn't feel anywhere near comfortable enough to let her guard down so far. One night would not an infection create.

She didn't pay any attention to what Tegan decided to sleep in, not that she could've seen much anyway given the dark. Working by feel, she left her jeans, socks, flannel shirt, and boots in a relatively tidy pile beside the bed, then leaned the Mossberg on the wall near the headboard and crawled under the blankets.

… and proceeded to stare at the ceiling.

The country had been quiet at night, even before aircraft stopped working.

In the stillness of the moonlit bedroom, Harper became aware of every tiny little sound: her breathing, Tegan's breathing, Jen breathing on the other side of the wall to her right. Billy and Chase tried to get the last word in saying goodnight to each other back and forth. Carl Sr. and Lena, apparently a couple, slept together in the master bedroom. Like a pair of tweens on sleepover, the two adults seemed to like staying up late and talking in the dark.

Better than having to listen to them doing it.

Her mind drifted to the topic of bandits. Jorge mentioned they might run into trouble here, but gave little detail about the extent of the problem. No one here said a thing about any sort of problem. Barring the lack of electricity—and the shootout with Theo—the trip felt like they'd gone to visit relatives she didn't know well who lived a long way off, as in completely normal. She couldn't remember the last time she had such a filling meal. Evergreen's farm hadn't quite 'hit its stride' so to speak. They didn't have pigs for ham, nor did they use the handful of cows for beef. The idea of there being multiple ranches down here all capable of producing adequate food opened the possibility of trade at some future point. Evergreen didn't presently have much worth exporting beyond the clothing Renee and her team made. She couldn't really think of anything Evergreen produced sustainably that the ranchers would want. At least they hadn't run out of toilet paper yet. The ranchers might trade for some, but Evergreen couldn't make any more, so they'd never want to give it away.

Harper squirmed, cringing at the thought they certainly would run out at some point. Probably this year. Everyone had to be worried about the subject, but no one spoke about it. Cliff's suggestion of bending over in the back yard while someone else sprayed her down with the garden hose—something he called a 'hillbilly bidet'—originally sounded like a purposefully embarrassing joke... but the potential reality of it once the TP ran out made her seriously uncomfortable.

I'd sooner take a cold bath every time I had to go rather than figure out what the heck to do with a freakin' corn cob.

The scuff of boots on dirt went by the window outside, reminding her of the bandit problem. Harper tensed, listening to the repetitive, even pace of a man walking. It sounded more like someone on sentry duty rather than attempting to sneak in. Still, anxiety won out. She slipped out of bed to the window. A man in a cowboy hat carrying a rifle went by outside, close to the house. He definitely appeared to be patrolling on night watch. She couldn't recognize him in the dark by face, but he seemed young… so it had to be either Julio, who looked about nineteen or twenty, Jorge, or maybe Will.

Anxiety settled, she crawled back into bed.

"What's wrong?" whispered Tegan.

"Heard someone go by outside." Harper exhaled. "Thought it might be bandits."

"Loud bandits."

Harper stifled a chuckle. "Everything's loud at night. I can hear the chickens digesting their feed."

Once she recovered from a case of the giggles, Tegan whistled. "Wow. We shouldn't stay up all night talking."

"I'm not trying to."

"Are you one of those people who has trouble falling asleep in new places?"

Harper shook her head, not that anyone could see it. "Not really. I'm specifically anxious about bandits. Talk about getting caught with my pants down. Maybe it's stupid of me to leave them on the floor."

"Hah."

A door creaked. Relatively light footsteps went by in the hallway toward the kitchen. A moment later, another, more distant door creaked, then shut with a soft *clonk*.

Harper cringed at the idea of having to go outside to use the toilet in the middle of the night. It would absolutely suck in the rain or winter... probably why medieval people invented the chamber pot. Of course, with only a fireplace for heat, the bathroom back home got really damn cold in the winter, too. Probably little different from an outhouse barring the 'getting rained on' part.

She tried to stop thinking about anything and go to sleep. *Of course, they didn't let Logan and me have a room to ourselves.* Even though it would've been way too awkward to do anything fun in someone else's house, she would've loved to snuggle with him innocently. No one bothered to ask about any potential relationships. For all Lena knew, she and Logan could've been married.

With a soft sigh, Harper allowed herself to fantasize about being with Logan.

MISSION CREEP

G unfire broke the peaceful silence. First a single rifle shot. A man—probably the one walking sentry duty— gave a howl of pain. Another rifle shot went off much closer to the house, followed by a barrage of incoming fire. Shouts of alarm filled the house.

"Shit!" yelled Harper. "I knew it!"

She rolled out of bed, diving flat to the floor amid the snaps and zings of bullets coming through the wall. A few *clicks* and *clanks* from elsewhere in the house confirmed a deliberate attack. Keeping low to the floor, Harper pulled her jeans on, grabbed the Mossberg, and crawled out into the hall. Tegan dropped about thirty F-bombs in four seconds and also dove to the floor. Men inside the house shouted 'stay down' as well as 'back left, kitchen, and dining room.' A deer head to Harper's left flew off its mounting in the hallway, crashing to the floor beside her. Glass shattered somewhere out of sight.

Harper followed the shouting to the dining room. Carl and his eldest son hunkered down behind the wall, firing bolt-action rifles out windows into the yard. She rushed over to a free window and took up a firing position. Ken zoomed across the room, heading for the kitchen. Logan came sprinting by, spotted Harper by the window, and swerved to join her.

Muzzle flare came from the darkness behind the house, four or five shooters spaced evenly in a line. Two fired rapidly, suggesting semiautomatic weapons. The rest shot more slowly, perhaps using bolt-action rifles. Harper aimed out the left side of the window; Logan poked his AK out the other corner. They crouched shoulder to shoulder like a pair of soldiers in a bunker facing an enemy charge. In the dark and unable to see the people firing on them, she treated the muzzle flashes like clay pigeons, hoping buckshot did most of the work. Harper fired three shots as fast as she could click the trigger at the most rapid muzzle flash, its pattern recognizable as an M-16 or M-4.

The rapid *boom-boom-boom* of a semiautomatic shotgun seemed to give momentary pause to both sides of the gunfight, but the break didn't last long. Whoever decided to attack Overton Ranch opened fire again.

At the sound of nine-year-old Chase screaming in pain, Harper's intention shifted deadly. Her first three shots, she'd been trying to scare people off. Upon hearing the little boy who'd hours ago been all smiles showing off his toys wail, she wanted blood.

Manuel and Jorge yelled back and forth in Spanish. Outside, Jen screamed in horror.

For the first twenty or so seconds of the attack, ninety percent of the shots had come from outside into the house. Carl and his eldest son, plus whoever happened to be outside, initially returned fire at a cautious rate. After the brief shock of Harper's initial volley wore off, Logan, and Ken engaged. The Carls picked up the pace. Unlike everyone else, Harper didn't fire randomly into the dark; she shot only upon seeing muzzle flashes, squeezing off two more shells before the hostiles went dark. In a matter of seconds, the balance of the fight had shifted dramatically in the other direction. All the shooting came from the house. The bandits either didn't expect significant resistance, or they'd only intended to shoot the place up and leave in a hurry.

"Stop," called Ken. "They're gone. Can't see shit out there. We're just wasting ammo."

Logan pulled his AK in the window, nodding once.

Whoa... Harper gazed in stunned shock at fifteen or so small holes in the dining room wall from incoming bullets. A lantern behind her had exploded, covering the table in oil. Fortunately, it hadn't been lit—or the whole house would be on fire by now.

"I'm gonna need light," shouted Tegan from the hallway.

Carl Sr., seeming furious, stormed out of the dining room into the hall. "Lilly, Billy, Chase, Becca, Jen? Sound off."

Chase yelled, "Ow ow ow ow ow."

Rebecca moaned like a zombie from down the hall.

Billy yelled, "Here!"

"Julio's dead!" screamed Jen outside.

Another zombie moan came from the same direction as her voice.

"Wait, no!" shouted Jen. "He's still moving."

Harper rushed down the hall after the Carls to the boys' bedroom. Chase lay on the floor, squirming. Billy knelt beside him, holding a lit oil lantern so Tegan could examine the smaller boy. Harper couldn't see much more than the child's feet and legs sticking out beside the doctor. She dreaded looking further into the room, so didn't.

Carl Sr. paused in the doorway. "Talk to me, doctor. What happened to him?"

"Bullets hit the wall." Billy looked up at his father.

"He's got a splinter in his ear," said Tegan.

"I'm okay," called Lena.

"Oh... is that all?" Carl Sr. scratched at his eyebrow. "Why's he screaming so much?"

Tegan glanced back at him. "The 'splinter' is three inches long and it's stuck completely through his left ear like a tiny arrow. He's going to need stitches."

"Doctor!" yelled Jen from the back door. "Julio's hit real bad. There's blood all over the place."

Tegan grasped Chase's hands together and stared into his eyes. "Look at me, kiddo. I know it hurts. But it's not anything to worry about, okay? You are going to be just fine. I need to leave the splinter there for a little while because Julio is in bigger trouble."

Chase sniffled. "Okay. I understand."

Tegan looked at Billy. "Stay with him. Don't let him fuss with it. Don't pull it out."

"Yes, ma'am," said Billy.

"Lil?" yelled Carl Sr. "Lilly!?"

Everyone stopped moving at the same time. For three seconds, the house fell silent.

Oh, no... Harper's mind leapt to the worst possible scenario: Lilly lying dead in her bed, hit by a stray shot.

Carl. Sr. and Lena crashed down the corridor, bumping into Harper, Manuel, and Logan hard enough to knock them against the wall on their way to the girls' bedroom. Rebecca moaned something unintelligible after they burst in the door. Tegan hurried the other way, heading for the kitchen, and out to the backyard.

"Lilly!" yelled Carl Sr., his voice so desperate Harper choked up.

She ran through the tangle of bodies in the darkness, stumbling to a halt at the door of the girls' room. A few bullet holes in the wall let in tiny horizontal shafts of moonlight, though none appeared close enough to the beds to be terrifying. Carl Sr. and Lena felt around the room until Drew arrived with a lit lantern, revealing a complete lack of Lilly. Poor Rebecca Vargas looked like she'd jumped headfirst into a massive poison ivy bush. Rashes reddened her face, neck and arms. Her throat appeared mildly swollen as well.

At the total lack of Lilly—or any blood—Carl Sr. went blank-faced.

Whew... no body. Crap! Where is she? Harper's stomach bottomed out as she remembered someone going by her room. "Mr. Overton?"

He shifted his gaze to her, his eyes cold and lifeless.

"I heard someone go outside like right before the shooting started," said Harper. "Maybe she's hiding in the outhouse?"

Carl Sr. closed his eyes. "The bastards were right by the damn outhouse. If Lilly was in there, *we* probably shot her."

Harper swallowed saliva, already suspecting as much. "She'd have gotten down, right? Soon as the shooting started. They opened fire first."

Julio's agonized wail came from the other side of the house.

Carl Sr. took the oil lamp from Drew. "You got a point. May as well look. Damn sure don't wanna see what I expect to be there, though. Not like her to stay quiet and ignore me when I call for her. Gotta do it."

He led a grim procession down the hall. A scene of chaos unfolded in the dining room as Tegan and two men from the ranch positioned Julio on the oil-slicked table. He appeared to have been shot somewhere in the chest. Between the poor lighting and all the blood, Harper couldn't tell exactly. She didn't dawdle to stare, too worried about Lilly... and what they might find in the outhouse.

With all the energy of a robot, Harper followed Carl Sr. outside, scarcely noticing her lack of shoes. Carl Sr., Carl Jr., and Logan all wore jeans, no shirt or shoes. Ken appeared to have gone to sleep fully dressed except for his armor and belt, since he couldn't possibly have had the time to put everything back on. Jen and Lena milled around outside the back door in bathrobes as the Carls, Harper, Logan, Drew, and Ken started across the field behind the house.

"Leave the lantern here for now," said Ken. "If the bad guys are still out there, light will make for a target."

"Yeah." Carl Sr. handed the lantern to Lena.

Harper raised her shotgun, scanning the darkness for any sign of motion. The outhouse jutted up from the open ground like an obelisk of shadow, stark black against the bluish moonglow surrounding it. Not even chickens appeared to be scurrying about. Distant cows murmured their disapproval of all the loud noise. She, the Carls, Ken, and Logan fanned out in a line. Urgency to get to Lilly as fast as possible in case she needed help fought with the fear of finding a dead girl there pushing her back. Carl Sr. crossed the yard too fast to be careful, clearly unconcerned for his own safety.

He stopped near the murky obelisk, giving no outward reaction to what he saw.

By the time Harper caught up, her eyes had adjusted to the dark enough to notice the door hung open and no young girl lay inside, alive *or* dead.

"Son of a bitch," whispered Carl Sr. "The bastards got her."

"Better than finding a body," said Lena from a few paces behind, startling Logan.

"Not much." Carl kicked the outhouse door closed, but it bounced open. "Them sons o' bitches have been harassing us for months. Now they got Lilly, they're gonna stroll right up to the goddamned door and demand whatever they want. Cows, food, the whole damn house if they feel like it. What am I gonna do? Tell 'em no, and have 'em kill her?"

Carl Jr. grabbed his father's arm. "No way, Dad. I'm tired of this shit. We go get her back."

"They see us coming, they'll just kill her. Maybe they'll kill her no matter what we do." Carl Sr. tapped his foot, gazing into the dark clouds overhead. "Maybe you got a point, son. We oughta just be rid of them once and for all."

"Uhh, boss," said Jorge. "Esos locos bastardos have muchas armas. We got tres rifles and a revólver."

Harper stared at the spot she and Lilly spent hours sitting and talking earlier. "You have at least one more gun. I'll help... get her back or get revenge, whatever it ends up being. Any idea where they are?"

"No. That's the problem." Carl Jr. kicked the outhouse door; again, it bounced back open. "Months now, they show up at night, leave notes with demands. When we don't set a bunch of food and stuff out for them, they come back and break shit, set fires in the crops, shoot guns at the house... then disappear. We can't find them."

"If they're far enough you can't find them," said Ken, "they must be using horses, bicycles, or some other kind of vehicle."

Carl Sr. chuckled. "We never hear any engines and there ain't no way they're riding bikes out here. Gotta be horses."

"Perfect." Harper looked up at Carl Sr. "I should be able to track them. My, uhh, stepdad's been teaching me some stuff."

"Harp's in, I'm in." Ken nodded. "What's a little mission creep?"

"Me, too," said Logan.

Ack. Harper bit her lip, full of worry for the boy she finally admitted she loved. Volunteering him for a potentially foolish and deadly 'mission' hadn't been her intention. She didn't want him to get hurt. *He probably feels the same way about me.* Guilt churned in her gut. It wasn't fair to Madison for her to risk her life out here... but how could she not help? If anyone kidnapped Madison, she'd burn a swath of flames across the wasteland to find her, not giving a single flying crap what happened to her in the process. Carl Sr. appeared to be on the same wavelength, and the man still had two other children to care about. Harper only had... no... she had a whole family, too.

We're in this together. Normal, good people and the idiots. She gazed down at the suddenly heavy Mossberg in her hands. Had she known all the responsibilities it would entail to join the Militia a year ago, she might not have done it. In the emotion of the moment, her brain hadn't gone much past 'no, I can't give away Dad's gun.' Much to her surprise, she didn't want to turn back the clock to that moment and make a different decision.

Only forward from now on. If anyone ever grabbed Maddie, Jon, or Lore, I'd hope like hell someone like us happened to be around to help.

"Got one here," called Drew from a distance to the left. "Half his head's gone."

"Say what?" blurted Carl Jr.

Drew gurgled in disgust. "Looks like he took a bullet under the nose. Top part of his head is just... gone."

Ugh. At least I know it wasn't my shot.

"Good for the bastard." Carl Sr. slung his .30-06 over his shoulder on its strap. "Hope he ate one of my bullets. Someone gimme a hand draggin' the bastard off the property. Buzzards can have him. Rest of ya go on back inside. Ain't trackin' a damn thing in the dark. Won't do Lilly any good ya get lost, ruin the trail, or end up shot."

Harper bit her lip. She *really* didn't want to wait... but having daylight on her side—as well as boots—could only help. It sounded as if these bandits intended to use Lilly as leverage for making the Overtons give them food and supplies since threats and vandalism hadn't worked.

Odds seemed good they wouldn't hurt her... yet.

A BALANCE OF INNOCENCE

MAY 5TH

Harper didn't expect to sleep much.

Between her anxiety over Lilly and the endless screaming of Julio down the hall, she'd resigned herself to hours of staring into space. Surprisingly, it seemed like only a few minutes between when she curled up on top of the bed and Logan shook her awake. Tegan lay sprawled across the other bed, wearing a thigh-length yellow T-shirt Harper had never seen before. Her hair still looked damp. *She must have been a bloody mess.* Assuming the doctor had been up for many hours after her, Harper tried to be as quiet as possible as she got up, pulled her boots on, and followed Logan out of the room.

Billy stood alone in the dining room washing blood from the table. Tears streaked his face, though he appeared as furious as he did heartbroken. Harper assumed he'd had an argument with Carl Sr. over going with them to find his sister. She agreed. If it had been Lorelei or Jonathan abducted, she'd never have let Madison go with her to hunt down the bad guys.

Working with Cliff for the past several months added phrases to her vocabulary she'd never have taken seriously in her former life. Things like 'search and rescue' or 'sweep and clear' came to mind. At the sight of little Chase padding out of the kitchen with a bowl of oats—his left ear wrapped in bandages—another phrase came to mind: seek and destroy.

These bandits rapidly found themselves in the same category as the Lawless as far as she cared. They'd been harassing the ranch for months and definitely knew children lived here. Anyone capable of shooting randomly into a house they *knew* contained kids didn't deserve her sympathy. Sure, everyone could claim desperation, but some actions remained evil.

Logan headed to the kitchen. He gave Billy a 'we'll find her' sort of nod on the way by.

The eleven-year-old stopped wiping the table as Harper neared. "Lilly's nice to everyone. She doesn't deserve bein' kidnapped."

"Yeah. You don't need to talk me into helping your sister. I'm already there." She gripped his shoulder. "They won't hurt her. If they did, they couldn't make your dad do what they want."

Billy looked down. "Yeah. Dad said the same thing. They should take me instead of Lilly."

"Hey..." Harper squeezed his shoulder firmly. "Don't do anything dumb, okay? Idiots like those guys won't just let Lilly go home because they have you. They'll keep you both."

The boy's expression gave off a 'so what, I'd at least know she's okay then' vibe. He appeared torn between grabbing a gun and going off to find her on his own or trading himself to the bandits for his sister. Perhaps the only reason he hadn't run off in the night is he had no idea where to go.

"Your mom wouldn't want you in danger. Not until you're grown up." Harper smiled. *Cheap shot, but I hope it works.*

"She'd still be mad." Billy grumbled and resumed mopping up blood. "I could be older than Dad and she'd still not want me doing dangerous stuff, even for good reasons."

"That's how moms are." Harper couldn't help but think about her mother *not* complaining at all when Dad handed her the shotgun to defend the house. Of course, attempting to stop a home invasion and going on a search-and-rescue mission happened to be two entirely different situations. Danger had come to Harper's family whether they wanted it or not. Now, she certainly wanted it. "Just sit tight for a bit, okay?"

He nodded.

Harper entered the kitchen.

Jorge and Carl Sr. stood by the counter munching on toast. The air smelled of last night's ham seasoned in gunpowder and lamp oil. Two coffee machines beside the sink remained there as a shrine to what once was. Neither looked to have been used in a long time. Ken sat at the kitchen table with Carl Jr, Lena, and Jen, all eating toast. The women looked exhausted. The younger Carl stared at Harper, radiating frustration. She expected him to jump out of his chair at any minute and demand to go with them due to not being much younger than her. Not her call to make, but she wouldn't object to a sixteen-year-old coming along. The line between a too-young kid and 'old enough to be shot at' didn't truly exist in any concrete form. Even once Madison turned sixteen, she'd be hesitant to bring her on any sort of excursion away from town. Mila could probably handle it now, at least mentally, but no reasonable person would dare put a ten-year-old in harm's way.

"Have some toast," said Carl Sr. in a voice as dry as the bread he offered on a plate.

She took the plate. "Thank you."

Logan leaned against the counter next to her. "Chase is gonna be fine. He's a tough little guy. Didn't even scream much."

Harper, mouth full of toast, stared at him.

"You didn't hear them?" asked Ken, eyebrows up.

"Don't know how you slept through that," muttered Carl Sr.

"I didn't sleep through it all," said Harper around a wad of chewed bread. She swallowed. "I remember Julio screaming. Not Chase, though. Shocked I managed to fall asleep at all."

"No anesthetic." Logan folded his arms. "Chase and Julio were awake the whole time Dr. Hale worked on them."

Harper gasped.

"Can't fault the kid for crying." Logan cringed. "Gave him a rag to bite on when she pulled the shrapnel out. Bled tons. Dr. Hale said it looked worse than it was. He might have a little scar on his ear, but he'll be okay."

"Good." Harper exhaled. "How's Julio?"

The room fell to a grim silence.

"Bullet tore up a lung." Carl Sr. pushed off the counter. "If your doctor hadn't been right here, he'd have been dead. He's still probably going to die. She did everything she could, gave him about a forty percent chance of making it."

"The bastards shot him first." Carl Jr. pounded a fist on the kitchen table. "He walked Lilly to the outhouse, stood guard outside. They saw him standing there and just shot him, cold-blooded like."

Ken scooted back his chair, stood, and picked his M4 up off the table. "Carl mentioned they hadn't shot anyone on purpose before."

"S'right." Carl Sr. nodded once.

"I'm thinking," said Ken, "they came by probably intending to do whatever usual crap they do, saw Lilly going outside and decided to grab her."

"Why shoot up the house then?" asked Logan.

Carl Sr. shifted his gaze back and forth between them.

"Panic? Maybe sending another message?" Ken slung the M4 over his shoulder. "They didn't stick around too long after we started giving it back to them… and they didn't take the time to grab their dead."

Harper found it difficult to frown while devouring toast as fast as she could chew. She didn't like the thought the bandits scrambled to get away fast to keep Lilly from being shot by accident. Thinking of them trying to protect her humanized them too much for her present mood to like. Of course, a dead kid couldn't be used to extort food and supplies. Their interest in keeping her intact could easily come from a heartless value perspective. Also, 'normal' people wouldn't have started a gunfight that put children in danger to begin with. Giving them 'humanity' credit for trying to drag her away before she got hurt made no sense.

"They didn't expect y'all to be here," said Carl Jr. "They been on our ass so long, they know me and Dad only got a couple of guns. When y'all lit up the night, they took off like the damn cowards they are."

The thought of Tegan performing chest surgery on a fully conscious Julio like a scene straight out of the Civil War made Harper squirm. Getting shot had never been high up on her list of things to do. Realizing what lay in store for her if she took a non-fatal bullet made the concept of doing anything more reckless than hiding behind a barricade in Evergreen and 'camping' like she used to do in *Call of Duty* sound moronic.

If Darci and Carrie can squeeze a watermelon through an opening the size of a quarter, I can deal with a gunshot. She ate the last piece of toast in three bites as it seemed the entire room waited for her to finish. *Better not to get hit in the first place. Don't hesitate. Don't do risky crap.*

Lena hurried over to take the empty plate from her. She gave Harper a brief, grateful smile, then shot a hard look at Carl Sr. "I should be going with you."

He shook his head. "The bastards already got Julio. They probably got Lilly, too. Don't want to let them take everything I hold dear."

"Not fair to me, Carl. What if they take you from me?"

"Ain't much of my problem at that point." He put an arm

around her. "Not my thinking to do, but if it takes my life to get Lilly back here safe, she's going to need a momma like you."

Carl Jr. leapt to his feet. "Dad, I'm—"

"Gonna stay right here and look after Billy, Chase, and Rebecca." Carl Sr. glared the teen back into his chair. "It ain't about you not being man enough to do this. It's about you being man enough to do what you *need* to do, not what you want to do."

"But what if you—"

"Get killed? Boy, if I get killed, we'd both get killed and where's that leave the rest of the family?" Carl Sr. spun, grabbing his .30-06 off a wall peg. "End of discussion."

Ken, Logan, and Harper exchanged awkward glances in the following silence. She couldn't think of anything to say without sounding cheesy, so simply offered a weak grimace of a smile, then followed the elder Overton out the door.

Drew Bullock and Jorge waited in the field behind the house with six horses, three from the ranch plus the ones Harper and her friends rode here. Jorge wore a revolver on a hip holster, likely a .357. Drew had a bolt-action rifle slung across his back, possibly the one the dead bandit dropped. Carl Jr. stepped outside the house, but didn't go far from the back door. He, too, carried a .30-06. Lena came out to watch as well, carrying Julio's rifle—or so Harper assumed due to all the blood on it.

More than any competition she'd ever participated in—even the one televised live on ESPN—it felt as though the entire world watched her. Thinking of shooting sports as a neat hobby and not something she planned to hang the rest of her life on prevented her from being too wound up in winning. However, she faced much worse consequences for failure here than simply getting a bad score while a couple hundred thousand people watched, if even that many. If she failed today, a family could be destroyed, a daughter might be lost forever, and she'd blame herself for it no matter how much anyone tried to convince her otherwise.

'I can track them' sounded so damn stupid to her now. Sure, Cliff taught her a few things about how to spot tracks and identify trails. She didn't consider herself very good at it. She'd gotten to a point where she could find and follow the kids during 'training exercises.' Madison, Jonathan, and Lorelei loved helping out. To them, it became a weird form of hide and seek. Harper could even tell Madison's tracks apart from Lorelei's when her sister tried to fake her out and go barefoot, too. Not difficult at all, given the size difference.

However, she still hadn't had the least bit of success attempting to track Cliff. How a six-foot, 250-pound—well closer to 190 now—man could move through the woods without leaving a trace baffled her. Of course, he'd been through Army Ranger training and spent as long in Special Forces as she'd been alive.

Well... as long as these jackasses aren't former Rangers, maybe I have a chance.

Trying to hide her nervousness, Harper approached the outhouse and studied the ground.

Everyone rushing out there last night definitely made things more difficult in the immediate vicinity. After a few minutes of crouching near the doorway, she identified Lilly's tracks as well as boot prints unlike any shoes worn by people belonging to the ranch. It appeared to be the tread of a combat boot, though didn't match Cliff's, which meant it likely didn't come from the same manufacturer that supplied the military.

Lilly's bare footprints indicated she'd gone into the privy but not out. Harper suspected she'd been grabbed and carried by the man in the imitation combat boots. Assuming he'd have wanted to run with her directly away from the house, she stood and walked around the outhouse, picturing the way he'd most likely gone. Compression marks in the grass lined up generally with where a man might have stepped.

Thinking back to last night, Harper couldn't recall hearing the girl scream. Despite all the gunfire, if Lilly had cried out for help, it should've been noticeable. Either she fainted, he covered her mouth, or threatened her at gunpoint to be quiet.

Hard to hold someone at gunpoint while carrying them.

She scanned the ground. No sign of any footprints belonging to a twelve-year-old.

Carrying her. Maybe a knife at her neck or hand over her mouth. Marks in the grass are deeper on the left. He had her on that side. He's right-handed. Stride is randomly spaced. He's running, ducking gunfire.

Thirtyish steps past the outhouse, her job became much easier: hoofprints.

She'd thought Lorelei easy to find since the girl made no attempt to conceal her passage, but horses made the child seem like a master ninja. Both Madison and Jonathan tried to make things more difficult on Harper by stepping on rocks or roots whenever possible. It worked at first, but Cliff showed her how a stepped-on rock sometimes had a little gap between it and the dirt. Following Lorelei had been as easy as tracing a spray-painted yellow line on the ground. A group of horses would be even simpler.

"Here." Harper pointed. "This is where they left their horses."

Carl Sr. waved at Drew and Jorge. The guys rode over, leading the other four horses. Carl Jr., carrying Julio's bloodied .30-06 rifle, accompanied them, his face slightly red, his expression all puffed up and 'hard' as if he expected to get into a wicked argument with his father about going vs. staying home.

Aww, crap. She stared at the animals. Riding had been one thing while Tegan took care of controlling the horse. Going solo added a new wrinkle. In her mind, the horse stopped short abruptly enough to send her tumbling forward out of the saddle to a painful dirt-eating faceplant. It made no sense whatsoever for her to be so afraid of falling off a horse like she did as a kid.

Carl Sr. glanced at his eldest son, nodded once, and said, "You're with me."

Harper blinked at his complete lack of argument. *Wow. Okay...* She shifted her attention back to the horse and sighed. *Bet Lilly is more frightened right now than I am of horses.* Grumbling mentally, she walked up to the same animal she'd ridden the previous day.

"Hey, pal. We're cool, right?" She patted him on the neck.

The horse didn't react too much, almost a 'yeah, sure. Get on with it' attitude. Expecting to enjoy a face full of grass, she grabbed the saddle and jumped up. Though she felt far from graceful, Harper mounted without a problem. She slid the Mossberg into the saddle sheath, picked up the reins, and waited. What little 'introduction' she got to the horses from Adriana at the Express office gave her the basics on how to get the horse moving, stopping, and changing speed.

Carl Sr. also noticed the horse tracks, which at least spared her being the only one capable of leading. Maybe he'd take point and her horse would instinctually follow the others so she wouldn't have to worry about controlling it too much.

The younger Carl got on the horse behind his father. Harper almost chuckled at his expression. The boy'd gotten himself so worked up and prepared to make an impassioned argument for why he should go with them... only to face no resistance. His father almost appeared proud of him deciding to defy the order to stay home and come anyway—though equally nervous. Once everyone mounted up, she made a soft clicking nose. Her horse shook his mane a bit. She gave an encouraging pat on the shoulder, clicking again. That time, the horse proceeded to walk forward. The undulating saddle with no Tegan to hold onto unnerved her for the first few minutes. She rode to the right of the bandits' trail with Carl Sr. keeping pace on the left side. Logan pulled up beside her, slightly behind as if trying to make a V formation with Ken further to the right and behind him. Drew and Jorge did the same behind Carl Sr.

If they'd been riding for any reason other than hoping to rescue a kidnapped child before her abductors hurt her, Harper might have remarked about feeling like she'd been sucked into a spaghetti western movie. *People aren't supposed to do this crap for real.* She kept half her attention on the hoofprint trail, half on the world around them. *I guess they used to. Those movies had to be based on something, right? Billy the Kid and Wyatt Earp really existed. Guess we're the posse.*

A girl her age would probably not have been allowed to ride out with a gun to do something like this in the real Old West. Honestly, part of her would've preferred to 'sit at home fretting' while someone else did the shooting. However, she no longer considered herself a child. Kids got to remain at home in safety. She couldn't do that anymore. They might have been staying in a house with no electricity and riding horses into the middle of nowhere chasing bandits, but as Wild West as her present reality felt, one aspect of the modern world remained. No one told her to sit down and stay out of it for being a girl.

On the other hand, not even nuclear war changed the reality of being female. She had no doubt what might happen to her if the wrong sort of guy got a hold of her in a bad situation. The Lawless certainly made no secret of their plans for her, or Renee. To this day, she still couldn't believe they kept their hands off her friend over a lie about age.

Guess it's true what they say happens to kid-touchers in prison. Not even the Lawless tolerate that shit.

Unfortunately, Harper could not pass for fourteen. If this trail led them to wherever the bandits lived, some manner of conflict would invariably occur. She didn't even consider the idea of attempting to talk them into letting Lilly go. These men shot up a house knowing it had children inside. They—probably—killed Julio. Attempting to negotiate with them would at best fail and at worst lead to an ambush. Ending up a kidnap victim herself, unable to get home to her family and enduring whatever those men did to her did *not* encourage her to seek a peaceful solution. More than any other point in her life, the itch to 'simply go in shooting' seemed like the best choice. It went against everything she believed in.

Sadly, the world had changed. So had she.

The truly depressing part of it all was how she didn't think people changed all that much. Organized law disappeared, and with it, consequences. Her father used to complain about religious people trying to pull the moral high ground argument by saying something to the effect of those who do good—or at least avoided doing bad—only because they feared punishment aren't good people, merely bad people on leashes. There certainly seemed to be a lot of 'bad people off their leashes' around lately. Like Steve Pratt. He'd seemed normal, quiet, and harmless... but what might he have done if police didn't exist?

Join the Lawless and shoot everyone who 'disrespects' him. Exactly like he said he did.

She stared up at a mostly cloudless sky. Nature decided to be beautiful today. All the ugliness came from humans.

People can really suck.

29

BROKEN HARTSEL

The trail of hoof prints led across the meadow south-southwest from Overton Ranch.

Harper had too much more to worry about than being uncomfortable riding a horse to pay any attention to discomfort. She guided the animal along at an unhurried walking pace, past mostly open land marked by an occasional sign of lost modernity like the blackened remains of a small helicopter or creepily out of place pieces of larger buildings, scattered around the grass like toys a giant child forgot to clean up.

Not seeing any obvious large cities spoke wordless testimony to the power of the weapons dropped on her home. She found it unfathomable to think a mangled bit of fire escape or the pole from a gas station sign could've been flung a hundred miles through the air.

Doesn't a nuke just vaporize everything? Oh, wait... the fireball does. There's also a huge blast wave.

Scraps of a rather morbid conversation she'd had with Cliff haunted her thoughts. Nuclear weapons created several 'zones of destruction,' one of which being what he called the YPS zone, short for 'your problems are solved.' Depending on the size of the warhead, everything within a given distance of the impact point would simply cease existing in an instant. No more problems. From there, destruction radiated outward in the form of a concussive blast wave, heat, fires, and flying debris. So, yeah, the bombs definitely could throw things.

It still felt surreal to see scraps of buildings as well as smashed cars out here in a field, miles away from civilization. She considered it extremely unlikely for a car to 'crash' into the ground directly below it, so figured the handful of debris piles with wheels had to have fallen out of the sky at some point.

The dichotomy between open meadow and pieces of city added a seriously eerie undertone to her already uneasy stomach. Maybe the sight of such destruction could make people give up, adopt a 'nothing matters' attitude, and do crap like these bandits or the Lawless. Did they hope to die easy to a gunshot before nuclear cancer got them? How much of Carl Senior's bravery came from expecting death due to his trip to ground zero and hoping a bullet spared him a long, agonizing demise years from now?

Several miles from the ranch, the tracks joined with a small road. No hoof prints appeared on the opposite side, making Harper reasonably confident the bandits followed the paving. Adriana's voice echoed in her head, advising her *not* to ride on paved roads since it could hurt the horse's legs. She nudged her horse up to a somewhat faster walk on the dirt beside the pavement while keeping alert for any signs the riders veered away into the meadow.

"Comin' up on Hartsel," said Carl Sr.

"Think they're holed up there?" asked Carl Jr.

"Last we checked around here, it was a ghost town," said Drew. "Honestly, we never even thought they'd be here. Too damn obvious."

Harper looked over at the men. "How long ago did you come here?"

"Been a while, about a year now. Wasn't long after everything went to hell." Carl Sr. scratched at his right eyebrow. "Time don't really have the same sense it used to. We didn't know what we'd find. Maybe the town would still be there, people willing to talk or trade. Ended up being empty. Looked like some kind of skirmish happened. Place was all shot up. We took as many critical supplies as we could carry and got out."

"Doesn't make sense they'd nuke anywhere close by." Logan shook his head. "Nothing important enough to hit out here."

"Spite," said Carl Sr. "Either they hated America and everyone in it, or wanted to really kick us in the balls for starting it."

"Or some weapon had a guidance problem." Ken fussed at the bandage above his left ear, which kind of resembled a Rambo headband, only white.

Harper rubbed a hand down the horse's neck, thanking him for not being mean to her. "Does anyone know who fired first?"

"Oh, I'm sure someone does." Carl Sr. chuckled. "Whoever pushed the buttons damn sure knew if they did it first or as a reaction. Joint Chiefs, CIA… stuff like that ain't important for us little people to know. Hell, they didn't even give us any warning. Figure all the satellites and high-tech crap they had, they'd have seen the missiles coming. News didn't say a damn thing until the detonations started."

"Yeah." She sighed, trying to avoid going down the path of feeling guilty for living in Colorado instead of on the East Coast. While those people would've been well into their morning and not still in bed like her, they had no idea anything went wrong until they caught fire. Hundreds of thousands of innocent civilians along the East Coast simply stopped existing without even realizing danger approached. She couldn't even say their sacrifice helped people west of the Mississippi survive. 'Sacrifice' implied they made a conscious choice. "My dad said the government didn't want people to panic. Wouldn't have helped. No one had enough time to do anything, anyway."

Murmurs of annoyed agreement came from everyone.

At the first signs of a small town up ahead, Harper brought her horse to a stop. She sat up tall in the saddle, shielding her eyes from the sun. The town of—probably—Hartsel looked shockingly tiny, almost like a Wild West city made from more modern materials. A loosely organized collection of mismatched buildings, one with a red roof, several appearing moderately run down, filled an area not even a square quarter mile.

A large tree-covered hill a few hundred feet to the right of the road offered a perfect place to observe the town from an elevated position of relative concealment. Compared to the houses, the top of the hill roughly equaled a six-story building for height. Harper veered toward it. The others followed her past a seemingly empty house with a barn, up the hill into a tiny swath of pines. Near the top, everyone dismounted.

"You'll stay here with the horses, make sure no one runs off with them," muttered Carl Sr.

The 'aww, Dad!' look on the teen's face seemed more like he'd been denied a request to borrow the car, not been told to stay out of a gunfight.

"You're a decent shot, son." Carl Sr. grasped the teen by the shoulders, looking him in the eye. "If you want to cover us, sniper like, from up here, and you think you got it in you to kill a man… do it. If Lilly is in that town somewhere and those sons of bitches are there, too, we're gonna need these horses."

Carl Jr. scowled. "Dad… we can always walk home. Sure, it'll suck, but—"

"You watched Julio on that table." Ice practically shone from Carl Sr.'s eyes. "Are you ready to be in his position? Are you ready to put someone else there?"

The boy swallowed hard. "I don't want to, but if they're gonna hurt Lilly, I damn sure will. Better me on that table than her."

"Well." Carl Sr. broke eye contact with his son, seemingly not expecting the answer he got. "Not gonna be much walking if we have a bunch of bullets in our ass." He swung his rifle off his shoulder. "What good's it gonna do Lilly if we all bleed out trying to walk back."

Okay, I know he's trying to scare him into staying safe, but damn. What the hell did I just sign up for? Are we about to take on an army? Harper moved to the eastern edge of the hilltop, sheltering behind a tree. Logan and Ken took positions on either side of her.

She observed the town from up high. Somehow it simultaneously looked like a place that belonged in a post-nuclear wasteland and also existed before. Abandonment after the strike made it seem even more like a movie set for the apocalypse. Four straight north-to-south streets ran through the main part of the town, the second most distant one from the hill being quite tiny. A few not-so-straight streets ran northwest to southeast. From the hilltop, she had eyes on the entire town.

People moved around a little past the intersection at the middle. Without a scope, she couldn't make out too much detail beyond them being all men in various forms of green or desert camo. Many hours spent on gun ranges helped her estimate the distance from her position to the center of town at a little less than 300 yards. She could probably hit a man from here with iron sights, but not while using a shotgun. The people in town might also not be the bandits they hunted, but it didn't seem likely they'd be anyone else.

Need to make sure before we start shooting or we're worse than the Lawless.

"Can't see much from here," said Harper.

"Couple of them have bandages on their arms. Looks fresh," said Ken.

She glanced over at him. He held his M4 up in a firing position, sighting through the scope. The optics might be small, but a 4x beat the naked eye. "Think it's them?"

"Ninety percent likely. Not going to start picking them off from here, though. Range is a bit much for a short barrel." Ken lowered the M4. "Also, we don't know where Lilly is. I do not want to risk hitting her by accident."

Carl Sr. nodded. "Appreciate that."

"Okay. We go in for a closer look." Harper pointed to her right. "Down the south side of the hill. We go straight in, they'll see us coming... besides, east face is pretty steep, basically a cliff. Need to use as many buildings as possible for cover."

Carl Jr. finished tying the horses' leads to trees and walked over to where everyone had taken cover near the edge. Without a word, he stretched out on the dirt, setting his rifle over a root for support. Despite being sixteen, he appeared younger in the face—and frightened.

Did I look like that before? She flicked her thumbnail at the Mossberg's safety. *I probably looked even more terrified. He seems so damn young. Only a year younger than me when I had to kill someone. Hope he doesn't have to do it.*

Heart heavy, she pushed away from the tree and started down the south slope. Ken, Logan, Carl Sr. and Drew all followed her... at least until Ken scurried forward to take the lead. She didn't feel patronized by it. Sure, someone might think he wanted to draw attention first to protect 'the girl' so she could get home to her little sister and family. However, she knew Ken. Protecting her certainly factored into it, but he also trusted her to be fast enough to tag any bad guys before they could shoot him. Also, he had a police-issue vest on. It wouldn't do any good against a direct hit from a rifle, but it beat a T-shirt for stopping power.

They hurried down the relatively steep, rocky slope to the back of modest-sized building made to resemble a log cabin. A plain steel door hung ajar, already broken open. The inside appeared to be a combination convenience store-slash-outdoors supply. Ken went in first, in full 'cop mode' pie-slicing the room. Harper followed, doing the same to the other side.

Shelves held various items like camping or fishing stuff and 'cowboy souvenirs.' Racks where T-shirts and clothes had been lay mostly bare. Only hats remained. Since the building had no one in it alive or dead, they largely ignored the place and proceeded to the front door, exiting near a pair of gasoline pumps.

Harper turned left, heading east into town. Across the street, a refrigerator-sized propane drum stood by the wall of a wood-sided house to her left. *Do not shoot anywhere near that.* Attached to the same house, a fence made of sheet metal and scraps enclosed a yard loaded with all manner of junk. It totally looked like the sort of place a gang of wasteland crazies might live. Fortunately, it seemed devoid of human habitation.

She turned left again, following a road identified as 'Mariposa' by a small hand-painted sign, then turned right at the first corner, once more heading east toward the center of town where the probable bandits congregated. In the interest of not being ambushed from behind, Harper approached the house coming up on the left. She nudged the door open with her foot, shotgun ready.

What might once have been a living room contained trophy cases, shelves, and tables filled with sneakers as well as some jerseys, balls, and sports memorabilia.

Oh, yeah. A dude lived here alone.

Logan whistled barely loud enough to be heard. "Whoa."

"What?" whispered Harper. "Sneakers. Who cares?"

Carl Sr. peeked in the house for only a second before continuing by.

"Damn..." Ken leaned closer to a trophy case full of pristine shoes in various colors. "I think that's an original pair of Jordans, like from the first batch they made."

"Some of these have autographs." Logan gestured at a different case. "Card by this one says the pair is worth twenty grand."

"Was," muttered Harper, shaking her head.

"This stuff might not be valuable anymore, but it's historically significant." Logan gazed around.

"We're not here to sightsee," said Harper. "Just looking for bad guys."

She jogged out and continued following the road, a few paces behind Carl Sr. The idea of sneakers being worth thousands of dollars sounded stupid and ridiculous even before the war. It made no sense to her how 'he wore them during a game' turned an already overpriced pair of designer shoes into a ridiculous collectible.

If I'm going to buy new sneakers, I don't want them to come pre-funked up with someone else's sweat. She sighed out her nose. *I've almost forgotten what it felt like to* buy *anything.* While some people in Evergreen seemed to prefer the new arrangement of sharing necessities, taking found salvage, and trading, not having money —or being trapped in the endless rat race of a full-time job to get it—came with its own set of problems. On a shallow, selfish side, she missed nice things like going to Starbucks or going out to a restaurant. From a more practical standpoint, the present system relied heavily on people being kind and caring about each other. Humans had a tendency to come together for the collective good in times of extreme crisis. However, as the proverbial dust settled and civilization began to develop again, that survival-slash-concern instinct might fade.

Ugh. I need to focus on still being alive next week. What's the point of worrying about where the world's going to be in ten years? I might not live that long. She froze in her tracks at sudden motion up ahead. *Might not live another ten minutes.*

It used to feel stupid to stand there in the open like a statue. The tactic worked much better at night, but still beat a hasty panic-fueled leap to the ground or worse—running for cover. Cliff's voice said *the human eye goes to motion* in her mind. Standing stock still reduced the chances of being noticed.

Something small and furry slinked out from between two dead cars.

She exhaled. *Whew. Just a... critter.*

Harper resumed walking, following a dirt path to an area somewhat behind the town's 'main drag.' Voices murmured in the distance, sounding casual. The men here did not seem to be aware of their presence yet. She leaned around the corner of the place with the red roof far enough to peek at two men sitting on steel folding chairs in front of a square, white one-story building. She couldn't see into the large windows on either side of the door from this angle. Two vehicles close to the corners effectively formed side walls of a 'courtyard'. The nearer one, a beat-up dark blue Ford pickup, had a machine gun mounted on a pole in the bed. Someone spray painted 'Promise Keepers' along the side; the other vehicle appeared to be a police car with all its windows shot out.

Directly across the street from the white building, a larger group of guys hung out on the covered porch of a bar-slash-restaurant that took the concept of 'tries to look like a log cabin but isn't' to new heights. More people moved around inside as mere shadows thanks to the lack of electric lights. None were small enough to be a twelve-year-old girl.

"How's it look?" whispered Ken.

She retreated from the corner, turning to put her back to the wall and looking at her team. "I see at least seven guys. Two on the right. There's a truck with a machinegun. Five on the porch across the street. More inside. Too dark to count. No sign of Lilly."

"They probably got her cooped up inside a place somewhere." Carl Sr. scowled. "She's not gonna just sit still, content to be taken. Minute they took their eyes off her, she'd be running."

Rage burning out from his hazel eyes hinted at all the fears rattling around his mind about what these men might've done to his daughter. Harper knew the sentiment well. She'd spent many hours dwelling on the same fears in regard to Madison if the Lawless—or other similar gangs—got their hands on her. Being forced to labor on a farm and kept in chains while sleeping, like the people they'd found in Kittredge, seemed like the mildest scenario. If the look on Carl Sr.'s face meant anything, he intended to kill everyone here for what he imagined might have already happened to Lilly.

"Probably have her locked in a room somewhere," said Logan.

Harper peeked around the corner again. Cop car. Plain white building with no signs. *That looks like a tiny police station. They seem to be using it as their base. If we're in the right place and Lilly is here, they probably have in there, maybe even in a jail cell.* "I think I know where they might be keeping her. If these really are the same bandits and not just some random group."

"A random group in a place where the tracks go right to?" asked Drew.

Jorge nodded. "Must be them. No sense not to be."

"You figure we go up and ask them?" Ken chuckled. "If it *is* the bandits, they're not going to be too friendly."

"So, we sneak in and take a look." Logan shifted his weight onto his left leg. "If they're *not* the people who kidnapped Lilly and they see us creeping around, they might assume *we* are the bandits."

Harper pulled away from the wall. "We followed the tracks here. If these guys *aren't* the bandits who've been bothering you, wouldn't they be in the middle of a shootout with the bandits? Give me a minute. I'm going to go around for a different angle."

"Is that a good idea?" asked Logan.

"It's either that or let you hold my guns and I go in there acting innocent, hoping they don't throw me over the nearest car and rip my pants off."

Logan stared at her. "That's not happening."

She wagged her eyebrows. "No. It isn't, because I'm not going to risk it. Be right back."

At first, it seemed as though everyone intended to wait right there as she scurried off, backtracking to the west to avoid anyone between the police station and restaurant seeing her. Ken, however, decided to go with her. She paused to let him catch up, then continued circling around.

They headed past the restaurant one block distant to the north, then moved up along the side of a large cinder block building, formerly an appliance store. Harper crouched, peering around the corner. Ken leaned past the wall above her.

From this angle, she had a clear view of the white building. Large handmade flags hung on both front windows on either side of the door, bearing the words 'Promise Keepers' in big lettering above smaller text 'Sons of the Founders.' The windows had gold-painted lettering as well, but the flags covered it. The front room contained a half dozen steel desks, a water cooler and multiple tall cabinets. Numerous plaques on the wall resembled giant police badges.

In addition to the two men on chairs out front, four more sat at the desks inside the building, one with his feet up. They all appeared quite casual, but not at all like cops. A chubby man with an oval-shaped face in green camo stood in the middle of the room, laughing at something one of the others said. The way he carried himself gave off a sense of authority, not so much being in charge of this group, more like he had a position of responsibility—perhaps quartermaster, or the guy who managed their weapon inventory.

"That idiot on the ranch won't be so tough now," said a man she couldn't see around the distant corner to the right, likely on the restaurant porch.

A handful of guys laughed.

"Wish I could see the look on his damn face when he realizes we got him by the balls," said another.

"I hope he don't cooperate," said a third guy with an eerily raspy voice. "If we gotta send him a bit of encouragement, I wanna do the cutting. Little bitch bit me."

Harper squeezed the shotgun hard enough to make the frame creak.

"Give it time. Let Mr. High and Mighty stew for a couple days first. We'll give him the same chance we give everyone else. Kid's just a kid. No need to get shitty if he plays along."

The man who wanted to 'do the cutting' growled.

"Aww man," said a different guy, his voice thick. "I can't wait to taste bacon again. Overton's got a whole bunch of pigs."

"Shit, Hank. You never said your family lived there."

"Fuck you," muttered the thick-voiced guy.

The others laughed again.

"Hank…" The 'I want to cut her' man gave a wheezy chuckle. "Do you even know how to turn a live pig into bacon?"

"Nah. That's their job. Civilians do what we tell 'em."

"First order of business, they hand over ammo," said the first man. "We're damn near out."

"Sixty's got a full belt." Hank coughed.

"Yeah. Sixty's for defense. We don't take it nowhere. B'sides, that's different ammo. Can't run 7.62 through an AR or an AK."

"AK *is* 7.62," said Hank.

"Dumbass." The man who wanted to cut Lilly spat. "Them things take Russian shit. Smaller brass than NATO."

"AK-47 uses 7.62 by thirty-nine. NATO uses 7.62 by fifty-one," replied another man who sounded a hair more educated.

Ugh. They're as picky as Harry Potter nerds arguing fanfiction details.

A phlegmatic cough came from the right. "We gotta do somethin' soon. Them ranchers figure out we're runnin' dry on bullets, they might try somethin' stupid."

"They won't," said the dry-voiced guy. "First of all, they don't know we're low on ammo. Second, they're too scared of what'll happen if they don't behave themselves."

Men chuckled.

Harper retreated from the corner. Ken locked stares with her. They nodded simultaneously, then crept back around the way they'd come toward where Logan, Carl Sr., Jorge, and Drew waited. *We found them. Lilly is here... somewhere. Probably in the police station.*

Her stomach did cartwheels. Honestly, this wouldn't be the first time she participated in an assault. The people treated like slaves at Kittredge needed help, and the Evergreen Militia went on the offensive. Of course, they'd been so close as to basically be part of the Militia's territory—unlike this place. The whole time she snuck back to the rest of her group, Harper pictured Madison staring up at her, three months after the end of civilization, the first Christmas they'd know without parents. Her little sister said she didn't need any presents ever again if Harper could give her only one thing: don't die.

Dammit. If I get killed doing this, Maddie is going to be a freaking wreck. Harper swallowed the saliva building up in her mouth. *If I don't, Lilly suffers who-knows-what. No telling if these guys are at least pretending to be somewhat human like the Lawless. How young is too young for them?* She scowled, disgusted at her own train of thought. The one guy wanting to cut Lilly made Harper think he'd seen too many gangster movies, and likely intended to lop off a finger to send back to the ranch if Carl Overton refused to cave in to their demands. *No one told him not to do it. Or even called him sick for suggesting it. We can't leave her with these people.*

She couldn't weigh Madison against Lilly. What kind of person would she be if she left one child to suffer torture so another one might not be sad? Attacking these 'Promise Keepers' didn't necessarily mean she would get killed. Good chance, but not guaranteed. Attacking them also didn't mean they'd win and get Lilly out of here. For all she knew, Harper might end up dead, Lilly would remain kidnapped, and Madison would never know what happened to her. For a moment, she considered going home while she still could… but pictured Lilly screaming as some big, hairy thug held her arm down and sliced her finger off.

No… Walking away from Lilly wasn't going to happen. She could be careful. She *had* to be careful. Best to just do it and think about the risks afterward.

We already came all the way out here.

30

WORSE THAN IT LOOKS

A faint child's scream cemented Harper's resolve.

Judging by the look on Carl Sr.'s face when she and Ken made it back to the rest of their group, they'd all heard it too. Thankfully, the scream had a plaintive quality, not fear or pain. Still, picturing Lilly trapped somewhere screaming to be let out infuriated her.

"Was that her?" whispered Drew.

Carl Sr. narrowed his eyes, seeming uncertain.

"It's definitely them," whispered Harper. "I overheard them talking. Mr. Overton, I need you to stay calm, okay? I'm going to say something that's gonna piss you off."

He raised an eyebrow. "All right. Don't wanna ruin our sense of surprise. I'll stay quiet."

"Good news is, they are complaining about being low on ammo." Harper did some mental math. "By my guess, we're looking at somewhere between nine and fifteen guys. Maybe more since I couldn't see into the restaurant. But I don't think all of them have guns anymore."

"That's good." Logan smiled.

"What part of that is supposed to piss me off?" asked Carl.

Harper took a deep breath. "What one of them said. I think Lilly bit him. They're going to wait a day or two to make you worry, then send a demand letter. If you don't do what they want, this one guy said he would cut her finger off and send it to you."

The moment Carl Sr. made the decision to kill every Promise Keeper in Hartsel showed as obvious on his face as a tornado stormfront over the plains. He remained outwardly calm, but the change in his eyes worried her.

"Don't worry, boss." Drew patted Carl's arm. "They won't get the chance."

"Yeah. Totally." Harper shifted her jaw side to side, thinking. "They believe the ranchers are too scared to do anything. Maybe they think no one knows where they are. Either way, they're not going to expect a counterattack."

Drew grinned. "They didn't expect y'all to tear them up last either. Ran like hell when you folks unloaded."

"So, you're totally sure this isn't a settlement?" asked Logan.

"Absolutely." Harper gave him side eye. "If there are any women here, they're hiding. Most of the guys I saw are wearing body armor vests and camo."

Ken nodded. "They're more of a gang. No women, no kids living here."

"Ex-cons?" asked Logan.

"Don't really think so." Harper rolled her eyes. "They had flags up on the windows. Promise Keepers or something like that. Sounds like one of those militia groups."

"Great. We're dealing with 'super patriots,' and I mean 'patriot' loosely." Ken took the magazine out of his M4 and swapped it for a full one. "Those guys are all dressed up in tacticool."

"What?" Harper blinked.

Carl Sr. almost chuckled.

"Bunch of idiots dressed up like soldiers," said Ken. "Did you see that one guy's rifle? He had nine pounds of useless junk strapped to it. Flashlight, forward grip, extra rails, mag holder, tripod... now there's a guy who has never once in his life needed to hump gear on a forty-mile hike. They got all their shit from Army/Navy surplus stores, focus on looking 'cool' rather than being functional."

"Oh." Harper pursed her lips. "Does that mean they don't know how to shoot?"

"Not necessarily. A 350-pound Meal Team Six member might still be a decent shot... as long as he doesn't have to get up out of his chair." Ken winked. "Don't assume they're not dangerous. However, there is a good chance they'll shit themselves once they really start coming under fire."

"Depends on what they've been through since it all fell apart." Drew spat to the side. "Soft ones wouldn't still be around."

"Fair point." Ken looked at Harper. "Assume they're all dangerous and skilled. Better to overcompensate than take stupid risks."

"Yeah. Already there." She moved to the opposite corner of the red-roofed building.

"What's the plan?" asked Logan. "Guessing 'jump out and start shooting' isn't going to work."

"My son's probably losing his mind watching us just stand around." Carl Sr. looked west at the big hill overlooking town. After a moment, he held a thumbs-up sign. "He's got us covered."

"Surprised you let him come, boss," said Drew.

"Lilly is his sister as much as she's my daughter." Carl Sr. heaved a resigned sigh. "And we needed someone to watch the horses."

"Heh." Drew covered his mouth to silence a laugh.

"We basically have two ideas," whispered Harper. "Frontal assault or look for a way to sneak in and get Lilly out as quietly as possible."

"Police station probably has a back door." Ken peered around the corner. "Place this small, they're not going to have all the nice security shit from a city station. We could walk right in."

"What's the setup?" asked Carl Sr.

"Here..." Harper squatted and traced lines in the dirt. "This is the restaurant. This is the police station across from it. Road." She drew a rough map with her finger, adding x's for people. "Two guys on chairs here. Four or five inside the front room of the police station. Unknown number possibly deeper in the building. Five on the porch of the restaurant. Unknown number inside it. They got a machine gun in a pickup truck here..." She traced a small box.

"M-60," said Ken. "It's conveniently set up pointing at the restaurant."

A gleam flashed in Carl Sr.'s eye.

"Before you think about that... we need to make sure Lilly isn't in there." She eyed Ken. "Let me borrow the Colt for a sec? Want the optics."

Ken removed a pair of binoculars from a belt holder. "Here. These zoom better."

"Nice." She took them, then pointed up at the red roof. "Boost please."

Logan and Ken lifted her. Harper pulled herself up onto the roof and belly-crawled far enough across to have an unobstructed view of the street. It almost made her laugh how freely she and Ken could roam around here without being noticed. The Promise Keepers posted no patrolling sentries, no one standing on rooftops to watch out for problems. Even to her, they seemed like amateurs, just a bunch of guys hanging out with not a care in the world. Perhaps they technically were amateurs by comparison, considering she *had* some training from both Cliff and Roy Ellis. An Army Ranger and a former SWAT officer knew some stuff. Then again, from what her father said, groups like this often had at least a handful of actual military vets along with the CCPs, or 'camouflage couch potatoes.'

The binoculars gave her a better view inside the restaurant. More guys in camo or T-shirts sat at tables drinking from cans or eating. A few remained moderately overweight. The only two men she spotted *not* wearing an armored vest probably *couldn't* wear armored vests. How anyone remained obese a year and change post-Armageddon spoke to how prolific their looting must have been.

Damn. There are a lot of them. Maybe fifteen inside. We're almost up to twenty-five hostiles now. This is sounding worse and worse by the minute. Don't see too many weapons, but they could be on the floor.

Curtains in the small windows along the upper story blocked her view inside. If they kept Lilly in that building, she'd have to be upstairs, in a back room, or in the basement, assuming the place had one.

"Incoming," said a man on the street.

For an instant, her heart nearly stopped, until she processed his casual, unworried tone. She hadn't been spotted. 'Incoming' must refer to someone else approaching, far enough in the distance not to have alarmed the bandits. Harper panned the binoculars away from the restaurant to the street between it and the police station. Five Promise Keepers gathered in a line, all holding rifles, the two men from the chairs and three from the restaurant porch. All faced east.

Harper shifted her attention out along the road, zooming in on two people. A man with short, black hair in his early forties and a slightly younger ginger man pulled a flatbed trailer loaded with a mound of vegetables. The trailer appeared to be similar to the type landscapers in her old neighborhood used to lug their equipment around, maybe ten feet long, made to be pulled by a pickup truck or car. They'd rigged an improvised front wheel so the men didn't have to support the weight normally held up by the hitch.

None of the Promise Keepers in the road did anything more than watch as the men arrived in town and approached them. A shaggy-haired guy wearing a camo ball cap and Kevlar vest stepped forward from the bandits. He walked around the wagon once as if inspecting it, then seeming satisfied, nodded at the two men.

The ginger-haired guy approached him, gesturing at the police station. A brief, though tense conversation followed, too quiet for Harper to make out more than the word 'arrangement' or 'good faith.' Though he seemed annoyed by whatever the ginger man said, Camo Cap Guy waved him to follow and crossed the street to the door. Both went into the police station.

A group of fifteen or so Promise Keepers came from the restaurant building, only two bearing firearms. All had at least a knife on them, while several carried swords, sledgehammers, or axes. They descended on the wagon, grabbing bundles of vegetables, bread, and eggs, which they carried back inside. Harper held still, watching this unfold. If any of the men happened to get the random urge to look up at rooftops, they'd probably see her. She didn't want to risk moving and attracting attention.

The men finished unloading the wagon and disappeared back into the restaurant, except for the four who'd been standing in the road waiting for them initially. The black-haired guy glared at the Promise Keepers with thinly veiled contempt, though said nothing. He didn't appear to be armed, not even a knife.

Around fifteen minutes later, Camo Cap Guy and the ginger man emerged from the police station. The rancher's face almost matched his hair for color. Tears streamed down his cheeks and he appeared to be fighting hard to keep some degree of composure. Grins and chuckles came from the Promise Keepers. Several waved goodbye in mockingly polite tones, saying things like 'thanks for dropping by' or 'see you next month' as the two men took their empty wagon and trudged off down the road to the east.

What the heck did I just watch? Harper slid backward until the edge of the roof concealed her completely from the road. *Oh, shit... they must have his kid, too. Or maybe wife. That's what that asshole meant by they would be too scared to do anything.*

Shit.

TACTICALLY UNSOUND

Careful not to make noise, Harper shimmied to the back side of the building and lowered herself to hang off the roof. Ken and Carl Sr. reacted the fastest, grabbing her legs and easing her down to ground level.

"What the heck took so long?" Logan raced over. "You scared the hell out of me."

"Couldn't move or I'd have been spotted," she whispered. "We have a serious problem."

"Knew that already," muttered Drew.

Harper sighed… and told them what happened. "I think that guy went into the police station to visit his kid or wife or something. I didn't see Lilly in the restaurant. Just a bunch of guys eating and hanging out. Couldn't see upstairs or into the back."

"Sounds safe to open a shooting gallery then," said Drew.

Carl Sr. replied with a chilling nod. "Yeah. Sure does. These fools have been running around demanding food and supplies from all the ranches in exchange for protection. They declared it their territory, spouting some kinda 'new republic' bullshit, and we needed to accept them as the law around here. Anyone doesn't give 'em what they want, it leads to violence."

"Yeah, them guys been around here a while. Even before the war." Drew rested his .30-06 over his shoulder. "Some kind of militia thing. These fools couldn't wait for the end of the world so they could swoop in and become the new power to replace the old government they pretended to love."

"This is gonna end today." Carl Sr. looked down. "If you're right and these boys are running out of ammo, they're gonna get desperate. Only thing more dangerous than a fool with a gun is a *desperate* fool with a gun. Can't ask you three to get involved. This is our little war. My daughter."

Ken raised both eyebrows. "Dude, there's no way the two of you plus that kid back on the hill are going to take on this entire group with a couple Springfields. We're happy to help."

"Drew, Jorge... same goes for you two." Carl Sr. looked at them. "Not gonna ask you to get shot at for me."

"Damn, man." Drew whisper-chuckled. "I ain't volunteering to get shot at for you. Doing it for Lilly. Let's kick some ass."

Jorge patted Carl Sr. on the arm. "Abriste tu casa para mi familia y para mí. Nos hemos convertido en familia. Lilly también. Le ayudaré."

"If I'm not around to say it after the smoke clears, I'll never be able to thank you enough." Carl Sr. opened the mechanism of his rifle to check the chamber, then looked up. "Whatever happens, only thing I care about is getting Lilly home in one piece."

"Not a good idea going in expecting to get killed." Ken smiled. "If it happens, I'd prefer it be a surprise."

"What's the plan?" asked Drew.

"I'd like to try quiet first." Harper crouched over her dirt map. "If we can get in there and find Lilly, bring her out, then we can back off and maybe engage from the hilltop. High ground and long range."

Ken cringed. "I don't think we're going to be able to make it into the police station unnoticed, even from the back. We can probably get inside, but we're going to be seen."

"Hill's bad." Carl Sr. sighed. "You said they got an M-60? I don't want that thing turned on us. While you try sneaking into the station, I'm going to hop on that pickup truck and give those bastards something to bitch about. They're all obligingly packed tight up in the restaurant. Gotta take the opportunity."

"Umm… machine gun nest is painting a giant target on yourself." Ken bit his lip. "Might be better to disable it."

"Nah. Rather use up their ammo. Even if we lose, they won't have it to mess with anyone else." Carl flicked the safety off his rifle. "Got a feelin' you're right about these fools. They're going to panic, or sit there for a couple seconds confused as all hell."

Harper didn't like any idea. Her brain practically shorted out trying to come up with a tactical plan that minimized risk to them, so she ended up clinging to her original suggestion of stealth. "Okay. I'm going to try to sneak into the police station from the back. They won't know who I am. If anyone sees me, I'll act like I'm just out here on my own wandering. I, uhh, don't think their first thought is going to be wanting to shoot me." She blushed.

"No way. I'll do it." Logan rested a hand on her shoulder.

"Thanks, but"—Harper grabbed his hand—"I'm a better shot, and they'd just shoot you on sight. Me, they'd kidnap. You guys would have a chance to get me out."

Logan hardened his brows. "You need to get home to Maddie."

She tensed, her mind going in ten different directions. "You gotta get home for me and Luisa."

"You both need to get a damn room," whispered Ken.

Harper made an odd noise, part laugh, part sob. Between fear, worry, and embarrassment, she couldn't force a single word out.

Carl Sr. kinda pointed at Harper, Ken, and Logan, waving two fingers back and forth. "You three go for the police station. See if you can make it in quiet, maybe get Lilly out. I'm gonna move up on the side, wait behind the truck. Appreciate it, Drew, if ya cover me. If it goes south, I'm jumping on that machine gun and making hamburger in the restaurant."

Logan clenched his jaw, seeming pained. After a few seconds, he huffed a heavy sigh. "Better I cover Carl. He's going to need more than a bolt rifle supporting him to hold that gun position against a large group. My mag is half gone and it's still holding more rounds than the Springfield."

"Uhh…" Harper stared at him.

Ken lightly whacked the back of his hand into Logan's bicep. "Swap to a fresh mag. Start off full."

Logan changed magazines.

"He's right." Ken nodded to the side in a 'let's get going' way. "You saw yourself, most of these guys are in the restaurant or outside. Only a handful in the police station. Maybe we'll get lucky and they have her in a back room. Might be able to slip in and out unnoticed."

"Yeah, sure." Harper rested her head against Logan's shoulder.

"All right." Carl shook Logan's hand. "Appreciate it. You're right. These Springfields aren't made for war. Drew. You and Jorge want to head around behind the restaurant? Best thing is if they're catching fire from more than one side. It'll keep them from throwing everything they have at me. I'll take the M-60. Logan watches my back. Mr. Zhang and Harper, you do what you can to get Lilly out of that building unhurt."

Ken gave a thumbs-up.

"You got it, boss," said Drew.

Jorge nodded.

She dreaded Logan going around the side to the street— especially right next to the machine gun, which would undoubtedly draw the most hate. Thinking he'd be moderately safer than Carl Sr. because the Promise Keepers would focus on silencing the M-60 first made her feel like a garbage person.

Obviously, she'd be more upset about losing the boy she loved than a man she'd only known for a day... but still. Consciously acknowledging her bias seemed wrong. She didn't wish anyone dead... except the kidnappers.

Ken checked over his M4. "Plan is solid. Carl gets on the 'sixty and deals with the restaurant and street. Drew and Jorge pincer from behind the restaurant. Logan watches Carl's back. Harp, you and me hit the cop shop. No one start shooting until or unless shit hits the fan inside the police station. The longer we have before they realize we're here, the better the chances of getting Lilly out unhurt. Guys..." He looked at Drew and Jorge. "Watch crossfire."

The two men nodded before hurrying off to the left, circling around wide to get into position.

Harper reluctantly lifted her head off Logan's shoulder and exhaled. "Okay. Let's do it."

Carl and Logan crept around the corner of the red roof building, hustling toward the police station while trying to stay out of sight. Harper closed her eyes for a second, thinking about Chase screaming in pain, thinking about the ginger-haired guy who probably got a far-too-brief meeting with someone he loved. She imagined people like this taking Madison and forcing Evergreen to give them food.

Doing this before I overthink it.

She opened her eyes and fast-walked out from behind the wall.

32

THE COP SHOP

A chain link fence enclosed the backyard of the police station.

Green metal slats woven among the links made it impossible to see into the yard without climbing. A padlock and chain secured a gate big enough for a car where a small driveway met the fence opposite the building. Ken jogged across the alley. In a smooth—obviously practiced—move, he dropped his M4 to hang on a strap and vaulted the fence.

Harper didn't feel confident enough to fling herself over like that, so she stopped long enough to shoulder the Mossberg, then grabbed the pipe running along the top of the fence to climb.

"Hey," said a man to her left.

She whipped her head around, staring at the oval-faced guy she'd seen inside the police station earlier. The man had puffy cheeks, an unkempt brown beard, and almost too much belly to squeeze into a Kevlar vest. He also pointed a silver Desert Eagle at her. Standing there with both hands gripping the top of the fence and her shotgun hanging on her back didn't give her much in the way of a tactical advantage. In fact, she couldn't have felt any more vulnerable at the moment if she'd been naked.

They stared at each other for five seconds that seemed more like five hours. He practically peeled her clothes off with his eyes. As much as she could, she ignored the creepiness, taking in the details. He wore full baggy camo with all the accessories: Kevlar vest, knee pads, elbow pads, shin guards, and knuckle protectors, three silver magazines for the DE on his belt stuck out of holders intended for AR-15 style magazines. No rifle. One grossly oversized 'movie combat knife' with a compass in the handle… and a keyring worthy of a high school janitor hung next to the mag azine pouches.

She fixated on the keys with almost as much desire as he fixated on her chest.

"Nice shottie," said the guy, sauntering closer. "Why don't you go ahead and put it down. Don't drop it. Too nice to mistreat a weapon like that. Mine now."

She didn't move.

His expression took on a lurid, greedy quality. "Sidearm, too. Don't think I didn't notice the handgun. Matter of fact, just take off the whole belt."

No wonder he isn't shouting for backup. He wants me alone. "If you're thinking what your face says you're thinking, just shoot me." *Ack. What the hell is wrong with you, Harp?*

He chuckled. "Nah. We're gonna be real good friends. I'll treat ya right, sweetie." His smile vanished as he pointed the gun at her head. "Now, get that belt off."

"Hey, Meal Team Six," called Ken from above the fence.

He jumped in shock, released a clipped fart, and spun to aim the Desert Eagle up to his left. The instant the weapon no longer lined up with Harper, Ken fired, putting two rounds into the guy's chest, one into his face. Tiny puffs of Kevlar fiber burst out of the pinholes made by 5.56 green tip ammo. The back of his head blasted out in a sluice of dark red and brain. He fell over backward, arms out to his sides.

"The lady said no," deadpanned Ken.

Harper resumed breathing again. She pounced on the dead man, ripping the keys straight out of their nylon strap before grabbing the three pistol mags, which she tossed into her hip satchel, then nabbing the hand cannon. *Yikes. This thing would break my damn wrist.* She stuffed it in the hip satchel, too, thinking of giving it to Cliff, or maybe Deacon, when—if—she got home.

"Who the fuck is shooting?" yelled a guy from the street, sounding more annoyed than worried.

Carl Sr. might have yelled 'I am' or perhaps she only imagined him doing so as the M-60 started firing.

"Crap!" She leapt for the fence, scrambling over it while all hell broke loose out in front of the police station.

33

PROMISES BROKEN

Watching war movies, even in an IMAX theater, had nothing on being within a hundred feet of a real M-60 going off.

Danger likely made the sound seem ten times louder. Intermittent cracks and booms from smaller rifles went off like a spontaneous fireworks display. Men screamed both in pain and surprise. Glass shattered, metal clanked, and every so often, a ricochet made a weird zinging noise like a laser out of *Star Wars*.

The yard contained two more police cars bearing Park County Sherriff markings, a trash dumpster, and a broken-into wooden tool shed. Ken struggled at a plain grey steel door in a featureless cinder block wall, evidently stymied by the lock.

She raced over to him. "Sorry."

"Not your fault." He sighed. "We're out of luck. Unless your shotgun works as a key."

"How about an actual key?" She fanned the keyring out in her hand, searching for one the right size to test on the door. Alas, they all looked roughly the same. One appeared more worn than the others, so she tried it.

"What are the odds the guy with the keys is the one who catches us?" asked Ken.

The knob turned. Grinning, she hauled the door open and stuffed the key jumble in her pocket. "Pretty good if more than one dude has the keys. Kinda dumb to only give it to one person."

"True." Ken hurried in through the doorway.

Harper raised her shotgun into a firing grip and followed him inside. The first room contained a desk with a computer on it, some small metal cabinets, and a little lockbox on the wall holding several sets of car keys. More yelling came from further inside the building, along with shouts of 'they got the sixty' or 'they're everywhere,' lots of cursing, even more screaming... and a child shrieking in terror.

A man in camo and body armor appeared out of a doorway thirty-ish feet down the hallway, running toward them. He gave a strangled yell of surprise, then shouted, "Breach in back!"

Harper hesitated for a half a second because he had no weapons in his hands, until spotting a handgun on his belt. She fired, aiming for his head to bypass the armored vest. Ken shot the guy at the same time, making two tiny holes in the Kevlar.

He stumbled backward as if punched in the face, careening over dead.

Harper rushed three steps forward to the left, taking cover in the first side room while keeping her weapon trained on about thirty feet of hallway leading to a door, beyond which had to be the front room. Two more doors on the left side in front of her remained closed. A doorway opposite her position looked in on a tiny conference room with a whiteboard covered in crudely drawn penises, US flags, and almost childish depictions of people shooting each other. Midway up the hall on the right, the telltale moving shadow of an approaching person darkened the floor of a branching corridor. Past the offshoot, another door on the right side stood closed, no windows.

Ken sheltered at the corner of the first room, aiming down the corridor.

Screaming an incoherent war cry, a Promise Keeper stuck a submachine gun out of the side passage blind, only his hand and the weapon exposed.

Harper dove into the little office as the guy ripped full auto blindly around the corner. In two seconds, his magazine ran out. A haze of gunpowder smoke and plaster dust filled the hallway, rolling into the room with her. Ears ringing, she pushed herself upright and whipped around the doorjamb, aiming at the corner where the now-empty submachine gun still stuck out into view. Sure enough, the idiot peeked to see if he hit anything.

She pulled the trigger, blowing open the upper right side of his head. Before he could even start falling, a bearded guy wearing some manner of camo-patterned armored facemask, a ballistic vest, knee pads, and tacticool gloves rushed into the hall from the lobby door at the end of the corridor. Harper aimed and fired as fast as she could react. Her shotgun went off a fraction of a second faster than his M-16. Buckshot slapped into his facemask, knocking his head back and half twisting the 'protective' gear off his head. A spray of 5.56 stitched holes in the wall and chipped the linoleum tiles a few feet in front of her. Staggered, the man fell backward against the doorjamb. Moaning in pain, he attempted to sprint for cover in the main room—but ran straight into the wall, thanks to the twisted mask covering his eyes. Ken fired two shots into his side. The man grunted and collapsed to the floor, mortally wounded.

A loud metal *clang* came from the front room along with a child's terrified scream.

Harper tried not to think about how close Ken's bullets passed by her head on their way to the idiot in the facemask.

The machinegun fire outside slowed from a constant pummeling to long bursts separated by several seconds. Constant F-bombs and other, more colorful phrases came from multiple different voices. Logan cried out in a way that could've been sharp pain or a battle cry.

Her heart nearly stopped. *No! Please...*

Overcome by reckless concern for him, she bolted out of the doorway and raced to the door at the end of the hall. Five Promise Keepers hunkered down behind the two long windows, sheltering behind metal radiator cabinets, alternatively firing at the corner of the restaurant across the street and at a sharp angle left toward the pickup truck. Two lay dead near them, perhaps shot by Drew or Jorge from across the street. So much gunfire and chaos raged in the street out front, none of them noticed her enter the room behind them. Empty rifle brass lay scattered everywhere: on the radiators, floor, the dead bodies, even atop a few desks.

A maze of large steel 'cop desks' stood between her and the front wall, arranged around four concrete columns holding up the ceiling. A cage-type prison cell like out of a Wild West jailhouse occupied the right, rear corner. It appeared large enough to hold six people, but had no bed. A barefoot girl in a nightdress with long, light brown hair curled up on her side beneath the lone steel bench in the cage, trying desperately to put something metal between herself and bullets. Multiple gouges marked the bars where incoming fire struck them. Most of the shots entering the police station lobby appeared to be coming from the restaurant across the street.

That's Lilly!

Harper tightened her jaw. Without hesitation, she opened fire on the Promise Keepers by the window while simultaneously rushing to cover behind the nearest concrete column. Starting from the left, she exploded two heads before the other three noticed they had a serious problem in the room with them. The third dove in a panic out the window. Not wanting to shoot him in the ass, she shifted aim to the fourth. Ken rushed in, firing on the guy clambering out the window. Two rounds to the back left a corpse slumped over the radiator, head and arms dangling out of the building. The last two Promise Keepers spun, firing wildly into the room in an uncoordinated frenzy. Cringing, Harper hastily sent the last two shells in the Mossberg at them, then ducked fully behind the concrete.

Ken triggered so rapidly at them it sounded like his M4 ripped fully automatic.

Seated on the floor with her back against concrete, Harper stared up at him 'combat walking' into the room like some kind of five-foot-nothing version of a Terminator. Her hands shook enough to complicate the process of stuffing more rounds into the shotgun. Reloading under pressure didn't usually bother her... but incoming bullets made her far more nervous than worry over losing a few points of score for time.

... *Seven, eight, nine.* Harper racked the bolt and shoved another shell in, then zipped her hip satchel.

A few feet in front and to her right, Ken engaged more Promise Keepers from a position behind one of the desks, firing out the window into the restaurant. Harper swung the shotgun around the column and scanned the street for threats. Somewhere between seven and twelve corpses lay in the road. Every ground floor window on the street-facing side of the restaurant had been shot out. More guys lay dead on the porch, one in the doorway. A few people appeared to be crawling around in the back of the restaurant's main dining area.

"Clear in the police station," shouted Harper.

"Probably clear," said Ken, only loud enough for her to hear. "Could be more down the hallway on the right."

"Wouldn't they have come after us?"

He shrugged. "Probably, but they might not have ammo."

"Good point."

"Mr. Overton's hit," shouted Logan.

Hearing his voice made Harper light headed with relief. *Thank you...* Her gaze fell on the dead in the room with her as well as on the street outside. As the adrenaline of the moment faded, horrified revulsion took over. She hated *having* to do it more than doing it. Kidnappers, thieves, and criminals they might have been… but still human beings. Harper closed her eyes. *I'm sorry for ever complaining about having to wake up early for school. Can I go back? Wake up out of this horrible dream.*

A moment later, she opened her eyes to the same carnage, and sighed.

Guess not. Had to try.

NIGHTMARE FUEL

Twenty seconds after the shooting stopped, a sniffle came from the holding cell.

"This is the most dangerous part," said Ken in a near-whisper. "Clearing the scene. Be wary. Not everyone who looks dead is dead. Could have bad guys hiding anywhere or pretending to be dead."

"Logan?" yelled Harper. "You… okay?"

"Yeah," he shouted. "Got it handled. Looks quiet out here, but we're in cover."

"Let's check our back door, then go across to the other nest," whispered Ken.

She nodded to him, then peered over at the cell. The girl she assumed to be Lilly still huddled under the steel bench. It felt *wrong* to leave her in there, but it would be worse if she ended up getting shot because they failed to 'secure the scene' as Roy Ellis put it.

"Lilly?" whispered Harper.

"Yeah," replied the girl.

"It's Harper. You're gonna be okay. We have to make sure it's safe first. I'll be right back, then we'll get you out of there."

Lilly mumbled something incomprehensible.

"Crap," whispered Ken. "I'm down to three rounds."

Harper pulled the Desert Eagle from her hip bag and offered it to him, plus the three magazines.

"Damn, what a cannon..." Ken swung the M4 over his shoulder before grabbing the big handgun.

A few shouts and intermittent gunshots went off inside the restaurant. Harper took point, hurrying around the back of the police station to make sure they didn't have any problems hiding in offices or conference rooms. The branching hallway contained two bathrooms and a secure steel door. Its narrow window offered a peek at a dark stairway going down. At discovering it locked, she decided checking out the basement could wait for the scene to be cleared. It didn't seem likely any bad guys would hang out behind a locked door in the dark.

Satisfied no Promise Keepers remained in the police station, Harper jogged to the front room. Two men lay dead in the doorway, so she climbed onto the radiator cabinet and slipped out the massive hole where a window used to be. Both flags lay on the ground amid a scattering of shattered glass. With her focus—and shotgun—on the restaurant in front of her, she didn't notice a 'dead' man in the road moving until he whipped his arm up and pointed a handgun at her.

A blast of gore flew out the side of the man's head a second before the *crack* of a distant gunshot came from the hilltop.

She squeaked. *Shit...*

Somehow, she brushed the near-death experience aside with about the same level of anxiety as when she'd run over a safety cone during her first driving school experience. She continued toward the restaurant, though divided her attention between the bodies around her and the ones in front of her. Ken stepped over the dead guys in the police station doorway, following her to the porch.

The stink of spent gunpowder, shat pants, and skunked beer

from half-consumed cans on the porch tables brought her close to gagging. She got even closer to throwing up after climbing in through the windows, and the smell of cooked meat added to the milieu.

"Ugh. Hijo de puta," muttered Jorge.

Harper looked toward where his voice came from, a doorway leading to the kitchen. She started across the room, sweeping her shotgun around at each body in case any of them played possum like the man on the street. All the tables and chairs had been chewed up to hell from the M-60 shredding the room. Splinters, scraps of seat foam, smashed plates, and all sorts of debris had seemingly exploded everywhere. Seven guys sat slumped over tables, dead, shot where they'd been sitting. Three other bodies clustered near the front windows, rifles still dangling from their lifeless hands. It looked as though Carl Sr. got more than half the Promise Keepers within the first several seconds, before any of them had the chance to even get up.

A man burst out from under the table of a booth seat, firing three rounds from a handgun into Ken's chest at a range of about twelve feet. Ken barked like a kicked goose, staggering backward. Harper aimed and fired at the Promise Keeper in under a second, shredding most of his face and sending most of his jaw flying.

The men's room door burst open. Another Promise Keeper rushed out with an AR-15. He had Ken dead to rights but... for some reason, didn't shoot in the two seconds it took Ken to recover and pump two .50 caliber slugs into the guy's chest. A massive spray of blood painted the bathroom door. The man collapsed, gurgling, rifle clattering to the floor nearby.

Harper stared at the ejection port of the rifle, slide locked back. Empty. *Out of ammo. What the heck did he charge at us for?*

Ken gasped, swooned to one side, and caught himself on a table. "Oh... that's a rib. Damn it."

"Are you...?" She stepped toward him.

"Vest stopped it. I'll be okay. Sore for a month, but okay." He gingerly coughed. "Good thing he only had a Sig. This freakin' DE is a monster. It would've blasted a hole right through this 3A."

"Ay mierda... Drew..." Jorge groaned from the kitchen.

Harper approached the flapping door. "Jorge?"

"Yeah. They got Drew."

"Coming in. Don't shoot." She nudged the door aside with her foot.

The kitchen looked like a scene straight out of a horror movie. A dead guy in camo lay on the floor in front of her with a meat cleaver embedded in the front part of his skull, eyes crossed. Another man slumped over the food prep counter, his left hand pinned to a butcher block with a carving knife. It appeared he'd been struggling to pull the blade out when someone shot him in the side of the head, spraying the contents of his skull into a nearby sink. The bodies of two more Promise Keepers sprawled on the rubber floor mats by a huge industrial stove. Both still held onto bayoneted AK-47s and appeared to have been shot to death.

Drew Bullock sat with his back against a steel oven, one hand clutching his slashed throat. His pale grey eyes couldn't possibly open wider, gazing into the next world. It looked as if he'd bled to death while trying futilely to stop the bleeding. Both he and Jorge sustained multiple bruises, slashes, and stab wounds—though hadn't apparently been shot.

Jorge looked up at her, smiled, then let his head rest back against the leg of a metal table, using both hands to clamp an improvised bandage around his knee. A bloody combat knife lay on the ground next to him.

Crushing guilt flooded the corners of Harper's eyes with tears. She started to feel responsible for Drew's death... until it occurred to her he, Carl Sr. and Jorge probably would have attempted this without help from the Evergreen Militia. It hadn't been her idea to attack this place. She'd been trying to talk everyone into a stealthy approach. The guilt devil taunted her with the notion she'd led them here following tracks. However, the other two men with the wagon of vegetables knew where to go. Even if Carl Sr. hadn't known where the Promise Keepers hid out before, they would have told him where to bring his 'tribute' of supplies. Sooner or later, a bloodbath would have taken place.

Carl Sr. did not seem to be the type of man who would meekly surrender to being extorted.

She couldn't believe she stood in a building among twenty or so corpses… especially the dude with a meat cleaver between the eyes. *Great. More nightmare fuel.*

Since she couldn't blame herself for Drew being dead, her subconscious mind changed tactics and blamed her for walking away with only minor injuries, a few scratches and scrapes. Stinging revealed a grazing cut on the left side of her head, likely from a fragment of cinder block or concrete blasted loose by a bullet hitting a little close. These 'Promise Keepers' appeared to have fulfilled Ken's prophecy about them. The ones who had the nerve to shoot back did so in a frenetic, panicky way. Seeing all the bodies gave a sobering statement of how lucky they'd been to face an army of untrained guys who had likely never been shot at before. It also helped that many didn't have ammo. Jorge and Drew walked into a meatgrinder when they tried to assault the restaurant via the rear entrance. None of the dead bandits in here used firearms, only bayonets, knives, and at least one baton.

They outnumbered us five to one. We should all be dead. What the heck was I thinking?

Months ago, Mila tried to 'do magic' to keep her safe. Harper didn't know if the girl sincerely believed lighting candles at night and chanting would help or merely did 'witchcraft' as a way to give Madison some mental security. Initially, she thought the creepy little girl weird, but her talk of the Shadow Man turned out to be a completely mundane problem. So, maybe she really didn't believe in magic.

Sure feels like something *helped me.* She sighed, wondering if karma balanced itself out in the grand scheme of things. Taking the nuclear war as personal bad luck didn't feel right since it screwed everyone. Losing both parents, however, fit in the bad luck column. Maybe she had 'Wyatt Earp' luck. The man supposedly walked out in the open in a raging gunfight and escaped without a scratch on more than one occasion. While she in no way felt anywhere near as badass or cool as him, freakish circumstance sounded like the most reasonable explanation.

Ken loped into the kitchen, favoring his left leg. "Oh, man..."

"Yeah..." Harper stared down.

"You all right?" He gave her a once over. "You look ready to throw up."

"Kinda stunned we're not all dead."

Ken waved dismissively at the corpses. "Half these guys didn't have ammo. They got by on intimidation."

"Dude from the bathroom had no ammo." Harper rubbed a hand up over her head. "What the hell was he thinking, rushing at us like that? Did he *want* to die?"

"Who knows? Maybe he gambled on me surrendering since he got the drop on me." Ken crouched to check on Jorge's knee.

"You shot an unarmed guy? No guilt?"

Ken shook his head. "Dude ran at me with a rifle. I don't have x-ray eyes. Didn't know he had no bullets until after. It sounds like a shitty thing to say, but I'd rather ponder the ethics of shooting an idiot without bullets after the fact than find myself a ghost. It's on him for rushing at me and pointing a gun at my face."

"I guess." She backed up. "I'm gonna go get Lilly."

"Okay." Ken helped Jorge up to one leg. "We'll be right behind you."

Carl Sr. moaned in pain outside.

Holy shit. He's alive! Harper rushed through the restaurant and out onto the porch. Across the street, Logan helped Carl Sr. down from the bed of the blue Ford pickup. The M-60 no longer had an ammo belt dangling from it. Blood covered Logan's entire face, dripping onto his shirt; however, he didn't move in a way to suggest he'd been seriously hurt. Carl Sr. on the other hand, clutched his side and limped. Harper stared at Logan, barely able to breathe at seeing him so bloody.

I can fall to pieces in a minute. Lilly's gotta be terrified.

She hurried down the porch steps and ran for the police station, practically playing hopscotch over all the bodies littering the street.

35

THE NEW REPUBLIC

A chill ran down Harper's back as she re-entered the police station.

Soft childlike sobs echoed over a room of dead bodies. It felt as though she'd stepped into a movie where the director dubbed sad music or eerie sound effects while the camera panned across the fallen strewn about the battlefield.

All we're missing is some atmospheric fog and maybe a white dove.

Harper did her best to ignore the dead as she made her way to the holding cell in the back left corner. Lilly hadn't moved much from where she'd been moments ago. She still lay curled up on the floor under the bench. The cell had no toilet, unsurprising due to it being right out in the open in the front room. Seeing a white bucket left in there with the girl got Harper angry all over again, chipping away at what little regret she had.

Bastards couldn't even give her privacy.

"Hey. It's over. All the bandits are gone." Harper pulled at the cell door, to no effect. "You probably want to avoid looking around too much."

Lilly scrambled out from under the bench and crawled over, grabbing her in as much of a hug as she could manage with bars between them. Quiet shivering burst into loud, shuddering sobs. Harper held her tight, hoping the girl's meltdown came purely from being trapped in the midst of a gunfight and nothing worse the men did to her.

"Did they hurt you?" asked Harper.

The girl shook her head, still trembling. "N-no. They told me I had time to decide which finger they would cut off if my dad didn't give them what they wanted." She sniffled. "If I didn't pick one, they'd cut them all off."

"Unbelievable. What the hell is wrong with people?" whispered Harper. "They're just bastards, okay? Wanted to mess with you."

Lilly exhaled hard, then looked down at her hands as if she needed to remind herself she still had all her fingers. "You don't have'ta lie. I know he was serious. He had evil eyes."

"Sorry… just trying to help." It occurred to Harper she hadn't seen the face of the man with the dry voice who talked about cutting fingers off children. "I'm pretty sure he's dead. Heard him on the porch and that's the first place your dad opened fire."

"Good," said Lilly. "Sorry if I can't stop crying. Never been so scared in my life."

"No shame in it. You're safe now." Harper looked at the door. "We'll get you out of there."

Logan and Carl Sr. dragged themselves into the room. Jorge arrived seconds after them, his arm across Ken's shoulders for help walking. Harper looked over at the guys. Logan appeared to be bleeding from a nasty cut on the forehead. Carl Sr. took at least two bullets, one somewhere in the lower left chest, the other to the right shoulder. His shirt had been shredded into a bandage, likely Logan's doing. Other than having the wind knocked out of him and seeming a bit stiff, Ken seemed okay. Jorge suffered a stab wound to the knee as well as numerous shallow slices or punctures from knives all over. For obvious reasons, Drew Bullock didn't walk in.

"Daddy!" yelled Lilly, grabbing the bars. "No!"

Why doesn't it feel like we won? Harper glanced at the girl. *Maybe we sorta did.*

"Lil." Carl Sr. limped over to the cell. "Tell me what they did to you."

"Not much, Dad. Just grabbed me. Said they'd shoot me if I made any noise. The man had a gun against my head. They brought me here and put me in this cell." The girl looked down. "I tried to get away, but couldn't. Bit one guy. He slapped me in the face."

"Don't gotta feel bad." Carl Sr. kissed the top of her head through the bars. "None of it's your fault. Tell me everything."

Lilly blushed. "They made me use the bucket in here... and they told me to choose which finger they'd cut off to send you if you wouldn't give them what they wanted."

Carl Sr.'s face reddened in an instant. He whipped his Springfield rifle up, aiming at the keyhole in the cell door. Fortunately, he stopped himself before Lilly could even scream and jump to the side. "Dammit. Where's the key?"

"Easy." Harper grasped the rifle, lifting it. "You might hit her. They have a key somewhere. We'll find it."

Carl Jr. jumped over the dead guys in the doorway. The sixteen-year-old's eyes said 'whoa holy shit' but the rest of him appeared calm-ish. "Dad... you're hit."

"Yeah. I know. Lilly's stuck in that damn cell. Help look for a key." Carl Sr. took a step toward the dead guys by the windows, but careened to one side. He dropped his rifle to catch his fall on a nearby desk.

"Dad..." Carl Jr. rushed over to help hold him up.

Jorge, Ken, and Logan got started searching the dead. The keyhole on the cell door looked like some old-fashioned thing from the early 1900s. None of the keys on the bundle Harper took from the oval-faced guy would come close to working in it.

As the others rummaged the dead, she checked desk drawers and cabinets.

"Damn, these guys have been eating well," muttered Ken. "Better than us."

"No farms around here." Logan rolled a dead man over to get at his pockets. "Think they have a big stash of cans somewhere?"

"No." Harper frowned. "Remember those guys who brought the wagon of veggies? These idiots threatened all the ranches around here. I bet they've been getting 'tributes' from multiple families."

Lilly tugged at the cell door, rattling it. "I heard other kids yelling before when that man came in. I don't think I'm the only one they kidnapped."

"Where...?" Ken looked up.

Harper furrowed her brows. "Basement. Gotta be."

Carl Sr. grunted as if merely existing hurt.

"Logan," said Harper. "Please get him back to the ranch. Tegan's there, and he really needs her right now. It can't wait. I'll deal with this place."

He looked at her, his expression giving away an internal argument between knowing Carl Sr. needed help fast and not wanting to leave Harper's side. Before Logan could come up with a way to argue and not sound like a jackass, Carl Sr. yelled, "I ain't goin' nowhere with Lilly stuck in that damn cage."

"Daddy, go see the doctor," said Lilly past sobs. "Don't die. Please. The key's here somewhere. They'll find it. You don't have time to wait."

Carl Sr.—with his son's help—staggered over to the cell and took her hands. "Lil..."

"I'm okay, Dad. Please go to the doctor. I need you alive." Lilly sobbed. "It's gonna feel like my fault if you die."

"Don't you dare for a second think that way, kiddo." Carl Sr. reached into the cell, pulled her closer to the bars, and held her.

"All right. You girls have a good point. I can trust you to handle this if it means I get to see you grow up the rest of the way."

Harper tugged on his arm. "The key's here somewhere. It's just a matter of time searching for it. You are bleeding. Go to the doctor so she still *has* a father."

Lilly covered her mouth, still crying.

"I can get him back," said Carl Jr. "Thinkin' Logan wants to stay with y'all."

"Naw. That boy's bleeding like a shot pig." Carl Sr. grabbed Logan's shoulder for support. "He needs the doc too. I'm all right with it. Got more a piece a them than they got me. Boy, do me proud, all right?"

"Okay, Dad. If you're sure." Carl Jr. grimace-smiled at Logan in a 'sorry, I tried' manner.

"It's fine." Logan hugged Harper. "Be careful, okay? Don't know what kind of surprises they left for us."

She didn't want to let go, but each second she clung to him shaved seconds or minutes off Carl Sr.'s life. "Hurry."

Logan nodded to her, then helped Carl Sr. outside.

"Horses are right there." Carl Jr. pointed out the windows. "I brought 'em into town. By the truck."

Ken and Carl Jr. dragged a few of the bodies out to the street while Jorge and Harper continued searching for the key. After returning from the third trip, Ken paused to look at Lilly padding around the cell like a caged tiger. "Any idea why they put you in there?"

"So she doesn't run away," muttered Jorge.

Lilly cry-laughed. "Uhh, they made up some bullcrap about charging me with a crime."

Everyone stared at her in disbelief.

"Say what?" blurted Harper.

"They accused me of being a traitor to the New Republic for helping Daddy conspire against them to deprive them of 'supplies and materials needed for the reconstruction.' They said he failed to support the New Constitution."

Carl Jr. whistled. "Wow. Those guys were crazy."

"Not entirely crazy." Ken rubbed at the sore spot on his chest. "*Crazy* would've been thinking they established a new republic *without* nuclear war happening. Not like there's a government left. Charging a little girl with a crime because her family refused to be extorted, that's just evil."

"Yeah." Carl. Jr. nodded. "It sucks having to shoot so many people, but I think it's for the best."

"I really hate that you're right." Harper shook her head. "By the way, thanks for taking that guy out. Saved my ass."

The boy nodded. "You're welcome."

She glanced over at him. "You okay? Ever have to kill someone before?"

"No. Not 'til today." He shrugged. "Shot a couple of them trying to sneak up on the truck from behind or chargin' across the street. Doesn't feel like it really happened, yanno?"

He's the reason Logan is still alive. Harper paused, overcome with gratitude for a moment, then looked at the floor. "Yep. Been there." She gestured at Lilly, stuck in a jail cell with only a nightgown on. "Might not happen today. Maybe not even this week or this month. However, you're going to have a moment where you can't stop thinking about shooting those guys and thinking you did something horrible. When that moment comes, remember this sight. Remember the look on your little sister's face right now. The guy you shot wasn't just going to kill me, he helped kidnap Lilly… and they were going to hurt her."

Lilly sniffled.

Carl Jr. exhaled. "Yeah. I know. It's why I had to do it. Had to go with y'all. Don't feel it yet but, guess you're right. I will."

"You said they had other people locked up here?" Ken started dragging another dead guy toward the door. "I was really asking why they put Lilly up here instead of with the others."

"I dunno." Lilly squished her toes into the floor. "They didn't say why. Just kept talking about finally 'beating' my dad. So stupid of me to go outside at night. They hadn't caused trouble for almost a week. Thought I'd be okay." She gasped. "Julio! They shot Julio! They didn't even say anything. I was sitting on the toilet and just *bang* a gunshot right outside. Is he okay?"

"He's hurt bad." Carl Jr. bowed his head. "Wanted me to tell you he's sorry he couldn't stop them and you shouldn't feel responsible for him."

Harper spotted a grey metal box mounted on the wall. It had a 'first aid' symbol on it, but she decided to check it, anyway. Much to her surprise, a four-inch key hung on a sticky hook attached to the inside of the door. Most of the medical supplies had long since been taken.

"Got it!" She swiped the key off the hook and held it up while fast-walking to the cell.

The huge key fit the equally oversized lock. As soon as Harper pulled the surprisingly heavy door aside, Lilly rushed out and grabbed her older brother in a fierce hug. The girl hid her face against his chest, no doubt to avoid having to look at all the blood.

Carl Jr lifted her off her feet. "Watch your step, Lil. There's mess everywhere, and you got no shoes on."

"It's clear out back." Ken pointed at the hall. "Might wanna bring her out to the backyard. The road out front's a… situation."

"I saw. Good idea. Holler if ya need me. I'll be out there with Lil." Carl Jr. approached the hallway, carrying his sister. "More in here. Close your eyes, Lil."

"They are closed," whispered Lilly. "Sorry."

"Stop apologizing."

Harper pulled the mess of normal keys out of her jeans pocket. *One of these has to work on the basement door.*

36

COLLATERAL

S tanding by a heavy steel door peering through a narrow window at a dark stairwell going down did little to ease Harper's nerves. Fading adrenaline from participating in yet another shootout, the elation of finding Lilly unharmed, the shock of seeing Logan as a bloody mess, plus the anxiety of what waited for her behind the door all pushed her proverbial dial up to eleven. The key bundle jingled like sleigh bells in her shaking hands as she cycled through them, searching for one that worked.

Even though she knew beyond all doubt nuclear war destroyed civilization, wandering freely around—breaking into—a police station still made the hairs on the back of her neck stand up as if there might be some tiny chance she imagined everything and she'd get in serious trouble.

What's down there? It's dark. More Promise Keepers? No... can't be. Lilly said they had other kidnap victims. Why else would the people on the various ranches just give these morons food and supplies? Key six failed to move the knob. *Grr. Okay, threat of violence. Give us the shit or we kill you always worked. But... they didn't have much ammo left.*

"Easy," said Ken in a soothing voice.

"What? I'm putting keys in a doorknob, not defusing a bomb," she whispered.

"Your hands are shaking. Relax."

She stared at the key bundle. "I'm not frightened. I'm anxious. What if we're too late? I don't want to see dead children or kids with fingers lopped off or..." She rested her forehead against the cold steel door and started to cry. "Maddie's gonna kill me if she finds out how much of a shitstorm this turned into. I had bullets hit the wall like inches away from my face. That one dude out front almost shot me."

"Hey..." Ken rested a hand on her shoulder. "We did a good thing here. Remember the look Lilly gave you when you opened that cell door. I think even Drew would agree it was worth it, especially if there are more kids than just Lilly stuck here. I can go first if you are worried about what's down there."

She exhaled, steeling herself. "Thanks. It's okay. I can handle it. Worst case, I see what horrifies me the most and no longer think of the people I shot as human beings."

The ninth key worked.

Harper wiped her eyes, then put the keyring back in her pocket, swung the shotgun into firing position, and pulled the basement door open. The smell of people stuck in a confined, poorly ventilated space smashed into her face. Fortunately, it didn't carry any notes of decaying corpse and by another miracle, the odor of urine, though detectible, seemed quite weak. Ten grey concrete steps led down to a landing where the stairwell curved around to the left, barely visible in the feeble amount of sunlight making it into the hallway from office windows behind her.

Okay. This is not too bad. Doesn't smell like anyone's dead down there and it's dark, so I won't see the grisly details if there is anyone.

She crept down to the landing and peered around the corner. Another ten stairs led to a small alcove in front of a second steel door. No light leaked out from the tall, narrow window spanning roughly half the door on the right side. Ken unclipped a crank flashlight from his vest, wound it up, and provided a somewhat-more-than-pathetic amount of illumination.

"Nice… how long does that thing last?" she whispered.

"About two minutes per crank."

"I mean… like, how long until it wears out and stops working entirely?"

He shrugged. "No clue."

Harper advanced to the door and grasped the knob. Before she could even test to see if it was locked, children's voices murmured from the other side.

"The shooting stopped," said a pre-teen.

"What happened?" whispered another kid.

At least two different kids cried.

"I dunno."

"Don't hear anyone now," said a boy. "I think they left."

"If everyone's dead, how are we gonna get out?" asked a young girl, her voice saturated in fear.

"I wanna go home," whined a smaller child.

All the anxiety and guilt festering in Harper's gut exploded into a second wave of anger. "Shit," she whispered. "Okay, maybe I don't feel guilty about shooting these bastards."

"What are you seeing?" whispered Ken.

"A door." She glanced back at him. "It's what I'm hearing that's bothering me. Kids."

Harper tried the knob. It turned easily, unlocked. She stepped through into a completely dark room. Even holding a shotgun didn't help ease the primordial fear caused by staring into the gloomy basement of an abandoned police station. The way her breathing echoed suggested a fair amount of open space. Ken panned the weak crank-light around, revealing a desk, a long table with various pieces of equipment on it, a camera rig facing a height-measurement on the wall—likely for mugshots. She guessed the equipment was used to do breath tests for drunk driving. Two tall metal storage cabinets stood against the far wall, one on either side of a corridor.

A small square of dim light on the left caught her eye. It appeared to be a teeny window in another steel door on the left side of the room. Since this place had zero electricity, the only explanation for light had to be casement windows or something similar.

"Ken, what's that? Left? The window."

He aimed the flashlight at it, illuminating a solid white door with the word 'holding' on it.

"That's gotta be where they are." Harper crossed the mostly empty room to the door.

The sound of kids crying grew louder.

Ken moved up beside her. They lost light for a couple seconds as he wound the crank again, brightening the beam. This door appeared to have a more high-tech lock than a simple key, though the Promise Keepers had already blasted it open with gunfire, likely months ago. She grabbed the handle and pulled the door aside to reveal a short hallway containing four jail cells. Small whispers fell silent at the metallic screech of the door. Daylight, no doubt from windows in each cell, cast the shadows of bars on the floor between them.

The odor of confined bodies reached new levels of unpleasantness, though fell short of eye watering. Fear from those stuck inside this place practically hit her like a solid force. She took in the scene for a second or two, adjusting to the funk in the air.

"My name is Harper. I'm not one of the buttheads who put you guys in here. All that shooting you heard before was us. The bad guys are gone. My friends and I are going to get you out of there and help you go home."

Children appeared at each cell door, grabbing the bars and struggling to look out at her. A grungy, blonde girl with pale green eyes, maybe ten, and a redheaded girl a little older than her occupied the nearest cell on the left. Red ringed the maybe thirteen-year-old's eyes, as if she'd been crying quite hard not long ago. Opposite them, a scrawny fourteenish girl held a seven- or eight-year-old girl as if clutching a teddy bear for protection. They both had the same shade of brown hair but didn't appear related. The smaller one still sniffled, not quite done crying, but also gave off a sense of hopeful surprise. In the far cell on the left, two boys, one about nine, one a year or two older, jumped up and down, cheering. A pair of terrified brown faces peered out at her from the distant cell on the right, twin girls not yet tweens, in matching coral-hued dresses.

Harper stepped forward in complete, horrified shock that anyone could put school-age kids in jail cells. The sight infuriated her so much she almost screamed. Unlike the one upstairs, these cells were only a third the size. Instead of a bench, they had two stacked beds with a single thin blanket each and a steel sink-toilet combination. Judging from the lack of overpowering poop smell, she assumed the toilets worked still. Small, barred windows near the ceiling in the cells looked out into sunken wells. They let in a bit of daylight, but offered no view of the outside world.

Each cell also contained a random selection of stuffed animals, toys, and a few books. The blonde girl appeared the grungiest, as if she'd been wearing her nightgown for months. Every child appeared to be in dire need of a bath and clean clothing. None had visible injuries, nor did they appear malnourished... or even bruised. The blonde girl appeared to be the only one—other than Lilly—abducted in the middle of the night, as none of the others wore pajamas or nightgowns. Several pairs of handcuffs hung on a wall hook near the door out of the holding area, some open. The haphazard way they'd been draped there implied the Promise Keepers had used them on their kidnap victims.

Harper glared at the restraints, unable to stop herself from snarling.

"They only put cuffs on us if they make us go somewhere," said the blonde ten-year-old. "But they never ever let us out, so they don't really use them. They never open the door once we're inside."

"They treat us like criminals." The oldest girl frowned. "Except, criminals got showers once a week."

"I can't even." Ken spotted the flashlight on the nearest cell door, revealing a relatively standard keyhole, not the Wild West nonsense like the cage-type cell upstairs. "This is just..."

"Yeah. Let's hope this whole situation here is just a bunch of crazies and not a sign of where society is going." Harper slung the shotgun over her shoulder and pulled out the keyring.

"Holy crap," said the older of the two boys. "Ryan, you didn't say you had an older sister who's a badass."

The redhead sniffled, staring intently at the keyring. Tears poured from eyes a pure shade of cornflower blue. "She's not my sister. We just have the same color hair."

"This is a dumb question, but I gotta ask." Harper tried the first key. "Are you guys okay?"

"Kinda," said the blonde girl right in front of her. "Mostly scared. Tired of being locked in here. I want to go home."

"They didn't really hurt us." The tall, slender fourteen-year-old bit her lip. "They almost cut one of Laura's fingers off, but she screamed and cried too much, they couldn't do it to her."

The eight-year-old stuffed her hands under her armpits defensively.

Harper almost dropped the key bundle thanks to a surge of fury. "You don't have to be scared of them anymore. They're all gone."

"Yeah, all they really did was kidnap us and keep us locked up." The younger of the two boys stuck his arm out of the cell to point at the blonde girl. "Sage has been here the longest. Like six months."

Sage rattled the door. "Come on. Please open it! I didn't do anything wrong. I wanna go home. I hate it in here."

"Whoa. Sage?" Harper stared at the filthy child. "You're Lilly's friend, right?"

The girl nodded.

Son of a bitch. No wonder her parents wouldn't tell Lilly she died—she didn't die. Harper snarled under her breath. *These shitheads probably threatened to hurt her if the parents told anyone what happened. Can't go letting people start taking precautions to protect their kids.*

"I know none of you did anything wrong." Harper put the third key in—and it worked.

Sage and Ryan rushed out of their cell.

Harper caught them in a sorta-hug. "Slow down. Please wait long enough for me to let everyone out so we can all go up there together. Don't run upstairs yet, okay? It's a mess. I don't want any of you to see certain things. You'll get bad nightmares."

The girls clung to each other.

"Okay," whispered Ryan.

Sage glanced back at the open cell door, looked down at her bare feet as if to confirm she no longer stood inside the cell, then broke down in heavy sobs.

Growling to herself, Harper tried the same key on the opposite cell. It didn't work, though the next one did.

The older girl politely stepped out into the hallway. "Thank you. Are you really going to let us go home?"

"No take fingers," whispered Laura. "Mine."

"Of course we're going to let you go home." Ken sighed, seeming saddened by the kid's assumption she might have only changed captors.

"Yes." Harper smiled at her. "Soon as I figure out where you guys need to go."

"I'm Amber Rollins." The older girl exhaled hard. "I was kidnapped from a farm about twenty miles southwest from here. The people I lived with didn't care when these guys kidnapped me since I'm not their kid. They basically laughed and said 'whatever, she's your problem now.' But these idiots didn't let me go."

Ken scowled.

"Not their kid?" Harper studied her face. "Wait, did you say Rollins?"

"Yeah."

"Okay, this is crazy, but..." Harper wince-smiled. "Is your dad named Jim?"

Amber covered her mouth. "Wow. Yeah, but he's dead. He was in Denver when the bombs came down."

"Holy cow." Harper stared into her eyes. "There's a Jim Rollins where I live. He's like our guy in charge of all the farms. What are the odds there's another farmer named Rollins? Don't want to get your hopes up, but, like... he might be your father."

Amber bit her lip.

"Ooh. Jim's gonna be pissed if that's his kid." Ken scratched his head. "Weird, he never mentioned having one or tried to go to her."

"Uhh..." Amber stared down at her dingy sneakers. "My parents got divorced five years ago. Mom took me to Colorado Springs. Our place was like *just* far enough away from downtown, we survived the fireball. Mom got sick, radiation I think... she died a couple months ago. I tried to go back to my dad's place out in the country, but other people are there now. When I told them it belonged to my father and I used to live there, they kinda felt bad and let me stay."

Harper shifted her jaw side to side. This girl *might* be Jim Rollins' kid, but she couldn't say for sure. "Well, you might as well come with us if you want. Best case, he's your dad. Worst case, you have a place to live that *will* care if idiots kidnap you."

Amber made a noise part giggle, part sob.

"Will you let us out, please?" asked the older boy.

"Help," whispered one of the Latina twins.

"Yes." Harper hurried over to the boys' cell. "I'll sort out who all of you are and where you need to go in a few minutes."

"Please, can I go outside?" asked Sage, still trembling. "I don't remember the sky anymore."

Harper's heart nearly shattered. She glanced at Ken. "Can you go with them? I'll get the other two cells open and be right up."

"You sure? It's dark." Ken wobbled the crank-light.

"Yeah. It's a big, open room. We'll be okay." Harper tried the next key in the cell door.

"Okay." Ken waved to the four kids no longer stuck in cells. "C'mon. Follow me close and don't look to the right when we get upstairs."

The children nodded.

"Are you a cop?" asked Sage.

"Used to be. Guess I still sorta am." Ken smiled.

"Did you arrest the bad people who kidnapped us?" asked Sage.

"Umm. Not exactly." Ken cringed.

"Sage," called the older of the two boys. "They shot them all. There's no arresting anymore."

"Yeah..." Harper paused, staring at the keys. "Those men can never hurt any of you again."

"Oh." The blonde seemed to relax slightly, then clung to Ken, shaking.

He picked her up to carry, then led the other three out into the larger room.

Harper unlocked the last two cells once she found the correct keys. Both boys and the twins mob-hugged her. The boys continued jumping up and down, cheering. The twins barely made a noise, though their big brown eyes radiated such gratitude it brought Harper to tears.

"C'mon. You guys need fresh air." Harper backed toward the door until the kids finally released their hug, then turned to lead them out.

Does it make me psychotic that I no longer feel the least bit bad about killing those guys?

Harper decided it did not.

37

EVERYTHING SHE NEEDED

O nce Harper escorted the kids outside to the yard behind the police station, she took a moment to enjoy clean air. Jorge, Carl Jr., and Lilly joined them in the yard, all seeming shocked at the discovery of eight children being held hostage. The instant she recognized Sage, Lilly pounce-hugged her and burst into joyful tears. The two girls seemed to be trying to squeeze all the air out of each other.

"You're okay... not sick," said Lilly past sniffles.

"Sick?"

"Your parents told me you were sick and couldn't come out." Lilly wiped her eyes.

Sage stared helplessly at her friend.

"The bad guys probably threatened to hurt you if your parents told anyone the truth." Harper exhaled hard. "Doesn't matter now. You're okay and will be back home soon."

After a brief moment of uncontrollable sobbing, Sage erupted in giggles and ran around the yard waving her arms, basking in sunlight.

"What now?" asked Ken.

"Now? We figure out who they are and where they need to

go." Harper glanced at Amber. "Except for her. She's going to stay with us."

"Sounds like a plan." Ken chuckled. "I sense much walking in our future."

Though Harper felt a little guilty at prolonging her return home, these kids definitely deserved her time. She gathered them in a group and tried to collect pertinent details.

Sage Appleton told her she'd been the first kid taken by the Promise Keepers after intimidation and threats failed to convince her family to give up food and supplies. Two men came in her window at night and grabbed her straight out of bed six months ago. Ryan McFadden got kidnapped while walking between ranches to visit her friend, who hadn't—yet—been abducted. Men in camo ran up on her like cops arresting a suspect, throwing her to the ground and cuffing her hand and foot before tossing her over a horse like a sack of grain. Nine-year-old Tommy Haywood reported being grabbed from behind while leaving the outhouse on his family's farm right before dinnertime. The eight-year-old, Laura Burke, explained to Harper how she'd been sitting on the floor inside her house when one of the men simply walked in and grabbed her. The rest of her family had been out with the cows and garden.

Joey Milford, the eleven-year-old, spotted a man running with Laura over his shoulder away from the next ranch over and tried to stop the kidnapping, only to be caught off guard when he chased the guy into a group of six Promise Keepers... at which point they'd abducted him, too.

Natalie and Ximena Morales ashamedly admitted to falling for a big white teddy bear left at the base of a tree. When they slipped past their ranch's fence to check out the plush animal, Promise Keepers grabbed them. Surprisingly, the men allowed them to keep the big white teddy bear in their cell.

Having something of an idea where each child needed to go, Harper tried to come up with the most efficient way to get them all home. The kids came from farms or ranches all within forty miles of the ruins of Hartsel, the sort of homes where the nearest neighbor lived two miles or more away.

"What's on your mind?" asked Ken.

She set her hands on her hips. "Trying to figure out the best way to get them all back where they belong. It's going to be a little challenging trying to put eight kids as well as us on four horses, then figuring out how to get to where they live. Dunno if the kids can point the way."

"Carl Sr. know people," said Jorge before looking at Carl Jr. and speaking in slow Spanish.

"Yeah. He's right. My dad knows everyone around here." The teen smiled uneasily. "Even if he, uhh, you know... why don't we just bring everyone back to our place for now? They all look hungry and could use a bath, new clothes, and a decent meal."

The kids didn't give any sign of being against the idea of staying together a little longer.

Anything has to be better than stuck in that damn basement. Harper sighed at the building, hoping with all her energy situations like this remained crazy outliers and the entire world wouldn't turn into *Mad Max* during her lifetime, or at all.

Sage jumped at the idea to go to the Overton ranch, as she'd visited it many times and it wasn't *too* far away from her home. Ryan and Laura demanded assurances going there would only be a temporary stop. Harper, Carl Jr., and Ken promised them they would go home as soon as possible.

"Do you have any food?" asked Tommy. "They didn't give us anything to eat yet today."

Harper nodded. "Yeah, there's food... those two men brought an entire wagon of stuff in right before we kicked the hornet's nest. Where did they put it?"

Ryan bowed her head and wrapped her arms around herself.

"In the restaurant." Ken pointed a thumb back over his shoulder at the police station. "It's still a heck of a mess out there.

Everyone wait here. I'll go grab something for them. Sorry, but it's gonna be vegetables. Not gonna sit around here long enough to cook any of the meat. Besides, the kitchen's not exactly in the most sanitary shape."

Remembering the bloody scene, Harper grimaced.

Not one of the kids complained, in fact seeming quite interested in vegetables.

Harper blinked. *Wow. The world really did end.*

Ryan sniffled.

Oh, shit. The ginger dude who they let into the police station. He must be her father or maybe older brother... She approached Ryan. "It's okay. You're safe. We'll get you back home soon."

"I know." The girl wiped her eyes. "You... saw my dad?"

"Yeah. I was hiding out on a roof watching the town, looking for the best way in." Harper let out a long exhale. "All that food belongs to your family."

Ryan pulled her hair off her face, taking a few deep breaths to collect herself. "It's okay. We're all hungry. I don't think my dad would mind. It's just those Promise Keeper bastards he hated feeding. Lazy, good-for-nothing leeches. All they did was sit around playing cards and laughing while everyone else worked." The girl fumed, gone from weepy to angrily ranting about how much she hated the Promise Keepers and how they'd kept her locked up for two months, only let her father see her for fifteen minutes every two weeks, and how if 'you guys' didn't kill them all, she would have—if she ever got out of jail.

Jorge muttered, "Pelirroja típica. Esa niña parece que quiere pelear. Como Harper."

Carl Jr. appeared confused for a few seconds, then laughed.

Harper couldn't help but feel somewhat mocked, but his tone didn't seem mean-spirited, so she ignored it. *Probably said something about all redheads being furies.*

Most of the kids stretched their legs running around the yard, grateful to be out of the tiny cells. Amber wandered over and asked about Evergreen and Jim Rollins. So, Harper rambled about the town and its farm coordinator. The more she talked, the more teary-eyed Amber became.

Oh wow. Maybe he really is her dad. This is going to be... interesting.

Not having spent much time around Mr. Rollins, Harper didn't know him *too* well. He'd become Evergreen's 'farm coordinator' because he owned-slash-ran a big farm before the war. She remembered talk of him returning to his property to collect various supplies as well as livestock for the town. While he already had a big farm, the strike annihilated his crops and did a number on his cows. They'd brought the healthiest back to Evergreen. He didn't trust the land to be safe, either from contamination or crazies with guns. A town up in the mountains offered much greater security, so he'd gone there. She knew the man as quiet, pragmatic, one of those guys who never seemed to smile. He didn't come off as mean, more 'got a job to do, no time for frills.'

Wow. It might make so much sense now. He thought his daughter died.

"Yeah, they're right back here," said Ken from inside the police station before yelling, "Clear! It's just me. Ryan, someone to see you."

Harper, Carl Jr., and Jorge all turned to look at the building simultaneously.

Ken emerged carrying a wooden crate of various vegetables. The ginger man and the other guy Harper observed bringing the wagon into town earlier stepped out behind him. Ryan gave a startled squeak before sprinting into an embrace. She crashed into her father so hard the man almost went over backward. Ryan ended up hanging on him, her feet off the ground, as they both wept tears of joy.

"Damn fine work," said the other man, nodding to Ken.

"Wha?" Harper blinked. "Where'd they come from?"

"Heard all the shooting," said the dark-haired man. "Didn't really know what to think of it, but Jason was in a mood after that damn son of a bitch cut his visit with Ry short. Figured if someone started shooting up the Promise Keepers, he was gonna storm in there and get his kid back."

Ryan cried a little louder.

"Except..." The man sighed. "We heard that machine-gun going off and it looked like a total shitstorm. We just had the one little 9mm hidden under the wagon, so we decided to wait for the dust to settle."

"Mr. McFadden!" yelled Sage. She ran over and clung to him, tearfully telling him about how mean the kidnappers had been to her, mostly leaving her in the cell and never letting her out, sometimes forgetting to feed them for a day, and how they almost cut one of Laura's fingers off.

Ryan's father hugged both girls, too overcome to say much.

Damn, I miss my parents. Harper looked away from them. She didn't feel jealous or begrudge the girl getting her father back, nor any of these kids getting their families back. But seeing the reunion made it painfully clear she could never experience such an event. Rather than think about how much she missed her dad, she helped Ken feed the other kids.

The kids tore into the raw vegetables like a pack of dogs on raw meat.

From the conversation going on between Ryan, her father, Joey, and the other guy, Lane—a former ranch hand, now basically family—Harper learned the boy lived on the next farm over and knew their family quite well. He and Ryan had been friends before their abduction.

Mr. McFadden and Lane brought their wagon back. Ken and Carl Jr. helped bring the food and supplies out of the restaurant and load it onto the wagon while the kids remained behind the police station, out of sight from the carnage. That done, Ryan, her dad, Lane, and Joey headed off to the east as a group.

While Jorge—and his messed-up knee—kept an eye on the remaining children in the station yard, Harper, Ken, and Carl. Jr. ran around collecting weapons and ammunition from the dead as well as taking a modest cache of ammo from an armory in the station basement.

Harper discovered a crude stable the bandits set up inside a former auto garage. Bones from other horses littered the yard nearby, suggesting a grim end to other animals that the Promise Keepers had likely eaten. Unable to tell if they'd killed the animals for food or merely used the meat after poor care and neglect killed them, she tried not to think about it. Since it would be cruel to abandon the three surviving horses here with no one to care for them, she ran back to ask Carl Jr. for help moving the animals to what had basically become their rally point behind the police station. Once all useful ammo and weapons had been collected, Harper and Ken gathered the kids and moved as a group, heading west toward the hill where they left their horses.

Lilly and Sage hadn't stopped talking since the little blonde girl's burst of energy at the sunshine on her face waned. Harper stopped by the one house to grab all the formerly expensive sneakers and sports jerseys. No sense leaving the stuff to rot, useless. Someone could wear them. She didn't care about any 'collectible' value. No one had money anymore, nor did anyone really care about famous athletes. Everyone had much more immediate and direct concerns, like not starving to death.

Jorge, thanks to his knee injury, rode one of the horses. Amber rode on one of the bandit horses, accompanied by little Laura. Sage and Lilly, both fairly competent riders took the other two, each girl sharing it with one of the twins. Tommy rode with Carl Jr.

THE TRIP BACK TO OVERTON RANCH WENT BY MUCH QUICKER THAN the original trip to Hartsel.

Not having to follow tracks made much better time. Lena—basically Lilly's new mother—and Jen came running out of the ranch house as soon as they noticed the group approaching across the field. Billy zoomed out a moment after them.

As the women came to understand the true scope of the Promise Keeper's actions, the initial elation of having Lilly home safe and realizing Sage hadn't died of a mysterious illness shifted to shock, then anger, then satisfaction. Carl Jr. mentioned plans to go with Manuel and possibly Clayton to recover Drew's body so they could bury him here.

Upon taking in the state of the kids, Lena lapsed into full 'mom mode,' ordering them to follow her around back to get washed up. She sent Jen off to gather some clean clothes, Carl Jr. to begin filling the big washbasin, and asked Jorge to get a fire going to heat the water. Upon noticing his knee, she grimaced, then looked at Harper.

"Sure. Just tell me where the wood is and where to start a fire." Harper smiled. "I don't mind helping out."

"Oh, you did enough, sweetie." Lena hugged her. "I'll get Clayton to do it. He knows where everyone is. Go on inside and rest."

"How is Carl?" asked Harper in a quiet voice.

Lena sighed. "He's resting now. Your doctor friend is 'cautiously optimistic.' She thinks he's got a better chance than poor Julio."

"Sorry." Harper looked down.

"You don't got a thing to apologize for, hon." Lena nudged her.

"I meant that in a general 'sorry this happened' sort of way." Harper managed a weak smile.

"Yeah. Don't we all. You folks did right by us here." Lena

patted her on the arm. "Don't be strangers. You'll be stayin' for dinner again, I hope?"

Harper looked up at the sky. Trying to go home now would definitely result in at least two or three hours of travel in complete darkness before they'd even gone half the distance—and needed to sleep outdoors, anyway. "Yeah. If you'll have us. Bit late to set off."

"Of course we'll have you." Lena squish-hugged Lilly. "You brought our Lilly back to us."

The 'geez mom, not in front of people' expression on the tween's face almost made Harper laugh for being such an ordinary reaction to an absolutely abnormal experience. Lilly insisted on rushing inside to check on her father.

While Lena and Jen took the kids around back for a bath in a giant outdoor round tub, Harper headed inside with Ken and Jorge.

Tegan, still seemingly exhausted, pulled herself up off the couch. "How bad is it?"

"The situation?" asked Harper.

"No, your injuries."

"Entirely emotional," muttered Harper, mostly sarcastic. "Where's Logan?"

"Using the outhouse. He's fine." Tegan offered a weary smile. "Cuts to the scalp bleed much more than you'd think. Couple stitches is all it took. I think a bullet hit the truck, ricocheted off, and hit him in the forehead… but it lost most of its energy on the truck so it didn't pierce his skull. Probably knocked him loopy for a few minutes. He'll have a headache for a while. I didn't detect any signs of a concussion."

Harper sighed in relief.

"Ken, you good?" asked Tegan.

"Little sore. Took a couple rounds to the chest. Vest stopped them, but I might have cracked a rib. Jorge needs you first. His knee's tore up. Bayonet probably. It's gonna take me an hour to get the vest off."

"I can help," said Harper.

Over the next couple hours, Tegan tended to Jorge's leg, examined Ken's severely bruised chest, and checked on Carl Sr., Julio, and Rebecca. Harper mostly sat on the sofa holding Logan protectively.

The kids trickled into the house as they finished bathing, wearing clean, borrowed clothing. Tommy wanted to hear the story of the gunfight, as did Billy. The boys asking for it got the twins wanting details as well. Manuel tried to talk to them in Spanish, but the sisters didn't appear to understand a word of it.

Harper and Logan told a somewhat sanitized version of what happened in Hartsel, leaving out gory details. They did share that Carl Sr. jumped on a machine-gun knowing he'd likely get shot or killed for making himself such a target, but his doing so was the only reason the raid succeeded. The Promise Keepers had more men than they thought, and while some might consider it 'unfair' to cut down a whole restaurant full of unsuspecting guys with an M-60, after what they did to nine innocent kids, Harper couldn't summon the least bit of concern for 'unsportsmanlike' conduct in a firefight. She even hoped the man who wanted to cut Lilly's finger off took long enough to die he realized who shot him.

After dinner, Harper went to the back bedroom with Ken to see Carl Sr. He lay in bed, shirtless, blankets up to his waist. Blood-soaked improvised bandages wrapped around most of his torso. His breathing had a labored quality suggesting he really needed pain medication, though the only thing anyone had available came from a two-year-old bottle of Advil they happened to have in the bathroom.

Lilly sat attentively at his bedside, appointing herself full-time nurse. Sage obligingly joined her, happy to be reunited with her friend, and considerate enough not to talk too loud. Since the unspoken fear hanging over everyone gave Carl Sr. roughly fifty-fifty odds of surviving, she wanted to spend every single second he had left with him just in case he didn't make it.

Not wanting to bother him too much, Harper gave a brief account of everything that happened after he left. She and Ken made arrangements with him to get the other children back to their respective homes and also split the scavenged ammunition, weapons, and clothing.

Considering the temporary influx of kids, Harper gave up the bed she'd used the previous night to the twins and Laura. She ended up sleeping on the couch—with Logan who surrendered his borrowed bed to Tommy.

She climbed on top of him, lying chest to chest under a blanket, trying not to look at the bandages wrapped around his head. They couldn't really do anything there in the middle of the living room while Ken stretched out on a sleeping bag nearby and anyone might walk in without warning. Except for boots, they kept their clothes on and remained completely innocent, not even kissing. It didn't bother her. Holding him, surviving at all, having his heart beat so close to her chest she could feel it, gave her everything she needed.

PRECIOUS

MAY 6TH

Harper, Logan, Ken, Dr. Tegan Hale, and Amber stopped to camp for the night in the abandoned Platte Canyon High School off Highway 285. A convenient creek just south of the football field offered a place to water the horses.

With little else to do as they waited for sunset and allowed the horses to rest, Amber told everyone about how she'd left the outskirts of Colorado Springs, spent a few weeks roaming around scavenging food and such with her mother until the woman became too sick to function. They'd holed up in one of those dollar store type places somewhere. Amber did her best to take care of her mother and keep her comfortable for a few days, until she woke up one morning to find her dead. After doing the best she could to bury her mother, she spent about two weeks wandering alone, somewhat feral, sneaking around the ruins and avoiding anyone and everything that moved. Finally, she got the idea to try making it back to her father's farm, the place she'd lived from birth to age nine before the divorce.

She *did* reach the farm alive, though hungry, only to discover a group of total strangers had taken it over. None knew what became of her father or any of the people who worked with him. When she pointed out her old bedroom and accurately described some other things about the house and basement, they accepted she used to live here... so let her stay. The people hadn't been bad to her, but they hadn't exactly cared much, treating her more like some random adult they deigned to share room space with than a frightened and lonely orphaned child. She'd lived on the farm for five months before the Promise Keepers kidnapped her, mistaking her for the actual daughter of someone who lived there.

"I'm kinda surprised they didn't let me go," said Amber, her voice echoing over the empty high school gym. "I mean, being locked up sucked serious ass, but those guys didn't have to keep feeding me. Guess they thought Ben was lying about not caring what they did to me."

"Lucky they didn't start cutting pieces off." Ken cringed.

Amber bit her lip. "They talked about it. I begged them not to. Told them the people on the farm really were complete strangers and they wouldn't care."

"Damn... rough," said Logan.

"The worst part of it was watching the visits." Amber looked down. "Ryan just cried to herself, didn't make much noise. Poor Sage screamed for hours every time her mother got dragged away. I think I'm going to hear her yelling 'Mommy come back' for the rest of my life."

"Monstrous," muttered Ken.

"Maybe we should go back and bury them." Harper flicked at Logan's flannel shirt. "Wouldn't want the buzzards to get sick."

"Hah." Ken exhaled. "Don't go letting yourself get too vindictive. We did what we had to do."

"Yeah. Not taking pleasure in it. Just... glad we survived."

Logan squeezed her. "So am I."

MAY 7TH

They rode back into Evergreen late on the morning of the seventh.

Two of the Promise Keeper's horses remained with the Overtons. One, with Amber riding it, returned to Evergreen to become part of the Militia's resources. After riding up to the front of the HQ building, everyone climbed down from their horses. Logan went with Tegan to the medical center to have his wound cleaned and possibly re-stitched. Ken volunteered himself to bring the horses back to the stable and deal with checking in the scavenged guns, ammo, and clothing. This left Harper to bring Amber to see Mr. Rollins. As much as she desperately wanted to go straight home, it wouldn't take too long.

Harper waved for Amber to follow, then headed up Route 74. Jim Rollins, despite not having school-age children (or so anyone thought) took up residence in a house off Braeburn Lane, in the area up north where she usually patrolled. It allowed him to be close to both the big farm as well as the smaller one on the old golf course.

"Okay, so..." Harper glanced over at the younger girl. "Usually, when someone new shows up in Evergreen, they need to go to the medical center to get checked out. Dr. Hale already had a look at you, so I'm sure we can skip that step."

Amber nodded.

"If Mr. Rollins turns out to be just some guy with the same last name, I'll bring you back to see Anne-Marie. She's the town manager and will figure out who you'll stay with. You're kinda at the age where you might be able to be on your own if you really want to be."

"No." Amber shook her head. "I'm only fourteen and I'm kinda messed up. I really need someone... a mom or dad. I don't care. I don't wanna be alone anymore. Do you know what it's like living in a house with thirteen other people and still feeling like you're alone?"

"No, but I can guess…" Harper sighed. *She should talk to Tegan. Heck, we're all a little messed up now.*

A few minutes of walking later, Harper veered off the highway into the woods. Mr. Rollins' house sat a little more than a hundred feet in. Not the biggest place, but it had an asphalt driveway as big as a basketball court—a true benefit in a world with no working cars.

Harper knocked on the door. "Mr. Rollins? Are you here?"

"Yep," called a man from inside. "What blew up this time?"

Amber covered her mouth in both hands, emitting a faint squeak. Tears gathered in her eyes, and the teen appeared close to throwing up.

Holy shit! She knows his voice. Harper trembled from anticipation and joy. "Uhh, Mr. Rollins, you really should take a look for yourself."

"All right. Hang on."

The scuff of a sliding chair preceded footsteps thudding in the house.

Mr. Rollins opened the door, giving Harper an 'okay, let's hear it' sort of look. If the dictionary had a picture for 'pragmatic,' it would be his face. He looked to be close to her dad's age, mid-forties. Kinda thin, brown hair going gray, the sort of cowboy-hat-wearing guy they usually put on TV commercials for pickup trucks or beer.

"Daddy?" squeaked Amber. "You're alive!"

For the first time since she arrived in Evergreen, Harper observed an emotion on Mr. Rollins' face other than 'okay, now what.' He broke down in silent tears, seemingly unable to do anything more than stare at her.

With the two of them right in front of her, Harper had no trouble seeing a familial resemblance.

"How...?" whispered Mr. Rollins. "Colorado Springs..."

Amber pounced on him and sobbed, most of the strength leaving her legs. "Daddy..."

He wrapped his arms around her, shifting his disbelieving gaze to Harper.

"Right place, right time." Harper smiled at him, then sighed. "Some idiots were kinda shitty to her. Nothing overly bad. No need to freak out. They're all dead now."

Mr. Rollins nodded once, then buried his face against his daughter's neck.

"I'll, uhh, leave you two some privacy." Harper took a step back. "I need to go let my family know I'm back."

"Thank you," said Mr. Rollins, his voice cracking.

Harper cried happy tears the whole way home. She walked in the front door to find Jonathan and Mila sitting together on the sofa reading a comic book open across both their laps. They didn't look up right away when she walked in, so she set her backpack down and stood there watching them read lines, doing voices for various characters.

Aww. They really are kinda cute together. Wonder if this kid crush will grow into something more. She blinked. *Oh, crap... he's gonna turn twelve like next week.* She whistled in awe. *Time is flying.*

The whistle made the kids look up. Jonathan squeaked.

"Hey." Mila waved, casually. "Welcome back. I'm glad you aren't dead."

"Same here." Harper exhaled.

Jonathan ran over to hug her. Mila's blasé act cracked to a happy smile in only four seconds. She also rushed into a hug.

"Where's Maddie?" asked Harper. "And Lore?"

"Take a guess." Jonathan nodded toward the hallway.

Ugh. Expecting her little sister to be curled up in bed, too sick with worry to function, Harper jogged down the hall to their bedroom. Madison, barefoot in jean shorts and a purple T-shirt, sprawled on the floor with Lorelei. Except for the girls playing with dolls rather than a video game, Harper might have walked into her sister's room back in Lakewood before the war. Lorelei appeared to be trying to wear her frilly 'doll dress' as much as possible before she either outgrew it or it disintegrated.

Wow... Maddie outgrew dolls when she was seven. She's gotta be playing to amuse Lore... maybe to stop thinking about me being gone.

"Hey, guys," said Harper.

The girls jumped. Lorelei beamed. Madison looked up. Her expression went from calm to confused to worried to overcome in under a second. She scrambled to her feet and ran over, clamp-hugging her.

"Yay!" Lorelei cheered, then added herself to the group hug.

"How did it go?" whispered Madison. "Did you have to erase any morons from the gene pool?"

"Unfortunately, yes," said Harper on more of a sigh than voice. Madison shuddered.

"That's stupid," declared Lorelei. "Who wears jeans in a pool?"

Despite everything, Harper chuckled. "It got a little hairy, but this group of idiots kidnapped the daughter of the guy who ran the place we took Tegan to... and then it turned out they had eight more children locked up in a former police jail."

"Locked up?" Madison scrunched her nose.

"I'll explain later. Can you pause clinging for a bit? I really want a bath and to change. Been wearing and sleeping in the same stuff for days."

"Request denied," muttered Madison, still holding on.

Harper chuckled. "At least give me enough space to put the shotgun down. You can hop in the tub with me if you want."

"Okay," said Madison.

"I'm fully expecting you to activate super cling mode." Harper patted her sister on the back. "All I'm asking for is a couple minutes to get cleaned up and comfortable first."

"Correct." Madison relaxed. "And okay."

TAKING A HOT BATH FELT *AMAZING*, EVEN IF SHE HAD TO SHARE THE tub with both sisters.

After drying off and putting on a clean outfit—Harper decided on wearing the one dress she still owned since she wouldn't have to do Militia stuff for the rest of the day. She'd done plenty of adulting recently and no longer considered pants important... at least until tomorrow morning's patrol.

Despite being a little big to do so, Madison curled up in her lap when Harper reclined in one of the big living room chairs. Lorelei continued playing with dolls on the floor. Neither Jonathan nor Mila seemed to be self-conscious about reading the comic book aloud with an audience, though they did stop to listen as Harper told Madison a relatively honest version of what happened. Again, she left out the gore. She also kept apologizing for doing something so risky.

"You had to. I understand." Madison fidgeted at her hair, twirling it around her finger, releasing it, then doing it again. "The ranchers didn't have enough firepower. You helped those kids. That's really cool."

The front door opened.

Everyone looked up as Cliff staggered in doing an impression of a zombie. He didn't even need much makeup considering the dark circles under his eyes and 'shoot me now' expression.

"Whoa." Harper blinked. "What happened to you?"

Cliff emitted a moan worthy of any 1950s era horror movie.

Jonathan laughed.

After closing the door, Cliff scaled back the overacting and rubbed a hand up and down his face. "Welcome back. Also, some day you will have babies who refuse to sleep for more than a single hour at a time. You will then know my pain. Excuse me." He stumbled off down the hall toward the bathroom.

"The babies are adorable." Madison smiled.

"They poop soooo much!" Lorelei flailed.

Harper snickered. "Babies tend to do that, yeah."

"So…" Madison stared into Harper's eyes. "You got shot at."

"If you want to be technical, none of them really shot *at* me. The ones who would have shot *at* me, I nailed before they could fire… the rest of the bullets, it would be more accurate to say were fired in my general vicinity."

Madison gave her a clearly unimpressed look. "You know my price."

"Yeah."

"I am going to be clingy for the rest of the day." Madison snuggled tighter. "Maybe two."

"That's totally okay."

Harper closed her eyes, let her head sink back against the recliner, and squeezed Madison. *Every minute we get to have together is precious.*

fin

ACKNOWLEDGMENTS

Thank you for reading *The World We Make!* When I originally conceived Evergreen as a short story for a post-apocalyptic anthology, I never expected the awesome response it would get—nor that it would grow into a (now) six-book series. I am grateful to all the readers who shared their reactions to the series that prompted me to keep it going.

Additional thanks to Lee Sheridan for editing and Alexandria Thompson for the cover.

Author's note: some readers may notice a few odd shifts in the timeline. The mention of the one-year anniversary kinda snuck into book 5 as a one-off line and had little attention paid to it. So much so when I started working on this book, I believed I still had the one year touchpoint to cover. I ended up writing a more involved treatment of the survivors dealing with the day and my editor suggested keeping that (as it was far more engaging for her than the throwaway line originally in book 5).

That said, some things in book 5 have changed around a bit. Book 5 has been updated to fit the timeline presented here. (If anyone is wondering why most of the chapters are dated now...)

ABOUT THE AUTHOR

Originally from South Amboy NJ, Matthew has been creating science fiction and fantasy worlds for most of his reasoning life. Since 1996, he has developed the "Divergent Fates" world, in which *Division Zero, Virtual Immortality, The Awakened Series, The Harmony Paradox, and the Daughter of Mars series* take place. Along with being an editor at Curiosity Quills press, he has worked in IT and technical support.

Matthew is an avid gamer, a recovered WoW addict, Gamemaster for two custom RPG systems, and a fan of anime, British humour, and intellectual science fiction that questions the nature of reality, life, and what happens after it.

He is also fond of cats.

Visit me online at:
    Facebook: https://www.facebook.com/MatthewSCoxAuthor
    Pinterest: https://www.pinterest.com/matthewcox10420/
    Goodreads: https://www.goodreads.com/author/show/7712730.Matthew_S_Cox
    Email: mcox2112@gmail.com

Prophet of the Badlands Series

- Prophet's Journey
- Prophet's Mercy

Divergent Fates Anthology

(Fiction Novels - Adult)
The Roadhouse Chronicles Series

- One More Run
- The Redeemed
- Dead Man's Number

Faded Skies series

- Heir Ascendant
- Ascendant Unrest
- Ascendant Revolution

Temporal Armistice Series

- Nascent Shadow
- The Shadow Collector
- The Gate to Oblivion
- The Queen of Discord
- The Burning Alchemist

Vampire Innocent series

- A Nighttime of Forever
- A Beginner's Guide to Fangs

- The Artist of Ruin
- The Last Family Road Trip
- The Phantom Oracle
- How Not to Summon Demons
- Ordinary Problems of a College Vampire
- A Vampire's Guide to Surviving Holidays
- An Introduction to Paranormal Diplomacy
- A Vampire's Guide to Adulting
- How to Stop a Vampire War in Six Easy Steps
- Ancient Vampire Death Cults and Other Annoyances
- Hunting Vampires for Fun and Profit

Standalones

- Wayfarer: AV494
- Axillon99
- Chiaroscuro: The Mouse and the Candle
- The Spirits of Six Minstrel Run
- Sophie's Light
- The Far Side of Promise anthology
- Operation: Chimera (with Tony Healey)
- The Dysfunctional Conspiracy (with Christopher Veltmann)
- Of Myth and Shadow
- The Girl Who Found the Sun

Winter Solstice series (with J.R. Rain)

- Convergence
- Containment
- Catalyst
- Catacombs

Alexis Silver series (with J.R. Rain)

- Silver Light
- Deep Silver
- Silver Quarrel
- Silver Crucible

Samantha Moon Origins series (with J.R. Rain)

- New Moon Rising
- Moon Mourning
- Haunted Moon

Vampire For Hire series (with J.R. Rain)

- Moon Master
- Dead Moon
- Lost Moon
- Vampire Destiny
- Infinite Moon
- Vampire Empress
- Moon Elder

Maddy Wimsey series (with J.R. Rain)

- The Devil's Eye
- The Drifting Gloom
- Dark Mercy
- Primal Wrath

Samantha Moon Case Files series (with J.R. Rain)

- Blood Moon

Immortal Operative (with J.R. Rain)

- Broken Ice
- Broken Wing

Four Elements series (with J.R. Rain)

- The Elementalist
- The Black Rose
- The Wakefield Curse

Witches series (with J.R. Rain)

- The Witch and the Hangman

Young Adult Novels

The Eldritch Heart Series

- The Eldritch Heart
- The Cursed Crown
- The Sapphire Soul

Evergreen Series

- Evergreen
- The World That Remains
- The Lucky Ones
- Nuclear Summer
- The Nuclear Frontier
- The World We Make

Progenitor Series

- Out of Sight

- Out of Mind

Diary of a Teenage Fey

(Short story series)

- Elder Horror
- The Hag of Barrow Falls
- Babysitter's Nightmare
- Lharakki
- Bauble for a Soul
- Simulacrum
- Amorphous
- Manticore

Standalones

- Caller 107
- The Summer the World Ended
- Nine Candles of Deepest Black
- The Forest Beyond the Earth

Middle Grade Novels

The Adventures of Ubergirl series

- My Dad is a Mad Scientist
- Aliens Ate My Homework
- The End of all Halloweens
- Dr. Infinity and the Soul Smasher

Tales of Widowswood series

- Emma and the Banderwigh
- Emma and the Silk Thieves
- Emma and the Silverbell Faeries
- Emma and the Elixir of Madness
- Emma and the Weeping Spirit

Standalones

- Citadel: The Concordant Sequence
- The Cursed Codex
- The Menagerie of Jenkins Bailey

www.ingramcontent.com/pod-product-compliance
Lightning Source LLC
Chambersburg PA
CBHW020508260626
47156CB00006B/1927